DEC   2002

The
Winter
Zoo

The Winter Zoo

A NOVEL

John Beckman

Henry Holt and Company

New York

Henry Holt and Company, LLC
Publishers since 1866
115 West 18th Street
New York, New York 10011

Henry Holt® is a registered trademark
of Henry Holt and Company, LLC.

Library of Congress Cataloging-in-Publication Data
Beckman, John.
    The winter zoo : a novel / John Beckman.—1st ed.
    p. cm.
    ISBN 0-8050-6904-6
    I. Title.

PS3602.E33 W56 2002
813'.6—dc21   2001039696

Henry Holt books are available for special promotions
and premiums. For details contact: Director, Special Markets.

First Edition 2002

Designed by Margaret M. Wagner

Printed in the United States of America

1   3   5   7   9   10   8   6   4   2

for Katy

He's no end of fun, for all you say. . . .
A human, if ever we saw one.

—Wislawa Szymborska

The
Winter
Zoo

Prologue

MY DEAREST COUSIN: There's a photograph I took here in Kraków, and I've got it lying on the desk. It has me kneeling by the flower vendors on the main square, surrounded by a flock of pigeons. Some hover, some land, some eat crumbs from the folds of my skirt, one takes off from my left shoulder. Behind me in the photo is a man in a Harley jacket, retroflex and shouting in Polish, showering me with a burst of crumbs. His name's Dick Chesnutt, but never mind him—it's just a photograph.

I also have one of you that I call Age Eleven. Your arm's locked straight, propping you against a tree. Your red curly hair's flat in the wind. Your lips are simpering but your eyes are shy. Overexposed Portrait of a Boy in Shorts. Maybe you remember it. It was my very first photo.

Well, you had your chance.

I'm taking my Polish utility scissors and driving a point through the photograph (the one of you). I'm cutting across the tree, through your arm, all around the outline of your head, and plop! there you are: Boyface, floating on the woodgrain of my desk. I had no choice. I've written you a dozen invitations, but you haven't stirred. I've spread your name like the flu throughout this city, throughout the cafés, the mead cellars. Now you're all the whisper in the university halls. Go! Come! Outside my window, heat lightning rolls through the clouds, searches the city's domes and spires, flashes the crooked spine of the castle. The cut was decisive. Somehow I know you're coming at last.

Anyway, I press my thumb to your boyface and lift it up off the desk. I dab the back with flour paste and graft it onto the other photograph, right over the defiant face of Dick Chesnutt. A near-perfect fit—except your face is in more vivid color, and it's teetering Humpty-Dumpty on your reckless new body.

Your loving cousin,
Jane

Book One

Halloween
Feast

One

FREUD WOULD HAVE CALLED IT OVERDETERMINED. It was a moment so heavily hung with meaning that it sagged like an overdecorated Christmas tree. Gurney felt sure his chest would collapse. Why had he waited so long? Now he was responsible, standing six foot five in the cool whirr of a recovery room, holding his newborn daughter. The morning was overcast. He had a bachelor's degree. She was seven pounds, six ounces, swaddled in flannel, and her hair, like his, was red and curly. She hadn't even taken her first bath yet, and already he imagined her growing out of control—walking in a year, talking in two, television at three, school at five, tall, then awkward, chatty, smart, choosing colleges, getting an attitude. Already she was looking everywhere for her father.

She's a doll, a young nurse whispered, poking her head into the room. You must be so proud. She's got your hair, your eyes. No question who the father is!

Gurney swallowed and looked at the baby, whose eyes fell on inscrutable things.

What's her name?

Her mother likes the name Sarah, he said softly. Gurney looked at Sheila, the mother, who was sleeping. I guess her name will be Sarah.

You're so lucky, she said. Baby Sarah!

He smiled and gave his daughter a proud little bounce.

This must be the happiest day of your life, she said, lingering for a moment, then leaving the room.

In Sarah's eyes, now just open like fresh-cracked eggs, he felt judged. He looked for solace, for a combination of her blotchy face, her ketone breath, and some base instinct that would stir him to joy, but as when choosing a necktie or reading an ink blot, he felt unequipped. Was this beauty? Was this joy? The child gasped. She blinked and sighed. Throughout the pregnancy he had felt unequilibrated, but now he positively wobbled. She had gravity, how she grunted and gurgled, tugging at his shirt with her mighty little fists, but even so she offered him a choice: he could clamber with her onto the land, trudge the dusty roads of paternity while his boyhood blubbered off into the clouds, or he could drop her into the arms of her mother (with whom he had long ago scissored the ropes) and lift from that room and out the open window, squiggling a handkerchief in brutal farewell.

Nothing bad had ever happened to Gurney. He had swerved through life like Mr. Magoo. Not even the pregnancy, when she'd announced it the winter before, was such a bad thing. They were sitting in the Union, drinking coffee, looking over the frozen Iowa River, when Sheila said she was keeping the baby. Keeping it! But then she said he had obligations neither to her nor the baby. She could tell at a glance that he wasn't ready. She said, All I ask is that you be nice to us. The next day he brought her a pint of Chunky Monkey ice cream, but right away she threw it up. She asked for three Zagnuts, but when he brought them, she threw them up. She wanted arugula, tapioca, tuna fish, and beets, but then, in turn, she threw it all up. For two weeks she ate only spicy-crazy noodles from the Thai Star Café, and every day she threw them up. For that first trimester, they were happy to focus on her appetite. In the second trimester her tiny breasts became hard and full, her hips grew stocky, and her underwear drooped under the slope of her belly. She had never looked more beautiful, but she was treating him like a child. She swam twenty laps a day, pumped her bicycle to class, planted azaleas in her window box, and she gave an expert paper in her seminar on Bergson. She galloped through springtime like Joan of Arc; Gurney dallied behind like Sancho Panza. In the third trimester, when the weather was hot and sweet and balmy, Sheila became ornery, refusing his phone calls, never answering the door, twice leaving town without letting him know, and he knew he had failed. She was healthy as ever, in burly condition, but she was vomiting again. He brought her Chunky Monkey, but she left it sitting on her porch to melt. One morning he brought flowers and stood behind her, watching her work a crossword puzzle. After several minutes she told him to stop mooning. Do something, she said. Are you ever going to do anything? I'm having this baby in two weeks, maybe sooner. What are you going to do? Gurney, who of course had no idea, said nothing. Fine. That was fine with Sheila, who said she was tough as a horse and quite ready to do it herself, but if Gurney had plans to continue mooning, she would much rather he answer the silly letters from his cousin Jane, go to Poland, and moon over her instead. He knew she meant it.

He felt he had been rather slow to mature. As a child his understanding of the world had developed with blocky certainty: at five he was proud to infer that sugar, when wet, was sticky, but that that stickiness could be washed away with even more water; oil, however, was oily in spite of water, no matter how much, until soap was added. Such apprehension increased gradually, like moss over a rock, then onto some trees, then throughout a grove, by which time he was in high school and reasoning that Ophelia committed suicide not because she grieved for her father, or even because Hamlet had murdered her father, but because without her father's restraints she found the world to be a merciless welter, not at all what she had expected. Now, for the first time, Gurney found himself standing in the eye of the vortex of that same welter, holding his own daughter, and somehow he recalled his father sitting alone with a scotch in his library, staring madly off into the corner while Ravel's *Bolero* usurped him like an army of belly dancers. That was his father's escape. All at once, Gurney understood. He wanted to call his father and share that feeling, but the thought made him shudder because he knew that whereas his father really was a father, having earned his escape, Gurney was incapable of being a father, and his own escape was as real as setting the baby in the arms of her sleeping mother and walking out the door.

He mooned over his daughter. He mooned over Sheila, who

turned on her side and popped open her mouth. After twelve hours of labor, after chewing on towels, clawing the mattress, cursing Jesus, cursing her midwives, writhing, twisting, torquing, and, at last, squeezing a screaming child from her body, Sheila slept like a warrior. He feared her waking up. He laid down the child. He feared the decision he was playing in his head. How could one person make such a decision about life, especially when it would reverse the life of this infant, the life of this woman? His leaving would send seismic tremors into everyone's future, send rifts and splinters through so many possible lives. Only an evil world would allow him this option. But he had waited too long, and Sheila had made it clear that he was never really there: she had said he was pacing on the perimeter like a jealous tomcat. So it was okay. It was expected. He looked out the window, over a field, where the shadows of clouds coasted across the land like his myriad futures, darkening vectors of space, then leaving the field unchanged. Why should he abandon Sheila? She had given him acres to hem and haw in, yet he wanted more. But what? Did he hope to find better? Did he hope to be free?

Freedom, it seemed, wherever he might go, was out of the question. Wherever he might be, the child would keep developing, growing off her mother like a nut or a fruit, in the absence of Gurney, in spite of him, and she would study his photo and curse his face; she would be strong like Sheila and rue his pale blood that mixed with her own. If he were to stay, would her face grow differently? Whether or not she had Gurney's hair, Gurney's eyes, Sarah was a tiny model of her mother, an annex of her mother's flesh, and only with heroic effort would he ever assert his influence. If he were to stay, he feared, he would grow like a second plum on Sheila's tree. Fun, it seemed, was out of the question, but still he had this nagging suspicion that, at twenty-two years of age, there was still so much more fun to be had. The baby sighed. The walls were blank yellow in the hospital room. Out the window, on the horizon of the field, pearly steam gushed from a smokestack.

As of August, he was a college graduate. He had announced to his cousin Jane he would arrive in two weeks; she was delighted, but he was sure she wouldn't be so welcoming if she knew he was leaving behind a child. He had received his passport, reserved his ticket, packed a bag. He had vowed to himself not to turn back. His plane was leaving at midnight tonight, but still there was no one—not his parents, not his sister, not Sheila, not his daughter, not a soul—who could have known that he was going. So he could stay. He could still be a father. Poland, with its crooked castles and concentration camps, was at this point the scariest place on earth, maybe the last place he wanted to be. So he could stay. Nobody would know that he had thought such thoughts.

On the nightstand was a notepad advertising yellow pills called Demerol. Beside that was a ballpoint courtesy of Xanax. Gurney picked up the pen and swirled its dry tip over the notepad, but no ink came. He scratched the words *Dear Sheila* into the pad, then swirled it more urgently, then zigzagged, then, choking back a weep, dropped the pen to the floor. Through his tears he saw the baby moving her arms. A name was being called over the intercom. Nurses walked by out in the hall. The floors were shiny, the ceiling white. An answer wasn't coming from anywhere outside.

As it is told, Ophelia drowned herself. She wandered out of the court with her dress falling off, leaving a trail of flowers and bawdy songs. As with all suicides, she was on her own when she chose to climb a tree and throw her body into the pond. Just so, Gurney was alone when he leaned close to his milky daughter, kissed her, and whispered, I hate myself. He looked once more at Sheila, planted there, permanent, and he felt once more as if he might collapse. But instead he edged himself sideways out the room, briskly walked to the nurse's station, and left the brief message that he had gone to Poland. Before they could question him, he started to skip, then started to run—down the hall, down the stairs, out the doors.

Two

GRAZYNA WOKE AT FIVE and sat up in bed. That morning Jane's cousin was arriving from America. The night before she had straightened and swept and dusted the flat. She had propped a folding wall between the beds in Jane's room. She had leaned her best paintings and charcoals around the flat. She had poked torch lilies into her paintbrush cups. And that was all she was going to do. What more could he want? If he was disappointed, he could find a hotel. She left her bed unmade and went to the bathroom, her blue tile bathroom with its periwinkle tub, its egg-blue toilet and ocean-blue towels. A daisy tilted in a glass on the sink, but blue was her favorite color. She lit the gas and started filling the tub.

Though Zbigniew, her ex-husband, had been gone more than a year, she kept his shaving brush in its mug on the sink, its bristles stiff in the dry, pocked foam. She carefully moved it to make the daisy more prominent. She undressed. She squirted Pepsodent onto her toothbrush and brushed her teeth, watching in the door-length mirror as her hips and breasts swayed in two directions. She spit and rinsed, then looked again at the fogging mirror. Her straight brown hair curled off her clavicles. She stretched her torso, making her breasts rise off her rib cage. Once, many years before, maybe when she was still nursing Wanda, Zbigniew had taken her breasts in his hands and said: The French have a beautiful word for breasts—*saules*. He'd pronounced it with his chin protruding, as if he were rolling Cointreau on his tongue. *Saules!* he'd said. It sounds like they're billowing in the wind! He'd lifted them and made them float like lily pads. *Saules.* She'd been too modest to tell him that the word was *seins,* and that *saules,* most curiously, were willow trees. *Saules,* she now said, protruding her chin and lifting her breasts, and now, at her age, with the elastic giving out, it sadly seemed more appropriate.

A knock came at the door as she was testing the hot water with her foot. Wanda walked in with her hair tangled on her face, wearing just underwear and that Sonic Youth T-shirt. She looked tiredly at Grazyna, who pulled her foot out of the water.

You go first, Grazyna said.

Wanda shrugged. No. Go ahead.

Go first, Grazyna said and sat on the cold toilet seat, crossing her legs.

Wanda pulled off her T-shirt, walked out of her panties, and looked at the foggy mirror before stepping into the tub. She was shorter and more solid than Grazyna. Her shoulders were broad and her thighs were blocky, but there was something playful about her long, conical breasts. Grazyna had grown so weary of Wanda's severity, her hard gray eyes, her set jaw, her disgust with either communism or capitalism, her malaise over the divorce, that it pleased her to watch her daughter's breasts bounce about. Wanda dropped to her knees and soaped herself with a washcloth. Grazyna picked flakes of polish from her toenails. So what do you guess he's going to bring us? she said.

Who?

Jane's cousin.

Mother!

I was just thinking. When your father came back from America he described this machine for making bread. You put yeast, flour, and water in the machine—maybe nuts, raisins, seeds—then you just turn it on. It stirs, it kneads, it shapes. She pantomimed this in the air in front of her. You leave it there on the counter and it bakes your bread for you. It even bakes!

Mother! We have bread from the bakery every morning.

But the smell of baking bread.

I don't think he's bringing anything, and you shouldn't expect him to.

I certainly should. She pounded her fist on her knee, then smiled.

Well, expect something small. If he gives me something, you can have it.

Like perfume. Paris or Poison or Opium.

He's not coming from France. I mean small like a baseball.

Or a bread-making machine.

Wanda shampooed her hair and rinsed it slowly, over and over with the handheld showerhead. She stood and Grazyna tossed her a towel. She dried herself and fastened it over her chest. Grazyna tossed her another.

Why this?

Wrap it around your head. Like a turban.

Wanda tossed it back and stepped out of the tub, her hair ratty and snarled over her face. She stood at the sink fumbling through the brushes and bottles of lotion, making a racket in the cabinet until she found her toothbrush; it was where it had always been, in a glass with Grazyna's. Grazyna stepped into the tub and stood in the hot water, watching her ankles and calves grow pink, prickly, and speckled with myriad bubbles. She lowered herself down. Wanda spit a long stream of foam into the drain, tossed her unrinsed brush into the cabinet, and, hesitating, picked up her father's shaving mug. Grazyna sat up with a splash. Wanda dislodged the brush from the mug. She raised them high above her shoulders like the Eucharist. She turned to her mother and, scowling, said:

Why?

Please.

Every morning I look at his filthy dead whiskers on this mug and brush.

I know. I do too.

Why?

I don't know.

It makes me want to puke.

Please.

Puke, I said. She took a couple steps toward Grazyna, holding the brush and mug like pistols. Get rid of them.

Please.

Do it.

Wanda.

Then I will.

Wanda!

Here they go. She raised them high above the wastebasket, ready to dash them, rousing Grazyna to her feet, but then started to laugh. A small, thorny laugh. She jammed the brush into the mug and sent it rattling across the back of the sink. Grazyna sat down, feeling embarrassed. Wanda mumbled: It makes me want to puke.

They will be here soon, so I need you to run to the bakery and the grocery. Okay? Can you do that? We need oranges, eggs, bread, yogurt. Anything else?

Oranges, eggs, bread, yogurt, Wanda said. Poppy-seed cake.

Thank you. And Wanda?

Hmm?

Can you wear a dress?

Oranges, eggs, yogurt.

And bread, Grazyna said, smiling.

Poppy-seed cake.

IT WAS SEPTEMBER 1990. Trains were loading up at Berlin-Lichtenberg and pumping like blood to the capitals of the East, bringing TVs, appliances, exotic new foods—the relief was to be fast and fun and expensive. Among these trains, Gurney's was filthy, coughing and wheezing its rattly old lungs, slugging along through thick pine forests, pulling wagons of boxes and wagons of people whose sleeping bodies were slack and sweaty, whose heads were full and drooping like tulips. He awoke. He nodded. He awoke. He nodded. He kept shifting his head from the cold glass to the curtain, watching power lines rise and fall, the dark story of Poland lit by streetlamps in the countryside. Boxes crammed every free space on the train—teetering in the luggage racks, shifting in stacks about the narrow cabin floor. He'd been seeing those lousy boxes for days. When his train from Amsterdam had first arrived in Berlin, he'd found scores of pedestrians near the Zoologischer Garten bent under one or more such boxes. At first he'd thought that a department store had been looted, or that someone was throwing a great German giveaway, but day after day the boxes kept coming. At the National Gallery, Brandenburger Tor, everywhere he looked people were hauling boxes. Only when he was boarding his train for Kraków did he realize that the boxes were all destined for the East. All of them were coming with him to Poland. All he'd wanted was to stretch his legs. All he'd wanted was a good night's sleep. But there was to be no chance of that. In one of her last letters Jane had explained that those same tracks, with that same two-step knocking, had once carried cattle cars of prisoners from the West to the death camps smoking throughout the East. In a photograph she'd sent along with the letter, she stood at the spot where the tracks stopped in Birkenau. Listening to the tracks, the knocking of the tracks, his mind kept turning the whole night through, and he kept watching the trees and distant passing houses until morning light soaked the sky. Though the ride was interminable, as they passed greenhouses and factories and the block houses of Kraków, he wanted the train to roll and roll, faster and louder into ugly daylight. So long as he was moving he felt forgotten. He gripped the tacky vinyl of the seat, wanting to go forward, wanting to go backward, dreading the sticky moment of arrival. But inevitably, with a piling screech, he arrived.

He wandered the atrium of Kraków Głowny. He searched the peddlars, beggars, and travelers for what he remembered of his cousin Jane. Somewhere amid the drizzle in his head, amid the squawking intercom and the boiled-cabbage smell, he expected her to appear on yellow plastic roller skates, an eleven-year-old girl chasing her dog. Five drunk soldiers, arm in arm, swayed through the crowd like a sinking sailing ship, cracking the whip, sluggish but dangerous. He moved to the wall to give them room. Everyone did. They shouted and stomped, hurled Slavic curses, and accused the room with their tiny red eyes. They swung their attention to a woman in orange coming through the doors twenty yards away. They stumbled toward her, leaning forward and gaining momentum. They spread out their arms and threatened to consume her like a Venus flytrap, but she slipped nimbly past them, calling them fucking troglodytes in clear American English and proceeding headlong to the center of the floor, letting them crumple in a heap of hooting laughter. An American! he thought, watching her stride closer, black jeans, orange turtleneck, long brown curls rippling behind, but not until she'd recognized him and begun hurrying toward him did he register that this pretty American was Jane.

The last he had seen her was three years before, when she graduated at twenty-one from the University of Chicago. After the ceremony she shaved off all her long hair and took him to industrial Art Institute parties, where they ate tapas, smoked dope, and snorted one of her professors' coke. From his sheltered Iowa City perspective, that night was a thrill. She ignored everyone but Gurney, as if she had finished with all her other friends. She talked of nothing but moving to Europe. And that was the night she first invited him to join her, painting him into her autumnal cityscapes—in gondolas, rathskellers, *bateaux-mouches* on the Seine. She secreted him into a red-lit room and crouched him down on an unmade futon. With her glowing scalp and tricky face she looked older than he did but younger than ever, like either Gandhi or the devil, insisting he find her when he finished with school. But then how did it happen? She was whispering and insisting, and then she kissed him deep and garlicky, licking at his mouth with her eyes wide open, nosing up his neck and face, clasping his wrists behind his back—then she stopped with an apologetic laugh. She had written to him many times since, but never once had she mentioned that night. Neither had he, of course, and though he thought of it sometimes and got aroused, he knew their relationship was much larger than that; they were best friends, cousins, childhood conspirators, and if one night became a little erotic, it was a small and wonderful contradiction. But now, in that instant, as she came rushing

at him with her rushing hair and eager smile, blurting his name in that
ugly old place, he recalled that night with startling fear—what if they
fell in love? Where would he go? She kissed his cheek, then his other,
then his neck, then embraced a long time rocking side to side, her hot
breath down his collar, her hair smelling sweet like nuts and molasses.
When she started to talk he simply said Shush. When she tried to pull
back, he squeezed her all the harder, as if shielding her from all the
terrible things that had followed him from America.

You're so huge! she said, her green eyes awake despite her tired
face.

The Gurney Green Giant, right?

The Ostrich Man!

The Poplar Tree! he said, hoisting up his backpack.

Gargantuan! She grabbed his big hand and marched him across
the floor to the atrium doors, and with this grand gesture the dreary
place was resuscitated, like a bread factory illumined by kids on a field
trip.

Who are the troglodytes? he said, indicating the soldiers who now
leaned against the wall.

Apes, she said. Average gorillas, loose from the zoo.

They drink on the job?

What job? They're useless now. We don't need soldiers in today's
Poland!

Outside the station it was cold and wet. She said the walk to her
flat would be fifteen minutes tops, and she led him into the chilly blue
fog that swept the streets and the shapes of buildings. The spiny roofs
with their greenish onion spires reminded Gurney that they were
close to Russia. Motors rumbled, people argued, somewhere metal
clanged on metal, and his cousin Jane pulled him straight into it all.
They passed by kiosks and vegetable stands, through regions of smells
that hung in the fog—burning rubber, bubbling tar, some gaslike,
foodlike, fetid smell that came and went like the breath of a rhino.
Jane didn't seem to notice, stepping past a drunk wrecked up on the
pavement, leading him down into a cat-piss tunnel. All at once, he felt

young and awake, and whatever was clanging out there, Jane was laughing in that concrete tunnel with her wicked curls, her smirky mouth, her jerky, sexy, Janey walk! Kraków could have been anywhere, so long as Jane was there with him. He recalled following her deep into the Maquoketa Caves, following her flashlight into the roothairy recesses where she promised they would find relics of the Black Hawk tribe but where they found only a pair of footprinted panties. He hadn't been disappointed because she had made it an adventure, Tom with Becky Thatcher, and in the same way, he trusted, she would not disappoint him now.

Who are these people? he said as they emerged out of the tunnel onto a narrow strand of park where, near and far, bodies slumped on benches and under shedding trees, stuffing the alcoves along a great stone wall. A sparking streetcar bashed through the fog, but not a single body stirred.

What people, my dear? Grazyna and Wanda? Your new family?

The pack was cutting into his shoulders. He paused to adjust it. Tell me about them, he said.

She took his hand and kept walking. There's not much to tell, she said. Zbigniew moved out, so I—we!—live in his studio. Grazyna, his ex-wife, is Wanda's mother. She kind of reminds me of an antelope because she's so tall and refined, with all her noble Polish blood. But Wanda's a little wood-weasel. She's sixteen or seventeen, totally oblivious in her teenbeat little world. She won't bug you much. She stays in her room. How are your folks?

Huh?

Your parents!

He shrugged a bit, nodded feebly.

Did they kick and scratch when you said you were coming? Uncle Leonard always went ballistic if you just drove into the city! I'll bet he flipped.

They were cool. He said this without missing a beat.

I'll bet.

I'm an adult now, a graduate, he said with a laugh.

They're finally letting little Gurney grow up. That's sweet.

They stopped inside a grand medieval gate. Set into its brick wall, in a simple glass grotto, an icon of Mary with slashes on her face sadly flickered behind a few white candles. Ever since he'd arrived in Europe he'd been surprised and confronted by images of the Virgin Mary—morose paintings and twelve-foot statues, coddling her child, her pious eyes averted from Gurney's. But this one seemed especially tortured, so young and pure and human that the Hail Mary began rotating involuntarily in his head.

God, Jane said, scoffing at the icon. Get used to that thing, the Black Madonna, it's fucking ubiquitous here. Every house, school, shop has one. Lech Wałesa even wears one on his chest! Totally creepy. Anyway, this is called Florian Gate and it's the entrance to the old city, which is surrounded by this park, which used to be a moat. Way back when, there was a drawbridge here and probably some cracker telling jokes about King Kazimierz. Aren't I a good tour guide? Wake up, dear. Don't look so glum. If it weren't so foggy you could look down the street and there you'd see St. Mary's Cathedral. It's just three blocks away and that's where we live.

Great.

You coming?

He followed her down the cobblestone street all hazy with coal smoke, jammed with old buildings like buckling teeth. She called it Ulica Florianska, and now she walked with such ease and belonging, traipsing in and out the crowd, that he felt revived by the sharp smell of autumn, the morning smells of bakeries and waking sugar shops. It occurred to him all at once that his travels were stopping there, that he was going to live there, and as he always did in September, he felt that back-to-school thrill of something in him changing, but this time the sense of loss was much sadder, the anticipation much dizzier, and the two currents met in a sickening whirlpool. They neared the main square and he wasn't entirely unhappy, but the smell of dead leaves, even as it mingled with this alien fog, evoked nothing so keenly as an image of Sheila, kneeling on newspaper in front of their daughter, carving triangle eyeholes in a plump little pumpkin. He stopped beside Jane and they stood there looking, the narrow street opening onto a colossal bay of fog.

It's like Moby Dick, she said, meaning the main square. You can never see the whole thing at once. Even on a clear day, it's too huge and there's always some big thing in the way. The clock tower. The Cloth Hall. It's like standing on the edge of God's chessboard.

Gurney couldn't see any of this, but he took Jane's word for it. High above them rose a creepy cathedral, its two mismatched towers— a pencil-tip spire, a green onion dome—stiffening against the tumbling clouds. As he stared into the square's foggy space, blocky shapes began to emerge.

You poor cabbage, she said with a wink. He took her hand. You look so sad. Are you tired?

Yes.

Are you hungry?

Yes.

Are you homesick?

Yes.

Turn around, she said with a smile.

He turned around to see an elegant yellow building standing four stories high. Its window frames were cast with wedding-cake curlicues.

This is home, she said softly, pointing up to the top-floor windows.

WANDA MADE HER WAY AROUND THE KITCHEN TABLE, spooning soft-boiled eggs into the four silver eggcups that Jane had brought back as a gift from Salzburg. Dim morning light came in from the courtyard. Jane's crazy cousin had been twenty minutes in the bath. Ten German candy bars, Ritter Sport bars in all colors of the rainbow, were stacked like poker chips on the kitchen counter. This was the much-anticipated gift. Jane and Wanda's mother smoked and talked, acting as though they were sitting in a Parisian café.

Life with Jane had only confirmed her opinion that Americans were loud and excessive and rude. She'd hated America at least since 1987, the year her father taught at Stanford (where he'd met his first mistress) and returned with a ridiculous, middle-of-winter suntan, sneering at Poland and anything Polish. But then that morning, upon meeting the cousin, her heart had reversed. He was nothing at all like cynical Jane. He was the pure and simple American myth: eyes blue as Montana skies, hair red as the Painted Desert, legs long as a Texas giraffe's. He wasn't even gloomy, like dear Dick Chesnutt. He was one of a kind, an American orphan—shaking her hand, dropping his bag, shyly ducking through the bathroom door. He'd been in the shower for almost half an hour.

Gurney! Jane called, but he didn't respond. His running water hissed through the walls. I'm sorry, she said to Wanda's mother.

It's fine, Wanda said. The eggs are still hot.

He's very finicky, Jane said. They might be a little slimy for him, maybe a little too much like oysters.

Wanda used to be finicky, said her mother. She'd only eat potatoes and noodles and soup.

Wanda thought her mother was wearing too much lipstick (it made her lips snap when she talked) and too much blue eye shadow.

My mom was so mischievous, Jane said, sitting up, spreading her hands out on the table. Once, when he was about fifteen, she served him a catfish with everything intact—the eyes, lips, whiskers, everything, like it had jumped out of the river and died on his plate! He got so scared, he left to go to the bathroom and didn't come back for two whole hours. He just left! Jane laughed.

Wanda liked Jane's stories, but she was always jealous of her storytelling Polish, how she spoke very well but freely made mistakes, slipping into English, sometimes even German or Yiddish. Wanda's English, by contrast, clapped like wood.

Before long Gurney came into the kitchen, big and exuberant, his wet hair jangling over his eyebrows and ears. He filled the doorway in his brown shirt and jeans, reminding her of a big exotic tree, like a baobab in *The Little Prince,* brought thousands of miles and planted in their kitchen.

I'm so happy to be here, he said. It's a gorgeous place.

Jane stood up and put her arm around his waist, her head barely reaching the height of his shoulder. This is Grazyna.

Her mother held up her hand to be kissed, but Gurney turned it sideways and shook it like a man's. Grazyna means grass, she said too carefully.

Grace, Jane said.

That's pretty, he said, smiling. Gurney means hospital bed.

Grazyna is a local painter. She is very famous—locally. And you know Wanda.

We've met, he said, sitting, but now I'm all awake and human.

And hungry? Wanda said.

Those are poppy-seed rolls, Jane said. This is BoboFrut. It's fruit juice for babies, but we drink it anyway.

And this, I presume, is a soft-boiled egg? He knocked around the top with the back of his spoon, deftly scooped it off like a lid.

Nobody talked. The breakfast table clanged like a construction site. For over a year it had been just the three of them, three women, every morning joking about the neighbors' noisy sex life, judging Wanda's stupid teachers, praising Jane's amazing students, getting her mother's gossip on the Grand Teatr. But before Jane had moved in and Wanda's father had moved out, the breakfast table had been a minefield—Wanda and her mother on pins and needles while her father stabbed at his sausage, the three of them acting as if the fate of the world depended on his fucking peace and comfort, and for a while there she'd really believed it did. Now, once again, they were on their best behavior, called to order by the trumpet blast of a man. If Gurney weren't so adorable, soapy, and smiling with that robin's nest of hair, she might have been compelled to chase him away.

I have a headache, he said. I think it's from traveling.

It's from pollution, Wanda said. The air in Kraków is poisonous.

Jane's pretty face went sour.

What did she say? her mother asked in Polish.

Taking breaths in Kraków, Wanda went on, is like smoking two boxes of cigarettes every day.

Jane translated this to Wanda's mother, who wiped her mouth, ready to scold.

Wanda continued: My mother wants me to tell you that Communists like my father are guilty for making all the pollution. It is my father in particular, she wants you to know, because he's the director of the Academy of Metallurgy. Or he was until they fired him. Because he was a Communist, of course.

Wanda's father, Jane said, was indeed a professor of metallurgy. His name is Zbigniew. You may just meet him. He had nothing to do with the Lenin Steelworks, however, which are now called Nowa Huta, which is where the pollution comes from. Watch out for Wanda— she's an Earth First kind of kid.

Who's your father? Gurney asked Wanda, plunging an orange slice into his mouth.

All this is my father, she said, indicating the flat with a sweep of her hand. Do you think all Poles live like this? You're wrong. Zamoyskis are special. We're the *nomenklatura*. Most Polish flats are just little boxes, three meters by three meters. That is what Stalin said every person needs. Three meters. But some people, like us, need a lot more than that.

You're a Marxist? Gurney asked.

My father was. The Party loved him because he read Marx and Engels like a normal person reads the newspaper—every morning, as if it had changed in the night while he was sleeping. But nobody else is Marxist, not even the Communists.

Right, he said.

Nowadays Poland is nothing at all. (She was proud to use the word *nowadays,* but was afraid it was a little too British for him.)

Poof! said Jane, obliterating Wanda with a wave of her hand. Poland wants money, like everyone else. Open your eyes, girl!

Does anybody really know what they want? he said. Nowadays anything goes, doesn't it?

You're not going to be one of *those,* said Jane, are you?

One of what?

Some kook coming over here trying to save Poland?

I'm not trying to save anything. I just think it's kind of exciting.

Well, nothing new's going to happen here.

Something new's already happened.

Right. Corporations are at the gate, drumming their fingers, and Poland's pissing its pants to let them in. Money, sweetheart. Money's what's happening.

Boring, he said. Money's boring. I bet they just want to have fun.

Can't have fun till they get some money. It's a natural law.

Boring, Wanda echoed. We want everything, everything in the world, and then we want to put it on fire. But who is going to pay for it? Do you want to pay for it, Gurney?

I'm not paying for squat! he said. Let's just steal it, you and me.

Wanda blushed. Matka looked worried at the tone of conversation. Wanda assured her it was all about bread machines, but she wasn't in the least bit amused. Buttering a slice of poppy-seed cake, she said they should make Gurney feel welcome.

Oh! Jane said, grabbing his arm. I almost forgot your letters!

What letters? he said.

I'll go get them. She glared at Wanda as she ran from the room.

Oh yes! You must be very popular, Gurney. Already you have letters.

Is that possible? he said, wiping his hands and mouth, as if he'd been asked to leave the table.

Who's Sheila? Jane said, appearing behind him, leafing through three identical airmail envelopes. One is from some Sheila Sleeve, one is from a Mr. Robert Q. Sleeve, and one's from Uncle Leonard. Maybe it's just some *boring* money! She laid them next to his plate. He didn't pick them up.

Well, he said, Sheila's just a friend. I didn't know she had this address. But, then, of course she must. I guess I gave it to lots of people. I hope you don't mind. He looked around, blushing.

Of course not! Jane said.

Why would we? Wanda said, laughing.

So who's Sheila?

I dunno. A college student. You know.

She's written twice. She must be a good friend, like almost a *best* friend.

We're close, he said, touching the envelopes, fanning them out like Tarot cards.

Something had happened that Wanda didn't catch. Gurney blanched. He brought juice to his lips and glanced about the table. Wanda fought an impulse to reach out and touch him. She really wanted to kiss him, grab his hand right then and there and drag him out and show him the city—get started on their international stealing frenzy—but when he met her eyes she quickly looked away. They continued to eat in clattering silence.

She was running late for school. Reluctantly, she excused herself and grabbed a couple of candy bars. She slipped off to the privacy of her messy bedroom and started dumping books and tapes into her bag. She passed the candy bars from one hand to the other. Marzipan and raisins. Disgusting! Marzipan, as she recalled, tasted vaguely of vomit, and raisins in chocolate were like fat mushy bugs.

THAT FIRST NIGHT AT BEDTIME, AFTER A CHILLY DAY OF SIGHTSEEING, he leaned out the French windows and took in the view from his safe European home. Coal smoke chuffed from the neighbors' chimney pots. Dome-shaped lamps swayed on high wires, casting friendly shadows along the sleepy old buildings. He closed the windows and sat on the divan to look once more at his unopened letters. The lightest one was from Sheila; the thickest one was from her asshole father; the most dreadful one, addressed in that unmistakably pharmaceutical script, was from his own benevolent father. Just looking at the envelopes made him feel like a fool. Burning them, of course, would have made him feel sinister, but opening them would have been no fun at all. He wasn't at all sure what he wanted to do with them. He looked around for a safe place to hide them away.

Although Jane had lived there for a year or more, there was a sad look of abandonment about the place. Mammoth rugs covered the bare plank floors. Bookshelves and tapestries covered the bare stone walls. He couldn't decide if it was cozy or creepy. Jane called it the wreckage of Zbigniew's studio, the room where he had once tutored his young lady students. He liked imagining a young lady of metallurgy— a vestal virgin, or as Jane had said, a Vulcanian vixen—seated beside Zbigniew in the warm light of the desk lamp. He imagined Zbigniew looking like Hephaestus, maybe crippled and rather ugly, with his hand clamped onto the student's thigh as he explained the smelting of iron ore. He imagined Grazyna's ear pressed to the door.

Jane appeared in front of him, toothbrush jutting from her foamy mouth, T-shirt barely covering her yellow underpants. Her T-shirt read, The University of Chicago, Where Fun Comes to Die. He stuck the letters under his arm.

Is there someplace to keep these? he said.

Aren't you going to open them?

I just want a safe place to keep them.

Aren't you going to read them?

I want to keep them safe.

Right, she said wryly, showing him to a desk in the corner, fairly hidden beneath heaps of cosmetics. Here's a good place, she said. She opened the drawer and lifted some magazines. Put them under here. She slid shut the drawer, just missing the tips of his escaping fingers. She stood looking up at him, still brushing her teeth, the sound barely audible behind her closed lips. She went to the bathroom to spit. He had no reason to think she knew anything about his daughter, but somehow she seemed to be participating. Very strange. Very Jane. When she padded back into the room, flashing triangles of yellow as she walked, he had all but forgotten the menacing letters. She didn't seem to care that he kept glancing down, distracted by her body as if by a television with the sound turned off—she seemed to expect it. Her nude breasts slid around in her shirt. She pushed the T-shirt between her legs and sat cross-legged on her bed. How like it had been more than ten years before, when she was just a girl holding him ticklishly at her mercy, when little boyish nibs started showing through her Holly Hobbie nighty. He didn't sit next to her. He crawled into bed, safe on his side of the folding Chinese wall. She turned out the light and muttered something into her pillow. A short while later, the trumpeter high in the cathedral tower played his shaky eleven o'clock song.

Three

EVERY MORNING JANE WHISKED him out onto the streets, following a quixotic plan that would fizzle by noon and land them in some cellar café, smoking cigarettes and drinking brandy. Halloween in Poland, she said one morning as she led him down Ulica Grodska, is like sex in a cloister. It is absolutely unheard of, righteously ignored, but those of us with the horn for it never fail to sniff it out—and then what pleasure! She spoke to Gurney's heart, his cobwebby conscience, well aware that Halloween was his favorite holiday. The end of October was a few weeks away, but she wore a purple cape that billowed from her shoulders and rippled through the streets like a man-of-war jellyfish. Gurney stopped to press five thousand złotys into the hand of a Romanian girl, then ran to catch up with Jane. She was determined that day to find him a costume.

They shopped in department stores and drafty boutiques that smelled faintly of lavender and halitosis. One shop was a cellar with stone walls and low thresholds, its concrete floors heaped with used clothes imported from Vienna and sold by the kilo. In the center of the shop, hurried by their mothers, boys and girls changed pants and dresses, shivering but unashamed of their naked bodies. The mothers were more discreet, changing behind bedsheets or under their sweaters. Gurney bought a Tootsie Roll watchcap. Jane bought an orange-and-black striped bodysuit, expecting it to be a little tight.

They ended up in the most prestigious shop, with its vaulted ceilings and sycophantic salesman, but even this place seemed desperate for business, offering red leather pants and frilly lingerie next to Scandinavian hand mixers and Russian snow skis. Jane rifled through clothes racks for possible costumes. Gurney looked on, over the dressing-room curtain. He tried to be a good sport about it, but he knew each time, as he ducked out into the open, that the characters he portrayed (Sherlock Holmes, Jack the Ripper, someone whom Jane called Queen Jadwiga) had been neither redheads nor midwestern giants. He started to think he was impossible to disguise. But then Jane discovered the red velvet robe, rich and regal with feathery lapels. She tore it from the rack and passed it over the curtain. He wore it onto the floor, arms outstretched, while she and the salesman circled him like wolves, striking a bargain in Polish. The salesman stole glances down the front of her sweater while she tugged at the shoulders and groped the lapels. Her eyes kept returning to Gurney's face. Something wasn't right.

King Midas! he said.

Yes! Midas! Jane agreed. Touch me. No—touch this little lech who keeps looking down my shirt. Turn him into a lump of gold.

Gurney clutched his shoulder, making him quail.

Touch him all you want, Jane said. He'll do anything to make a sale.

The robe was fun and gave him a swagger. In the mirror, it clashed with his copper hair. Jane's face appeared under his arm, nudging through thick red folds of velvet.

I'll buy you the robe, she said, even a crown and a big long scepter—I'll even give you the golden touch. Just make one little concession.

Anything, he said, tickling her ribs, making her wriggle in his freckled hands.

We have to dye your hair black.

What?

Black.

In the mirror, his face fell slack. Red hair had always been his alibi. He knew redheads who were beautiful, redheads who were dignified, but he had always felt that *his* red hair, like his size, was an excuse to be puckish, even churlish. Hadn't Pinocchio been a redhead? Redheads never really grew up. But maybe Jane knew better. Maybe his essence was elsewhere. Still, when he imagined his red hair black, the difference was split between a gentleman and a criminal. Jane touched his chin with her finger, tracing a line through the valley of his cheek.

Look at yourself, she said. I remember when we were kids looking in the mirror, you'd always avoid your face, like it was a dirty picture. But you'd *gawk* at mine, like it was *also* a dirty picture! Even then, I thought someday you'd get over it. You should *enjoy* your pretty face—those full lips, that noble nose, those dreamy, aquamariney eyes. But we've got a serious problem here. So serious that I am willing to pay 190,000 złotys for you to be the King of Halloween, just so I can be your vampire queen. I'm willing to sacrifice an entire case of vodka in order to buy this gorgeous robe. What are you willing to sacrifice? Tell me that.

He flattened the lapels and smiled at the mirror.

So black it is, she said.

Black it is not.

After the final No there comes a Yes, she said.

And a No.

No, black it is.

Red.

No.

Yes!

So yes it is, she said.

No, yes it is not.

Yet later that afternoon, as rain throbbed against the windows of their room, Jane encouraged him to strip off his shirt, roll back the rug, and kneel over a kettle in the center of the floor while her gloved fingers worked dye into his eyebrows and hair. It smelled terribly of ammonia and turned her gloves purple. When she'd finished, she sat him facing the window and brought him a warm bottle of Żywiec beer. She brought him newspapers and magazines, but he mostly watched the cathedral, blurring and slithering in the rivulets of rain.

Half an hour later he was standing at the mirror, looking straight into his sallow face and thinking it looked like a wartime photo, captured alive in a tragic time and place. He had concealed his identity, blackened his boyishness, but now his face was fake and blue, and his deepest secrets were out in the open. In the mirror, over his shoulder, he saw Jane walk through the door in her new orange-and-black body-suit, which was in fact too tight, articulating every pit and curve of her body.

You're so debonair! she said. Like a young Errol Flynn.

Like an old Vincent Price, he said. I look dead.

He reclined on the floor in front of the mirror, starting to think he liked this rakish new look. Her striped silhouette looked naked in the mirror. She put on a record and dropped the needle. Gershwin's oboe wiggled through the air. She walked behind him, back and forth across the creaking floor, wearing neither panties nor bra.

She used to make him dance way back in junior high, back when his shyness made their nearness more exciting. Once she'd made him dance with his hands on her bottom, to feel it shift as she moved her legs. He would never forget that. And that same old fear was rising in his blood—for what was stopping him? A smile flashed over his face as he turned from the mirror and grabbed his cousin by the tiny wrist—by the ribs, by the waist, like a sailor, like a spy—and made her dance under the crooked mobile as it circled the room like thieves on bicycles. The music gleamed. Her neck was luscious. The tight, striped cloth was soft as skin, pushing on her breasts and hardening her nipples. She planted her open hand on his chest, and her face—mouth open and eyes open—looked back at him, full in the face, look-ing like Jane but so unlike a cousin as the horns resumed and rattled the picture frames that he started getting hard in his trousers and swiftly pivoted away from her, tripping three steps and upsetting the kettle, spilling purple-black dye in a lake that seeped into the grains and grooves of the wood, soaking the edges of the fat rolled rug.

ONE COLD AFTERNOON AS THE WIND SHOOK THE WIN-DOWS, he reclined on the divan in his new red robe, reading *Gar-gantua and Pantagruel*. He took great pleasure in wearing the robe—its broad fluffy collar, its fat furry cuffs—though Jane said it was to be worn just once, on Halloween, and then burned on All Saints' Day. But she was off teaching. His attention was starting to drift from his reading, stretching across continents of floorboards and rugs to a twisted black shape by the door. It was a pair of Jane's underwear, right where she'd sloughed them off.

Earlier that day, after lunch, it had been as if she'd been reading his guilt-wracked mind. She plopped down beside him on the divan and, as if out of nowhere, shared her unconventional ideas about morality. Morality, she said lightly, is a circus tent. The big top. It's gilded, gawdy, flocked, and garish. High, pointy, righteous, and mighty. (She shaped this out with her hands, molding a two-foot circus tent in the air in front of them.) It looks gorgeous from above, and it keeps us hidden from the eye of God. We love morality. We need it. We like it. Just like we like our traffic laws. But it's really only there for what's hidden inside it. Inside the tent—that's where we get to cheer and scream. Inside's where we eat teeth-rotting food and fly the trapeze, where we walk the tightrope, drive the animals crazy with whips and chairs and meaty treats. There's no good. There's no evil. Morality is nothing but a flimsy old tent, the pretense of knowing right from wrong in a beautiful world where anything goes!

It had been a pretty idea, and strangely inviting, especially how she punctuated it by lying back on the pillows, but the fact remained that Gurney loathed the very *thought* of morality. Where he came from, there was nothing fun about it. Maquoketa morality was as implacable and thick as the coarse woolen skirts worn by the nuns. It was the heavy paneled door to his parents' bedroom. Maquoketa morality hid horrible things. Maybe Jane, he thought, having grown up in the city, had been raised in a carnival of good and evil where both were equally fun because everyone agreed that both were for show. Gurney, however, having grown up in the country, had been raised in a place where fun was kept in a cage, a monstrous freak to be jeered at and mocked. As for him, he had secretly courted that freak, sneaking out to visit it whenever he could. Now it kind of felt as if he'd eloped with it.

And then there was the question of Jane's underwear.

One summer back in grade school, playing hide-and-seek in a neighbor girl's house, he'd swiped a pair of panties from her dirty-clothes hamper and stowed them safely under his mattress. At the time it hadn't felt bad at all. After all, had this girl, whose father was a doctor, really *needed* this one pair of underwear? And could she ever have prized them as much as he had, cherishing them for months, holding them to his nose, reverently touching them to his dry open mouth? He recalled their fabric being almost immaculate, *almost* concealing the girl who once wore them. They had put him on intimate terms with the girl, without his even having to strike up a conversation. This girl, who was garrulous and popular at school, was soft and vulnerable in the privacy of his bedroom. This girl, who was a state-ranked tennis player, had left him exquisite spots of pee. He could still taste of those fine spots of pee.

Stealing those panties had been an ethical decision, not a moral one. He had broken every rule of society. He had acted on his own sense of what was good, boldly dipping into the neighbors' clothes hamper like some kind of Nietzschean Übermensch. And now here he was, twenty-two years old, living with his cousin in Kraków, of all places, eloping with fun on the frontier of ethics—a beautiful world where anything goes!

He crawled across the carpet, following a faded ivy pattern that bloomed and branched toward the twisted black shape. Sliding two fingers into a leg hole, he lifted the satiny article to his face. She was so small! In his mind, she was big, a tall tornado winding through the city, but dangling from his fingers, with a narrow little crotch, with simple bands of lace sewn around the hems, she was actually quite small. He unzipped his jeans. He looked out the window at the flat gray sky. He expected her panties to be spicy like rosemary, strong like garlic, maybe rainy and earthy like a forest. Holding them out in front of his face, he imagined her body all warm on top of him, crawling all over him as the two of them tumbled through a chilly garden, a wet one, at night, with tubers and flowers and sticky soil, her breath combining with onions and jasmine, her small body sliding and pulling and squeezing, tugging up the length of him. But then when he put the cloth to his face and ran it all over his nose and lips, the smell was too vague, artificial, flowery, a perfume she'd never have worn above the waist. He kept masturbating, not finding the smell he was routing for. He searched the cloth for a trace of his cousin, an auburn hair, a spot of pee, something to bring her a little closer. Nothing. Even the perfume started to fade, leaving him nothing but the softness of cloth. Oh—but she'd felt that softness against her bottom! That same soft cloth had clung to her crotch—and now he was feeling that slinky cloth—feeling it soft against his face!

When he came, slashing semen across the carpet, he was muttering the words Jane is soft. When he sat back on the rug, black panties in hand, he thought how silly those words really were.

He was beginning to doze off and have wonderful dreams when in walked a gentleman with a close-trimmed beard. It didn't alarm him to have a stranger in his room. Wanda and Grazyna kept a steady flow of visitors, talkative Poles who had no sense of boundaries and carried their conversations all over the flat, talking louder while sitting on the toilet, louder yet while flushing the toilet. Sometimes they'd wander in and loiter at his window, drinking aperitifs and smoking cigarettes. Gurney didn't know Polish, so he never knew how to get rid of them.

This afternoon's man had a noisy sense of purpose. In Gurney's hypnagogic state, the man became the character of Pantagruel, a great foolish giant full of sweetmeats and venison, maybe still swaying from a battle on horses. Gurney groggily turned his face to the pillow, listening to Pantagruel clear his throat and shuffle through books and papers in the corner. He was dreaming a donkey had clomped into the room and was munching on paper when he heard the desk drawer squeak open. He looked up to see Pantagruel sweep orange peels to the floor, remove the drawer, and set it on the desk. Meaty hands removed magazines papers letters and rudely began rummaging through them. Gurney sat up. The man was holding the letters to his face, almost as if he were smelling them. He plunged his thumb into a seal and then stopped. He addressed Gurney in English with a mild Polish accent.

Huh? Gurney said.

Are these letters yours?

Are you holding seven letters?

He counted them out and said that he was.

Are they addressed to someone named Gurney?

Yes.

Then they're certainly not yours.

They're unopened, the man said, turning back to the desk.

And?

Aren't you curious, in the least bit curious, what they say?

Gurney didn't answer. He rubbed his eyes, swung his feet to the floor. Right there was the wad of Jane's underpants. Right next to them, rather suspended on the fuzz of the rug, was the long slash of semen. It was absurdly slug shaped, like the letter S on his father's old Spalding squash racket. He smeared it around, feeling it cold and slimy through his sock. He brushed the underpants under the divan.

The man turned around, saying, Aren't you in the least bit curious who *I* am?

You're Pantagruel, he said, not really thinking.

I am Pantagruel.

No. I've no idea who you are.

No idea?

Gurney shrugged.

He tossed the letters on the desk and took a step toward Gurney. These books that you enjoy, he said, indicating the bookshelves, some of which Gurney had left spilling onto the floor. They are from Russia, Germany, Italy, and France. They are from America, Mexico, Brazil, and Argentina. Have you any idea how they got here? And how did these rugs come all the way from Pakistan? This folding wall from Hong Kong? This mobile from Canada? Oh, don't answer. You lie on that sofa, which I brought here from Austria, dressed like a king and acting like one. That is very good. Let me tell you there are no kings in America. Let me tell you that. You lie there in the middle of the day, reading a book that I brought here from England, translated to English, for your convenience. You will find maybe four of its kind in all of Poland. I give you all the world, right here in this room, and yet you laugh and call me Pantagruel. Yes, I am the dreaded Pantagruel.

No, he said. Accept my apology.

So, then, who am I?

You must be Zbigniew Zamoyski. You don't have a beard in the pictures.

I am Zbigniew Zamoyski, he said, extending his hand and shaking hard. You are bigger than I thought you'd be. What can you do with your size?

Pardon me?

Are you an athlete?

I play basketball. Pickup games.

Do you box?

No.

Do you wrestle?

No. Well, I did in grade school.

I suggest you take up boxing and wrestling. Zbigniew pulled four books from a shelf and removed a hidden bottle of *vinjak*. He uncorked it, took a swig, and held it out for Gurney, who also took a swig.

I see you are enjoying my studio, he said. Do you make sure to give your cousin her privacy?

Of course I do.

Zbigniew Zamoyski recorked the bottle. And you have a job?

Not yet.

Not yet. Not yet. He carried the bottle around the room, taking good strides in his ankle-high boots. He walked behind the folding wall to where Gurney slept; he lingered for a moment, then appeared out the other side. He looked before sitting down on Jane's unmade bed. You are just visiting, then?

No. I'm staying.

But you haven't a job. I don't understand. Does your cousin give you money?

I have savings. They're running out, but I have savings.

You are a gambler, I see. I think you should work at the Kasino. You will find a brand-new casino on Florianska Street. It is called the Kasino Kraków.

I'm going to teach.

In that robe? Hmm. With your hair like that? An interesting ambition, but a teacher in Poland must be respectable. You should work
at the Kasino.

It disturbed him to see this man lie across Jane's bed, but after all
it *was* his home, and he hadn't invited Gurney to live there. Still, Gurney indulged himself in a little bit of insolence, saying, I'm not looking for respect.

Very good, he laughed. That much I believe. But then you have
more reason to work at the Kasino.

Gurney had nothing to say to that.

Zbigniew walked the bottle over to the window, which creaked
and strained in the October wind. He drank and gazed out long into
the distance. Gurney considered reaching out for the bottle, but then
thought better of it. They stood there in silence, looking out at the
city, listening to the glass, and just when Gurney was about to offer
him a Ritter Sport bar, Zbigniew spoke: On a very clear day, he said,
stroking his beard, from this very window, you can see the Tatry
Mountains on that far horizon. The wind clears away the fog and the
smog, and the mountains can be seen over the tops of those buildings.
More than two hundred kilometers away, the glacier shines like gold
in the sun. I have seen it. It is amazing to see. He stared for a long
time, the wind beating the glass. He stared as if hoping that, with a little bit of effort, he could manage to make the mountains emerge.

Gurney flattened out his robe and said: You can't tell me I'd be a
bad teacher.

Zbigniew looked at him, surprised. He uncorked the bottle,
drank, and held it out to Gurney, who also drank. Gurney looked at his
stocking feet next to Zbigniew's shiny boots.

I've been teaching for fifteen years. I have been a student, a lecturer, a university professor. I know a student when I see one, and you
are *perhaps* a student, *perhaps.* But you are not a teacher. You will
never be. If you have talents, you will find them elsewhere, perhaps at
the Kasino Kraków, but who knows.

They watched the vendors on the square, scrambling to tie down
flowers in the wind.

Grazyna says you are a nice boy, but she thinks you are lazy. To be frank, from what I have seen today, you may never find a real job. He paused, as if allowing room for rebuttal, and again turned to the window, nodding.

Jane says she knows of two good teaching jobs.

As for me, I don't care if you are a nice boy. I don't care if you are intelligent or stupid or honest or proud. I don't care if you call me Pantagruel. I don't care. Zbigniew's voice was shaking and low, as if he really wanted to be shouting. But if you hope to live in this flat, the same flat as my teenage daughter, you will not be lazy. For some reason, Americans are examples to our children. And if I learn that you are a bad example, and this is a promise to you, I will put you on the streets with the drunks and the Gypsies.

Gurney fought the urge to swallow. The wind picked up a vendor's umbrella and dragged it swiftly across the square. He stayed by the window as Zbigniew made his rounds about the room, returning the bottle to its place, collecting papers and textbooks and portfolios and shoving them into a portable stack.

On his way out the door, Zbigniew paused. A promise, he said. Your choice. You find a job, or you live on the streets. I suggest the Kasino, he said, clicking shut the door behind him.

Gurney looked at the letters thrown across the desk. Three were from his parents. Three were from Sheila. One was from Sheila's father—his daughter's other grandfather, a mean old grouch who, in Gurney's opinion, was much too much like Zbigniew Zamoyski. He gathered them up and looked around the room. Under the rugs? Behind the paintings? In the plants? Thinking fast, he slid them between the records in an old boxed set of Shostakovich.

PRIVACY, HE THOUGHT, meant nothing to Jane. Her mother had lavished her with American toiletries—pantie liners, pads, tampons, and douches—and Jane kept them strewn about the floor like bait. More to the point, she told him everything—not only that she'd cheated on her SATs, but that for a brief period, back in college, she had worked out of her dorm room for a phone-sex company. She did a demonstration for him of her Stained Jane monologue, riding low on the corner of her bed, rocking back her slender neck, cupping an imaginary telephone to her face.

As such, his cousin was proudly public.

But then one night, merely by accident, he learned she too was keeping a secret, or more than likely *many* secrets. Most nights he'd be writhing awake in his sheets, listening to the cats and drunks on the square, while Jane slept soundly on her side of the divider. But one particular night, when nerves had kept him up especially late— sometime after three o'clock—Jane flicked on her lamp and crept in her underwear to a stack of portfolios that he'd never really noticed before. Casting birdlike shadows up the walls, she took a bound black notebook from somewhere in the middle. As he drifted off to sleep, she furiously scribbled and scratched away, as if she'd been waiting impatiently all day, storing up fables, riddles, confessions, unscrupulous things even her tongue wouldn't utter.

He discovered she did this several nights a week. During the day he passed the folders with reverence, pleased to think she had secrets of her own. But at night he imagined invading her diary and discovering she had children in the capitals of Europe. He imagined her writing them letters she'd never send, promises and apologies she'd leave in her will. Once he dreamt of her funeral in the Alps. Her casket was open and strange kids looked on, more interested in her face than sad that she was dead. It was Gurney who stood at the pulpit, reading long passages from the secret black notebook, solemnly addressing a windblown crowd.

Four

JANE TOOK OFF FOR VIENNA ONE FRIDAY AFTERNOON, leaving Gurney in Kraków for the weekend. Wanda thought this was unspeakably rude. Jane had often disappeared for days at a time, off to the mountains or up to the Baltic Sea, sometimes to Vienna or Berlin or Prague, once to Helsinki. She claimed to have friends all over Europe, but Wanda just knew she didn't; she imagined Jane moping around in Vienna, alone in McDonald's, dreaming of America. Inside the Jane they knew was a colder Jane, then a mopier Jane, a sadder Jane, then a tiny little lonelier Jane. Wanda had a hard time feeling pity. She kind of felt bad for Gurney, however, and that night she looked in to see if he wanted company.

She stuck her head in around seven o'clock (the door was ajar) and was shocked to find him in the open window—crouched down and silhouetted against the sunset, surrounded by pigeons and talking to himself. Naturally, she feared he was pondering suicide, but she certainly didn't have to yelp the way she did, startling him there in the window frame. Afraid he would fall, she ran to the window and clutched her arms around his chest, his big and muscular Gurney body. She actually dragged him from the window to the floor, feeling his heart beating against her forearm. She held his face just inches from her face, adoring his gleaming toothpaste smile. He smelled fresh and young, like minty shampoo, and she was very near to kissing his mouth when she realized he had a loaf of bread under his arm. He airily mumbled, I *do* love her.

Wanda was certain she had heard those words, so certain she let his head drop to the floor. Love who? she wondered. Jane, of course! She paused to breathe and said, That is normal, but she was violently jealous of the sparkle in his eyes, knowing of course that it wasn't at all normal. He didn't even seem to recognize her, at least not until his eyes dried out and he sat up as if he'd awakened in the middle of the street. He got to his feet and shooed the pigeons, waving the stick like crazy Petrushka. She took the hint and left him alone.

After that he left the flat and didn't return until well after midnight, tripping over something in the hall. She suspected he'd been drinking—probably by himself. She tiptoed after him and listened at the door as he kicked off his boots.

The next morning was cool. It looked like rain. She canceled the thought of a picnic in the meadow, where they could look at the castle and find animals in the clouds, all towering and white, and thought they might visit the salt mines instead. But when she knocked on his door at five past nine, he was already gone. He didn't come home until that afternoon, and he spent the night behind closed doors.

Now it was Sunday and she was doing her business on the side streets and the main square. She had a cup of tea at the Zalipianki, where she met her cool friend Mateusz Słowokowski and his crummy friend Władek, who was showing off a camera he'd stolen from the German electronics store. She wasn't impressed. He was more than twice her age and should have known better. He pointed it at her, screwed with the lens, but he didn't even take her picture. It was probably broken. She didn't go with them to the Gallery Strawberry. Instead she thought she might check out the new Indian shop on Florianska, since it was the only store in town that was open on Sunday. It was then that she saw Gurney on the street.

He looked okay. Brown jacket. Black backpack. He was much taller than the rest of the crowd, like an Iowa scarecrow, his black hair perched like a crow on top, and he was intently watching something. She sidled up behind him to see what it was. It was Igor, of course, the blind Bulgarian fiddler who had played on Florianska since she was a child. Small and crippled, he sat on his chair, gazing sightlessly around the crowd as if forever pleading for silence. Then he lifted the fiddle to his chin and sawed it. He made beautiful music but he always looked perplexed and wild, as though trying to scale an incorrigible fish. Gurney smiled and nodded, watching Igor wrestling the fish, with scales flying off in all directions. The music was colorful, earthy, anguished, seducing listeners from the crowd streaming past, earning their trust, stealing them away to the unscrolling fields of Bulgaria, prompting Gurney to stop his smiling and close his heavy, dreamy eyelids. Her father had always warned her not to listen to Igor, not even to walk on Florianska Street because the music was just a decoy for the pickpockets and Gypsies, but in her seventeen years she had never known a single person to be robbed. It was just her father's racism and classism, the same paranoia that kept him hiding in the woods. All of a sudden, however, Gurney shouted and wheeled around, looking angrily over the heads, shouting, Stop! Stop! but to nobody in particular. She hurried over to him and he greeted her with relief—genuine relief. Igor played louder, more fiercely now.

My wallet! he said.

Was it taken? Who took it?

He shot his eyes around the crowd, thrusting his hands into the pockets of his coat. I was listening to that song and then like that my wallet was gone.

She pushed her way through the crowd, knowing she'd never find it, but trying to make it look as if she could. What kind of traveler keeps his wallet in his pocket? But here was her chance, she thought, and began scrutinizing and accusing every man, woman, and child, accosting the Gypsy women who gathered around her, tugging at her bangs, making the cross, waving playing cards in her face. Though she usually enjoyed their antics, she berated them in the voice of her father. The boiled-corn vendor suggested she steal one in return. The old policeman on the corner, who probably knew her father and hated him, and knew her friends and hated them, called her a revolutionary and laughed at her through his dirty brown teeth. Fortunately, Gurney didn't see any of that—he had turned his attention back on Igor, ready and willing to be robbed again. She assured him she had notified the police.

She bought him a bowl of ice cream at the arcades on the square. She liked how the waitresses dressed like mountainfolk but wore their hair in pink and purple, shooing pigeons from between the tables. She was proud of their yellow building, sharp against the sky on the northeast corner, its arches like eyebrows over Jane and Gurney's windows. She was proud of him, too, even with his hair so ghastly black, even if he was silly enough to be robbed on the street. She was glad to see him shoveling ice cream into his mouth.

Aren't you getting any? he said, pausing with the spoon halfway to his mouth.

No, I am okay, she said.

Do you want some of this? he said, pointing it at her mouth, unaware how sexy it would be to eat off his spoon. Know that I'm paying you back threefold.

It is my gift, she said, proud of how much he was enjoying it.

I can't believe I was robbed. I'm very distracted today.

Why are you distracted?

No good reason.

Now that she had him captive, she wanted to ask him so many questions: Why, for instance, was he such a lunatic—leaping a meter whenever the phone rang, drinking and eating everything in the kitchen, laughing and smiling when his eyes looked so sad? Why was he so distracted? And no bullshit this time. And where did he get his money, whatever was left of it? Did he like to draw or dance or sing? Did he like to kiss with those ice-creamy lips? Did he like the Pixies? Did he like the Clash? Did he dream of sneaking into her room and waking her up with a kiss on the neck? Did he ever think of her and masturbate? Did he ever fuck Jane? Had he ever fucked at all? Was he gay? Was he impotent? He tilted back in his chair, facing his cheery face to the sun, his freckles brightening, his blue eyes sparkling, but then the light drowned like a rat, disappearing into his dull black curls. His skin was flawless, like Dresden porcelain, but then his eyes started squinting and his mouth opened wide—a sunlit yawn, showing the black fillings in his snow-white molars, showing the walls of his cheeks and gums, and his tongue drew back to the dark cavern of a throat all stringy and dribbly with vanilla ice cream.

Did they take your passport? she said, not caring.

No, he said, clutching at a squarish lump in his shirt. Thank God I keep it around my neck.

How much money did they take?

About six hundred thousand złotys.

My God. That is horrible. Is that all of your money?

Huh? It's just sixty bucks, right? I mean, it completely sucks, really. Especially because I don't have a job. But, you know, I'll get a job. The way I look at it, whoever took it needs it more than I do.

You say that today, but someday you will need to steal wallets yourself. He laughed and looked away. She wondered if they were flirting.

It's just another warning to get off my butt. I should be ashamed, goofing around at my age. Anyway, your dad's gonna toss me out if I don't get a job.

My dad? she said, startled. He doesn't even know who you are.

Well, when he came by last week, he got all pissed at me for not having a job. He said I should work in the Kasino. Like I'm going to do that.

He was at our flat? That's impossible. I haven't seen my father in two months. Why did he come? Did he ask for me?

I guess you were at school.

But did he ask for me? Was my mother at home?

All I know's that he came into my room, which isn't my room, I guess, and he started firing questions at me—why I'm here, where I get my money, blah, blah, blah. Then he insulted me. Then he left. He's pretty intimidating.

What does that mean?

He, uh, startled me. Not really scared me, but he got my attention.

Did he ask for me?

He did say that I'm a bad influence on you because I don't have a job, which is exactly what my own dad would say . . .

Gurney went on about his father and his job hunt, but she couldn't be bothered to decipher his English, distracted as she was by her fury at her father: first, for sneaking into their home (she would change the locks at once); second, for thinking Gurney could influence her; and third, for not even leaving a note. He broke into their house, took God knows what, did fuck knows what, and didn't even tack a note to her door!

The waitress came and Wanda ordered Cokes, assuming Gurney had nowhere to go. The clouds were bulging, whipped up like meringue over the cathedral, but she had no desire to look for animals. Then she saw Mateusz and his creepy friend Władek walking toward them from across the Rynek. They barged through the tables and sat on either side of Gurney, who yawned and said *Dzień dobry* as if they were old childhood friends. She was sure they'd never met.

Mateusz was in Wanda's level in school. He was a clownish boy with messy hair who always smiled wide to brag his missing tooth. He and Piotr, another good friend, had a cabaret show called Wujo Płujo, an act that made fun of old people like her parents—the artistic, academic, and political elite. It was mostly just gags and dirty sock puppets, but Wanda never missed their shows. She loved them, but she hated the crummy old drunks they hung out with—especially this particular asshole Władek, who took a swig of her Coke the minute it hit the table and rudely spoke to Gurney in Polish, saying, You're too old for this pretty girl.

He's *not* too old, she said, but anyway he's just my friend, and he doesn't speak Polish. Certainly not *your* kind of Polish.

Mateusz poked his tongue through his gap.

Władek laughed and asked if Gurney was German, but she snubbed his question, turning instead to Mateusz and suggesting he practice his English with Gurney.

Oh, he's American! Mateusz said in Polish, with mock admiration. And an English teacher? I should've known—he does have that missionary look. Except he's got that Britpop hair. But I bet he's blond underneath. No, I bet he's a redhead. Just like Ronald McDonald! I'm good at this. He's a redhead.

She stifled her laugh because Gurney was catching on, nodding like a sport as he rummaged through his backpack.

Mateusz swiveled to face Gurney. He raised up his eyes as if conjuring a spell and started uttering English words: Blood metal dog wheel . . . feel motor . . . fool water . . . full bloody well!

Good words, Gurney said, cooperating, his hand still searching around in his bag.

Yes, words, Mateusz said, looking into Gurney's eyes as if reading his future. Storm eggs. Rain snakes. Snow fish. Earth worms. Birth words, he said significantly.

Gurney needs a job, Wanda said in Polish.

Get him a job at the Kasino, Władek said, swinging his lens around to Gurney. They always want Americans to run the roulette.

She immediately thought of her father, of course, and looked for his lizardlike resemblance in Władek. They had the same thin selfish lips, the same wide foreheads, the same long black Japanese cameras. Gurney's a teacher, she said, disregarding him.

Has he talked to Dick Chesnutt? Mateusz said.

I don't know, why? she said.

Dick Chesnutt? Gurney said, surprising all of them, making Wanda wonder if he secretly spoke Polish. Who's Dick Chesnutt? Is he like some biker guy? Jane mentioned him in a letter before I got here.

I think she hates him now, Wanda said, but Dick Chesnutt is very cool. He was my first English tutor, long before Jane. And he taught me how to play guitar. He has lived in Poland for many years and all the young people love him here. She wanted to boast about her first real kiss, that one wintry day in her bedroom, when in the middle of a guitar lesson Dick Chesnutt eased her back onto her pillow and kissed her with his rough and manly face, lashing his expert tongue against hers. But nobody on earth knew about that. It was their little secret.

He has a very famous penis, Mateusz said in Polish. His penis is very active in politics!

Matek!

He's an asshole. I gave him some money to buy hash in the Netherlands, and that's the last I heard of him. That's where he belongs, fucking Don Quixote. But I bet he'd get your friend here a job. Slimy Americans stick together.

He'd pimp him, Władek said, focusing his lens on Gurney's face. You know, Dick Chesnutt works for the Kasino. I think he's a pimp.

You're disgusting, Wanda said. Anyway, Mateusz, Dick Chesnutt's a brilliant idea.

What about Dick Chesnutt? Gurney said, removing a small brown book from his bag. It was a diary, the kind they sold in leather shops around town.

Maybe he will get you a job, Wanda said.

Jackpot Chesnutt, Mateusz said, firing an invisible pistol at Władek.

But what kind of job? Gurney said. I heard you say casino. I'm not working in some filthy casino. I could have moved to Vegas for that.

Very Polish, Matek said, admiring Gurney's diary. Very expensive.

A leather love book, Władek said to Wanda. He can use it to write secret notes to you.

Gurney reached for it, but Matek dangled it well out of reach, letting its pages flutter in the wind; only the first one had been written on. Gurney snatched at Matek's wrist and pried the little book from his hand. He angrily stuffed it back in his pack. Matek rubbed his arm. Władek focused his camera on Gurney's pissy face, waiting as it twisted into an angry pink grimace, then, with a chuckle, clicking the shutter.

Matek clapped his hands and said: The very first exposure on a new stolen camera! Film is a precious substance, you know. We must conserve.

Gurney got up and zippered his bag. He apologized to Wanda, glowered at Matek and Władek, and made his way across the square, ducking under umbrellas, shrinking as he got closer to their building, disappearing through their tiny door. Turning, she was caught by Władek's big lens. He snapped the picture. Mateusz snickered. Fuck them all, she thought, inhaling big and exhaling even bigger, squeezing these filthy boys from her lungs.

Mateusz and Władek whispered back and forth, as if arguing how she would taste. They decided something and nodded in agreement. Władek reached into his coat pocket and slapped a wallet down on the table. It was thick and black, bulging with złotys.

Private property, Matek said.

Open it, Władek said.

She scooped it up, flipped it open, and was met by Gurney's glowing face. His hair brassy red, beaming from an identification card. Did you take any money? she sternly said.

They hesitated. Władek tossed down a twenty-dollar bill. Mateusz produced a ratty five. They said they left his złotys alone. She flattened them out, green side up, and slipped them back into Gurney's wallet. She consciously kept from smelling the leather. She consciously kept herself from smiling. How'd you do it? she said.

Elementary.

It couldn't have been that easy. I was there. I didn't see you anywhere.

We sure saw you, Władek said.

You were ogling your American like a porn show.

Mateusz! Really, how'd you do it?

Here's the truth, he said, gesturing at Władek, who was putting the camera back in its case. He just saw you when we were walking by. But the instant he saw you, he had to have your picture. The camera *loved* you. Your chin was up, your lips were open—you looked like Echo, your eyes all weak for that goony Narcissus. So he stepped back a bit, thinking he'd get the whole scene, Narcissus included, maybe even that Orphic Igor. He thought: Step back, save film, get it all! But then he saw it, down there in the right-hand corner of the frame—the wallet pushing out of his pocket, pushing and slobbering like the tongue of a moron! It was more than simple—it was a *gift*. It leapt into his hand and we disappeared in the crowd. You should've been there—but I guess you were!

You two are scum, she said, smiling.

Mateusz looked thoughtfully down the arcades. No, he said, not exactly. Thieves are quite the opposite of scum. Thieves have never been scum in Poland. They've always been aristocrats and royalty. I'd think a Zamoyski would know at least that much. I figure if I play it right, I might just be the next in line.

So why'd you give it back?

I didn't give it back. Neither did Władek. We just gave a gift to a pretty Polish girl.

Right, she said. You know I'm giving it right back to Gurney, and you *know* I'm telling him just who took it. She shoved it into her bag and stood to leave.

Giving it back? That's a pity.

Aren't you scared? she said. Gurney's big. He could tear both of you to shreds.

Gurney's a schmuck, Matek said, laughing.

Gurney, Władek said, is the enemy.

THAT NIGHT GRAZYNA was at the height of her powers— evoking creases with crude thumb smudges, making pubic hair creep like ivy. She did seven-minute charcoals of Julian Zagórski, the famous young actor and bon vivant who was rehearsing to play Hamlet completely naked. She'd been commissioned to paint his image for the playbill.

He crouched in front of her, refulgent in the soft brown light. He appeared on her easel in short stark strokes. With one leg stretched behind him, flexing but steady, his body had a classical symmetry. His back was arched inward, his arms were thrown upward, and his wild curly head hung defeated. The skull in his right hand was thrust straight in front of him, gazing brazenly into the future.

But it was far too serious. She thought once again of the play she was promoting: Hamlet's swinging penis would have a tragicomic role, shrinking from Claudius, bouncing at Polonius, swelling for Ophelia, raging for Gertrude—or maybe raging for Claudius, who could know? She looked at the penis, which, since the beginning of this pose, seemed to have increased a couple of inches in length. Unless Julian had it strictly disciplined, she thought, his penis would lend real spontaneity to the play—like a puppy scampering around the stage on a leash. But this pose wasn't in the least bit spontaneous; it was pained and contorted, Prometheus Nude. She told him to relax and tacked fresh newsprint to the sketch board.

She walked over to him, making him stand straight, then went to work shaping him, lifting his chin with her index finger, tilting it thoughtfully from the left to the right. His head swiveled at her touch, alcohol bloomed from his lips. She stepped back and looked at his torso and hip, and saw that, in the past couple minutes, he had slackened and lengthened and was swelling in the glans. Forthright, she said, and he snapped his hips forward, tensing his stomach and stiffening his thighs. Careless, she said, and after a pause, he made like he was hurling the skull over his shoulder. Perfect!—except for his thighs, which with a brush of her fingers widened into a randier plié. She backed up to her easel and sketched his midsection, but just as she was suggesting the shadows encroaching his rib cage, the studio door flew open and let in Wanda.

Wanda, go away, she said and kept sketching, smudging out a nipple with her index finger.

I'm not waiting.

Go away.

Talk to me about my father.

Let me work! And we have company—he deserves his privacy. Julian looked arrogantly down at Wanda. She sassily smiled back, knowing he couldn't move.

He can listen, Wanda said. And you can talk. Anyway, I like to watch you work.

Not tonight. No arguments.

Good, she said, pulling out a desk chair. I hate arguments.

Wanda, she whispered, you're being a brat!

All the world's a stage, Julian said, presumably speaking in Hamlet's voice. Don't stall your lives on my account. I need practice being nude.

See, Wanda said, this guy's reasonable. Tell me one thing, then I'll go. Who's been letting my father into the house?

Don't be silly, Grazyna said, startled. He hasn't left his cottage for months! She hated lying, and she was terrible at it—and why was she lying, anyway? She had promised not to report Zbigniew's comings and goings, but she had insisted, more importantly, that she would never lie about it to Wanda.

You're lying, Wanda said, taking a stroll around the model. The skull shook in his hand.

I have never lied to you, honey.

Well, I can smell him. This place reeks of him. She followed her nose across the floor, striding past Julian as if he were furniture, sniffing dramatically at the air. I can smell him in here, and my nose never lies. It smells, she said, clambering onto the bed and burying her nose deep in the duvet, it smells just like my father's sweat and cologne have been rolling around on your bed!

Wanda! Out! This instant!

Julian's arrogance was melting into agony.

Deny it, Wanda said, looking up from the bed.

I deny it. Absolutely, she said, and this was the truth. Now go.

But Wanda didn't budge from her spot on the bed.

Very well, dear, Grazyna finally said. She continued sketching, but now imbuing Hamlet with all of her household woes: Jane's cruelty, Gurney's sloth, Wanda's bitterness, Zbigniew's pout, all of it dashed, rubbed, and scrawled onto the prince's reluctant frame. But then it wasn't Hamlet at all. In truth, it wasn't much of anything. She tore away the page and told Julian to stay put.

Wanda curled up on the bed, there to stay.

Grazyna tacked up another page. Julian sagged, then flexed his muscles. His penis grew red, thickened with blood, unrolled its length. Wanda shifted, creaking the bed. Grazyna kept sketching, not ashamed to be aroused by her art, not even in front of her teenage daughter, who had every right to be aroused as well. If only Zbigniew could have witnessed this little scene! But he was in no position to be pointing fingers. He'd committed any number of crimes, against the family, against the state. And now look at him, smutting around out there in Ojców. So damned righteous! So *prawa*, she thought, making a face. He was so *menaced* by anyone's pleasure—Grazyna's, Wanda's, even his own—so *mad* that he couldn't control it, couldn't contain it, and it was no wonder that he went off like a big Russian missile. But Wanda was young and free. She deserved to be spared all that. She deserved to have some fun.

Why couldn't Grazyna be a teenager, too? And why was it her job to keep them apart? Why couldn't she be shameless like Julian's penis, now pulling itself upward, nosing outward, maybe goaded by her daughter in the bed? Wanda sat up. It stretched straight out, fell against his hip. Should she draw it that way? Zbigniew allowed himself absolute freedom, but what did he do with it? He lived in a shack, afraid of his country, afraid of his daughter, madly intolerant of anybody's pleasure. Why should *she* waste *her* freedom too? The model was straining, his expression melting into a lascivious scowl, and his cock—it was rising tall against his belly. Wanda! she said quietly. Wanda was crouching on the edge of the bed, her mouth parted as she looked at Julian. Wanda, you're going! she said with a start, taking her daughter firmly by the elbow and forcibly leading her out to the hall.

Five

THE FRIDAY EVENING THAT JANE had gone to Vienna, Gurney had clawed crumbs from the heart of the loaf and scattered them into the blackberry sky, trying to attract the pigeons four floors down. The birds didn't budge. Changing his tack, he stepped to the ledge, filling the French windows with his breadth and height. Smelling the rich October air, he felt affection for the people about the square—how wild and disconnected they looked in the distance, like ants tumbling out of a gouged-open hill. Indeed the whole city, splotched and smoking, its roofscape dark to the blue horizon, seemed to be itching under blankets of smog. He leaned a little farther out, tossed crumbs more liberally into the sky, and all at once the pigeons rose up, spinning in a helix above the vendors' umbrellas, rising to the height of the cathedral spires and clattering and cooing all around his feet. Their talons scratched the green copper ledge, their beaks pecked at nothing, at crumbs, at nothing, their eyes stuck like stickers to their smooth little heads. Smooth little pigeons. Stupid little pigeons. Are you the smart one? he said to the dark one. You the homing pigeon? Tell you what. If I give you a note, could you bring it to my girl? It's really very easy. Fly from here to Berlin to Amsterdam. That part's a cinch. Cross the Atlantic along the coast of Greenland . . .

He was imagining the flight routes he'd seen on the plane, sweeping arcs in green, yellow, and blue that festooned the oceans and islands and continents, making the world seem manageably small. But then, seeing these pigeons' earthbound bodies, and to imagine them flapping thousands of miles, struggling far beneath the jet stream, he was struck by the actual distance home—not two points on an imaginary globe, not the leapfrog of two or three airports, but thousands and thousands of unclosable miles . . .

Suddenly a clamor came from behind him. Wobbling and startled, he reached for the frame, sending birds flying outside and in. Two birds fluttered around in the room, and there was Wanda rushing toward him. Someone shouted from far below. She was surprisingly strong, clutching him around the chest, pulling him to the floor. He'd never noticed how pretty she was, and wouldn't have dreamed how strong she was, panting her warm sweet breath in his face, clutching him firmly to her teenage breasts. He felt a kiss about to happen, swelling on his lips, tingling in his spit, so close that he raised his open mouth.

Klunk. She dropped his head to the floor. What? What had happened? He squirmed out from beneath her and got to his feet. Grabbing a yardstick, he chased birds from the room, hissing and shushing them into the sky. He broke more bread on the ledge until he heard her feet softly padding from the room.

He shut the windows, pulled on a sweater, and grabbed a feathery pocketful of złotys. He had to get out. He slipped out through the flat—down the stairwell and into the night.

BELLS GONGED, TRUMPETS BLASTED, tiny cars whined in the darkening streets. Communism was dead, corporations were circling, people were bursting with October ecstasy. Folks laughed in tavern doorways; punks threw firecrackers from the Mickiewicz monument; two teenagers had a dry ride right there on flagstones. Even the flower vendors were passing the bottle. Jane may have gone to Vienna for her fun, but all of Poland was there on the square, looking to find the next new thing. He, too, wanted his piece of the city—a cabaret, a supermarket, a Busy Town brothel, someplace even Jane didn't know. He'd been cooped up for weeks in the rooms of his secret, and enough was enough, so he turned down fashionable Ulica Grodzka and joined the mob flowing southeast of the square.

He was starving. He went looking for food in the darker parts of the city. After walking half a mile past caged-up shop windows, past a feast of appliances and dinosaur tools, he took a left turn down an even darker street, toward a yellow-lit sign maybe three blocks away. The pollution got heavier, coming from something big like a Safeway, some beast of a factory that kept people indoors. It smelled, as he imagined it, like cyanide gas. The thickening pollution made him want to turn back, back to the club, back to his flat, but he kept on walking, turning right and left to escape the smell. He'd lost all concept of the calendar recently. He counted back the days as he walked along. It was Friday, he remembered, his baby's birthday. She was exactly five weeks old tonight, but what did that mean? Could she laugh and lift her head? Had her eyes cleared up? He wanted to know. By day the city coursed with strollers and prams, milk-fed babies with fat little faces, a bumper crop of babies taking the nation by storm, and day by day he dealt pretty well. But tonight, as he walked, drunk and peckish, he felt he must have some genuine knowledge—not menacing information like he might find in those letters, not words and facts and photographs. But knowledge. He wanted to hold that baby to his face.

The yellow sign ahead turned out to be nothing, a closed petrol station.

She'd be twelve in less than twelve years, he thought. On September twenty-first, she'd walk home from school alone and her mother would be working until six or seven. She'd unpack her schoolbooks, open a pudding pack, sit in the kitchen, and look out the window—look at what? Where would she be? What city? What state? What country? She'd be old enough to want nothing but a visit from her father. Old enough to wonder why her father was gone, old enough to judge him with the mind of an adult. He approached the streetlamp and watched it flicker, its light lifting up and falling to the ground. He stopped and had a look at its noiseless moths, spinning in love for a fickle bulb, due to die over the next couple weeks.

An alley he'd been following stopped short. He'd reached, he feared, the Kraków clog, where dogs he'd heard yelping would come bounding after him and plunge their teeth into his tired legs. But there were clinks and voices behind a wooden gate. He pushed it open. Across a bumpy grassy court, dull red bulbs pulsed in basement windows and people laughed above the city's rumble. Going to the windows, he saw people drinking and, yes, relief, some were eating! Was it a private club? They were mostly men, boozing and smoking, maybe priests or mafioso. He tried the door and it easily opened. He creaked down mildewy steps to the restaurant.

Przepraszam, pani, he said to a waitress swinging a tray of beers between the tables. She didn't see him. Nobody did. *Przepraszam,* he announced. *Przepraszam, pani!*

Tak? Co? she said, slamming down beers.

To jest, er, to jest restauracja?

Co?

Restauracja? He said, miming eating, well aware that people were watching him and laughing.

A fat-headed man insisted Gurney sit across from him. Someone cheered. Someone belched. The man was burly, shouting one word over and over, thumping himself in the chest: Gurney realized the word was Wojtek, clearly the man's name, and responded by thumping himself in the chest, saying his own name. He sat and a beer bottle slammed down in front of him. He sipped it gratefully, slaking his thirst. A fist banged the table. Two fists, three fists, then a chorus of walruses banging their fists and demanding he guzzle, or so he surmised. They hollered as he gulped and foam drooled over his jaw, the cataract cold down his raspy gullet. Where the hell was he? The night was askew. Another beer slammed down and they pressed him to guzzle. He gulped half of it, then returned it to the table. They began to sing and Gurney swayed with them, going along, feeling okay, until he noticed that the surrounding tables weren't amused. At the next table over, there was an empty seat and plenty of food, but he felt obliged for the beers he had drunk. He slipped ten thousand złotys onto the table, but as he rose, Wojtek rose with him, widening his eyes and baring his yellow teeth. He clutched Gurney's shoulders and forced him back down, grumbling reprovals with fatherly restraint.

Listen, Gurney said. Do you speak any English? The man's face went slack. Do any of you speak English? They laughed uproariously. Am I just talking to pigeons here? I don't want to drink. All I want is food. They howled. He slammed his fist, and they howled louder. I'm just hungry. I'm starving. My daughter's gone. My cousin's gone. I'm gone, he said, and it felt good to say this, but his words, rushing out of him, trickled but a stream through the factory of their laughter. He said: Tonight my daughter is five weeks old, and you know what I do? I whack off into my cousin's underwear. Been doing it for a week— now it's just habit. My daughter's five weeks old, in the middle of America, and I'm beating off into my cousin's underwear. I know you have daughters, I know you'd kill me if you could understand me now. So you might as well laugh, though you'd kill me for ditching a defenseless little baby. But someday you'll catch me. Someday you'll figure it out and kill me. Gurney rose once again to leave, but now a lighter hand closed on his arm. He turned to find the thick gray sweater and ornery smile of Jane's friend Linda. He started, panicked. Had she heard him mention his daughter? Jane's underwear? Had she heard his stupid speech? He said: What do these guys want from me?

We're sitting in the corner, she said and thumbed at a dark table where her friend Jackie sat alone, lit by a candle. They had food on their plates. You can join us, if you're done playing with these guys.

He didn't really know Jackie and Linda; he'd met them in passing a few times before. His snap judgment was that Linda was fake and Jackie was cute. It would be nice to have some company, nicer yet to have some food, but he had the uneasy feeling that he was crashing a date.

Where's Jane? Linda said.

She went to Vienna, he said, still standing, keeping an eye on Wojtek, who was still laughing with his comrades. Gurney wondered anew if Linda had heard his confession.

Told you so, Jackie said, smiling at Linda. Her smile was so easy he relaxed a bit.

Why didn't you go with her? Linda said.

I couldn't afford it, he lied. He would have gone along had she invited him.

Their food was still hot—cabbage, potatoes, and sausage. Jackie had a blood-red bowl of borscht. That's what he wanted. Potatoes and borscht.

Can you join us? Jackie asked, to which he smiled and took a seat.

Who is she visiting? Linda persisted.

Jane? I didn't say she was visiting anyone. Do they have menus here?

The kitchen closed half an hour ago, Jackie said.

They must have something. Some soup, you think? Bread?

Sorry, Linda said. They're pretty lazy.

But then Jackie surprised him by hailing a waitress. She spoke softly at first, in mellifluous Polish, but when the waitress shook her head and the revelers started pounding again, she pointed her voice and gestured toward Gurney as if he were dying of a tapeworm. He was both flattered and ashamed when the waitress deferred and urgently went off into the kitchen. Jackie went back to her soup, carefully spooning red pools to her lips.

Did Jane tell you about this place? she said.

No, it's mine. I found it myself. I turned left off Ulica Grodzka, then right, then left, right, left. I guess I'm lost.

You're hardly lost, Linda said. You're in Kazimierz.

Oh, he said, looking for Wojtek, glad to see him drooping over his beer.

You don't know Kazimierz? The old Jewish Quarter? Jane hasn't shown you?

Maybe she has, he said, positive she hadn't, though she'd mentioned it a couple times. He watched Jackie spooning soup.

I think you'd remember, she said sourly. It's completely haunted by the Holocaust.

He thought of the cyanide smell and shivered.

Then you haven't seen the graveyard, Jackie said, leaving her spoon in the half-empty bowl.

No, I haven't, he said, excited that she was excited. Whether she was Linda's lover or not, she had huge brown eyes that he was secretly enjoying. What's the graveyard? he said.

It's the best part of Kraków, hands down. Remuh Cemetery, just three blocks from here. You can't see it from the street because it's hidden behind this big wailing wall. You go in through this apartment building that used to be a synagogue and come out into this graveyard that's all crammed with tombstones, all in Hebrew and covered with vines. It smells *great* in there, like dirt and mulch and life. I only go there when the sun's going down—that's when the sky's still light but the trees are black and there are all of these oil lamps burning on the graves. More importantly, that's when the *snails* come out. That's why I really go there.

He waited for her explanation.

The place is just *crawling* with all kinds of snails, she said. Little brown ones, big black ones—but I only pick the big ones, bung 'em in my bucket. He imagined her sneaking through the graveyard, lamps and snails reflected in her eyes. Suddenly he wanted to know everything about her.

What do you do with them?

I poach them like eggs! she said with a laugh. Then I eat them with garlic butter.

They're scrumptious, said Linda, clearly imitating Jane.

Rudely, the waitress dropped a basket next to the butter. Lifting the cloth, he found half a loaf of bread. No jam. No cheese. Whatever. *Dziękuje. Dziękuje bardzo,* he said, bowing to the waitress, slathering a chunk with butter and gladly shoving it into his mouth.

Eat up, Linda said, patting his back.

Filling up with bread, he felt more relaxed. The waitress brought him a pint of beer. Linda did most of the talking, but he found himself distracted by Jackie in the candlelight, her chocolaty eyes, her cowlick tipped with ivory light. He couldn't stare, but he couldn't contain her in a single glance; she kept eluding him. All night long he had been swelling with affection, a poignant desire without an object, and now, though holding back, he felt it warmly erupting from his chest and flowing onto Jackie's pretty face and slender shoulders. He wanted to rub her and keep her warm, and that was a crazy wish, but the few times she met his eyes she held them for a moment, and in those moments he felt rich and alive, like snails and soil, like vines and moss, and when he looked away he shuddered, knowing he wouldn't rest until he met her alone.

What are you doing in Kraków? Linda asked him.

Having fun.

There's a lot more to it than fun, she said. But then again, you didn't even know about Kazimierz. Have you been to Oświęcim?

Where?

Auschwitz?

No, not yet.

We were thinking about going tomorrow, Jackie said.

You haven't been, either? he said.

Of course we have, Linda said. But it's good to go back.

Why don't you come with us?

I'd love to, he said, not at all sure what he meant by that, apart from wanting to see Jackie again.

They shared a cab ride back to the Old Town—Gurney in front, Jackie in back with Linda. When they parted in the park, Linda said they'd meet him at nine, at the bus station. She waved a bit as they turned away. Walking the familiar streets to the Rynek, he wanted to run back and kiss Jackie in the streets, but then he thought of her dreary chaperone. He wanted to believe that Jackie was free, that Linda was just her dour friend, and at the thought of kissing her and eating her snails Kraków became one big playground. They would go to the graveyard and go to the zoo and climb the mossy walls of the castle. And tomorrow, of all things, they'd go to Auschwitz.

HOLDING HIS TICKET AT THE STATION, a bit glazed with a hangover, he took in the Saturday morning bustle. He bought a Polish candy bar for later, predicting it would be bitter and waxy. The sky looked like rain and the air smelled fresh, despite occasional blasts of car smoke. He was squinting to see who was coming from the station—Poles carrying boxes, occasional lost-looking backpackers— when Linda ran up and said the bus was going.

I've been here fifteen minutes, he said.

Well, we've got to get on it.

Where's Jackie?

She's not coming.

Why not?

Who knows.

He had a passing thought that he wasn't coming either, but she'd already gotten behind him and was guiding him toward the bus. All the seats were taken, but he could see that the aisle was filling up anyway. There was no getting out of it. They stood in the rear, bracing themselves on the backs of seats as the bus jerked around and rolled out of the lot. He was too tall to see the sky, or much else beyond the adjacent lane of traffic, so he closed his eyes and pretended to be sleepy. He should have stayed home and slept off his hangover.

Sleepy? she said.

A little, he said, not opening his eyes. If they could be quiet for a few more minutes he'd be just fine.

I bought us a little breakfast, in case you're hungry. If you like sweets.

Sure. Thanks.

Pulling a sack out of her daypack, she offered sugary jelly doughnuts. *Pączki*, she called them. He chose one and took a big bite, making sure he got jelly, but the flavor was terrible: sweet and bitter and perfumy, like some kind of cleaning agent.

I guest you don't like rose hips.

Is that what this is?

It's an acquired taste.

I'll keep trying, he said, taking another bite but liking it no better. He was trying not to resent Linda, his vague acquaintance who had shown up late, without Jackie, bearing such offensive doughnuts. But he had to be nice. She was tall and blond and she wasn't unattractive; Anglo-Saxon, he thought. Not his type, too brash, but that was for the best. He would eat her lousy doughnuts, and he would even suffer the hours of getting-to-know-you. He would keep it light and simple. And he'd ask after Jackie a lot so they'd know exactly the one in whom he was interested.

She watched him with a neutral face. They rode in silence, the city streets giving way to open highway, and he thought he might actually get some rest when she said:

So what do you enjoy?

Why?

I'm trying to figure out what you mean by fun. You said you're here having fun.

Did I?

You did. What do you do for fun?

Jerk off in Jane's underwear. That's what he wanted to say. He just shrugged.

Do you and Jane have fun together?

We have lots of fun together.

They eventually got seats. He laid his forehead on the foggy glass. Headlights reflected yellow on road. She kept quiet for a time, but after a while she asked if he was ready for Auschwitz. He said he was and kept looking at headlights and wet little clumps of red and purple trees.

Do you think you'll have a good time?

He looked at her like she'd poked him with a stick, but he didn't have an answer, so he turned back to the window. Hills rolled along like they did in Iowa, but the farms were smaller, divided by gorse and rough stone fences. He'd known about the death camps for as long as he could remember—there were those books by Elie Wiesel and Jerzy Kosinski, there was that miniseries on television called *Holocaust*. Then he thought of a local poet who had survived one of the camps, maybe Auschwitz. His parents had introduced him to her. They'd told him she had a serial number under her sleeve. Even more than film reels of bulldozers and bodies, that rumor of a number tattooed on the poet's arm had rooted the whole thing in his young imagination. So maybe this visit could be an act of nostalgia, he thought, maybe he could manage to enjoy it that way. But of course this thought so rudely missed the mark that it only made him angrier at Linda's question. A good time at Auschwitz! He jammed his hands in his coat pockets.

I kind of like it, she said at length, in an almost confidential tone. I don't know why. I guess it's not a normal thing to like.

He didn't know what to say to that.

When they pulled into Oświęcim his hangover was fading. It did wonders to get off the heated bus. She said they could visit Auschwitz I or II or both.

Auschwitz I, she explained, is the small one right in town. It's kind of set up like a museum. You might know Auschwitz II as Birkenau. It's the big one on the edge of town. It's left pretty much like they found it. I don't care which one we see.

Let's go to the museum one, he said, hailing a cab.

The cab dropped them off in a wooded neighborhood with the usual stucco houses and wood smoke. It was quaint. He opened his umbrella for them, expecting they would have a good walk, but after half a block she said they were there. She pointed to a smallish, tasteful gate, arched with the words ARBEIT MACHT FREI.

Work makes you free, she said.

I know, I know. He had seen countless photographs of the gate.

They would meet in two hours, she said, at the Visitors Reception Center. She suggested falling in with a tour group. She left him under his umbrella at the gate. Two hours at Auschwitz! From the looks of it, it could have been a small college campus—lawns and flagstones sogged with leaves, its lush ranks of mossy poplars, uniform rows of three-story buildings whose brown bricks and red clay roofs looked a bit more German than Slavic. It was nice to be alone. In this oddly pleasant setting, he rather felt like a tourist again—not having fun, of course, just walking and looking, drips and drizzle pattering his umbrella.

After wandering around and seeing almost nobody, he bumped into a group of fifteen or more. All of them wore sky-blue jackets, each with a white Star of David on the back. Some carried tall Israeli flags. A couple of them smiled at him, but most were listening to the young American guide. According to the Polish government, he said, Auschwitz was to be a monument to the martyrdom of the Polish and other peoples. Those were the words they used. As we make our visit we will see special attention given to Polish Catholic martyrs, much more attention, in fact, than is given to the millions of so-called other peoples, namely the Jews. Gurney was impressed by the guide, who couldn't have been much older than he, and he kind of wanted to fall in with the group, thinking he'd get the true story. But as Gurney himself wasn't Jewish, and wasn't wearing a sky-blue jacket, he continued on in his own direction, arriving once more at the infamous gate, where, if he wasn't careful, Linda could find him still gazing at the trees. But the gate offered a pretty perspective on the camp. And rain on his umbrella made harmless, almost inaudible little taps. He listened.

Here he was, enjoying himself at Auschwitz!

Another group shuffled by—all ages, all sizes—and even though their guide spoke only in German, a fact that made him a little uneasy, he joined up as if he'd been waiting there for them. *Tag*, said a man in a Tyrolean hat. *Guten tag*, he answered and went along with them, having no clue what was being said—why that patch of grass was important, why one building that looked like all the others brought such an awful hush to the group. They stopped at a building in the camp's far corner. A sign over the door read BLOK ŚMIERCI, which the guide translated into German. *Auf Englisch?* Gurney asked the man in the Tyrolean hat. Block of Death, he said and looked away. They went inside.

The group squeezed into chilly corridors, peering through three-foot iron hatches into cramped living holes. He felt that the guide, who was clearly Polish, was laying it on thick for the German tourists. He had them linger at the shrine of a Polish priest who'd given his life so that a family man might live. Likewise, watching them bowing over hundreds of votive candles, he felt that the Germans, for their own part, wanted to show their sincere atonement. Standing amid them at the black cork muffling wall, where tens of thousands of prisoners had been executed, Gurney felt how very American he was—an interloper with no right to anyone's sorrow. Still, he'd traveled all this way. He wanted to get as close as he could. Trying to imagine such summary killing (hundreds of people shot dead each day), and wishing he could give at least the impression of horror (maybe by mustering sniffles or tears, maybe by closing his eyes in prayer), he was overtaken by un-usually strong fatigue.

The tour groups all mixed together in the next building—blue-jacketed Jews, atoning Germans, dozens of others he couldn't iden-tify, sniffling and coughing from one room to the next. He'd seen photographs of most of this stuff before. Everyone probably had. Hundreds of thousands of shoes and boots sloped the walls in one long room, as did glittering heaps of eyeglasses in another. There were mounds of prosthetics and mountains of women's hair—*Jewish* women's hair, black and blond and auburn and red, straight and wavy and shockingly braided. A roll of yellowing burlap stood alone, as did candles and soap and a canister of Zyklon B. Real burlap. Real soap. Real cyanide. The connection was clear; the meaning, well, opaque.

Then something struck him with genuine wonder. Small striped uniforms hung on display. A small checkered skirt. A small tattered blouse. And above the clothes were photographs of children, hun-dreds of kids, each one featured from the same three angles: profile, mug shot, looking upward to the right. Every day boys and girls had been torn from classrooms all over Europe and arrived at Auschwitz in the dead of winter. Some got on by dint of their innocence, some by dint of rage or wiles. This was what he saw in those photographs. Leonard Grosicki, proud and pudgy, managed to make himself sit up straight in spite of his homesick, watery eyes. Mamet Merenstein, a wiry little kid, managed to get by on his incorruptible sweetness—protruding ears, parted lips, wide eyes looking at a real-life monster. *Maria Matlak, ge-boren 1928, Häftlingsnummer 39847, mit einem Sammeltransport am 2. April 1943 nach Auschwitz verschleppt.* Maria Matlak, fourteen or fifteen when she arrived from someplace—Czechoslovakia, from the sound of her name—got to keep her dull blond hair, much the same color as Linda's or Wanda's, held back on the side by a simple barrette.

In profile she was frightened, a metal bar pressing at the back of her head. Full-on she was sad, eyes glassy, sorrow tugging at the corners of her mouth. But in the third photo, with her hair pulled back in a flowered scarf, her eyes looking upward and to the right, she had joined a generation that would rise above childhood, rise above puberty and safety and fun and take on their menacing photographers. *Helena Waholek mit einem Transport aus Krakau nach Auschwitz gekommen,* lost her hair, left her girlhood playing in the streets of Kazimierz. She came to Auschwitz ready to work—ready to work and set herself free. Looking at kids who died unspeakable deaths, he was struck by nothing so much as their beauty, their vitality, struck by the mettle of this steely generation and if just for one moment he was shaken free from himself. He realized, too late, that he had been smiling.

When he turned away, Linda was standing there looking at him.

I thought I might find you here, she said.

Why do you say that?

No reason. When you're done you should see the Krematorium.

I think I'm done.

It was a squat, brick structure, built into a hill. A little death factory with a trapezoidal smokestack. A group of them crowded into a concrete chamber. They followed the guide's finger to a hatch in the ceiling, a hole through which, as Linda translated, pellets of Zyklon B had been poured. Leaving the gas chamber, they followed the path bodies had taken to the rusty, cold, coffinlike ovens. Linda told him that the Zyklon B hatches had been added for effect sometime in the fifties.

It's a powerful effect, he said.

The guide explained the elevation system, gesturing with his arms like a flight attendant, showing how bodies were lifted by a conveyor and then inserted by fours into the kiln. Linda looked on with no discernible expression. Taller than the rest, he looked on from the back. Everyone was vital under bright caged lightbulbs, rainwater shining on gray and yellow slickers. Tousled gray hair and clear plastic scarves. Fidgety kids holding grown-ups' hands. He thought of the poet with a number on her arm, probably still living in northeast Iowa. He thought of Leonard Grosicki and Mamet Merenstein, Maria Matlak and Helena Waholek, all those children with their big brilliant eyes. And yes, as ever, he thought of his daughter, growing up in this modern world, and then as usual his thoughts fizzled into blankness until he was just looking over people's shoulders to the cold open mouth of a square black furnace.

TRAVELING BACK ACROSS SCRUFFY FIELDS, watching dark clouds sinking on the horizon, they said next to nothing at all. The land was wet and rough and still, but fifty years before it had been the Nazi frontier. Fifty years before, in a storm of tanks and planes and soldiers, Germans had crossed and encompassed those fields, trapping them up in a barbed-wire net, digging and slicing and building and stretching, stripping the flesh from the bones of a nation and building a monster, a pervert, a factory, the colossal sicko of their imagination. Fifty years before, Poland had been Germany's ethical frontier—but what kind of ethics herds people like cattle? What kind of ethics kills people like roaches? A new kind, he thought, a sinister kind. Anything goes on the frontier of ethics. No morality there to tell you what is good, you answer to nothing but your wishes and fears, and depending on who you are, depending on how you think, anything can happen. If you think in columns, if you hide yourself behind fantasies of racial purity, if you hide yourself in rows of men who goose-step headlong into a fantasy of power, then of course you will master that soft frontier, chart it out, pour concrete for new moral factories, new moral cities. And if you hate, he thought, then hate must be your towering good, hate must be your moral fuel, the white-hot fire in your moral ovens. For hate is absolute, it lets nothing else come before it. On the frontier of ethics, anything can happen, and nothing is sacred.

When they parted at the station, she must have been reading his mind, saying she would tell Jackie that he looked forward to seeing her on Halloween. He thanked her for taking him along and walked alone back to the Rynek.

He paused at the leather shop near his building, not yet ready to go upstairs and face the Zamoyskis. Through his wavy reflection he saw leather jackets, leather pants, leather luggage. At first he was revolted by it—pounds of shaped and twisted animal, curled and polished—but as he took in all the opulence and carnage, one small object caught his eye. It was a coat-pocket book, bound in leather. A permanent book. For some reason it was engraved with bulbous Hebrew, under which was printed the word POLAND in English. Why? Why on earth? But before he knew why he had gone in and bought it and was climbing the stairs up to the flat, flipping through its blank pages. He had bought it for his daughter, he realized. He would write all sorts of things in it for her—fun things about pigeons, solemn things about Auschwitz, maybe honest things about Jane and Jackie, even maybe something about Sheila.

WHEN JANE CAME BACK on Sunday night, he had been growing morose all day—his wallet having been stolen that morning, his reasons for staying having fallen like the leaves that were filling the city's soppy gutters. So when she burst into the room and dropped her luggage and said she had a super surprise, he hardly lifted his eyes from his reading.

Why so glum, chuck?

It's not you.

Is it you?

It's everything.

Natürlich. We've gotta get you out of the East one of these weekends. What are you reading? Petronius! That's not so glum, she said, sitting next to him. That's sexy.

I'm just reading words. I went to Auschwitz yesterday.

Oh, you poor thing, why the hell'd you do that?

Linda took me.

Linda? Good Christ. If Linda told you to jump off a bridge, would you do it?

It was good for me.

I can see that. Here, cabbage, I've got something that's really good for you. And no more nasty Auschwitz, you hear? Actually, I just have a picture of your surprise. She pulled things from her bag, looking for it. The real thing won't arrive until Wednesday. Here it is! She showed him a sketch of a man in a tuxedo.

You got me a gigolo?

You wish, Encolpius! It's the tuxedo. I've had one fitted to your grand old size, so you can wear it at your new job.

I'm going to *be* a gigolo?

You wish. You're going to be a croupier at the Kasino Kraków.

Fuck me. No way.

Don't be a brat, she said in all seriousness. She got up.

I'm not a brat. I'm just not a croupier, whatever that is.

Well then what are you? Are you a teacher? No. Are you going off with all your friends to medical school and law school and graduate school? No. Are you a musician? An artist? A movie star? Do you have a trust fund? If you're a traveler, well then travel, but it looks like you've come to a stop here, right? And you're going to need money, aren't you? You're going to need something. She slapped the picture down on the desk. I'm not your mother, I'm your cousin, and I stuck my neck way out for you this weekend. I even got a tuxedo fitted to your size, just so you wouldn't turn into a goddamned nobody. Remember that. Don't forget it.

She slammed the door behind her. After sulking for a while he walked over to the table. The gigolo had one hand in his pocket, smiling like a million bucks. She was right, of course. He had no money, and he had no business being a brat.

The door creaked opened and she came up behind him. She slipped her arm across his belly and said, Maybe you're right. Maybe you're *not* a croupier, honey, but at least you have to give it a try. The Kasino's a scream! It's about games and risk and stuff. It's all about fun. Everybody's dressed up and drinking martinis, whores walk around between the tables—*pretty* whores. You may not think so, but it's just your thing.

It couldn't be. It sounds awful.

She tickled his ribs and said that she'd show him *awful*. Close your eyes for a big surprise, she said. He opened them and found five new Ritter Sport bars.

Six

LATE ONE AFTERNOON, when Jane had finished her classes for the day, Gurney went to meet her in the Kawiarnia Jagiellonska. He followed her directions through drizzly medieval streets to a low iron doorway and a narrow stone stairwell that corkscrewed down into a gaslit café. The low, arched ceiling made walking difficult. Disaffected students read fat books by candlelight. They smoked wretched-smelling Caros, drank hot honey mead, and gave him looks that let him know he was a tourist. Such was the Jagiellonian University. When he found his cousin at a corner table, she was already holding court among some anglophone friends—Christine, Ralph, Linda, and Jackie, all of them looking jaded in the greasy cellar light. Jackie greeted him with an easy smile. He hadn't expected her to be there, nor had he expected Linda, who was looking as unreadable as ever, almost as if they hadn't had their trip to Auschwitz.

Sex among friends, Jane began, looking around the table, meeting everyone's eyes before going on. Sex among friends, like Halloween in Poland, should never see the light of day. Consider two friends. Consider, well, for example, Jackie and Linda, two of our dear friends who meet one day at the open market, the Nowy Kleparz, a chance encounter between the leeks and beets. It's Wednesday morning. It's cold and windy. The air is crisp and smells of leaves—in fact it's way *too* crisp for the jumper Jackie's wearing. She shivers and jiggles. Linda rubs her goose-pimply shoulders. They shake and talk and sort through the onions. They probably gossip about Jane's dark cousin who's recently stumbled onto the scene. Linda thinks it's safe to talk about a man, to deflect attention while she moves ever closer to shivering Jackie, whose big brown eyes crave the woolliness of Linda's gray sweater. They embrace. Why not? It's Wednesday in Kraków. There's really nothing else to do.

Gurney looked around the table: Linda was smiling, Jackie was looking sidelong at Jane. Christine yawned, and Ralph, who had the beginnings of jowls and smart square glasses that made him look stupid, coughed.

Let's back up, Jane continued, lighting a cigarette. No embrace, but Jackie still shivers, and Linda gladly gives up the sweater. They start to chat and pretty soon it turns out one of them was going to make Basque pie, and the other one was going to make leek soup. Linda insists they buy a bottle of bull's blood and make lunch together on her big ceramic coal stove. Jackie needs persuading, but of course she agrees, and off they go. Halfway home, as if Linda'd planned it, the sky turns black and it starts to pour, a total cloudburst, drenching the paper grocery bags and soaking our friends to their pretty little bones. When they arrive, all wet and sloppy, Linda lights the gas and stokes the coals and shows wet Jackie the way to the bathroom, which, as we all know, has no door. Of course Jackie feels the tension—she's felt it all along—but not until Linda is crouching over the tub and stirring the suds like a roiling cauldron does Jackie really consider her rump, now slightly parted, articulated by her dripping, *clinging* skirt. She's nervous, but she considers it. Linda's bottom.

Jackie reached for one of Jane's cigarettes, giving her a simple glance.

Of course Jackie has a dilemma, Jane explained. However much they might smell like rain, however wet and soggy her underwear feels, she knows that Linda just can't keep a secret. For even a dreadful secret, like the chirping sounds Jackie makes when she's . . . *happiest,* or the lemony way Jackie tastes when she's happiest, even a dreadful little secret like *that,* when trusted with Linda, will be loosed over the city like a hundred red balloons. But then Linda's got a dilemma, too. However eagerly she wants to unbutton Jackie's jumper and push up her breasts with her nose, she knows herself. She knows she'd have to tell someone immediately, and a few more people eventually, and thereby be exposed to all the other vultures who desire Jackie as much as she does. It's tough. We all know the economy of revenge around town. The Kraków rumor market. Anyway, this is all hypothetical. The whole story is hypothetical.

Of course it is, Linda said, laughing with such ease that the story in fact *did* seem hypothetical. She had straight blond hair and such a frank face that Gurney wouldn't otherwise have thought of her bottom. But now her frankness made her formidably alluring, whether or not the story was true.

Of course it is, Jackie said, as frankly as had Linda. But then she stood, put on her coat, and meeting everyone's eyes but Jane's, said she was previously engaged and had to go. She looked so dignified with her short, sandy hair that Gurney wanted to follow her out. At that moment he felt much closer to her than he did to Jane, but then she was gone, leaving an uneasy silence behind. He felt creepy. He felt accomplice to something—but to what? Could this possibly have been a true story? Had Jackie and Linda been out on a date the other night? Or was Jane just up to her old tricks? But what, for that matter, *were* Jane's old tricks? And what was she driving at? If she was trying to punish Linda for taking him to Auschwitz, her plan seemed to be backfiring. Linda urged her to continue the story.

Must I? Jane said with twinkling eyes.

If you must, Ralph said, you must.

Okay. So Jackie's standing and Linda's stirring bathwater, both of them still quite wet and shivering. The tub is filling, hot and steamy. Jackie says they should boil water for broth. Linda tells her to do just that. So Jackie fills a kettle and puts it on the stove, and while she chops vegetables, the flat goes foggy and sweat slides through the rainwater down her hot back, down her skinny arms. Hmmm. Linda watches from where she is in the bathroom, stepping out of her skirt, pulling off her shirt, unhooking her bra, loosening her hair, shedding all but her damp blue underpants. Even that sags to show some hair. Pretty sexy, huh, Ralph?

If you say so.

Well, it is and Linda knows it. But what's she gonna do about it? She could get in the tub like a good girl—soap up and get out. Maybe get dressed. Or she could go into the kitchen in just her knickers, grab herself one of Jackie's carrots. This is just what she decides to do. Jackie looks up, continuing to chop, but slowly now, fearing for her fingers. Linda tells her to go take a bath. Jackie laughs and tells her to go first. Linda refuses. Jackie points the knife at Linda, who laughs even though it's hardly funny, that big knife so close to her smooth white belly. Linda turns her back to Jackie and uncorks the bottle of bull's blood, showing off the fine muscles in her back and shoulders. Jackie watches. She stops her chopping, takes the wine, and *finally* goes into the bathroom. We've all been very patient with her. We all know Jackie's peachy peach jumper, right? *Dobrze.* It's sacred how she wears it, untouchable like Athena's aegis or something. Well, now she just doffs it like some old windbreaker. She unhooks her bra, steps out of her knickers, and slides, very naked, into the tub. Linda, taking this as a clear invitation, makes busy noise and then slinks into the bathroom. Jackie just dallies in there, suds wobbling from her swinging breasts, suds parting on the surface of the water, just enough to reveal snatches of leg. It's hard making conversation when your underwear's all wet, but Linda can hardly just up and leave, so she sits on the edge and assesses the situation: Should she be the aggressor and plunge a hand into the water? Should she grab a piece of slippery Jackie? Is sitting on the tub as close as she will come? Up to the last minute, the bathroom scintillates with possibility!

Jane laughed her mean little laugh. She sipped her tea and leaned back into the shadows.

Is that all? Linda said.

Finish it, Christine said.

It *is* finished, she said. The rest would be pure pornography. I think we're all above that now, aren't we?

Ralph wiped his nose on the back of his hand. Quite, he said.

I suppose I could give you the *moral* of the story, she added, looking down, smiling, but that's so obvious. And I'm sure all of you have more important things to do.

Quite, said Ralph, not budging. I'm previously engaged!

They all had a good laugh over that—even Gurney, though he felt like a fink for laughing at Jackie and it left him wondering how he would face her on Halloween night.

SEVEN

NEVER MIND THE AMERICAN dollars, never mind the six hundred thousand złotys—the fat leather wallet held even greater treasures, stuffed and meaty like a sausage pierogi. Bright as an orange on his Iowa driver's license, Gurney was beaming at six foot five, 190 pounds, residing at 900 North Dodge Street in Iowa City, Iowa. On frayed business cards were the names of restaurants—the Kitchen, Moti Mahal, the Thai Star Café—where he'd go to stuff his face, then lapse into talking over the spicy, greasy wreckage of plates. Yet what puzzled Wanda on that Thursday afternoon, as she sorted through the wallet for the twentieth time, was the absolute lack of photographs. Didn't he have friends and family? Was Jane the only person in his life? But then how could it be, in all her flipping and sorting, building the man from these cards and tickets, that she had never before noticed this one thin pocket hidden inside the bill compartment? It was sealed with some kind of glue. She sucked in her breath and sliced her thumbnail along the slit. Sure enough, there was a photograph in there, stashed upside down and backward.

It was a picture of Gurney and a mousy girl with dark hair, a crewneck sweater—American as hell. It was black and white, blurry, and, okay, so she was pretty, so they looked good together, but on closer inspection there was no mistaking their common misery. Just look at their eyes: total opposites. If Gurney was checking the sky for birds, she was checking the corners for spiders. Why did he keep the dumb thing around? The picture made her a little sick, not unlike the shots of her parents after their marriage, when they were beautiful young mannequins attached at the hands, faking their way through Communist society. Again, boring. Now that they were divorced, however, her parents were acting so much realer; maybe sometimes they acted like children, maybe they both did some really stupid things, but at least the house was alive for once.

Gurney would be needing his wallet back, she thought, since that night they had their Halloween. She wondered why foreigners made such a fuss over Halloween, and she imagined them crowding into the Jama Michalika, dressed like vampires, too drunk to be pretentious, sucking each other's necks with cheap plastic fangs. But she reasoned that the Americans could have their Halloween because it was nothing compared to Juvenalia, the best of all of the city's customs, when the key to Kraków was given to the kids so they could dress up in costumes and run torches through the streets and remind everyone how fake and awful they'd become. She'd have to wait for April for that, however, and Gurney and Jane were getting theirs tonight.

She lay back on her bed, the wallet flopped open on her chest, and listened to the soothing sound of the wind. Just one thing was wrong: she had taken too long to return the thing. She had planned to contrive a story to protect her friend Mateusz, and just about anything would have convinced Gurney, but she had grown so fond of the thing, emptying it, smelling it, opening and closing it (everything short of putting it down her pants!) that now she had to bother with telling Jane, too, who, the bitch, would start snuffling around like a nosy bloodhound.

A soft rapping came at her big door, behind her tattered print of *The Scream.* It came so softly that she thought she had dreamt it, for nobody was home. When it came again, louder this time, she clapped shut the wallet and stuffed it under her pillow. She sat with a creak but didn't respond.

Wanda?

She said nothing.

Wanda? came the voice again. It was Tati.

You shouldn't be here, she whispered—but why did she whisper?

Maybe I shouldn't, he said, trying the door, but as he should have known, it had been dead-bolted since the day he left.

Stop, she said loudly. Don't touch my door handle. I don't want you here.

That's what your mother says. But I want to talk about that. Would you let me come in, *kopytka*? Just for a minute?

Let me see, she said smartly. I've forbidden you from touching the door handle, and you can't possibly come in *without* touching the door handle, so I guess you're in a fix. Looks like you're staying out in the hall.

You could open the door for me, he wheedled, almost succeeding in making her smile.

Fat chance.

Listen, Wanda, honey. I'm sorry.

For what?

Everything.

List all the things that belong to everything.

Well, he said, pausing. I'm sorry I left your mother.

Don't be. I'm glad you left her. She's glad, too. What else? she said, getting to her feet and pacing the herringbone boards of her floor, creaking back and forth from the door to the window.

Well. . . . His voice trailed off and he was silent for a while.

After almost a full minute she asked what was wrong.

It's my stomach. Maybe it's my heart. I can't be sure until I've been to the doctor.

Are you okay?

I'm not well, he said weakly. I just stopped by to give you something.

What is it?

Open up and I'll give it to you.

She waited for a moment. She wanted to torment him, make him hurt, writhe in pain out in the hall, but curiosity got the better of her. Anyway, there was a small chance that he really wasn't well. She unlocked the door and looked up at his face. His face looked old and worn and defeated, but to her amazement he was lavishly dressed: fine black boots, tailored gray trousers, a gold mock turtleneck that had to be cashmere, and most astonishing of all, a heavy waist-length leather coat. She stepped back and mockingly admired him. Been playing the Kasino? she said.

He said nothing. He was a wreck. He passed his hand over his ashen face. She knew this look very well: a locomotive temper made regular trips through her father—cursing, pounding, chugging out steam, smashing chairs, smashing glass, threatening to flatten her and her mother; and then it left *this* shaky man behind, kicked from the caboose into the middle of nowhere. He shuffled into her room, hauling a stack of record albums and a beautifully wrapped gift. She didn't pity him, but she wondered who or what had gotten hold of him today. She flopped back on her bed. You look terrible, she said.

He didn't respond but walked straight to the window. Standing there, he looked hard at her tattered *London Calling* poster, the bassist frozen in punk-rock fury, smashing his buzzing guitar on the stage. Her father so loved all his own little toys that she doubted he could appreciate such raw destruction, even the destruction of something you love—yet, if only for a moment, it seemed he was trying. After a headachy silence he touched his chin and, looking out the window, asked if she still played guitar.

There it is, she said, thumbing at the instrument leaning in the corner, splattered with stickers, its tuning pegs wild with unclipped strings.

Of course you realize what an ordeal it was, dragging that thing back from America for you. He stank with smugness. Do you still take lessons?

Of all people you should know that I can't afford lessons, but I don't need them anyway. I write my own songs now. For a second she was nervous that he would ask her to play one, but true to his nature he didn't even turn around. Your mother and I had plans for you to be a musician, he said. Great plans.

Subtly, Wanda adjusted the pillow over Gurney's wallet.

He continued: Here's something I never told you because I was afraid you'd become arrogant too soon. Now it's too late for that. When you were about eight, not long after you'd begun playing the piano, our friend Jan Moczulski listened to you practicing; he raised his finger and said you had the touch of a prodigy. The touch of a prodigy. He would have known. Someday, we thought, someday our Wanda will perform at the Filharmonia! One day, Paris! One day, Vienna! You see, that's what parents do. They set themselves up to be disappointed.

Wanda had lived too long to take a compliment from her father, for she found they always came at a price. He was mixing something up behind his beard. Even so, she was surprised by this particular story, perhaps because she had adored Professor Moczulski, his Beethoven hair, his easy sense of humor, or perhaps because she missed his piano, the musty Steinway grand over at the university that thrilled her parents whenever she played it. But now, after five years, she wouldn't even know where to find middle C. Of course that was her father's point.

I guess we could never have known what was best for you, he said. But it only seemed right to start you playing the cello, too. That was also Moczulski's idea. Selfish advice, coming from a cellist. You liked it at first because you felt like a grown-up, controlling this big instrument with your chubby little knees—that's the thing about you, Wanda, you always wanted to feel grown up. That was the part of you I wanted to nurture. But then came the day you disappointed me. I was standing outside the door and you were playing your scales. It was always relaxing to listen to your scales—you took them so seriously, you played them so well. But that day you kept stopping and starting, and that is to be expected, I suppose, he said, flexing his jaw and staring over the city. But we had raised you to be respectful of the things we gave you, and up to this point you had behaved very well. You folded your clothes, you polished your shoes. You had been a gracious little plum. But that day you stopped trying and started throwing a fit, hurling your beautiful instrument onto floor, making such a racket I thought that you'd cracked it. I turned the door handle, like I did just now, and found it locked, and when I started rattling it—you spoke that word, that one awful word that only drunk men say, and I heard you proceed to whip it with your bow, shouting *Kurwa! Kurwa! Kurwa!* You didn't care at all. You didn't care about me, your helpless father out in the hall.

Wanda smirked. Was she supposed to pity him slouching there, hung like a sack of spider's eggs? Was he looking for a serenade? She made sure he was finished and then changed the subject.

What's in the package? she said.

Do you want to know? It is of the finest quality and I want you to have it, but only if I can trust that you'll take care to respect it.

Though he entirely misunderstood her, he always knew exactly what to get her. She was intrigued. The gift was smallish, odd-shaped, cubelike, and it was fastidiously wrapped in gold and green paisley—surely not the work of her father's clumsy hands, but that of a shop-keeper's or, more likely, a girlfriend's. He'd probably been traveling: that's when he guiltily bought her presents. It was awful, having to hate all the nice things she owned, having to trash her Yamaha guitar, but she did it on principle. She watched him set the gift atop her wardrobe, sadistically high, where she couldn't reach it without stand-ing on a chair.

So, he said meaningfully, turning toward her on his boot heels. Beneath his good looks and impeccable manners, the beast of her fa-ther was starting to show through. Something was up, and it made her nervous. He spoke: So you don't take guitar lessons, but you write songs on your own. That's progress. That's good. I like that. When was it, three years ago when you started guitar lessons?

Something like that.

Let's see, we started you out on a secondhand guitar—why was that again?

Huh?

You had a good reason, as I remember it. Someone said you had natural talent, he said, tapering off, finishing the thought with a twirl of his hand. Yes, I recall, it was that tutor of yours! That American gentleman. What was his name?

Don't play stupid, Tati, you know his name.

That's right, and then he was the one who gave you the lessons. I've been thinking. Maybe he was putting you on to make some money. In the final analysis, natural talent is very relative, don't you think?

I'd been talking about the guitar for years. You just didn't listen, but he did. He thought I'd be smart to start taking lessons. That's all.

Was he a good teacher?

Excellent.

Was he a decent man?

Just like you said, he's an American gentleman.

Naturally, you were young and naive, not much of a judge of character. Can't you remember his crooked eyes, his crooked teeth? Faces don't lie, my girl. I knew right away the man was a crook. An awful crook! Her father slipped into his professorial role and began lecturing at something invisible, something hovering in the air in front of his face: He had that wild greasy hair, those holes in his jeans, that heretical Rasputin look all about him that should have told me he was lousy from the start. I mean, I *did* know, I could tell, I could smell it on him like he'd shit his pants.

Wanda grimaced and said: Then why'd you let me work with him?

Her father smiled grimly, unable to answer.

How could you know anything about him at all? Wanda persisted. Tell me that. I'd be surprised if you ever really met him. How could you have? You were always gone.

Precisely! he said, his face lighting up. Approaching her slowly across the floor, he eased himself onto the bed beside her, faintly smelling of some rummy cologne. She drew her knees up to her chest. Now we're getting somewhere, he said. I was always gone. I was never around to supervise. And some days I'll bet you were left alone, all alone with this American goat, just the two of you here in your bedroom, is that right?

Mother was home.

Always?

She's always home. Yes, always.

Yes, always, he said, mocking her. An admirable thing about your
mother. All of Kraków could be dancing on the square and she would
stay home to watch the house. But then inside her house it's a whole
different goddamn carnival—foreigners milling around in their
bathrobes, her daughter locked up in her little bordello!

Papa!

Don't *Papa* me.

But you're wrong!

Don't *Papa* me, he said with a growl, pulling his knee up onto her
bed and facing off against her in a pouncing position. Wanda recoiled
up to the headboard, heart pounding, breath short. Wind whipped at
the straining windows. He spoke sourly: I can't so much as leave the
country, not for the good of this family, not for the good of the university and the good of metallurgy for the nation of Poland without
you women ripping off your clothes and trailing some Bacchus up a
hill! Isn't that so? Isn't that how it has to be! Don't *Papa* me, you little
harlot, you little *kurwa*, don't *Papa* me. The word *daughter*'s reserved
for the good little girls. Daughters are nice girls, decent girls, not
rock-star harlots! Not barefoot urchins!

He grabbed her naked ankles. He put his hair-flaming face up to
hers. She shuddered and squirmed, a nightmare scream trapped in
her throat. She felt herself getting younger and smaller. Fuck you, she
muttered in her shrinking English. Fuck you, Tati.

I'm going to ask you a question, he said, whispering, squeezing
her ankles, squirming his lips in their spiny nest of hair. Your answer
to this question will make all the difference. But don't hesitate to respond because silence itself may be all I need. As he paused to catch
his breath, his pores seemed to widen, his beard grew hairier, his icy
hands held her feet immobile. Much as she tried, she couldn't avoid
his detergent-blue eyes. Who? he asked. Who was your first kiss,
Wanda?

She narrowed her eyes and turned to the side.

Who? he said through sharp yellow teeth.

She hesitated a deathly long time, disbelieving that he could even
suspect the truth. Nobody, nobody on earth knew of her colossal first

kiss, that delicate moment that had been pressed for keeps. Nobody
knew but Dick Chesnutt himself, the sweet man who cared enough to
share it with her, the kind sweet man she promised never to betray.
Her evil father couldn't have known that, so what was he looking for?
What did he want?

You can't say, can you? Can you? Will you? Just as I thought. How
did he do it? Did he kiss your belly? Did he kiss your cheek? Her father pressed his hot hairy mouth to her cheek and made a vile wet
kissing noise. She swung at him, shivered, screeched, but he was too
big and strong, pushing her by her ankles up to the headboard. Did he
kiss your ears? Kiss your nose? Did this terrible man kiss your mouth?
As he pressed his animal mouth to hers, slobbering the sickest most
poison saliva, she fought with her nails, teeth, and limbs, kicking and
hurting this wretched thing that was her father. And it didn't stop
there now, did it? Does it ever stop there? Did he fuck you? Did he?
He fucked you! he grunted, laying his horrible weight on her. How
could he? How could you?

Mama! Mama! Mama! Mama! she shouted until, miraculously,
her father was off her. He stood, both feet on the floor. She didn't immediately register what was happening, that he was bemusedly looking through Gurney's wallet, delicately fingering its paper contents.
She started, then stopped when she glanced at his face; stranger than
ever, comically deranged, looking as far out as Job must have looked
when it finally occurred to him that everything was gone. He was a
land mine, a time bomb. Wanda stayed very still on her bed.

Him too. Him too, he said with a nod, folding the wallet and stuffing it in his pants pocket.

Father, please—

Stop! he shouted, thundering off the walls and windows and ceiling. He walked menacingly around the room, searching its clutter as
if for more clues. He picked up candles, tapes, and photos, all the
while muttering about Gurney and Dick Chesnutt, calling American
men just Turks in disguise, come to spread their seeds in Poland, run
their plows through the richest soil on earth. But they're happy-go-
lucky! he said with a snarl, shaking his fists in a mocking little dance.

Johnny Appleseeds! Perfect outfit for the wandering devil! But comes a day when the dirt bites back! Without looking down at her, he shuffled to the door, touching the wallet bulging in his pants. He went out, leaving the door wide open.

The front door of the flat closed with a squeak, his boots made a pattering descent down the stairwell. She stayed sitting on her bed for a very long time, letting daylight drain from the place through an imaginary hole in the middle of the floor. Watching the day swirl down the drain, she tossed her bad thoughts into the whirlpool, emptying her brain of all kinds of clutter: her unholy first kiss, all the motley things about her father that would always escape her understanding. How could he have known about it? Wanda was smart, but this was an answer beyond all fathoming.

When it was almost dark, she got off the bed and slid her wooden desk chair over to the wardrobe, snatching her gift from its lofty spot. It was heavy and well centered, not rattly and Polish. Even in the diffuse gray light, the fancy gold paisley winked. She ripped it open and felt sick. She revolved the shiny black box in her hands, flashing its cellophane, wishing it were fake: a Sony Discman. (A fake one.) With totally cool headphones. (Fake ones.) She turned it over in her hands, looking out the window and across the green copper roofs. She had wanted one forever, since she had known such a thing existed, but she had been careful not to tell a soul because she usually got what she wanted, and she knew for a fact she didn't want this. But how did he know? Here it was, the end of October, not a decent holiday in sight, and she was holding something she hated beyond hating. She sliced the edge of the cellophane with her thumbnail. She opened the flap of the glossy box and pulled the machine from its slot in the Styrofoam. Black matte. Smooth buttons. It was so *sexy* and *sophisticated,* opening with a kiss, closing with a click, smelling strangely electronic; she wanted it, yearned for it, but even though she held it right there in her hands, it was like dreaming about something in the window of a shop while knowing you'll never deservedly own it. It was stealing, and she knew she couldn't meet her father's one condition: she could never, ever begin to respect it. Not it, not him.

Winter was coming. You could tell because the window was hard to open, but with some shaking and pounding she managed to get it. And the rich night air was shivery cold, bringing drafty whiffs of coal-smoke memories, which Wanda tried to push away. First things first. The streetlamp was on, illuminating a broad orange circle in the alley. The crumpled wrapping paper took so long to fall, drifting here, floating there, she thought it would never touch the bricks below. The box, however, fell more quickly, hitting the ground with a little bounce. Yet the CD player, all gathered together with its friend the headphones, needed to make a brutal impact, preferably on one of its spinning corners. To execute this, she leaned out the window, raised it high above her head, and sent it whipping with a flick of her finger. Though its radical spiral glanced off the building somewhere near the second floor, it ricocheted nicely and smashed on the pavement, splintering its pieces in three different directions.

Eight

BY THE TIME HE'D GOTTEN TO THE GREEN BALLOON, sometime after ten o'clock, Dick Chesnutt's toes were frozen stony. His wig was stiffening and losing its flowers. His breasts had fallen into damp little clumps. And Jane's most cherished red velvet dress, which he wore with pride, was wrinkled and moldy from last year's Halloween, strangling his rib cage as it dried out. He was cross and cold and ill at ease, but that was just how he wanted to be. He knocked October wind from his ears. The pianist played *Die Blaue Donau,* but far too quietly for those high, ecstatic rooms. He wanted pomp and noise and trouble. He wanted them to notice his terrible arrival. He rustled against costumes, shook out his cold hands, and edged his way through the famous café—the city's oldest, most *grotesque* café—feeling he looked, sufficiently so, like a woman who had been dragged from the bottom of a pond. He wanted to be noticed. Having labored over the costume and then drenched his whole body, he felt he looked absolutely Ophelia.

He paused by display cases where, beyond his reflection, Punchinello puppets hunched on sticks: wisemen, hags, politicians, and bandits; dandies, princesses, pimps, and prostitutes. Their painted faces were stunned and guilty, their bodies just tufts of batting and taffeta. They were leftovers from a wilder era, not the little revelers they used to be. He fixed his lazy eye on them. He too was a leftover from a wilder era, from a time when he and Jane were famous around town and known as that sexy Western pestilence, two foreigners openly pleasuring themselves and making the locals want the same. Grotesque!

Tonight he would be more grotesque than ever, and if he had to have a reason why, it was to mortify Jane in front of her cousin, that shy but rather superior boy who'd just started working as a croupier.

Amber blobs drooped from lamps. Halloweeners lounged on tall green sofas, popping bottles of Bulgarian champagne, eating cookies and cakes and ice cream. Across the long and twinkling room, between the fat ceramic stove and the small cabaret stage, Dick Chesnutt's throne stood dark and empty. He sighed in relief and edged his way toward it, glancing around for familiar faces, wanting a Steppenwolf or an encrusted Des Esseintes but finding only a host of ingrates who reminded him that he was back in Kraków.

I've been to Prague, he said aloud, pausing for a moment in the center of the floor. Nobody listened. Who could hear him with all that talking? Voices scraped in his cold, wet ears; neither the gurgling of German glottal stops nor the salivary swishing of Polish syllables, it was the tin-can clangor of American slang, and it didn't give an inch for old Dick Chesnutt as he finally slumped into his hard red throne at the end of a long and crowded table. They didn't even notice him. But a card reading RESERWACJA had been set there for him. He smiled to think that someone had remembered, probably Jane. Maybe she was even looking forward to seeing him.

Looking down the table he recognized none of these blathering children. He couldn't even place their costumes. What in the world were they trying to be? They weren't even suave like the Americans in Prague, who decently kept their ugliness on the inside. New Krakovian cool was junky old felt and motheaten fur, looking like whores in piecemeal velvet with dumb red eyes gawking out from makeup. They tried to look more Polish than the Poles!

He helped himself to a glass of champagne and leaned closer to the stove, warming his stiff muscles. Champagne bubbles peppered his nose. The night was young but he was tired and content, like a possum returned from a long night of wandering. The person to his left, a young woman sitting in Jane's old seat with green glitter stubble smeared across her jaw, shoved his skinny shoulder.

Someone's sitting there, she said.

Fuck you, he said, sneering and sniffling, not bothering to tell her that this was *his* throne next to *his* old friend the stove, and if she and her goons tried to remove him, Halloweeners would respond with great hue and cry. But as the stove filled him with charitable heat, he wished he'd found a gentler way of putting it.

Mangy little mermaid bitch, she said.

A man in a fez and a pin-striped suit (a Freemason? a Turk?) turned from his conversation to say:

Seat's taken, mermaid. Talk that way to Cindy again, fucker, and I'll have to *dethrone* you.

Have you *throne* out! she said, stupidly, and laughed.

I'm Dan Quayle, said an American man who appeared behind Chesnutt, leaning on a golf club and looking nothing like the vice president. I say he stays. I say we honor the mermaid's reservation.

Here! Here! someone shouted from across the room, clearly referring to something else.

You just wait until the king gets here, she said, taking the card and waving it in the air. You'll see.

I think Cindy's a little delirious, Chesnutt said to Quayle, who'd vanished. He looked her costume up and down. Green glitter stubble and an orange jumpsuit.

The king's big and strong and *young,* she said. More than I can say for you! Hey! You drinking our champagne?

Hurrah! someone cheered. Dan Quayle leapt to the stage, without his golf club, holding two puppets he'd swiped from the cases. Chesnutt jolted upright, as if his own mother were being dragged away. Those puppets were fragile, the little darlings of Boy-Zelenski— they hadn't left their case for over seventy years, and now that asshole was swinging them like drumsticks! But he could see the crowd was ready for a puppet show. He reluctantly sat back into his seat.

The boy! Dan Quayle announced, brandishing in his right hand a cheery-faced boy puppet. And the shopkeeper! he said, brandishing in his left an aproned woman puppet. Negotiating a cigarette about his lips, he squawked out amateur puppet voices.

Clackety-clack, Miss. Clackety-clack.

Oh, you *boffersome* little turd, vot is it you vant?

Bread pudding!

Bread pudding? Vat's a scoundrel's lunch. You need a nice, fat *blood* sausage.

Bread pudding's the liveliest lunch, wench, provided it's crawling with wormy nuts.

Nuts, indeed.

A nut in need is a nut indeed.

The children today, said the shopkeeper, confiding in the crowd. Fay come from fe Vest, finking fey *deserve* all our bread pudding. Vy, you must *verk* for it.

Why work for it, wench, when I got the money to buy it? So make it quick: two big lumps of wormy pudding, a steamy heap of the devil's pierogi, and a kiss on the lips with a little bit of tongue so I can taste what it tastes like inside your mouth.

A boy your age. I vouldn't kiss you for all fe złotys in Vah-vel!

And I wouldn't soil my fingers with all those złotys! But here's a little effigy of Abraham Lincoln. A five-dollar bill. Now kiss, love, kiss!

The shopkeeper turned conspiratorially toward the crowd, then smashed so enthusiastically into the boy puppet that her delicate stick cracked in half. Dan Quayle burst into baleful laughter. Several people cheered him on. Throughout the show, Chesnutt had been gesturing through the curtained doorway, getting the attention of the squat coat check, who now pushed through the tables with a skinny little waiter, forcing past chairs, shouting bewildered reprimands at Quayle. They mounted the stage, grabbed the puppets, and dragged him laughing and shrugging from the cabaret. Several people booed and hissed. The piano played a gloomy dirge. Two Tatars at the end of his table, their heads ballooning in purple satin hats, cast deadly looks at Dick Chesnutt.

He wanted to explain. He wanted to say he too enjoyed the show. In an inspired moment he jumped to the stage and got the attention of at least the people up front. He toasted the room, gulped champagne, and started talking:

Why did the . . . , he began to say, cracking a smile. Um, what happened when. . . . Well, I heard this joke in Prague: When the Polish prime minister heard about a war in the Gulf he sent along ten thousand troops.

That's not funny, someone yelled.

Well, no, Dick Chesnutt said, raising his finger. But the president of Mexico didn't know what to do with them!

Nobody laughed.

Hey! Cindy yelled. How many racist mermaids does it take to screw in a lightbulb?

Smoke trickled up from a hundred bored faces, and there was Dick Chesnutt, forty years old, Jane's panties clinging as if he'd wet himself. Still, he refused to leave the stage. Before he could make a bigger ass of himself, however, a miracle happened in the back of the crowd: Jane and her stately cousin appeared. They moved majestically throughout the room. Jane wore a top hat and a sheeny black cape she swiveled around tables with her right hand raised, two fingers attaching her to Gurney's right hand, which he held at a gracious angle. People were greeting them! People knew them! As they came closer, their light grasp engaging and releasing over tables, even Dick Chesnutt couldn't help but smile. Jane waved a magic wand. Gurney trailed a spangled scepter. Though Gurney wasn't terribly handsome, something about the robe cascading from his shoulders, the crown cocked back like a sailor's cap, made Dick Chesnutt wickedly jealous. Even so, he had to smile. With no acknowledgment of Chesnutt but right under his nose, cackling her laugh of brambles and berries, Jane led Gurney up to his throne.

The king! thought Chesnutt, weakly stepping down from the stage.

Up you go! Jane told Cindy, who glowered in return, green whiskers shimmering. She waved the wand over Cindy's bushy head, as if threatening to speckle her face with warts, and magically Cindy relinquished her seat. She stood close by, as if thinking she might get it back. Likewise, Chesnutt stood behind Gurney.

Don't look now, Midas, Jane said to Gurney, but your daughter's behind you. She's back from the dead!

He wheeled around, crazily perplexed. Chesnutt took a step back.

My daughter? Gurney said. Chesnutt recognized the agony on this poor boy's face. Jane held the key to the boy's secret closet, and she'd just creaked it open to rattle its bones. Recreational cruelty, he thought, typical Jane. He started guessing what the secret might be— an abortion? Infanticide? Something severe.

Well, did you really kill her, Jane mused, or did you simply turn her to gold? Your Highness? Well? What's the difference, really, because here she is, almost good as new!

Wrong dead daughter, Chesnutt said graciously. Call me Ophelia, up from the swamp. He extended his bony hand to Gurney, who didn't want to play along.

Don't touch the king! Jane shouted. Swilling champagne, she admonished Chesnutt with her magic wand. He'll turn you into a mess of gold. Anyway, you're a suicide, you poor wretch. You'll give His Majesty all your bad luck!

Old news. So this is your famous cousin. Sitting in my throne.

Your throne? Since when did *Ophelia* have rights to the throne? They couldn't even give you a proper burial!

Now Gurney, she said, tapping out a Player, offering it around, then plucking it up with her red-delicious lips. Listen up, she said, lighting. Let Dick Chesnutt be a lesson to you. He came to Kraków— when? Eighty-two? Eighty-three? Sometime back in Solidarity, back when it was tough even for Americans. But, y'know, he had talents. He was smart and spoke Polish, so he got a job at the university teaching American poetry. He met some Commies who got him a good flat, a place with a phone down in Kazimierz. And he looked like this counter-culture clochard, playing these snappy punk-pop songs that all the kids thought so hep. Everyone liked having Dick Chesnutt around.

Now he's just that guy at roulette number seven, Gurney said. Now he's just some loser like me. Is that my lesson?

Wait a second, punk, Dick Chesnutt wanted to say.

That's pretty much your lesson, Jane said. Cindy got bored and walked away. Jane looked at Chesnutt but kept talking to Gurney. You know the jokes we make about old Americans in Kraków, how they pretend they're running from something big when they're really just afraid of their own mediocrity. Well, Mr. Chesnutt's a case in point.

She paused and gave him a chance to rebut, but he was feeling too hurt and betrayed to speak. She continued: He let everyone go on thinking he was some Ivan the Terrible, acting like his conscience was peering out of sewer holes and written on notes that his students passed around. Acting like Interpol was tracking him down. And it was fun for a while, a fun little gag, thinking we had a criminal among us. But we weren't stupid. He was no pop star, he was definitely no Ivan the Terrible. But he couldn't just leave well enough alone. He wanted his piece of Solidarity. He wanted to be the revolutionary superstar, and that's why he had to go blooey last spring with that incident at the Collegium Maius. He snapped, cracked, the poor man *popped,* and that was that for wishy-washy Dick.

What happened? Gurney asked.

Ask around, everybody knows. It'd be cruel to repeat it where Mr. Chesnutt might hear.

So where's *my* lesson? Gurney said, thumping his chest with the scepter.

Isn't it plain as day? He came here running from a mediocre past. You came here running from a mediocre future. Both of you are looking for trouble.

I'm not running from anything, Gurney said defensively.

Of course you aren't, darling.

Dick Chesnutt was feeling flimsy and flammable, as if he were made of papier-mâché. He knew cruelty when he saw it: when his father got drunk, the skin would hang around his cold gray stare; when his brother went off deer hunting he'd all at once look so heartless that Chesnutt would actually wish he'd have an accident; certain bullies he had feared, certain Party members, any gambler at the end of his rope, all of them would give off a scent like Jane was giving off now, a warning that things had changed and any terms were deadly ones.

So he left. He walked quickly from the table, through the noisier and noisier crowd, past the puppets and coat check to the dripping portico. He stood under the rusty cast-iron eaves and looked at rain pounding on flagstones. One block up, in the candlelit grotto, Dan Quayle could be seen pissing on the wall and leaning on his golf club.

Mermaid! he called out, still pissing. Mr. Mermaid!

Chesnutt looked the other way, down the shimmering orange stones toward the Mariacki Cathedral. In the tempestuous year when Jane was his lover, she'd made him promise never to tell her his secrets. She made believe he was guilty of unspeakable crimes. Riding his Suzuki through the hills of Hungary, digging for clams on the beaches of Yugoslavia, fucking in the golden valleys of Galicia, she'd murmur and call him her rapist and murderer, her mailbag robber, her weapons smuggler, and what a thrill when she'd nuzzle into his neck! So long as he glowed with hyperbolic offenses, she was glad to play Bonnie to his imaginary Clyde. He was a grown man, but she was just a kid, and for reasons he'd figure out much later she needed him to be rare and dangerous.

And how he'd wished he could meet that need! How he'd wished he really had a secret, something terrible he could give her, all tragic and important and wrapped in a box: snip the ribbons, rip back the paper, rifle through the tissue and take out the—what? The Fabergé egg? The pound of cocaine? The hammer all sticky with another man's gore? Throughout their relationship, the only real secret he'd ever dared tell made him out to look like a child-molesting pervert. So she knew he had nothing to give. She knew his crimes were base and unglamorous. And then after his dumb stunt at Collegium Maius, when they'd blacked out his dick in all the newspapers across Poland, when the world had discovered what a schlemiel he was, that's when she'd positively turned on him, becoming his first and cruelest critic, making him the butt of endless public jokes, nicknaming him the Man from Mapplethorpe.

That was about six months ago, and here it was Halloween again. He'd heard rumors that she was traveling with someone new, not Eulalia, not another woman, but a mystery man in Vienna and Berlin. He couldn't read her diary anymore, so he had no way of knowing for sure. And why did he even care? She was gone from his life. She could hurt only herself. But why, for that matter, was Kraków still hooked on her? She had ways of getting herself under their skin.

Evening, Mr. Mermaid, Dan Quayle said, approaching through the beating rain. I have a proposition.

Go away.

Hear me out. I want to rent your wig.

My wig? No chance.

I have five dollars. That's fifty thousand złotys. Just for ten minutes with your lovely wig.

That's sick. What do you want it for?

To sneak in and see the magic show.

What magic show?

Isn't that why you came tonight? Jane's been talking it up for weeks. She's a magician.

Magic show? He hated the familiarity with which he said Jane. He turned back through the door.

Hey! Wait! What about the wig?

Chesnutt stopped and grabbed the five. Quayle snatched the ratty wig from his head. Go in first, Chesnutt said. I'm making sure you don't do anything stupid this time.

Back inside, he felt more dignified without the wig. He walked brusquely toward the stage. Jane was already gesticulating with her wand. He took her seat at the table next to Gurney, who was distracted by his cousin and shoveling yellow ice cream into his mouth. Soon she beckoned him up to the stage.

King Midas! she said, rolling her top hat the length of her arm, presenting Gurney with a flip of her wrist. Upending the hat, she dropped two white rats to the stage. They scurried in confusion about the king's feet. People clapped. The piano boomed. Chesnutt moved to the throne and snuck some ice cream—French vanilla. Jane continued, puffing out her chest:

Allow me to remind you about the story of Midas, the greedy old king who got the golden touch, only to kiss his precious little girl and turn her into a twelve-karat mannequin. It's a tragedy of gluttony and stupidity, matched only by that fat kid in *Willy Wonka* who drowns himself in a pool of chocolate. Well, according to Ovid, the story of Midas doesn't stop there. His ignorance blossoms. Relieved of his hideous golden touch, he judges a contest between the hairy-arsed Pan piping on his pipe and the lofty Apollo plucking at his lute. Being a dolt in finer matters of aesthetics, Midas swears Pan is the better musician and Apollo punishes him according to his crime—disfiguring his head in a ridiculous way that Midas tries oh-so-hard to conceal. In fact, he reveals his secret to just one man in his kingdom: the barber, naturally. But the king's secret was so scandalous, so succulent, that the barber couldn't keep it for long. So he dug a shallow hole along the river, whispered the king's secret inside, and quickly closed it over with dirt.

Jane turned her eyes to Gurney, who was impatiently looking about his feet. What poor luck! To trust a secret to your dim-witted barber! Of course, like any secret once it has escaped, this one took on a life all its own, infecting the earthworms and feeding the birds, running with moles throughout the burrows, leaking deep into the water table and sprouting in the daffodils, daisies, and reeds. Soon the wind took hold of the thing, and then all the kingdom was in the know! But was it really such a secret? Was it a surprise to anyone? Jane waved the wand over Gurney's paper crown, saying, Was it really such a shock that silly old Midas was sporting the shaggy ears of a jackass?

She jumped up, grabbed his crown, and revealed a pair of droopy, hairy ears. Silence. Dick Chesnutt might have thought the trick was staged, but Gurney so urgently pulled at the ears that he gave the appearance of real disbelief. It had to be real. Gurney seemed incapable of such honest acting. The crowd was silent, then broke into cheers while Jane amicably patted Gurney's shoulder. Swept up in the frenzy, Chesnutt cheered too, but then as he trained his eyes on Gurney, who winced and struggled with his ridiculous ears, the gravity of it all began to sink in. It was one thing to take on a debauched ex-boyfriend, but here she was roasting her defenseless cousin, a pie-eyed boy who wasn't even looking for trouble. He wondered: Did she know his secrets? Did she simply know he was keeping secrets? Gurney was smiling now but tugging all the harder. He was plainly different from the other new Americans. Try as he might, the boy wasn't snide; he wasn't even a liar. He was just a kid with a healthy appetite, defenseless in a jealous old city like this one. Chesnutt wanted to warn him and protect him, maybe start probing after his secret. But he'd recline for another moment on his cozy old throne and sneak another spoonful of vanilla ice cream.

GURNEY DIDN'T KNOW WHAT THE HELL TO THINK. She had been fawning over him all afternoon long, feeding him trays of antipasto, serving him pitchers of Halloween sidecars. She had lovingly painted his face with makeup and painstakingly fitted his costume and crown. It had been feeling as it had when they were kids, despite how cold she had been that week. They had smoked hash under an umbrella on their way to the Wierzynek (the restaurant once frequented by King Jan Sobieski), and they had extravagantly dined to the other patrons' horror, the two of them claiming a table for six and filling it up with an American feast. They had started off with champagne and oysters and mussels, accompanied by several bottles of various reds that were so cheap they opened them all at once. They had ordered two great tureens of soup, a glut of sweetmeats and salads and breads, and in an inspired act of gluttony, had a bloody roast beef put at his end of the table, a stuffed rack of lamb put over on hers, and had hired a boy to move back and forth, pouring and passing and carving and spooning, blushing at Jane's untranslated advances. They had blown Gurney's money from the Kasino, her money from Uncle Sandy, and hadn't looked back all evening long as they devoured their way into a wild American holiday in Poland.

He should have made more of her dark transformation during dinner, the bloodthirsty humor that came over her during dessert when he started to tell her what she meant to him.

For now, onstage, everything was weirder than ever before. As if she'd been smelling his wish to see Jackie, and as if she'd been meaning to punish him in advance, she'd made a literal ass out of him by sticking big ears to his head—and they'd probably been there all through dinner! People cheered, flashbulbs popped, and while Jane was basking in the glamour of her punch line, he just stood there, the king of clamor, jerking at the goddamn things. So far as he could tell Jackie hadn't arrived, and he guessed Jane had won, for now he wished she wouldn't come at all.

He got down from the stage. Smoothing the rain-damp robe behind his legs, he sat on his throne and tucked his ears back under his crown. He avoided Dick Chesnutt, who was still sitting there in Jane's vacant seat. This guy was another disappointment: for months he'd loomed in Gurney's imagination, all fire and noise like the ferocious face of Oz, but in truth he was just that goof behind the curtain, pulling ropes and throwing knobs. Chesnutt looked from Gurney to his bowl of ice cream—two smooth lumps in a pool of yellow.

What? You want it? Gurney said. You can have it. I'm done.

No, thanks, he said, leaning closer.

Where's your wig?

I flipped it.

I see, Gurney said, glancing at his eyes, which pointed in two directions at once. Not wanting to stare, he tried to remember what such eyes were called. Stink eyes? Bent eyes? What did Jane see in this guy? Gurney saw nothing but a slicked-back fop, but of course he accepted a glass of champagne.

To your ears, Chesnutt said, clinking. How are they attached?

He fingered the tender spot behind his real ears where the donkey ears were fastened somehow. Some kind of glue, he said. I can't tell.

She does good work.

It was a damn good trick, Gurney said, as if he were in on it.

Who put the crown on your head?

She did. The crown, the robe, everything.

Of course, Chesnutt said, shivering, adjusting his breasts. That's how it was last year. She did everything. Painted my face, stuffed my bra, poked dead flowers all over in my dress. Her favorite part was dumping the water on my head. It took three buckets before she was happy, and even then the mascara wasn't runny enough for her. After that we went to the Wierzynek and made a big scene. A fine memory.

Don't tell me any more.

Naturally. Drink. But tell me, Midas, what's your secret?

Secret's out. I have donkey ears.

Let me guess. You're a redhead.

I'm blond. Dirty dishwater. What's your secret, Ophelia?

Let's drink, he said. They drank.

Tell me what happened at Collegium Maius, Gurney said.

That's no secret. Chesnutt smiled with big, perfect teeth. He drank. But it's a fair question, he said. So I shall tell you. He drank. It was 1989. Revolutionary spirit filled the air. The Party was going down and everyone knew it. But things weren't happening fast enough. It needed fuel. It needed a mastermind to nudge it along.

Isn't that what Lech Wałesa did?

So I got up a group of male students, an impressive group, smart young men who hated complacency—hated it almost as much as I did—and I marched them around the university courtyard. Oh, we chanted, and I had an excoriating speech prepared, but the part that raised a stink was, the truly inspired part was—we hung our dicks out our flies.

Your dicks?

They shut us down pretty fast.

You did this for fun?

We might as well have. I got nothing out of it—nothing but fired. Most people thought I did for publicity. Some said I'd been in Poland for too long, and they were probably right. But your cousin thought I did it for her, and I tell you here and now, I did not. We had a noble purpose.

Do tell.

Gladly, boy, but drink! Drink! There's always more where this came from. Poland's lousy with centuries of bad habits, and its worst one is this business of underground resistance—secret armies, lurking revolutionaries, young men in caves with puny little guns. It's a *stupid* habit and they always get creamed. They're far too Catholic to be sneaky. Every forty years they get themselves creamed. My thinking was simple, perfectly practical: they should get their money out in the open, put their guns and ideas up front. Whip 'em out, as it were. Whip 'em right out and let the Russians and everybody know exactly what they stand for.

Hadn't they been doing that anyway?

Chesnutt ignored this comment. Whip 'em out, I said, and so they did. It was a simple movement, very short-lived, but I think it gave us that last thrust to freedom. Poland, that is. It was all about honesty, all about power. The public missed the point, of course.

Sure they did. They were looking at your dicks! It was the stupidest thing he'd ever heard, but he didn't have the heart to say so. They drank.

I've just gotten back from Prague, he said. Boredom spreads in direct proportion to the influx of young Americans. They're all just mincing around over there, trying to get photographed for sleazy magazines. None of them are anything at all like you.

Me? What the hell do you know about me?

I know all about you. Drink.

You know nothing about me.

I know that you're very serious at heart.

Are you fucking with me? Gurney snarled, leaning forward. Dick Chesnutt's face looked strangely sympathetic. It was a voice that came from deep inside Gurney, from deep in his childhood, the voice bullies used when they were picking a fight.

No, I'm not fucking with you. I'm not fucking with you. Now drink. Timid little fakers around here. The boy and the shopkeeper! That bitch with the glitter! You're not at all like that, my boy, and here's how I know.

Spare me.

Drink. I know it just to look at you, but really I know it because of Jane.

What did she say?

Ah, now you're interested. She doesn't talk to me, she doesn't have to. I know just what she looks for in men. And you've got it.

You and me and Jane. Wonderful. I've gotta go.

Stay and drink. You'll want to hear this. The way you wear those hairy ears, thinking you're all fun and fancy-free, I know what torture's twisting in your soul. She wouldn't have anything to do with you otherwise. It's a little-known fact, but she wants her men to be serious, so severe and sick at heart that they can't control their own bodies. You think you're a hedonist? Flimflam! You're not one of these fluffy little creeps. Okay, maybe you've got that thick bottom lip, but let me tell you something about hedonism. In itself, it's nothing. Hedonism's just a big helium balloon—trying to lift up the bricks of your soul. And here's what Jane does: she pumps up the balloon and piles on the bricks. She makes her confusion your confusion. She's lonely is what she is, and so she gloms on, and she sucks the blood from every damned fool in town. Ever wonder why she still lives here? Of course *I* live here, of course *you* do, but she could make it anywhere— London, Paris, Tokyo, New York. Why settle for fucking Kraków? Because she owns the place, that's why. She owns Kraków, she owns you, owns me, and here's how she does it: she gets you drunk on her flowing teats, then she pries up treasure from the mud in your soul!

This is my *cousin* you're talking about!

Yes, you have a soul. Get used to it. You have a soul. But tell me this much. Tell me what you wouldn't do to kiss those tits.

Jesus Christ!

Tell me what you wouldn't do.

Gurney crossed his arms. Jane was flitting from table to table, spreading her magic, shocking people with her menacing little stories— stories that, if true, would demolish their reputations, though as ever the listeners were playing along, glad to be embellished in her stormy mythology. He thought of her white cleavage, her almond soaps and minty shampoos, and he shivered to think how thoroughly she owned him.

She knows what you're hiding, and she'll try to devour you. Chesnutt tightened his thin red lips, clicked his big straight teeth for emphasis. Jane loves secrets, he said. And she loves to keep them hidden, festering and boiling like ulcerous wounds. And she loves boys like you with enormous appetites—she bends over them like a nurse as they suffer in pain. But you can't let that happen. Here's my advice: Keep doing what you're doing. Follow your whims. Chase your desires. When you're dead your life will have an interesting shape. He paused to let all his wisdom sink in. Now you're just a croupier. Now you're just sliding your chips around—sending them out, dragging them in, stacking them up in little towers. But someday soon you'll be a dealer, and a dealer is the disinterested master of whim. That's in his job description.

Chesnutt's right eye fixed on Gurney, piercing and brilliant like a motorcycle's headlamp, but his lazy left eye trailed far away, looking on dark and miserable things. It was the left eye that Gurney kept trying to catch.

Here's what you're going to do, he said, taking Gurney's wrist in his icy hand. You're going to find out how much she knows. Here's how. She keeps a diary. She keeps it, or at least she used to, in a stack of folders by the door of her bedroom.

Our bedroom, he said, trying to get his wrist back.

You sleep together?

In separate beds—we're *cousins,* for Christ's sake!

Find her diary. It's a plain black book. I'm not sure what it says these days.

You've read it? You've read Jane's diary?

She was writing it for me, that was indisputable. She was baiting my fears, she was furnishing dark rooms in her imagination—just for me! It was so chilly in there I had to stop reading, but I'm sure she kept writing it—damnable things, beautiful things that must be read. So read it. It's the only way to keep on top.

You're sick.

Yes, I'm sick, but trust me. Read it.

Trust the man with his dick hanging out.

He drained the bottle into their glasses, and Gurney looked for something familiar, something stable to rest his eyes on. To sit there with Dick Chesnutt and talk about Jane's diary! Once again, he'd drunk too much. The cabaret was caving in. Babbling, chortling, zigzagging commotion was up and dancing between the tables—a smelly pirate with a perfumey queen, a bowlegged cowboy with a stiff-legged robot, shifty crooks with defenseless drunks. A whirling tornado, wound up in ticker tape, danced by itself—chasing Jane's voice near and far as it came and went in the clutter of bodies. But Jane herself was nowhere to be seen. Nor was Jackie. Read Jane's diary! The night was tilting, tottering, askew. He set down his glass and looked into his hands. His father had once told him to look at his hands if ever he was lost in the middle of a nightmare.

Halloween in Kraków, Chesnutt said, isn't about hiding behind brilliant disguises. It's about flaunting your dreaded secrets in public. Look at these jerks with their boring secrets. Green glitter girls and cowboy dykes. But isn't it nice to be Midas for a night? Being Ophelia really feels nice. There's a long-standing tradition here in Kraków. Keep all the best secrets alive and unspoken. And that's all the more reason to look into that diary.

Never, said Gurney, stroking his ears.

Do as you please, Chesnutt said, getting up. But beware your cousin's slinky charms.

Chesnutt walked off, wigless, into the crowd.

Nine

GURNEY HAD LEFT THE GREEN BALLOON ALONE, sometime after midnight, without ever having run into Jackie. But the very next morning, as he crossed the chilly Rynek, he saw her sitting on a bench. He stopped at a distance to take a breath and calm down. He was on one of those jags that overtook him lately: as when feeding the animals or buying that book whose pages he'd rip out after writing on them, that morning he was driven by the notion that only teaching could save him now. He was going to find a job at the university. The Kasino made him money and kept him busy, but the work was meaningless and the people were losers. He didn't want to become Dick Chesnutt, and he didn't want the curse of Zbigniew Zamoyski. But first he would see what was up with Jackie.

Her legs were crossed. Her naked knees shone from her skirt—purple plaid that playfully clashed with her tall argyle socks. Her cardigan sweater was his favorite mossy green. He wasn't sure at first, but as he got closer he was able to verify that, yes, she was occupied by a lunch box open on her lap—a school-bus-yellow Peanuts lunch box.

Hi! she said, holding a sandwich wrapped in wax paper.

It's kind of early for lunch, he said, pointing to the broken clock in the tower, its rusty hands stuck at four twenty-six.

It's breakfast.

You didn't show up last night. Neither did Linda.

I was tired. Did I miss anything?

Nothing, he said. Nothing at all. He gestured to the space beside her on the bench.

Have a seat?

He hovered for a second, then sat down next to her, close enough to see peanut butter and red jelly bleeding through the paper. That morning he'd awakened feeling old and lonely, and Jane had only made it worse—stinking and snoring like some drunk in the park. But now here was Jackie, changing everything, unwrapping a sandwich as if they were out at recess. God, he said. Where'd you find peanut butter?

It's Jif. Smooth and creamy. Every month my parents send me a jar. Last week they sent my grade-school lunch box! Too bad the thermos is gone. Want some? she said, offering him the first triangle.

He took the sandwich with both hands. It was a rarity in this country where not even the potatoes tasted like home. Even so, he just couldn't. He gave it back to her.

What's wrong with it?

Nothing. It's perfect.

I made it just for you.

What? For me? Did you?

November fools, she said with a laugh, taking a big bite and chewing it gratefully.

November fools?

It's November first. Halloween's over. Winter's coming. Only a fool would stay in Kraków for the winter. She swallowed. But I am.

What's so foolish about staying here for the winter?

If it just snowed snow it'd be all right, but it mostly snows coal. Big black flakes, pretty coming down, much lighter than snow, but then the streets and buildings and sidewalks get mucky, and your nose gets chapped from sneezing out soot. I can't blame my parents for wanting me to come home, but I don't want to. It's been three years, so they don't beg anymore. They just send things to make me feel homesick.

My parents couldn't care less, he said, wishing to put an end to the topic.

Really? That's so sad.

What else you got in there?

A freckled banana, she said, holding it up against the pale sky. A thing of strawberry yogurt. A Raider bar.

Wish I had something to trade for that Raider.

You can have the banana, she said and lobbed it into his lap, but no give-backs! And I won't trade it for the Raider.

He laughed, shivered, and studied the banana, if only to avoid Jackie's pretty face. It was easy at first—sitting next to her, chatting away—but the longer he looked at the pungent banana, the more he felt his confidence tapering off. Jackie's company was a very different thing. If living with Jane was a constant hide-and-seek, ducking behind trees and jumping down manholes, then Jackie was it and Gurney was caught. Something about her was boldly honest, free of makeup, an adorable pimple there on her neck, and when he looked at her his tongue got stuck.

Where you from? she said.

Iowa, he said, setting down the banana. The word wobbled for a minute in the air between them, a tedious bubble refusing to burst.

Funny, she said. What are you doing here?

Uh, running.

Unlike Jane's other friends, she didn't laugh nervously at this response. She didn't laugh at all. Running from what?

Expectations.

Whose?

My parents'. I, for one, couldn't care less what I do.

Then came the silence that naturally follows saying something stupid. He broke it by admitting she'd been missed at Auschwitz.

That's sweet. I've never been missed at Auschwitz before.

Well, you were. Why didn't you come with?

I'd already been there, and it was Linda's bright idea to go back. There's only so much of that a girl can take.

I'm sure. So why does Linda keep going back?

Because she's Linda. Because she's Linda the Unreadable Blonde.

I see. How readable are you?

I'm *very* readable. I'm like Jackie for Beginners.

That's good. I'm slow on the uptake. Where are *you* from?

Monterey. She started on the second triangle of her sandwich.

California? he asked.

California.

Never been. I read *Cannery Row*. Is it still like that?

Probably never was, but there's Steinbeck junk all over the wharf. Wax museums, T-shirt shops, crap. She waved this away, then continued the probe: What kinds of expectations?

My parents want me to be a pharmacist, he lied.

So you were a chemistry major?

No, uh, English. And philosophy.

Then you're off the hook. You're unskilled.

They're pretty fixed on the idea.

But you just said they could care less what you do.

Yeah, I did. What I meant was they could care less what I do because I don't really exist until, you know, until I'm back in school. Pharmacy school. His voice was growing smaller, his lie getting weaker. It bored him to continue this ridiculous story. A pharmacist? Bad move. He wanted to get back to plain old flirting, but before he could step even deeper into trouble, something much graver happened.

Don't look now, Jackie said and rolled her eyes.

Turning around, he saw it too: amid the pigeons, coming toward them at a reluctant pace, Jane was making her way to class. She'd been surprising Gurney all his life, turning up at the damnedest times, but only recently had this started to bother him, as if she had clones of herself patrolling the city and handing out social parking tickets. Unexpectedly, Jackie scooted closer, smelling like American laundry detergent. Having imperceptibly changed her course, Jane was heading directly for their bench. Her short orange dress was sharply November, very crisp, but as she came closer he could see that her face was dull and bloated.

Lovebirds, she said as a way of greeting them. Neither of them responded. Well, well, Jackie Witherspoon, she said. I can assume one of two things: either you so pity my poor skinny cousin you've taken it on yourself to feed him from your lunch box—and what a lunch box!—or you're flirting with him. Which do you suppose it is?

He's not so skinny. Actually I'm not sharing much at all.

So you're flirting with him.

Um, she said, looking quite naturally up at Gurney. Actually, we're flirting with each other. It's fun.

This answer came so fast that he could only blush, steal a glance at Jane's mirthless face, and smile at his Doc Martens kicking the stones. Somehow it was clear that she wasn't just playing, that she really meant it, but as much as this excited him it made him jumpy.

Gurney? Is this true?

Well, I was on my way over to the university because it seemed about time I started teaching, considering that's what I came to Poland for. I was going to get a job all by myself. But on my way over there I just bumped into Jackie—

And you started flirting with her. That's cute. I don't see why you don't believe me when I say there are no teaching jobs right now. Anyway, you've already got a job.

Do you need a job? Jackie said. Why didn't you say so? I work at the English teachers college, and they're always looking for native speakers. I've never thought they were very discriminating.

Nodding at Jackie, shrugging at Jane, he wanted to leave before the two of them started dueling, but he stayed put.

Maybe you didn't know this, Jackie Witherspoon, but my cousin's already a working man. He's a croupier at the Kasino Kraków, soon to be a dealer if he'll just put his mind to it.

She's fibbing, Gurney said, sneaking a severe and astonished look at Jane, who narrowed her eyes a little bit more.

I never fib! How could you say such a thing? After the risks I took to get you that job? Unforgivable, she said, and that's just what she meant.

So you really *do* work at the Kasino? Jackie said, ignoring Jane.

That's totally cool, much cooler than teaching could ever be. Keep the job you have. Totally. What do you do there? I bet the people are fascinating.

Which ones? he said. The gamblers? They're pretty scary. Both relieved and flattered by Jackie's approval, he felt silly for having lied to her about anything—but larger than the entire market square, blacker than the clouds that were forming overhead was the disgust on Jane's hungover face. Like sycamore leaves when they start shimmering silver, like horses turning to face the wind, a warning had drifted over Jane's green eyes and a storm was unavoidable now. He had seen this look before (almost every time she told her stories) but usually from the side view, as an onlooker and cheerleader, and it had always seemed like something out of vaudeville. Head-on the view was very different: her narrow face was refrigerator cold—cruel, carnivorous, self-preserving.

What's a croupier do? Jackie asked, touching his leg. If she wasn't flirting before, she definitely was now.

It's a pretty unamazing job, he said quietly, keeping a careful eye on Jane, patient but concentrating, as if waiting to step into two whipping jump ropes. I've got patent-leather shoes, a tuxedo, the works. I've got my place next to the roulette dealer, selling poker chips. All night long I pass out chips, sweeping them around with this long wooden cane.

Do you gamble?

Never.

Don't believe him, Jane said, smiling. Gurney's a fine gambler.

I've never gambled in my life!

I have, Jackie said.

He's lying. He's gambled all his life. Problem is, Jane said, Gurney never wins. Not to say he's a loser, really, but he always plays the impossible odds.

Exciting, Jackie said.

Very, very, Jane enthused, sitting down next to Jackie.

Don't you have to go teach? Gurney asked.

What do you care, gambler? Jane took hold of Jackie's sweatered arm. If I can tell you one thing about my little cousin, he's wild as a cowboy. Back in Catholic school he and his friends used to play mumblety-peg with their Swiss Army knives.

That's a lie!

What's mumblety-peg? Jackie asked.

Nothing, Gurney said.

Don't be modest, Jane said. Show her the scar.

He shoved his hand between his legs.

Once they caught him stealing dirty magazines from his own dad's drugstore, and his mom dragged him off to confession by his ear. Then they took away his bike because he thought he was Evel Knievel, jumping trash cans on his Schwinn Sting-Ray. I've got lots of Gurney stories. It got to where they wouldn't let him out of their sight. And then he was an altar boy! He'd get so drunk on altar wine that even the priest couldn't stop him. Once there was a funeral and Gurney went marching around the casket and tripping all over his gown, swinging the incense like a smoking yo-yo!

Jane and Jackie laughed. Gurney called her a liar, though he knew his protests would only make her more reckless. So what if he was being a bad sport—this time her stories were true, and she was using them to make him look like an ass. Then it occurred to him: she was challenging him to a duel.

It's the gospel truth, Jane said.

No big deal. You were just a kid.

He stayed calm, leaned back on the bench. No, no, listen to Jane. She knows all about gambling, he said. She's very smart, there's no doubt about that.

Huh? they said.

She's a smart gambler. But it took more than brains to get her into the University of Chicago.

How so? Jane said, innocently, too innocently. Was she really daring him to tell the truth? He wasn't sure.

Yeah, how so? Jackie said.

He paused, grinned, blushed, swallowed. I'm sure she'd have done just fine by herself—on the SATs, I mean. But like I said, she's a gambler. . . . Once more, he couldn't bring himself to finish the story, this time because the story was true, and already he'd said far too much.

You cheated? Jackie said with dismay. She shook Jane's hand from her arm. How could you? Did you really? But how?

Jane didn't answer. She hesitated. In the time it took her to cross her legs and smooth the folds from the orange flannel of her dress Gurney's mind made several revolutions, repenting what he had said, wondering where he would go if she banished him from her room. He recalled the two of them, very small, kneeling in her closet, pricking their fingers and mixing their blood and marrying each other, brother and sister. He wanted to apologize, but that would be exactly the wrong thing to do. Now it was her turn. To his surprise, she began smiling pleasantly, as if she didn't mind being questioned at all.

Of course I cheated, she said. And more than a few of my friends did, too. It was fun. Freaky. A *gamble*. Now you, Ms. Witherspoon, you went to *Stan*ford. Didn't you cheat on your SATs?

No, she said, frankly. Her hair shampooed, her face awake, Jackie cast a shadow over shabby, naughty Jane.

I knew that, anyway. Not a gambler. Jane got up and stood in front of them. Please beware of Gurney, though. He's the worst kind of gambler, and not just when he was a kid. I bet you're wondering what he's doing here in Kraków. I mean, even you came here with a handle on the language. You were fluent, right? Well, as you'll find, Poland could be anywhere for Gurney, and his reason for being here is really pretty shaky. She paused, as if allowing him to give a rebuttal. He had none. He looked at Jackie's lunch box. Noticing he had been holding his breath, he leaked it out slowly, hoping nobody would notice.

Who does have good reason? Jackie said. You sure don't.

You don't seem to understand. A year ago my cousin was scot-free, a college guy without a care in the world, maybe even thinking that he would never leave Iowa, but one day he wound up in the hospital. Now you might think I'm saying that he'd hurt himself—broke his arm, caught some virus—because hospitals are always half full of gamblers like him. But he hadn't been in a street fight and he wasn't drying out or recovering from drugs. Let me make this perfectly clear. One morning he had nowhere else to go. He was cornered, and like any animal when backed into a corner, he could see only two options: fight or flight. And, of course, he was stunned. Poor boy was caught like a deer in headlights, but instead he was looking into the face of his daughter, his newborn baby girl, straight into the eyes of his speeding future. Jane stopped and looked knowingly at Gurney, not judgingly, not with any real emotion at all. That, she said, was just few weeks ago, right before he turned up here.

He raised his eyes to the broken town clock. The time, as ever, was four twenty-six. Jackie folded her sticky wax paper. Jane got up and walked off to class. He had no desire to smooth over her story. It was remarkably accurate, almost as if she'd been there, but that was nothing new. He sat very still. Shoppers hurried under the darkening sky. He let the truth do what it would do.

ALL POLISH BATHROOMS WERE made from the same materials: burnt red floor tiles, sky-blue wall tiles, a chunky sink hooked to the bathtub with naked plastic pipes. Their simple mechanics were right out in the open: blue knobs drew water from the city's icy bowels, red knobs ran water through the wall-mounted gas heater. Even the blue hissing flames were visible. Yet in Jackie's little bathroom these same familiar fixtures seemed to be in miniature, nursery-school size. In fact, her entire flat was in miniature, a round little turret on the corner of a building on a crooked little street just southeast of the Old Town. A tiny kitchen and this tiny bathroom were attached to the round room, where his rain-drenched clothes dried on the stove. Gurney soaked, cramped up in the tub, hard rain beating against the copper roof. Eye level with his knees, he passed a hot washcloth over his chest and listened to her working in the kitchen next door.

Soaking there he retraced his steps, starting with the moment Jane had walked off and left him sitting exposed with Jackie. He was still bemused by Jackie's reaction: after a moment of silence she'd laughed and asked if she could take him home for soup. Easy as pie, he shrugged and said yeah. She snapped shut her lunch box and they went together through thunderclouded streets, him wondering what her flat would be like, neither of them speaking but holding hands, actually holding hands, and taking in her little part of the city—the relief carvings of harlequins and saints, the rushing about because a storm was coming. When he bent over and laughed like a nut at one point, Jackie didn't seem to mind a bit. And when it started to rain, big drops at first, then sweet heavy bucketfuls that soaked through their clothes and overflowed the gutters, and when he went stomping through rivulets and puddles and lakes, kicking plumes of rushing water, she laughed and cheered and egged him on, and for a minute nothing was wrong in the world.

Now, however, soaking naked in Jackie's bathtub, he was forced to think. Old fears crowded into the bathroom and he had to put them in some kind of order. Lathering his shoulders with a yellow bar of Dial, he thought of Jane and shivered. His scrotum constricted, his asshole tightened. Somehow she had found him out and that's why she'd stuck him with donkey ears. Twice. Even Dick Chesnutt had figured that out. A smart girl like her, it follows that she'd find out, but how exactly? Had his parents told her? Had hers? Had she read Sheila's letters? Had she intercepted more recent letters? How stupid to have kept it secret to begin with. To Jane his secret was just ammunition, and now that she had fired it, now that it had fizzled on the Rynek like some dud Polish rocket, she had nothing on him. She had no use for him. Did she even care that he had a daughter? Did she care about anything? Probably not. Fuck her, anyway. Still, he grieved the inevitable loss, the loss of his lifelong blood wife-sister-cousin, whatever the hell she was, and he didn't look forward to returning home.

Jackie knocked. He splashed his hands, trying to hide himself in the hot milky water.

Gurney? It was the first time he'd heard her say his name. Gurney? Can I come in?

I'm naked, he said.

We're in Europe, she said.

What could he say to that? Yes, he said quietly.

Accompanied by the hearty smell of soup, she padded barefoot into the bathroom wearing a short blue flannel robe, her hair still stringy with rainwater. In one hand were two tumblers, in the other a bottle of Hungarian bull's blood.

Drink? she said.

Hair of the dog, he said, glad for something to soothe his nerves.

She poured him a glass, cold and heavy, and sat down on the toilet seat. Very aroused, so nervous he was shivering, he crossed his legs. Naturally, things were awkward. She poured another and drank deeply from it. He splashed around. She shook her hair, coughed a bit. He took a drink. She rolled toilet paper around her hand and dabbed it at her runny nose. She blew. She shuffled her pretty feet on the tiles. He drank some more and sank down to his chin. But Europe or no, she too was clearly uneasy. He smiled at her. She looked serious for a moment, then turned away smiling, maybe poking fun at herself.

When will it be ready? he said.

The soup? She sniffed. No rush. Let's give it a while. Looks like you're making some soup yourself.

Cream of Gurney.

He pondered the etiquette of his situation. Since he was naked, and she was clearly naked beneath her robe, and they were seated in a European bathroom, was it appropriate to ask her to untie that sash and let the robe fall off her shoulders? Wasn't that fair? Her bottom, as he could tell, was firmly round and her breasts were defiant against the flannel, but the shape of her waist remained a mystery, as did her belly and the small private well of her navel. These he wanted very much to see. She sniffed and coughed. She shook her short hair back and forth. Could he make a request? He knew the answer, surmising that there were at least two types of nudity in Europe: the erotic kind and the everyday kind, and at least for now he was a victim of the latter. He was in the tub, she was in a robe.

What's her name? Jackie asked, as if finishing some unspoken thought. She stood, refilled his glass, and sat back down.

Whose?

Your daughter's.

He avoided her face and followed a pair of pipes up the wall to where they disappeared into a jagged hole, but when he did look at her she was calm and sincere, simply curious. Sarah, he said.

Did you pick the name?

Her mother did.

She coughed and sniffed. Are you still involved with her mother?

We were, uh, involved in college. But we aren't anymore.

I guess that's better. So then Sarah was an accident.

He didn't answer, sank a little deeper down. During the pregnancy he'd comforted himself by calling it an accident, but in just the few minutes he had been with Sarah he'd known there was nothing accidental about her. She was a baby and she looked like him. We didn't plan her, he said. If that's what you mean.

That's what I mean, she said, hesitating. Linda says you're really remorseful about it.

How the hell would she know?

She heard you confessing to those guys at the restaurant.

Oh.

And then she said you were all gloomy at Auschwitz.

Who wouldn't be gloomy at Auschwitz?

True.

So you've known about it for a week?

I've known what Linda told me.

And you didn't care?

I didn't know you.

I've been kind of pathetic, I know.

There's no right way to act, not in something like this.

Yeah, but there are hundreds of wrong ways and I've taken all of them.

Leave it to a Catholic boy to say that.

He splashed around, let the water settle. Can I get out now? I'm getting pruny. What time is it?

It's early, she said. About noon, I think.

I've gotta go soon.

Why?

I have to work tonight.

You have to relax, she said, crouching down beside the tub. That's what you have to do. She set down her glass on the tile with a clink. Just relax.

After a moment, he did relax. He took a healthy drink of his wine and squawked himself deeper into the water. His penis floated up, but he let it go. Europe, he thought. His mind wandered out of that room, to Jane's story from a couple days before, the story of Jackie following Linda home. Then, too, there was rain and wine and a bathtub. Then, too, it was steamy and sexy. The match was uncanny. Why hadn't he thought of it sooner? Because it had seemed so dirty the way Jane had told it. It hadn't felt at all like this—easy and real, like the natural thing to do. It was an entirely different kind of pleasure. He wondered if the other story had also really happened, if it had been easy and real before Jane came along and got her dirty hands on it. He flashed Jackie a sidelong glance, to which she playfully raised her eyebrows. He thought he should ask the truth about Linda, whom he'd grown fond of since visiting Auschwitz, but she promptly slid her hand behind his head and massaged the cords in his neck. He shivered and squirmed but of course let it go, glad that things were growing more intimate, even if it meant coming between Jackie and Linda.

I'm going to give you some consolation, she said, running more hot water into the tub. I'm going to tell you my own story.

Consolation would be nice, he said, and lost himself in her confident hands and the easy candor of her flowing voice.

It all begins with my first trip to Kraków. Every winter Stanford sent a group of us Slavic students to spend two months at the Jagiellonian. My year was really lame and most of them just stuck to the group, acting like they were on vacation, club-hopping and drinking and like that—and that's fine, I guess, but I mean it's not like we were in Spain or Greece. So I kind of ditched them after a week or so, thinking I'd make friends with the Poles. This was devilishly easy, of course, because Poles are so hospitable and half of them want to practice their English—it was so easy I was avoiding people pretty soon.

Once, when I was reading on a bench in my favorite part of the Planty, kind of behind the Wyspiański museum, I watched this funny man in tweeds with a nicely trimmed beard, stabbing a stick into the grass. He saw me watching him and he called me over to show me this snake hole in the grass—the only one he'd ever seen in Kraków. I told him that he'd never get the snake out that way, but he said he didn't want the snake because the hole itself was interesting enough. His English was perfect, but odd and stiff. This is how he talked: That a lone gray snake could adapt itself to this devastated city, this morass of ignorance and pollution and pain, suggests a primal ingenuity, a tenacity which exceeds that of most Krakovians. I asked him how he knew the snake was gray, and he said that was just how he imagined it. I told him that I thought Krakovians were pretty sturdy folks, and he told me that I was naive but very beautiful and that I should tell him more of this airheaded nonsense over dinner at the Staropolska. So I let him woo me, to make a long story short.

Did he ever start talking like a real human being?

Sometimes he did. She stopped the massage and sat on the rim, from where he was sure she could see all of him through the murk. He was unlike any professor I'd ever had, she said. He let his discipline run all over the place, but maybe they're all that way if you get close enough. He was a scientist first and foremost, but he had dozens of different things on his mind—politics, semiotics, all these ideas, most of them pretty far-fetched—and when he was on a roll he'd get them streaming all around us like ribbons from a Maypole. And the more beer we drank, because we were always drinking beer, I would watch his ideas dance faster and faster until we'd try to braid them into some beautiful cosmology, but usually we'd just get them all tangled up. One day we came to the conclusion that the universe was a big dump truck. Once he explained communism for me using this pornographic French cookbook. He used to have a great sense of humor, and we were always laughing about something, and that's what I really liked about him. Gurney looked at her face, upside down and turned away, and he wanted to cover himself, sure that he could never measure up to this character.

When I got back to the States I was bored and depressed. Yet before I could really recover from him, a letter came saying he'd gotten some grant and was coming over to do work at Stanford. Two months passed and there he was, living in San Francisco, his wife and kid halfway around the world.

He was married?

Regrettably. We picked up where we left off, this time without any worries—sometimes during the day, always at night, all over campus and the peninsula and the city. We'd been holed up for so long that we flaunted it for a while, and that was great. Sometimes he even took me to faculty parties, which was a trip. But right away I could see how awkward he was in the States, a bit less querying, a bit more sociable, and he took a childish interest in stupid things like shopping malls. I guess it was forgivable, considering how rough it was in Poland at the time, but you know, I was disappointed. Like, he insisted that we go to the Universal Pictures theme park, and it was really embarrassing to see him suck it all up. I wasn't even sad to see him duped by it all, I was just embarrassed. Isn't that awful? Then he shaved off his beard and started looking all healthy and tan and Californian. He might have looked more handsome to other people, but I missed the sickly Slavic look, you know? I still loved him, but like I said, I was disappointed. It got to where I didn't love him like I did at first, at least not at all in the same way, and I didn't want to be in public with him. Maybe I loved him out of habit and comfort, maybe even pity. Who knows. Whatever the reasons were, I couldn't just let him go when his visa ran out. I couldn't do it. Some dumb sense of duty made me see it through. Never do anything out of duty.

Don't worry about me.

I finished college and moved back over here. I didn't even consider my options. I found this flat, got a job, and I crept out to see him whenever I could, but we had to start going undercover again, because of his wife, which was good this time around because he still embarrassed me. He had his beard again but he was starting to get cynical, especially about the changes in Poland. He had completely lost his sense of humor. It was like he'd pawned all his fun and goofy ideas for a pile of smelly Russian newspapers. Now his big thing was that Kraków was like a metaphor for the decay of the West, and all the rest of the Eastern bloc countries were just rotten planets dropping like apples from their Soviet orbits. How depressing's that? It didn't even really make sense. Anyway, I didn't recognize all this at the time. Just like I didn't recognize how much he was to blame for how lousy I felt, or that any pleasure I still found in Kraków had everything to do with my sappy memories of it. I'm sorry. I'm just rambling now. You must be getting really pruny.

Forget about it.

I'll cut to the chase. I should have known I'd stayed too long when I started taking Polish contraceptives. Not even two full cycles had passed, and there I was, knocked up.

Shit.

It only seemed right to talk it over with him, but I wasn't thrilled by the idea. I had him over for dinner. I wasn't so against the thought of an abortion, until he told me flat out that I didn't have a choice. I told him I could do what I wanted—something I'd never really done before—and right away I knew why not. He didn't get up. He didn't even say anything. I had made this chocolate cake, with this mix my mother sent me, and it was sitting there between us on the table. And he just leaned forward, took the thing in his big awful hands, and *crushed* it, tearing it up right there in front of me, getting frosting and cake all over the place. I called him a child—because that's just what he fucking was—and that's when he really went off, beating the table, splattering frosting, shouting that the baby wasn't mine to keep, that it was a sickly, shriveled, shameful little thing that didn't belong to anybody! He kept shouting, really loud, and I remember bending over to protect my stomach. Imagine! You see how little this place is— it could hardly contain him when he started really flipping out, tipping over chairs, throwing shit, forcing me back in here, into the bathroom. I stayed in here for like an hour, a long time after he'd slammed the door.

What did you do?

That next weekend I took a train to Berlin, got the abortion, and came back here with no one to tell. Nobody in Kraków even *knew* about us. He tried to get me back for a couple months, but I couldn't even look at him. I put an end to it by saying I'd tell his wife.

She slid down from the rim and kneeled in front of him. Her brown eyes were wet and tired and honest. She told him it was important to her that he understand this much: I didn't have the abortion because he wanted me to. I guess at the time I thought I did it out of hatred, disgust at the thought of carrying his baby because I'd never seen anything so cruel as him. But now I know I would have done it anyway. I was just afraid, that's all. I was just afraid.

What's this guy's name?

That's not important.

I told you Sarah's name.

That's different. She's alive and a part of you. He's dead.

Is he really? Gurney was shocked.

He's dead to me. I haven't seen him in a year, even in this little city.

That's good, I guess. Gurney looked at his white and wrinkly hands. So do you have any words of wisdom?

She smiled. Just consolation. Just my story.

Thanks, he said, not wanting to sound ironic. Really, thanks. I'm quite pruny now. I gotta get out.

She stood, pulled a thick white towel from the rack, and held it open the way his father used to do. Still a little shy, he stood with a splash and let her wrap him up like a crêpe. She held him there, hugging him, and without any warning she straightened up and kissed him—on the mouth, long and deep, an unmistakably girlfriendly kiss.

From where he sat at her small square table directly in the center of her turret, her tall curved windows gave an unusual view of the city, as if the smoking buildings were collapsing all around him. Rain beat down on the conical roof. Her furniture was spare, but her rickety shelves burst with books. His clothes were warm and stiff from the stove. She set the table for lunch, still in her flannel robe, appearing and disappearing through the flowered kitchen curtain—spoons, butter, bread, wine. Reality started setting in again. Now that people knew what he had done, he would have to start explaining himself. What he was doing, why he had left. But even he didn't know why exactly. As Jackie had said, he'd left because he was scared. No, actually she'd said that about herself. Maybe he had it all wrong. He told people he was out to have fun, but whoever believed that, he thought, was every bit as stupid as he was. He acted as if he were adventuring on the frontier of ethics, but if that were really the case, he thought, he did indeed have fucked-up instruments.

She came through the curtain with two steaming soup bowls, an easy and fearless look on her face, and in that instant something shifted a few degrees for him, giving his problems another dimension. They rose like an image from a pop-up book: Jackie had had an abortion, a dangerous affair, massive things that could have crushed her, but now her life looked just perfect. Maybe it was because she had worked through her messes and dirtied her hands, and now she knew that life could always be worse. Perhaps his actions could also explain themselves. He could open the letters, write responses, send home Kasino money to pay for diapers, pay for jars of Gerber food. His life would get harder but his misery would pass, and people would start to leave him alone. He would start to leave himself alone. Strange, why did the greenish-brown soup in front of him make him think of stomping through puddles?

Eat up, Jackie said.

He did, voraciously, and for some reason his mind grew terrifically lucid. The lucidity could have come from any number of things—his yearning for Jackie, his soak in the tub, the sudden release of his secret into the world—but it seemed his pleasure was focused on the soup. Rich and nutty, vaguely prickly, its strange admixture of familiar spices played tricks on his tongue and excited his memory. Was it fruit? White wine? Vinegar? Sesame? What first tasted like seeds then tasted like soil. Garlic? Spinach? Mowing the lawn? There were trips to the zoo, to a best friend's farm, a canoe ride down the Maquoketa River to the mouth of the mile-wide Mississippi. There were the last days of autumn when the trees were naked but the Catholic girls had another week in skirts. Unable to stop, not wanting to cap the gush of memories, he noticed too late that he was eating like an animal—a sloppy concert of soup spoon and bread crusts that was keeping Jackie well entertained.

What's in this? he asked.

Do you really want to know?

Of course. He swallowed. It's fabulous.

Lots of different things.

Like what? What's the active ingredient?

She leaned forward and whispered, Earthworms.

What?

You heard me.

And he had. The bowl was half empty, still steaming. He lifted a spoonful and looked at it closely. It looked just like soup.

They're all minced up, she said. You never would have noticed.

Why? Why earthworms?

Don't think about it. Just eat.

Why?

Go ahead.

He paused. You know, it's really unlike me to eat earthworms, he said. Thinking about it, no one he knew would have eaten them.

You might as well change your ways, if you like them. Do you?

I do, unfortunately.

Then don't deny yourself. Eat.

With her cowlicked hair and worldly brown eyes, hunched with her elbows up on the table, Jackie was as trustworthy as Kraków got— which maybe wasn't saying much. And yet he did eat, cautiously at first but then as rapidly as he had before, spooning his way into a long forgotten memory of him and his mother playing catch with a tomato.

WALKING THE WET STREETS HOME from Jackie's, he shivered away his lingering pleasure with the fear that Jane would be lying in wait, flexed like the jaws of a brown wolf spider hiding deep in its

webby tunnel. In earnest, his fear was of Sheila's letters and his resolve to read them very first thing. But upon arriving home he found
Jane on the divan, looking harmless, illuminated by the floor lamp and
curled around an old fat book. Beside the mussed hair and touch of
pink around the eyes, she appeared to have recovered from Halloween all right. She greeted him with that faintest of winks and
closed the book over her finger.

He gave her a nod as he crossed to the records. Crouching down,
he was sorely surprised to find the long shelf all but empty—some
Dixieland, some Polish folk music ripe with mildew, but not a single
scrap of classical. He dropped to his knees and slapped the shelf.

Where's all the classical? Where's the Shostakovich?

Shostakovich? I didn't know you cared, honey.

Where'd they go?

Haven't you noticed? She slipped off the divan and crawled
toward him across the rug. She stopped, sat, crossed her legs. Look at
the bookshelves, the walls, the floor. I mean, do you notice anything?
It's emptying out. The records have been gone for days.

Where to? Gone where? He wanted to shake her.

Well, who owns all this stuff?

Where did he take them?

Where does he live, silly?

I don't know.

Ojców Valley. It's on the map. A short bus trip.

I can't just go there.

You went to Jackie's. You went to Auschwitz, of all places. You're
American. You can go wherever you want.

What did you do with my letters?

Oh, honey, she said, convincingly sincere; maybe she was sincere.
Oh, honey, do you really think I would read your letters?

I don't know what to think, after that crap on the square this
morning.

Let's not start on that, she said, stiffening. She got to her feet. You
don't want to start on that. Her voice was ice, and he felt that he had
finally blown it. She walked from the room and clicked shut the door.

Angry and tired, savage and alone, he sat there stewing. But then just like that, like a kid who realizes he's been bawling for effect, he felt just fine. He too got to his feet and spoke out to Zbigniew's echoey room: I'm American. I can go wherever I want. But he didn't really believe that.

Book Two

Inedible Feast

Ten

ZBIGNIEW'S SLEEP HAD BEEN SO TORN BY NIGHTMARES, so hounded by lawyers and Austrian soldiers, so crowded with fugitives in cold valley caves where he found his daughter after wandering in pajamas and then scrambling up a rushing winter stream, cracking his knees against the rocks, skinning his hands on the ice-crusted snow banks, that it felt much safer to be standing up, cold, in the middle of his floor. His big rumpled bed had done nothing wrong. The windows were black and all frosted over. Outside the valley was absolutely still. No one had followed him back from the city, and yet he was overcome by fear—first of his mattress, then of the bedroom, then of the library, then, of course, the closet. He paced around barefoot, straightening up, trying to make peace with his silent home. He touched the body on Grazyna's crucifix. He touched the glass of black-currant juice that had been sitting unfinished since yesterday morning, as if that night's horrible events had never happened. But the cottage refused to make amends. He had to get out. He shoved his naked feet into his boots and rushed out the door in just a nightshirt.

If seen across the valley that morning before sunrise, he would have seemed no more than a twitching in the dark. If seen from the woods, from across the road, or from one of the dark windows in the Słowokowski cottage over on its hill across the stream, across that winding ribbon of fog that made its way through dark and scruffy fields, he would have seemed merely a man up early, hacking away with shovel and hoe. But if seen from up close, from inside his own cottage, from behind the woodpile, or, say, from among the raspberries at the edge of his garden, there would have been no mistaking the guilt on his face, the bristly torment, the boots and nightshirt. As he rolled his eyes from ground to horizon, focusing and unfocusing, raising them up to the near-black sky, it would have been clear to anyone watching nearby that his digging was neither for treasure nor pleasure but for *distance,* and madly, racing with the daylight now blushing in the east. Gratefully, morning came gradually to the valley.

His hoe hacked and scraped the topsoil, dragging up onions and leeks and petunias, cleaning a roughly rectangular patch. He stood back a moment and took it all in, measuring the patch against the azaleas and peonies. It was half as large as the potato quadrant, twice as large as the carrot crib. A fecund smell was coming from the stream. It was the first of November and harvest was past: later that day he would turn it all over so no one could tell where the hole was hidden. He traded hoe for shovel and set to digging, tossing dirt so wildly about the garden that a watcher would have thought he had no intention of replacing it. But of course he did. He looked around, saw no one, and dug more quickly. The hole! The hole! the shovel seemed to say. The hole! The hole! The hole! He dug as if retreating back into the night, beyond black soil into muscular brown clay.

Trotsky would have called this an endless revolution, *this,* when capitalists fail and give way to Communists, when they fail one another and fail altogether and give way to a Church that gives way to capitalists, who are not quite dead, alive and well, zombies nuzzling from rock and clay, pushing up faces into the dim light of day, returning for the Communists in their tenured professorships. But Trotsky must have meant something different. The shovel struck rock. For what then, he thought, was Dick Chesnutt if not, in essence, a Trotskyite villain? Now American, now Pole, now capitalist, now socialist, now a lecturer on a penis brigade, now a transvestite with teats for muscles, a soggy and pathetic and unshaven woman—now alive, rebelliously alive, quiveringly so, Dick Chesnutt was as fretfully alive as Trotsky must have been for those few last moments in 1940 before

Stalin, or whoever, finally put him to rest. Trotsky/Chesnutt. Chesnutt/ Trotsky. It didn't really matter at this point.

He'd been carving the sides of the hole too neatly, trying to keep the shape of a box. He cursed himself and dug more quickly, more carelessly.

One thought kept resurfacing: a body, even one with teats for muscles, fights like mad for its last gasp of life. But life, though precious, is basically gruesome, and a grown man's neck, thick as a fence post, red and stubbly and greasepaint-slick, squirms like a toad when it's trying to save its whiskey-stinking windpipe. Toes frozen, hands raw on the wooden handle, Zbigniew wished for socks and gloves, but then with an awful surge of sympathy he recalled Dick Chesnutt's wild left eye, how it had swiveled in its lid, taking last snapshots of the world it was leaving. The fishlike right eye stayed very still, maybe amazed or already dead.

You sinister son of a bitch.

Those were Dick Chesnutt's last words in life, his last escaping breath before his trachea clamped shut. Pregnant as any last words would be, they raised all kinds of menacing questions: Who was sinister—Zbigniew or Chesnutt? Who was the son? Who was the bitch? Was Zbigniew's mother hovering near? At the time he'd managed to fight back the feeling, but it'd been awful watching that darting left eye, watching that quiet and complacent right eye. For he himself had always hoped to go with dignity, among family and friends. Live with pride and die with dignity. The dead man had lived the life of a savage, and so he'd died accordingly. It's hard to kill a man, even a savage. But it's easy, too. It's hard *not* to kill a man once you've gotten started—just as it's impossible to retract when you're already coming. Nothing can sway that beautiful drive. In fact, it was so very much like coming, *cette petite mort*, this little death of Dick Chesnutt, that he'd topped it off with a cry of pleasure, a big noisy finishing off. And then there he was, an exhausted murderer. And now there in the closet were the cold leftovers.

When the eye had stopped darting, when the body'd fallen slack and irrevocably dead, he had shaken its shoulders and pleaded with it to breathe. He'd even uttered a fatuous apology. But then he'd sobered. He'd let it drop to the scratched-up floor—bent and grotesque in its red velvet dress.

Like it or not, that's what he had gone there to do.

The cock crowed behind the raspberries. He was incapable of digging any faster. Pani Słowokowska appeared in her yard. She was a true peasant, a creature of habit, awake every morning at the blast of the cock, out to do her goat and eggs then back inside to push her beads. And there she was now, bucolic, Catholic, hunching over some filthy beast. He didn't wave, and neither did she, but he knew she'd seen him. She had her own idea why he was up so early and digging in his garden, but her darkest fantasies couldn't approximate the truth. They had owned this cottage for ten years now, but only his wife had befriended the Słowokowskis. He'd told his daughter that they were child eaters, for probably they were, and he'd forbidden her ever to go over there or to speak to their gap-toothed punk of a grandson. He'd assured her it wasn't a question of class, though of course it was. He'd told her it was a question of intellectual integrity.

He himself had encountered them only once. In 1979, he took a retreat at the cottage to escape the hype of the pope's visit to Kraków, only to find that the Słowokowskis had draped their roof with His Pious Face. All day long, it glared through his windows. That night, drunk with vodka, he staggered across the river stones, vaulted over their limestone wall, and landed clumsily on their property. Bring out your Jesus! he'd shouted out. Give me a Jesus! Any old Jesus! Bring him on, thorns and all, let me stick my finger in him! He'd stomped and clomped in their flowers and manure, shouting at the unflappable Jan Pawel II, not stopping until the now-dead Pan Słowokowski appeared at the door with a spade over his shoulder. He threatened Zbigniew, who responded with a fart. Shortly, wisely, he turned and shut the door.

Not only had Zbigniew been at the height of his powers, but at the time he was president of the Academy of Metallurgy and publicly favored by the local party. No man in the valley, not even the pope, would have dared clunk him over the head with a spade. Yet now that the Party was good and gone, Zbigniew bothered no one but himself. He was divorced, unemployed, hiding in the woods, living in a cottage that could be reclaimed at any time. Maybe, so far as Mrs. Słowokowska was concerned as she pulled warm darts of milk into her pail, Zbigniew Zamoyski, at this unholy hour, was at last out digging a grave for himself.

The sky was bluing, birds singing near and far, making the enterprise riskier and riskier. Beyond the fence, his own goat watched him with the yellow eyes of a devil.

Maybe the hole was deep enough now. Inside, he had to stand on tiptoe to see over the carrot tops, but then another foot deeper could be a good investment, maybe another hundred years for the body to rot, another century of privacy between the worms and Pan Chesnutt. Who would suspect a seven-foot grave? Surely not the widow Słowokowska. She was a traditionalist. But to see him in broad daylight dragging a body from his cottage—dumping it in the hole and covering it over—that would be certain cause for alarm. He cursed himself and shoveled faster. He shouldn't have gone to sleep at all. He should have started it the moment he got home. He should have kept working the whole night through. Stupid to obsess over the goddamn hole. But still he dug deeper and thought of his vegetables, wondering if his garden might someday be fertilized by this pedophilic Johnny Appleseed.

When he was finished it was already day, a gray sky framed by the edges of the hole. He leapt up to gain purchase on the rim of the grave, a good three feet above his head, but it crumbled in his grasp and showered down with him to the muddy floor. He tried again and again, each time crumbling a different wall, filling his boots and nightshirt with soil. His arms ached. His head was weary. The real work was finished; now he had only to get himself out, throw in the body, cover it over like blackbirds in a pie. It was so simple! Beginning to whimper with anger and frustration, he stopped himself. He propped the shovel at a ramplike angle. He'd nearly climbed the length of it before he slipped off and fell back down. Slipping from it twice more, he collapsed and wept in the crotch of the grave, raking his fingers, beating his fist into sticky clay. Then he collected himself. He balanced himself against the two walls and carefully walked up the shovel stick. This time he gained a good hold on the edge and smeared his way out of the hole.

Are you quite all right, Pan Zamoyski? Pani Słowokowska called from her gate. Some kind of animal was clutched under her arm. She'd heard him shouting.

He didn't respond. He was overcome by fear and fatigue. His nightshirt was filthy. The garden was cluttered with mammoth heaps of dirt. The valley was larger than he remembered it being, and the sky was filling with beautiful black thunderclouds.

Are you quite all right? she called again.

Why, yes, Pani Słowokowska, he yelled across, his voice high and weak and gravelly. Quite all right. Very good. It rather looks like rain.

She stood there watching him, petting her animal, then closed her gate and returned to her cottage. He hurried inside. Everything was dim. He tracked clay across the kitchen tiles, sliding along the bare boards in the hall. He caught himself on the closet door. It was open a crack. His heart fluttered, his throat restricted. Had the body moved? Was it possible? He eased it open, releasing a stench of feces and urine. The body was hunched in a sitting position, head on its knees, wrapped in a sheet. He reached one dirty hand beneath its legs, clutched another behind its back. He tried drawing the body close together, but it was stiff and wouldn't give. It was an awkward job getting it through the door, its stiffened shoulder knocking the frame, but eventually he managed and left it tipped over in the hall.

Wrapped in a sheet, the corpse was helpless and pitiable. Child-like. Once more, as he stretched out the resistant shroud on the floor, he found himself shuddering with something like sorrow. Not the sorrow he'd felt when his father died, nothing like grief. This was purely sorrow for himself—not self-pity but bony regret, wiry regret, dread that his life could have gone so wrong. How could it have happened in such a short time that Zbigniew Zamoyski, boy perfectionist, one of the university's most decorated scholars, a model husband and re-

sponsible father, could have become an adulterer, exile, and murderer. That such an honest and hard-working Communist could have
so easily become a speculator, a venture capitalist, a casino shareholder—smelling the shit of a murder he'd committed. It was all right
there in that rigid shroud. Looking at the crooked length of it,
unwashed, unburied, he searched for any indication that he'd truly
become a murderer. Yes, he'd committed a murder, but Zbigniew
wondered if he had intrinsically *changed,* as iron changed by blazing
coke, and he wondered if he was capable of killing again and if that
primogenital temper, once his charm, once his birthright, had now become a legion of cancers in his heart, rotting the fibers and sinews of
his morals. Had life in America cheapened his soul? Had life in the
country made him a beast?

Stocking feet extended from the shroud. The toes were blistered
and poking through nylons, caked with blood from a night in spiked
heels. At the thought of this man dressed as a woman, in a dress that
once belonged to Jane, whom Zbigniew adored more than maybe any
woman; at the thought of this fop swishing down the streets, sashay-
ing around on his American holiday; at the thought of him savoring
souvenirs of Wanda, the memory of kissing her, of swirling his ven-
omous tongue in her mouth, the mouth of a pubescent child, he tore
back the sheet. He clutched the cold ashen face by the chin. Its stupid
eyes were half open, its smeary mouth fixed in a grimace. He grasped
it by the neck and the front of its dress and dragged it along the wall-
paper. Its joints stayed locked in a sitting position.

You sinister son of a bitch! he said, knocking the head against the
wall. The face was slack, alcoholic—but its whiskers grown from the
night before. All in all, it was the same Dick Chesnutt, the lowly bastard who had disgraced the university, humiliated his students, parad-
ing them around the Collegium Maius, chanting Fuck communism!
Fuck capitalism! Fuck Mother Russia! making them swing their peck-
ers from their pants. Then and now, Zbigniew muttered, you are out
of control. He knocked the head against the wall. He hiked the body
off the ground. This body was wasted on your lousy soul!

Yet of course Dick Chesnutt's political life, if you could call it that, wasn't the thing that enraged him so. Dick Chesnutt was a political clown, and the papers had destroyed him in one fell swoop. So, no. What had provoked him to slide the body farther up the wall until its head was bent against the ceiling, then hurl it to the floor with a vegetable thud—to kick it—swipe at it—slather it with insults—this was provoked by elemental jealousy. Simple jealousy. Revenge is delectable, a one-inch slab of seared red steak, but jealousy burns inside like poison, it scorches and bleeds like a ten-year ulcer. He'd kept his cool on weekends with Jane, as cars whispered through the Vienna streets and she refused her expensive breakfast because the marmalade brought back painful memories. And he'd tried to contain himself the morning before, lying in the bath at the mercy of Jane as she told him in detail what Dick Chesnutt had done. And strangely enough, he'd even controlled it well enough to be sure he saw the man good and dead. But now there was simply no keeping it in. This husk of a man had made him a murderer, and mad jealous poison flooded his body, soaking like acid through his walls and membranes and turning him into a different sort of man—a poisonous man, a murderous man—and then, like piss welled up in a bladder, his fury cut free with utmost pleasure, and up and down the hall, cursing and coughing, he bashed the body from wall to wall, slapping its face, punching its gut, tearing its dress, dragging it around in a delirious dance. You sinister American son of a bitch, he said, tearing a hole in its filthy dress. It had been such pleasure to be in control, to master this filthy body that he had killed, this man he had killed with his two bare hands, that he was getting hard under his nightshirt. But no need for alarm, he thought. Nobody would know how much he liked it.

He went to the window. From what he could see Pani Sło-wokowska was inside, but he couldn't tell if the curtains were drawn. The cottage was yellow, the sky had grown blacker. He was about to turn away when she rushed from her door and began closing the shutters. Perfect! he said. She's afraid of the storm! In her efforts to unlatch the shutter she had somehow broken the bottom hinge, and now it seemed she was determined to fix it. He watched her make little progress in her work. He slid the currant juice out of the way and rested his head on the wood. He closed his eyes and fell asleep.

Deep cracks of thunder woke him up. Rain drummed the roof and rushed through the gutters. The distance was obscured by slanting sheets of rain. Beyond heaps of mud in the gouged-out garden, Pani Słowokowska's right shutter banged in the wind. A black rectangle of glass peered back at his property. Despite the weather, he had to do it. He put an oilcloth coat on over his nightshirt, rewrapped Dick Chesnutt in the dirty shroud, and hastily dragged him out to the garden. The body made a splash in the puddle that had already collected at the bottom of the grave. Muddy water seeped through the shroud, which pinkly clung to the dress beneath. The unholy position in which the body would spend eternity provoked a Hail Mary from deep inside Zbigniew. He stopped it midstream and cursed himself. He shoveled clay back into the hole.

Rain kept pounding as Zbigniew finished up. First he packed the clay down hard, then he replaced the soil as he'd found it. Last thing, he took a rake to the garden until the grave was flat and flush with the rest. He was catching cold. The sky was rumbling, flashing, pouring. Earthworms rejoiced in the growing puddles. Before returning inside to bathe, he paused to look at his lonely work. He leaned on the rake. The last person he had spoken to had been his daughter, and he regretted he hadn't been so kind. He hoped, in any case, that she was enjoying her gift.

Eleven

On the chilly afternoon of her November exams, on which she was sure she had done very well, Wanda and all the coolest students in her level coursed the leaf-rattling streets of the city, sweeping through the shops and crowded cafés and making noise in funereal galleries, too happy to stay in one place for long. The sky was so blue and the air so pure she found herself taking big hungry breaths, though Wujo Płujo (Mateusz and Piotr), with their short French cigarettes, did make smoking look attractive. Tall and thin in their frowsy black clothes, Wujo Płujo was the compass for the wayward group: they could make any suggestion sound so exciting, so forbidden and deliciously preposterous, that everyone, especially the girls, had to follow. Even their visit to the National Bank, with its looming ceilings and endless queues and zombified clerks tapping on typewriters, turned into a roast of the ornery customers, asking how much foreign currency they were making, how they would spend it, and how much they would donate to the Polish avant-garde. They accosted the eyes of the surveillance-box man, asking his forecast of robberies for that day, but they never did make it all the way to the counter.

Besides Matek and Piotr, they were: Monika, forever in American overalls; Kuba with his green, radioactive hair; funny Danuta, who Wanda didn't know so well; Iwona with big breasts and a good loud voice; Małgorzata, Wanda's best friend, who was a bore because she knew she'd failed her philology and who was deathly jealous of beautiful little Julka, cute as a muffin with straight black hair and a tiny brown dress that showed off her legs to Wujo Płujo. Long, slender legs. Of all of them, however, only Wanda knew Matek's secret—that he hadn't stopped shoplifting all day long. Not that she'd actually caught him in the act, but at different times—in the CD shop, the Italian bakery, the art-supplies store—he'd sneaked her looks that had little devil horns. This, she knew, meant shoplifting. The important thing was that he definitely did not look at the other girls, knowing, of course, that Wanda'd stay cool.

She stood with the boys at a newstand in staticky silence, looking far down Ulica Szpitalna, through the mobs to the edge of the square, where momentarily the other girls appeared, jaunty little specks in warm winter colors. When they came into earshot, Mateusz shouted out Yum-yum. *Smacznego,* princesses! He was referring to their big fluffy half-devoured waffles spilling with cream. He ran to them, demanding a bite from each one, and when the six of them came back striding arm in arm, Wanda ached with jealousy.

Change of plans, Mateusz announced, cozily between Julka and Danuta, his mouth a sticky white mess. Scratch the slogans and heads on pikes, we won't be storming the Bastille today. Instead, he said, lowering his voice and gesturing for them to gather around, we shall welcome the evening with a pipe of hashish.

Nobody responded. Everyone looked to the others' reactions. Wanda got nervous but not that bad—she'd drunk too much twice in her life, once without her parents there. But this, she realized, was an entirely different prospect. Małgorzata kept trying to catch her eye. Wanda, starting to smile, didn't look back.

What a bluff, Piotr said, laughing, clapping Mateusz on the shoulder. You've said that for a month now, and every night it's always the same, you and me slobbering over a bottle of Żytnia. So tell me, my dear, where is it coming from?

I'm glad you ask. Matek blew into his hands and rubbed them like a raccoon. Here's where the adventure begins. He looked at Wanda's purple Swatch, which read sixteen hours seventeen, thought for a moment, then spoke in a slow and measured voice: In exactly eight minutes, the nine of us will walk to the corner of Sławkowska and

Basztowa, where we'll catch tram number twelve to Dietla Street. We'll wait there for ten more minutes then jump onto tram twenty-one, which will deliver us from the safety of the Old Town into the dirty danger of Kazimierz. Night will fall, the wind will rise, and all of you will follow me through streets and alleys and hallways and cat-walks to the creepy residence of—what does Wanda call him?—Pan Dick Chesnutt? He paused for effect, let the name ring. He owes me a bag of Afghan hash. I've paid for it, I've waited for it, and who could refuse an ugly band like us? So let me hear it, who all's in?

The group fidgeted, puffed out clouds, exchanged a series of guilty looks. Her stomach twisted with moral tumult. Hashish in Kazimierz—that was one thing, but the forbidden Dick Chesnutt was another altogether. It had been ages since she'd last seen him around town (looking hunted and lonely among the trees of the Planty), but still she knew he was out there somewhere. His name lived a life all its own, connecting him to so many rumors and stories that very few of them, if any, could really be true. The real Dick Chesnutt! It intrigued and puzzled but most of all frightened her that Mateusz knew where he lived. That was something none of the kids knew, except Jane, who wasn't a kid. Would he recognize her? Shy from her? She imagined strumming his guitar again, drinking tea with him at *his* kitchen table.

But then there was Mateusz. He wanted revenge, he wanted his drugs, and things could get stupid or violent really fast. Dick Chesnutt might think she was hanging out with hoodlums, which simply wasn't true. She had to make sure they avoided all that.

All right, Mateusz, Wanda said smartly. Here's plan B.

It better be good.

It's better than yours. Look. We take the trams, the streets, the catwalks, we do all that. That part's good. The problem is how we deal with Mr. Chesnutt.

Wanda! Małgorzata whispered, nudging an elbow.

Czy?

Małgorzata said nothing, gave a hard look.

Go on, Piotr said.

We can't intimidate him because he's a friend of the family. And he's too sophisticated for your extortion or whatever.

Sophisticated family friend, Mateusz said. Go on.

Just let me do the talking and you'll get your hashish. All the girls looked at Wanda in dismay. Julka seemed to be impressed.

Fine, said Mateusz, nodding to Piotr. But if that doesn't work, I'm taking over.

Piotr and Kuba laughed. Matek made a macho whipped-cream mustache.

MOMENTS LATER THEY WERE on a tram—Wujo Płujo, Kuba, Wanda, and Julka. The other cowards had been expected home for dinner—as if Wanda hadn't been! It was crowded and clanging, so they didn't say much, just swayed from poles and watched yellow headlights flashing far behind. She felt underdressed in her jean jacket and flannel. People wore mittens and caps of all colors. She counted seven men wearing black wool overcoats, all of the same cardboard cut. And already it was getting dark, fluorescent green inside the tram, cobalt blue behind naked trees, arched and black over the busy streets. Kilometers of streetlamps blinked on at once, reminding her that Christmas was coming.

On the second tram, the thought of Christmas began to torment her. All of them sat: Piotr riled Kuba with his roiling fears for Lithuania, Mateusz charmed Julka by reciting poems of Julian Przybos's, and Wanda stayed silent, watching the Austrian-built estates of the Old Town give way to newer gray blocks of the forties, realizing how seldom she left the Center, sharply aware how privileged she was, and aware, with a cold lump of lead in her chest, that her mother was in the kitchen preparing a dinner that her daughter wouldn't be coming home to eat. And for the next month her mother would prepare for the holiday, fermenting the borscht, folding and freezing the crisp *pierózki*, shopping early for the compotes and gingerbread, the Christmas pike perch, mixing poppy-seed waffles and nut croquettes and all the foods of holidays past. All her mother's work for a broken family feast with Gurney sitting at the head of the table.

What's wrong? Julka said, clutching Wanda's hand in hers.

Me? Nothing! Wanda laughed. But she kept hold of Julka's soft and warm hand. Her jealousy changed into admiration—that Julka could make a brown dress look so fresh. Strange, she was grateful that Julka was along.

Is Dick Chesnutt really your father's friend?

Not exactly, Wanda said. The question made her pause. First, because it was so naive. Second, because of Tati's spooky knowledge of their kiss—a fact that added to the thrill of this adventure. First he was my English tutor, she said, then he taught me guitar.

But you said he's a friend of the family, she said.

Mateusz interrupted: He'd come by on Tuesdays to lick out the pots.

And he was a spy for the Kremlin, Piotr offered.

And an undercover agent for Ulica Sezamkowa!

Guy Smiley.

Kermit the Frog.

Oscar the Grouch, Kuba added.

Matek announced their stop. They bounded out into windy Kazimierz. Julka followed Piotr and Kuba, pulling Wanda behind by the hand.

Kazimierz proper was really quite small, clusters of streets that crept like vines from a small, deserted market square. Mateusz led them on a roundabout course, around sturdy synagogues and patched-up buildings, along the graveyard and under train tracks, down winding stone passages that ended abruptly, up grassy hills slippery with leaves. The village grew in complexity, doubling back on itself, transforming in sewer steam from what she'd known as a child into a funhouse of skinny cats and ghosts. They followed Mateusz, nobody speaking. Julka held tight to Wanda's hand, and sometimes their legs walked in step. Lights burned behind shaded windows. At one point a pianist could be heard playing scales. One drunk man, caught pissing in a trash can, was the only person they actually saw, and it was still early. She wondered who lived there and if it was by choice. Who'd *choose* to live in such ashes and ruins? Dick Chesnutt. He could have lived anywhere, but he'd picked this place. Weird. Watching her legs scissoring with Julka's, she recalled a dismal dream he'd once shared with her. In his dream, Kraków's black smog cover was filled with the restless spirits of Auschwitz. The ghosts hung over Kazimierz in one great vigilant mass—not in hell, not even purgatory, but watchful that history didn't repeat itself.

Matek stopped under a streetlamp, looking like he was getting his bearings. Think we're lost? he asked. He smiled and rubbed his hands together. He was beautiful in the slanting light. Girls should have faith in Wujo Płujo, he said.

Kuba laughed. Piotr sighed, scuffed his boot. Mateusz lit himself a cigarette.

Julka whispered into Wanda's ear: Have you ever smoked before? Hashish?

Julka nodded.

No. Have you?

No, said Julka. She was beautiful, too.

Are you going to try it?

Probably not. I mean, no. I'm not.

This struck Wanda as very funny and her laughter rang from the spooky buildings. Julka laughed, too, understanding her relief. Why had they come? Did they both have a crush on Wujo Płujo? Salty, sexy Wujo Płujo?

Piotr got jealous: Tell us your joke.

You wouldn't get it, Julka said.

Mateusz raised a finger: I've never heard a joke that could slip past Piotr, but if it does I'll scoop it up. Tell it.

Forget it, Wanda said. Let's go get you your drugs.

Right this way, he said, pointing.

She followed his bumpy finger up a dilapidated stairway. Stucco had fallen off the building, leaving ugly boards exposed. The first-floor windows were broken out. The second-floor windows were shuttered up. Her heart sunk. Dick Chesnutt lived there? It was unlivable.

Joke's over, Matek. Do you know where he lives or not?

No joke, Piotek. He lives in the back. You can't see it from the street.

If it'd been up to Wanda, they would have made a quiet approach, but Mateusz went up two stairs at a time, Kuba in tow. By the time she got there, they were pounding at the door. The windows were dark.

Shh! He might be sleeping!

Then we'll get him up, Kuba said. He continued to pound until Mateusz tapped his shoulder.

We should have called first, Wanda said.

He doesn't have a phone.

But it's Friday night. He's probably out. He might be at work.

Nyet, Mateusz said. He hasn't been to the Kasino in over two weeks. I've been tracking him.

Then where's he been?

Nobody knows.

Nobody cares, Piotr said.

Nobody but me, Mateusz said, turning the door handle and finding it open. He winked at Wanda and called inside: *Dobra nocy! Dobra nocy, Pan Chesnutt! Ty jest tutaj?* He called twice more, and when no answer came he stepped through the door. They listened a few moments, hearing a crash when he tripped over something. Then the light came on. Oh my God! he shouted. Come here, quick!

At first no one moved. Kuba went in first. Piotr followed.

This is stupid, Wanda said.

Julka took her hand and pulled her in. Inside, the place was devastated. Wanda squinted: one bare lightbulb back in the corner cast thick shadows about the room: a torn-apart couch, a slanting table with toppled chairs, books spilling from broken shelves. The boys stood about the room, darkly shaded, apparently hesitant to touch anything.

What stinks? Julka said. Wanda clutched her jacket to her face.

Something's rotten, Piotr said.

Something's dead, Mateusz said and began looking behind the dresser and under the bed, then threw back the curtain into the bathroom. Not in here, he announced.

It's in there, said Julka, indicating the darkened doorway to their left. I bet it's a kitchen.

Mateusz and Kuba stepped over and around the mess into the kitchen, flicked a switch that didn't work, and started banging things around. Wanda stayed with Julka by the door.

We found it! Oh man, we sure found it. Mateusz returned with a grimace on his face, a plastic garbage can held at arm's length. Kuba was behind him, holding his nose. He was in too big a hurry to finish his chicken! They took it outside, down the stairs. Wanda walked gingerly into the room. Piotr flipped through Dick Chesnutt's endless LPs. He blew one off and slapped it down on the turntable; it scratched and popped, rumbling like a train far off in the distance; then the innocent bells of Sunday Morning came tinkling through the dusty air. The Velvet Underground. What a relief. Theirs had been some of the first songs she'd learned. The music put her at ease, and she flopped herself down on the sofa by the lamp; but when the smell of musty burlap pushed up on her face she was sourly reminded that she was still intruding. It didn't help when Julka plopped down beside her.

There had been a time when this particular song recuperated Sunday mornings for her, changing the feel of them from a dressed-up, coifed-up hour in church to a free and milky walk in the woods, and listening to it now she missed her guitar teacher, his shaggy hair and sometime beard, the yellowed pads on his quick fingertips and his disgusting Dutch comic books.

While it embarrassed her to be sitting there, and scared her more than a bit, she wanted him to turn up stomping through the door and call her his crazy, amazing little fizgig. That would make her breaking in okay. Yet looking out the window, past chimneys into the orange nothing sky, she had a bad hunch that he wasn't coming back.

As that song fizzled out and let in the punching chords of the next, the boys showed up with two buckets of coal. Kuba lugged them to the kitchen. Mateusz and Piotr turned the place over, looking for drugs. Piotr ravaged a pink-painted dresser, dragging rivers of clothes from its drawers—widestriped turtlenecks, bright plaid flannels, a ratty brown fisherman knit she'd seen millions of times before. She picked it up while Piotr was digging through some pants.

She took off her jacket, pulled on the sweater. It was big and itchy and smelled like cigarettes. How do I look—in brown?

You look good, Julka said. Everyone looks good in brown.

Matek was acting the clowny detective, running his finger along the frame of an oil painting wherein, against a purple background, a nun brushed her teeth into a wavy mirror. He checked under the old Stalinist lamps, rolled back the yellow Ukrainian carpet, slid a Bauhaus commode from the wall—as if drugs would be hidden in those absurd places! She made a suggestion: Take a look in the W.C. He wrinkled his nose but slinked over to the water closet, uncorking a candle from a champagne bottle.

Look at that, Julka said, giggling, pointing to a short square dining table whose fourth leg had been replaced with an umbrella.

Look at those, Wanda said, pointing up at a curtain rod where the green drapes were held up by colored plastic clothespins.

But that's the worst. She pointed to a nest of cords and wires gnarling from the back of the television set into a rusted gray metal box. That's disgusting. This whole place is. I don't believe he's really American.

Americans aren't what you'd think they'd be.

Piotr squeezed in between them, all excited about a black leather book. Americans are perverts, he said. Take a look at this! A porno album! You may not want to look, Wanda. I think you know these people personally.

Open it, she said.

You sure?

Hurry up, Julka said.

You sure?

Damn it, Piotr, Wanda said, opening to a glossy Kodachrome, a woman bent and naked by a swimming pool. You could almost smell the shivery breeze: the sky was such a blue, the leaves and water rippled just so, the goose bumps on her thighs and ass were articulated

like tiny pebbles on a beach—even the curls of pubic hair were nice
and neat in the pale sunlight. Sexy photography, Wanda said, forget-
ting herself, even getting a little turned on. The next one was a shock.
In it, Dick Chesnutt was naked in a spa, holding his great, rigid cock
in his fist. Julka cleared her throat. Wanda's first impulse was to turn
the page, hurry it along, but she had to keep looking, amazed by the
honest bliss on his face (eyes closed, chin up) and shocked by his in-
humanly huge erection. Even the time she'd kissed him, he had acted
aloof, like a teacher. She couldn't have imagined him showing such
pleasure—and she couldn't have imagined it looking like this! She was
likewise stunned that he could look so vulnerable.

Mr. Chesnutt likes his penis, Piotr said.

He flipped the page too soon and there she was again, the nude
lady, wearing goggles, emerging from the water up into the camera.
From this angle her pert little breasts were beautiful, and so was her
smile—but toothy, uncanny, making Wanda hotly jealous. Who was
she? How could one smile seem so creepy? But then on the next page
there was no mistaking her: with Wanda's luck, it could only have been
Jane! Fucking Jane, naked Jane, prancing along the edge of the pool
as if she were walking a balance beam. Ignoring Piotr's hands and
Julka's pleas to slow down, Wanda whipped through shiny pictures:
Jane backstroking, Jane backflipping, Chesnutt pushing her backward
with a splash, then pulling her out to do it again. Unimpressed, she
skipped ahead, two at a time, past blurs of blue, skids of skin, until she
reached the inevitable climax: Jane from above, dragons of hair dripping down her shoulders, water streaming, her hard dark nipples,
a flush of red across her chest, her mouth, her nostrils, her green
eyes wide as she came in the face of Chesnutt's camera. Though
you couldn't see it, you knew he was inside her, filling her up with his
monster erection. Jane was coming. Wanda knew it. Totally disgusting. She closed the book.

The next song was the weird one about leather and sadism, darkening the weirdness already in the room. Piotr and Julka reopened the
album on her lap and inspected the pictures she had skipped over.

Wanda? Matek called out, appearing in the bathroom door with his candle. His face was adorable in the moving shadows. Could you come in here with me?

With you? In the bathroom? she said, flirting. Can I trust you?

Don't *trust* me, he said, showing the sexy gap in his smile. Just come here.

She went to him. Julka's jealousy hit her back like sunlight. Matek shut the door behind her, told her to have a seat on the toilet. The lid was hard, the room small. She tucked her feet back under the stool. Carved by candlelight, his face was boyishly smooth and ruddy, but as he eased himself closer to her, she could see manly lines about to smile. He squatted. She thought he might kiss her. She leaned back against the tile.

What did you want?

Are you ready for anything? he said, echoed.

No. Nothing.

You'll need to be.

What? You're crazy. And I don't feel like smoking hash.

Don't worry. He laughed. This is so much freakier than that. He sat on the floor and crossed his legs. Where do you think Chesnutt's gone to?

Traveling.

Be serious. He's gone. The place is destroyed. Something awful happened and he's gone now.

Let's say you're right. He's gone. Fine. So what?

Hold this, he said, giving her the candle. He rustled through his pockets. She expected him to show her his loot, and now even this made her nervous. Nervous because it was November. Nervous because it was after dark. I found something behind the toilet here, he said. Maybe you could tell me what you think of it.

Okay, she said, dribbling wax down the front of the sweater.

Here, give me the candle. He paused. Now you take this.

It was small, weighty, made of leather. Familiar. He shone the light on it, she flopped it open, and there was Gurney's grinning face. She flopped it closed and handed it back. He held it for a moment, his eyes puzzled, very young, then he put it on her lap. As if it were a tarantula scampering up her leg, she slapped it away. Keep it off me!

Shh. Shh. What does it mean?

Nothing. I don't know. What could it?

Were they friends?

My throat hurts.

Are you sick? Think. Think. Were they friends?

I don't know. *Who* friends.

Think.

At the Kasino?

That's it. Use your imagination.

Two Americans?

That's right. Follow that thought.

She closed her eyes and looked for the Kasino, even though she'd never seen it. Red carpet, chandeliers, Gurney in a tuxedo at the roulette wheel. Here comes Dick Chesnutt—black tie, no, itchy brown sweater. They shake hands. They speak English. They spin the wheel. The wallet shows in Gurney's back pocket, slobbering like an idiot's tongue. Jane appears, throws some dice. Jane strips. Jane comes. Dick laughs. Gurney laughs. Dick leans over and lifts the wallet.

No, she said. That's wrong. It's a lie.

You didn't say anything.

Shut up, Mateusz!

What? You didn't.

I'm sorry. Just shut up. Nothing.

Think, he said. How did it get here?

In her mind there was purple. And then there was Igor playing the fiddle. Then and there Gurney's pocket was picked, and that was the last he'd seen of his wallet. She knew this. She, not Chesnutt, had seen it last. That was when her mind went purple. Beyond the door, the music shrieked. Piotr and Julka laughed out loud, looked at dirty pictures together. The coal burned. Where was Kuba? Was he alone? Where was Gurney? The dark smelled like urine. *The wallet was smashed, dead on the tiles. It was right there on the tiles, dead and real.* But as the candle danced in their battling breath, shifting the features of Matek's face, making him stranger but not at all scary, the fact that he could have been anyone at all reminded her she was a long way from home. So she blew out the candle and smelled the smoke. She crouched down close enough to feel his warmth. Mateusz? I'm taking this with me. Listen. You never saw it, okay? She shuddered as she said this. Mateusz? She touched the nappy wool of his coat. She loosened his scarf and brushed her fingers over his sweaty neck. Matek? His breath whistled. Matek? He smelled nice and soapy. His hair was long and oily to the touch. His cheek was cold, his chin was whiskered, and his lips, at first, were startled by her kiss. Matek? Matek? But then, after a long and empty pause, his velvety lips startled hers in the dark, and then went their tongues, and then in the middle of the purple everywhere she found the place between his teeth where another tooth had been before.

THE BUBBLING KETTLE of mushroom bisque had breezed to the farthest rooms of the flat, and for some time the bread had been cool enough to slice. Jane and Gurney were probably ready for their dinner, but still she sat by her studio window, two fingers securing the wineglass on her armrest while she watched the light fade pinkly on the roofs. Wave after wave had rolled over the room: the orange wash of anger at Wanda's neglect, the violet terror that there'd been some accident, and now in the shadows of gray, blue, and black, she was a little bit drunk, despairing that her family, despite her efforts to fasten them down, had been lifted up by an inevitable gale and thrown to opposite corners of the night. Wanda this way, Zbigniew that way. And even if the door were to open right then, no matter, no matter, for Grazyna would still be holding the rope, its ends all hopelessly frayed and broken.

But the door didn't open, and didn't open. Instead of weeping she went out to the stove and ladeled bisque into three bowls. Blue bowls. Gurney appeared in his tuxedo, and Jane was there a moment later, sitting down and pouring herself a big glass of wine. No, that's fine,

Grazyna thought, sawing thick slices away from the loaf. No, that's fine. She pulled out her chair but then looked at her soup, where brown rubber lobes of mushroom poked from the gray cream swirl.

Joining us? Jane said.

I'm not hungry.

You need to eat.

She sat, but gradually, irritated that they hadn't mentioned Wanda. Gurney dragged a crust through the soup. Jane spooned away from herself, politely blowing with her brown-painted lips. Grazyna was actually rather hungry, and the soup appealed to her inebriated nose, but she was fearing she'd prepared it wrong, that somewhere between the sauté and the dollops of *śmietanka* she had—but what could she have done wrong? Had she left something out? The Americans seemed to enjoy it well enough. The Americans.

Jane said in her hushed and gossipy Polish: You have to hear this. I know you'll appreciate it. Gurney kept eating, looked at no one.

I'm worried about the soup.

Please, it's perfect.

You might not want to eat it.

You're being silly. I'm going to have seconds. Jane glanced at Gurney, who was contentedly eating, then continued: Last night I treated this boy from the cornfields to a limited engagement with the Tyrolean Quartet. She paused.

Ordinarily Grazyna might have been intrigued, even jealous, since for weeks all of Kraków had anticipated this event, yet now she only cared about the skin on her soup. She dabbed it with her spoon and absently responded: You mean at the Café Manggha.

You'd have known half the crowd, I'm sure. But good thing you weren't there. Here we were in this tiny theater, the two Westies seated up front, my cousin all handsome in his new car coat, me all vamped up like some kind of whore, all the Austrians getting a good look at how my cousin's roots are shining through.

Grazyna broke the soup's surface with her spoon.

I realize not everyone's equipped for contemporary music. But a certain decorum can be expected, right?

Dobrze.

You're an artist, you get it. But he didn't. He was all right for a while, but I got nervous when the music went silent for two minutes, during which time his hands started shaking and his knees kept clapping like he had to go pee. *Then,* to make the situation even *more* difficult, the clarinetist got up, took off the mouthpiece, and slipped it in his jacket pocket. Then the *viola* stood up, picked up a drum, turned it over, and held it out in the direction of the clarinetist. The other two musicians didn't budge. Finally, in a charming act of reciprocation, the clarinetist put his mouth to the *bell* of his instrument, pointed it into the hollow of the drum, and started to blow, softly at first, releasing at most a pleasant little squeak, but then puffing out his cheeks and filling up the theater with squawks of regret and quacks of shame and great big belching bellows of sorrow that had everyone deeply moved, I assure you. You should understand that it was all very authentic, very raw, and everyone looked on, perfectly composed—everyone, I'm afraid, but my hayseed cousin, who let off a titter, then a snicker, and then a longer and restrained sort of snort, and then even though I clawed my fingernails into his thigh, gave way with a stupid *guffaw* that echoed all around the room.

Grazyna hadn't even tasted her bisque, but she had finished her wine and poured another glass. Jane's story annoyed her. Maybe, she said, her voice a bit snotty, maybe laughter was the most appropriate response.

I have a fine sense of humor, Jane assured her.

Gurney got up for another bowl.

Oh, so maybe you do! Grazyna said firmly, fixing her gaze on Jane's righteous puss: her thick, dark, smirked-up lips, her quiet lines arched and plucked, her washed green automotive eyes—usually narrow, now almost lazy with watery self-confidence. When Grazyna spoke, it was more to this face than to the person behind it: But you force me to be candid. If you yourself had an ounce of etiquette you would have asked the whereabouts of Wanda. Did you even notice? Well, she's gone.

I'm sorry, said Jane, insincere as always.

Gurney seemed to notice that something was wrong.

Don't bother apologizing, and the same for your cousin, though I pity him almost as much as myself, the way you trample all over him, tapping little dents into his face and forehead, torturing him until even *he* thinks he's giggling. (Grazyna pushed back from the table, surprised and pleased by her own metaphor.) I don't think it's the least bit amusing, if that's really what you're trying to be. And don't think I don't know how you're trampling all over me, packing down the dirt over the grave of my marriage. That's clear enough, it always has been. I'm not stupid, I just want you to know that. You're just like him, you know that? You should know by now that he has no sense of family—just like you, so unconscionably mistreating your cousin!

Jane's face had fallen, she looked incredulous, and for an instant Grazyna felt she might have been mistaken—but then at the thought of Jane's little wink, how every word she said was in quotation marks, she had to laugh.

Maybe that's why I like you. You're just like him. And Wanda's turned out just like him, too. She could give a damn about family, our family, *any* family. Me neither! Why bother? Look at my family: you and your overgrown cousin—and yes, I agree, his roots *do* need fixing! I may like the two of you well enough, but that doesn't mean I care about you. I don't. You *do* pay rent, I grant you that. Wanda's even worse. She just takes, and her father keeps taking, and I keep giving, I keep giving like, well, like a long white hose of blubber, like a termite queen blubbering down there in her miserable termite hole!

Gurney looked on with curiosity and sympathy. Jane looked suspiciously at the neglected soup, now puckered on the surface, and politely pushed it away as if finished.

Twelve

IT WAS THANKSGIVING NIGHT. Gurney was at work, having a little trouble concentrating. Jackie was going to show up at any time, paying her first-ever visit to the Kasino. Later they'd be having roast turkey at her place.

He was starting to like it here, working at the Kasino. Since Dick Chesnutt's unaccountable disappearance, he had a roulette wheel all to himself and a little bit more job responsibility. It wasn't a skilled job. It didn't require years of professional school, and it certainly didn't take a genius; yet to do it right, he found, he had to affect the sober concentration his father used to show behind the counter at the drugstore. When Gurney put on his somber tuxedo, he kind of felt like a druggist of chance, as if he was leading people to the threshold of risk in that gleaming eighteenth-century ballroom. His instruments had the glittery precision of a chemist's. His posture was straight as a Popsicle stick. And when he spun the wheel—rolling the ball against that spin, sending it along its shiny silver path—he had to exhibit the utmost confidence.

But then, after he had released the ball and set it flying, once its momentum started failing against the oncoming chrome, something almost mystical happened. He became less the druggist than some kind of priest. For when it slackened in its trajectory and jumped up—*ping, pop, crack*—from the dish, he could only stand back and let it all happen, remove himself and sacrifice his gamblers to chance. Some gamblers even bowed as they walked up to his table, deferent as churchgoers hobbling up to communion, as if they had prepared themselves, through weeks of penance, to lose their fortune in one fell swoop. He even had a croupier of his own, an altar boy who scurried around doing all the real work while Gurney stood waiting to perform his trick. His name was Tomasz.

Since his promotion, all the croupiers were Polish, all the dealers were from either German- or English-speaking countries, and that was the way it was going to stay. It wasn't a terribly convivial workplace. The tables were well spaced out across the large floor—blackjack, craps, Gurney's roulette—and for some reason, all of the dealers kept jealously to themselves. The only women employed by the Kasino were either cocktail waitresses or prostitutes and thus were kept moving between the tables.

You look in pain, sir, Tomasz said that night.

The table was free, and the night was young. He wouldn't have said that he was in pain. But Tomasz's eager way of leaning forward made Gurney a little resentful. As if Gurney could help him advance to dealer! Both of them knew that would never happen.

Nobody wins at my table, Gurney said.

Sir?

I mean, they win small, enough to keep them playing, but nobody ever looks satisfied, and nobody ever walks away rich.

Is that your concern, sir?

Stop that. Call me Gurney.

Gurney.

I want to see someone clean out the bank. As he said this, a chalky-faced businessman (not successful, by the looks of him) approached the table with a short stack of chips. Gurney smiled, welcoming him from a distance. Bozena, in her orange-red evening gown, hungrily floated a few steps behind him.

That has never happened here, Tomasz laughed. At this Kasino, you win small. Not big. It is known.

Well, it isn't rigged.

Sir?

Fixed. It isn't fixed that way.

Of course it is not! I know that, we know that. Of course it is not, as you say, rigged.

So the next person to approach this table, even this clown, could quite conceivably clean out the bank.

I tell you it won't happen.

The businessman's confidence, how he slapped all his blue chips on square seventeen, made Gurney feel confident, too. Like a Virgin's predatory bass-line pumped from the ceiling loudspeakers. The man's silver wedding band, his thin gray suit, his tie too narrow for 1990—he had the distinguishing marks of a luckless man, but Gurney had a hunch that this was his night, and he felt a little sting as he set the wheel going, and he felt a little charge as he sent the ball whipping. He tapped his teeth as it scuttled in the dish. Eight black. Tomasz swept the chips. Bozena politely drifted away from the table. Glancing at her, the businessman made a hurt remark in Polish, to which Tomasz tried make some sort of repair. He stacked the rest of the chips on seventeen. Spinning this way, rolling that way, the roulette wheel repeated its mistake: eight black. Tomasz swept the chips. The man walked off, suspiciously looking back a couple of times—not at the wheel, naturally, but at Gurney.

See?

What? Tomasz said.

It's useless.

Yes, but it isn't rigged, Tomasz added, almost defensively.

And so it went for the next hour or so: three jovial Norwegian university students; an industrialist from Wrocław, bowing and scraping to his Korean associate (as well as to Gurney); the regular and compulsive Kasino Krakovians who habitually returned their paychecks to the company; and two *Let's Go! Eastern Europe* girls—a big redhead from Woodstock, New York, and a little brunette from South Orange, New Jersey. The two of them spoke with grating accents and bickered over the numbers they should pick. He was rather put off by their brazen Americana, but he wished them Happy Thanksgiving all the same. The big one gave him a piece of her mind: it was a holiday with a history of gluttony and theft and they were certainly glad to be missing it.

He liked the glitz and glam of the Kasino, but the fact of the place was rather sad. The regulars would arrive shortly after sunset, faces aglow with the hope of debutantes, even if he'd seen them lose a dozen times before. But every night they left looking cracked in half. There were two kinds of regulars: optimists and pessimists. The former drank fast and shot their whole wads, leaving in a rush in the middle of the evening, racing out to roll their mothers-in-law for change. He had to admire their reckless passion. But he couldn't stand the sight of the pessimists, the ones that fretted the night away, returning to his table with smaller and smaller bids, leaking away money with a drip drip drip until, at closing time, exhausted but unflappable, they had to be ushered out through the grand marble exit. Why did these chronic worriers even come to the Kasino? He supposed they returned in spite of themselves, believing they were maintaining a careful sense of balance as they followed their gradual descent into hell.

He understood the appeal of the Kasino—but he understood it objectively, as a dealer would. He himself didn't care much for money, though he could see the appeal of a world at risk, a pointless world of dangerous fun that teetered on the edge between depravity and joy, and he admired the ones who played so hard that they inevitably plummeted into the abyss. But the chronic worriers horrified him. That was no way to go through life.

That night the gamblers played their chips across the board, but time after time, with very few exceptions, the bead kept landing on eight black. Was it the exceptions that discouraged them? Some watched it happen three times consecutively and still resisted bidding on it—as if it could never happen for them! Most of them simply tired of the table. And why was seventeen so popular that night? It was obviously the wrong number. He was thinking of reporting his wheel to the management, even at the risk of suggesting it was rigged, but this thought was pleasantly interrupted when he turned in response to a tap on his shoulder.

Jackie had dressed up for a night at the Kasino. Her lips were lipsticked, her eyes were outlined, her breath-minted mouth chirruped in his nostrils. He pulled back an arm's length and took her all in. She must have arrived wearing a long, heavy coat because she definitely wasn't dressed for late November: her naked shoulders and arms were showcased in the pale Kasino light; her breasts pushed from the bodice of a tiny, tasteful cocktail dress; and her embroidered black stockings were tugged halfway up her thighs, revealing several inches of goosebumped skin beneath the inebriating breeze of fabric.

Pardon me? he said.

Your tuxedo!

Your dress!

Guess what? she said, cupping his ear.

What?

This. She directed his eyes into the leather, waist-level purse that could hardly accommodate all its red and blue chips. Fifty bucks, she said. And I'm spending it all at your roulette wheel!

He laughed. He was really glad to see her, could hardly wait to kiss her. He proudly introduced her to Tomasz, who brushed his lips over the back of her hand. She'd never played roulette before, so Gurney carefully reviewed the principles, as if it were something complicated like chess. She leaned far over the red velvet table, perusing its grid of ornate numbers, showing that much more of her breast. Very pretty, she said.

They say it's priceless. Its from an eighteenth-century casino in Budapest.

Well! she said, handling her chips with that edgy excitement shared by many first-time gamblers. It amused him to think that she fell into this category. Any suggestions? she murmured.

He glanced at Tomasz, who was preoccupied with his croupier stick and then, without thinking, and in a gesture that he would later interpret as perfectly harmless coquetry, he inconspicuously raised eight fingers and mouthed the word *black*.

Okay! she said, too loudly, and slapped down ten dollars in chips, all on number eight.

Is that the only number you want? he said, straining not to look at Tomasz.

Yes. No. Well, sure, I'll move three dollars to, um, seventeen. Now come on, dealer, let's play!

Sure as ever, he did his trick, but this time he didn't watch the wheel—he watched Jackie, drumming her fingers and biting her lip. He dragged the humming wheel to a stop and watched her face go shocked with glee.

You're a genius! she said, clapping her hands.

Gurney blushed. Of course he was glad for her, but she didn't have to be so demonstrative.

Tomasz calculated the winnings, and in the middle of counting, shot out a contemptuous blink at Gurney. It was evident that Tomasz knew and disapproved, although he smiled generously at Jackie as he dealt out her chips, now increased thirty-five-fold. She put aside her initial ten dollars and without hesitating stacked the rest on eight.

Eight black, she said. Gurney's lucky number.

Sure you want all of it on that number? The chances of you hitting it twice—you know, you're smart, the chances are negligible. Tomasz smirked at this attempt to save face.

Eight, she said defiantly. Black. Spin the wheel.

This time he watched the wheel, not her face, and he, too, had to smile when again it monstrously landed on eight black. Jackie screamed and spun on her tiptoes. Tomasz muttered his calculations at the ceiling. Gurney, keeping outwardly calm, softly laughed, gripping the sides of the roulette wheel as if it were the helm of a rattletrap ship. People rubbernecked from all parts of the room. Excitement like this was rare in the Kasino.

Again! she announced, resolutely pushing all her chips on eight, spilling them over onto the surrounding numbers. All of these, she said, are put on eight, on Gurney's lucky number!

Jackie, he pleaded, save some back, spread it around. That's a lot of money you're playing with.

She looked at him soberly.

Sir, Tomasz said censoriously, I must tell you that it is, how you say, *without ethics* for a dealer to advise a client in any way that, er, changes her bidding. Because if for some reason she wants to continue bidding on number eight, you must allow that, or invite another dealer to take your position. That is, if you feel your emotions are involved.

That won't be necessary, Gurney said, angrily.

Two waitresses had appeared at Jackie's side, balancing four trays of expensive drinks. She declined and ordered a Châteauneuf-du-Pape, saying she'd always wanted to try it. Bozena returned to his table, bringing a horde of curious gamblers. The music—no longer Madonna but swing-era jazz—was pumped up louder, the lights glaring brighter, none of it seeming to faze Jackie Witherspoon, who meditated on her stacks of high-stakes chips. Gurney could feel the management closing in.

Maybe you're right, she said.

Please, Jackie, don't take my advice. It is *without ethics.*

Okay, she said, sizing up her chips. (Everyone but Gurney looked on jealously.) Okay, I'll set aside a thousand, butter-and-eggs money, and leave the rest on number eight. Now would you spin the wheel, please, sweetheart?

Now, while rueful Tomasz counted out chips, others began putting markers on the board, among other numbers on seventeen red, but none of them dared join Jackie's eight black, on which spot she was bidding a startling sum of money. Gurney perspired. He even wished against Jackie's mounting fortune that the ball would go fickle and land on seventeen. He searched his mouth for saliva, watching the swift approach of Herr Messersturm, the Kasino's local manager, whose broad blocky face forced an overlarge grin. Gurney paused, didn't spin.

Naja, I t'zee, he boomed, inserting himself between Gurney and Jackie. Vee haf a lucky new klient at ze Kasino Kraków. Ziss iz *wunderbar, ja? Naja,* protzeed, shpin ze veel! Shpin ze veel!

And so he did, this time with extra force, rolling the ball with ex-

tra verve, prolonging the moment when the refractory little bead
found its way to its inevitable slot. Eight black. Cheers and groans.
Even Herr Messersturm had joined the fun, clapping his square,
fleshy hands. He turned his back to Jackie, so as to have a private word
with the dealer: Vot, I zay, *vot* iz hop'ning hier?

A stroke of luck, Gurney said, as if it were Jackie and not himself
he was defending.

A shtroke? I tink vee are looking at hundreds off tausends off
dollars!

But it's a casino.

The man's red face was a visible roar.

Things like this happen, right?

No more bets. Klose ziss table—at once! Zen you come to meine
office! He walked away smiling meatily at Jackie, clasping his hands in
a congratulatory way. She wasn't surprised when Gurney closed the
table; she rather looked relieved. What alarmed her, it seemed, was
his jumpy behavior and that Gurney had been summoned to Herr
Messersturm's office. She asked if she could help, if maybe she could
go with him and speak on his behalf—these kind offers went straight
to his gut, as did her confidence that he had done nothing wrong.
Hundreds of thousands of dollars. Hundreds of thousands! Could this
be true? It had all been up to luck, she assured him, toasting a glass of
rare wine to fortune.

Luck! he said, throwing up his arms.

They arranged to meet at Jackie's place for their late-night Thanksgiving turkey dinner. But Tomasz was less cheerful, agreeing to help
Jackie cash in her chips, nodding loyally to Gurney as if to a captain
who has one last request before walking the plank.

HERR MESSERSTURM'S OFFICE WAS SMALL AND CLUTTERED
but richly appointed, the walls tall and primary blue, decorated with
framed international currency. The wide gleaming desktop would
have commanded a larger room, but in here it looked cramped and
rather embarrassed. Behind it sat Herr Messersturm, who, upon Gur-

ney's entrance, puffed himself up like a defensive thrush but then relaxed and reclined, a youthful glow behind his mantle of cigar smoke. He no longer looked the despot of moments before. Gurney was ready to raise his hand and concede to him, no apologies necessary.

But he didn't apologize. Nor did he offer Gurney a seat. He nestled the cigar into its ashtray and let the disgust return to his face. I haf shpoken mit ze kasa, he said.

Pardon me?

Ze Kasa! Ze Kasa! *La caisse. Rozumiem? Verstehen Sie?*

The cashier? Gurney asked, touching the back of an armchair for balance.

Ja, on ze telephone, no? No? You know how much Geld ist gone? Gold? Gone?

Geld. Money. Dollars. From your roulette!

No.

No? You don't? You should.

I don't. How much?

I vill not tell you. I vill not, but ze zituation, ze zituation, it iss katastrophal! He was leaning forward on the desk now, frustrated with his English, pulling hard on his cigar to keep it lit. Much money. Und I am not satisfied vy much, *naja,* vy many dollars haf been lost. Are you?

No, I'm dumbfounded. How much was lost? he brazenly asked again, trying to recall the stakes of Jackie's last spin.

Vy do you care?

I'm dumbfounded.

Vot iss zat verd you say now tvice?

Dumbfounded? Shocked. Stunned. Er, um, *erstaunen? Erstaunlich?* No, surprised.

Surprised? *Das ist alles?* You zink ziss Kasino ist das Bundesbank? Surprised? Doch! Tell me vot hoppent. Shpeak zlowly.

Gurney straightened his jacket, clasped his hands behind his back. I was simply doing my job. A customer came to my table—

Vy, er, who iss ziss customer?

A customer. A gambler.

Do you know her?

What? he said but then had pause at the recollection of Tomasz kissing her hand. Yes.

Yes! Ja! Herr Messersturm shouted, puffing hungrily on his moist cigar. Zo interressant! I am dumbfounded! Tell us about her, she iss very pretty, ja?

I suppose. Well she isn't much of a gambler, but she had a lucky streak.

Lucky shtreak. Lucky shtreak. I know dieses verds. Ferry klever. *Natürlich,* luck *ist falsch.* Good luck *ist falsch.* How do you know her?

She's American. I know lots of Americans. Nothing strange about that.

Tell us vot hoppent. Shpeak zlowly, tell us eferyting zat hoppent.

This was when Gurney grew seriously nervous, afraid of anything he might utter accidentally, or even on purpose. He had to acknowledge his actions' repercussions, far flung from his wheel like bats from a cave, draining the coffers, spooking the night, making Jackie devilishly happy, making him wonder again about this mysterious Austrian, the shadowy man who'd made Gurney his tuxedo, made it fit too tight. Could Gurney actually die from this? This seemed a real option, as did prison, as did torture, all of the means at Herr Messersturm's disposal, terrible options that streaked and flushed and streamed like smoke from his fat Deutsch-sprech'n face.

Tell us eferyting zat hoppent. Eferyting.

But then what he told, in the muddiest English he could muster, only partially reflected what had really happened: To be honest Mr. Messersturm I've never been superstitious in any real way, no rabbit's foot, no salt toss, no Irish Catholic hocus-pocus that has everything to do with the potato famine and fairy rings and nothing, really, to do with me . . .

Zlowly, zlowly—*langsamer, bitte! Langsamer!*

But this only encouraged him to pick up the pace, to natter in a frantic, roundabout way that not even he could follow very well but that bought him time all the same, bought confusion, sketched an impossible portrait of Jackie who connected with the wheel like some do with dogs, how she made the animal whimper and purr, heal and shake, give up the bone. The content of what he said was unimportant. All of it was lost in that hazy little room, on that angry little man. What mattered was the mad divinity in Gurney, the knowledge that *he* was the madman at the knobs, spinning eight black, spinning out yarn, flinging words into the smoky air, flinging money, flapping and swooping on klutzy leather. As long as he flapped, blame was suspended, slung in the radical swing of chance, and so he flapped, gesticulated, talked.

Halt!

. . . regardless, I guess, that the wheel goes clockwise, the ball counterclockwise, and the two must meet absolutely at random . . .

Halt! Halt! Halt! Herr Messersturm stood, planted his knuckles on the inflexible desk. Shtop! I zee you are ferry ekcited, und zere ist no point to ziss diskussion. Zo, halt. Ve vill haf a big investigation, you know, und zer vill be many, many kvestions. First, ve take your veel in pieces. Ve must inspekt its machine.

Absurd. Gurney smirked.

Ja. Absurd. Ve vill zee. Now go. Go home. Do not return to verk until ve telephone for you!

GURNEY CROSSED THE OLD TOWN ON FOOT, filling his coat with wind and leaves, filling his face with spicy city smoke. Too hungry to wait for the turkey, he picked up a quick *zapiekanki* along the way. It was still early and the vendors in the arcades were still cheery, liberally dusting his tort with paprika. He wasn't thinking directly of Jackie's money, but all at once the streets were prosperous and the pigeons well-fed, and fleshy faces, cinched at the neck, dribbled with pepper sauce and grinned and chortled with a deep-down giddiness that mocked the gravity of Herr Messersturm. Dismantle the wheel! Capture that crooked culprit chance! Good luck! It was as if pipes had burst beneath the streets and released streams of laughing gas into the air.

Gurney enjoyed the greasy yellow crust as he ambled past a busy kiosk, coasting his eyes across pornographic magazines. His clothes fit uncomfortably, his appetite was edgy, and yet Jackie's money, for all its immensity, was like the strawberry chutney she might add to the turkey, the carmelized onions over new potatoes, the hint of leg beneath her dress. Jackie's new money embellished her fecundity, adding to the cravings and delights that he hoped to sacrifice on her little round table. She'd taken it upon herself to find him a turkey, roast it and baste it, dress herself up in a tiny maroon dress. Tonight, at last, he feared they'd do it.

The holiday meal, he said aloud. The brave American holiday bird! Ironically, the first Thanksgiving he might actually enjoy was to be spent in exile, in a miniature turret above the honks and squeals of Stradom. He was entering the unspared section of town. Buildings were speckled with liver spots and scars, crumbling about the lintels with syphilis and neglect. He was entering the thankless side of town, while across the globe, he thought, on the backroads of Iowa, pickup trucks were mounting snowy hills, portaging twelve-packs to grandmother's house. Back home it was the middle of the afternoon and American families were sitting down to eat—his father was uncorking a bottle of white wine; his mother, with potholders, rushed a casserole to the table. (Would anyone speak his name? Would they remember him in their prayers?) And at Sheila's parents' house in sleepy Marshalltown, beside a table surrounded by hatchet-faced Iowans, a well-fed baby didn't know any better, couldn't have fathomed what mad world she'd been born into, couldn't have fathomed that her *zapiekanki*-eating father had perhaps once again changed the shape of her life.

Blessed art thou among women, he repeated as he walked, drumming his fingers on the leather book in his pocket. And blessed is the fruit of thy womb.

From two blocks off, through the bare branches and tram lines, he could make out the honeyed safety of the turret. Ducking between two buildings to piss, he pointed his stream between a downspout and trashcan, onto a heap of dark rotten refuse that might have been leaves or rags or excrement. He thought as he pissed that it might have been a corpse, or someone dead drunk, or maybe someone innocently sleeping with nothing to be thankful for but sleep itself—until along comes Gurney to pollute even that; but he had to smile at his own superstition when he respectfully directed his stream to the wall.

Here I am, he said, zipping up.

Inside the building, halfway up the turning stairs, he jumped back quick. Linda was there, sitting in the dark in the middle of the steps.

Dinner smells good, she said bitterly.

He panted, gripped the railing. Can't smell, nose is cold.

I wasn't invited.

Oh.

Were you invited?

I guess so.

You have a lot to be thankful for.

He sighed, annoyed. So I do.

Jane won't like this.

Jane's up there?

No. I just came by to warn you.

What?

That's all.

Warn me what?

The door opened at the top of the stairs. Gurney? Jackie called.

Warn me what? he said more discreetly, but Linda slipped past him, padded down the steps and out the door, sending a draft back up the stairwell.

Who's there? Jackie called.

Just me, he said, leaving it at that.

It was warm in her place, rife with the smell of holiday bird. Everything shimmered, lit by countless guttering tapers—all colors, sizes, and proportions, short ones dotting the bookcases like plums, tall ones coiling behind the sofa, ellipsoid jade ones inching along the baseboards. A smattering of purple and blue and crimson clustered like a bonfire at the center of the table, flames tickling the wine bottles, challenging dry flowers. She stepped from behind the door, into the shaking light.

Candles, he said.

I blew my whole fortune on wax!

He bent a little, touched his stomach. Please let's not talk about the money, he said, aware that it was stashed somewhere in the turret.

Did you get in trouble?

Not really. I'm just dumbfounded. *Erstaunen.*

Me, too. But enough. Plus it's rude to talk about money. She unbuttoned his car coat, dropped it to his feet, and did the same to his tuxedo jacket. Relax now. She stepped up onto a chair and kissed him—warm mouth, dry wine, waxy lipstick. His hands fell on her silky stockings, just above and behind the knees. Now . . . no bow tie, no studs, no patent-leather shoes. (Kiss.) Take off your watch, take off your belt, undo this springy thing on your trousers. (She gave up on this after much fumbling.) And isn't it more polite to talk about luck? Money's dirty, but luck's freaky. He could tell she was a little drunk.

He accepted a sloshy glass of wine.

This is the best Chardonnay between here and the Kasino. I would have searched the whole Eastern bloc, but I'm rich on such short notice!

Happy Thanksgiving.

One hour left.

It's filthy out there tonight, he said.

She went to the kitchen. She came back and her eyes looked a little droopy, her mouth a little messy. She bumped into the table and flopped down next to him. Hi. So. Are you religious?

Never touch the stuff.

Me neither.

Are you hungry?

Sure.

She kissed him midlaugh and told him to get the wine. The place was so small—or he was so big—that he snatched the bottle off the table from where he sat. Her skirt flipped up in maneuvering on the sofa, but he politely looked away.

What's the turkey stuffed with? Mealworms?

No!

Snails?

No, just stuffing. Please. But that's why I asked you about religion.

Huh?

There's something I want to show you. But you can't call me crazy. Hand me that, she said, pointing to a slim leather volume on top of the shelf. Be gentle. He reached it easily, put it in her hands. This is my prized possession, she boasted. It's an emblem book from the Italian Renaissance.

God, is it original?

I found it in Sofia.

That's Bulgaria.

You know emblem books?

I have a bachelor's degree in English literature.

As if accepting this as a qualification, she put the flaky book in his hands. He delicately opened it and turned its soft pages, naturally lost by its Latin script but enchanted by its stark, hand-painted woodcuts.

It's called *A Covenant of Earthworms*. Most experts I've shown it to guess that it's an Old Testament parody, in which case it would be fun but pretty unremarkable. But I've got more and more reason to think it's esoteric apocrypha. This is what I do at the Collegium Maius every day. I follow its trail. They have excellent Mediterranean collections there. I've traced the hand-made paper and this oddball binding to these sixteenth-century artisans in Florence.

Hard work, he said, his mind now vaguely returning to the turkey.

The watermark's the telltale clue. See? She held a page so close to a candle that its ink and fibers throbbed with light. See the watermark? See that? Fifteen-oh-seven. See the wreath of segmented worms? I can't find it anywhere in the papermaker's register. It might be a secret guild—or, as I surmise, no guild at all. See this stitching? It's really worn down, but see how the leather looks like twisted-up nightcrawlers? Very special. She became a charmingly drunker version of certain professors he'd had in college, saying: I'd argue that, just as the church kept its wine holy by having it made in its own monastic vineyards, this earthworm sect kept its secrets, um, muddy, by enlisting its own members as earthworm bookmakers! And with the help of this biochemistry student I know I've discovered that even the ink has an organic constitution. Probably worms. More wine, she said. Please. He topped her off.

So what's it about?

The story! Of course! She reopened the book between both of their laps. It felt like storytime at the Maquoketa public library. It's a postdiluvian episode, she said, so it assumes the flood and the ark and all that, and it begins on the forty-first day, when, as you can see from this funny picture, the ark has plopped itself down on a hill. In this next emblem, Noah's all beaten up from his voyage. I think that's animal dung all over his legs. Delirious and drunk, he sees a rainbow in the sky, and according to this verse—I'm paraphrasing, it's really all open to interpretation. Actually, I think this book's all about interpretation, especially since it's an emblem book and being an English scholar, of course, you know that emblem books are just little hermeneutic puzzles.

Back to the story. Maybe the rainbow really *was* there, and because Noah was all slackjawed and woozy and gullible, stomping up the shore with shit on his boots—now I'm paraphrasing *and* interpreting— he saw this pretty rainbow and decided everything would be okay. He comforted his family by calling it a Covenant. He assured them they wouldn't get seasick anymore. But according to the book he was putting them on.

You tell this very well. He passed his hand through her short, shiny hair.

So far this part's straight from the Bible. Even this next plate, where Noah's so drunk he's passed out naked in his tent. See his little penis? Now here's where Ham comes in, ogling his father's voluptuous rolls—I like how his hair curls up, almost like a cap and bells. A real Ham. But then the joke's over. Enter Shem and Japheth, the two party-pooping, dad-fearing sons walking in backward to cover Noah with a blanket. The shame! At last, as we see, Noah wakes up with a roaring headache and curses poor Ham and all his offspring for feasting his eyes on the patriarchal loins.

What fun!

It gets better. The rest is apocryphal. Here we have the excommunicated Ham. See the ark and Noah way off in the distance? You can see the rainbow starting to fade. Here's the goat he takes as a companion. You can tell the goat's female from her udders. I'm not fully decided on what that means.

Lovers.

Oh, sure. All that's implied. Of course this divided sky, with the sun on this side and moon on that side, means they wandered day and night, stopping in an open pasture. The goat's chewing his medieval pantaloons. Ham's driving his hands into the soil and pulling up, as this page shows, a squirming mass of soil and worms. Yum. Ham is fascinated by it, watching the soil alive in his fingers—alive with *meaning,* to be precise. Like father, like son. He interprets what he sees, and even takes it as another kind of covenant. But that's where the similarity stops. Ham resents God. He reads it as a promise of social confusion. He reads the worms as a sign that postdiluvian life will bring all kinds of landlocked miseries—miseries that are sugar-coated by a pretty rainbow. That's why, when it rains, we get all those night-crawlers out on the street.

Now the big promise, as I read these verses to say, is that creation was supposed to disseminate like vermiculi, androgynously, blindly. Earthworms eat the soil, excrete it, live in it, and die in it. Rain's their only relief. That's when they wash up out of the dirt and bask in each other's company. Just like worms, people yearn for the same kind of pounding rain that will wash them up into the light of day. It's a complex little trope, but it works. For instance, worms are lonely in their tangled communities, and so are we. Earthworms have fluid and fracturing identities, so do we. And except at night and on rainy days, worms cherish their dirty privacy, and so do we. They have conflicting emotions coming from eight little hearts, and so on. *The Covenant* is so open to interpretation, it's such a puzzle, it's such a knot, that it's the perfect centerpiece for an intense little religion. So here's my hunch: that there was an esoteric and hermeneutic sect, one that would have been especially refreshing during the Renaissance because instead of justifying the received doctrine, it devoured it, and it devoured it from the inside like logophagous worms, and instead of aestheticizing religious ideology it looked for beauty in the perfectly ugly, it looked for sense in utter nonsense.

It sounds like alchemy.

It's so different from that, she said, turning to the last page, which was severely damaged. Ham was featured in close detail, feeding himself in a sacramental manner, coiling a worm like a Slinky onto his tongue. Gurney felt queasy.

So this is, like, your religion?

I'm not religious, she said sternly, drunkenly. But I can see this becoming my field of study.

In a weird way he could see it too, and he was jealous—jealous that with a jolt of scholarly mania she'd managed to build a career out of so little, a shabby book she'd picked up in an old Bulgarian junk shop.

She straddled him like a wrestler, letting the book fall between them, into the valley where their two crotches met. Trapped there, he unrolled her stockings and stroked the inside of her thighs until she laughed.

So it's no religion, he said, stroking. But you still eat earthworms.

She blushed. He didn't press it. He ran his hands up the outside of her legs, over her underwear, onto her smooth and warm lower back. Ice flakes tinkled against the glass. The perfume was fading from her chin and neck. They kissed some, lightly smashing the open book between them. Gurney gently placed it on the table. She pulled her maroon dress over her head, releasing her ivory body into the candlelight. Her waist was narrow with firm little muscles, her breasts ferocious in her snug black bra. Light brown hairs curled from the hem of her plain black panties. She lifted off his shirt and undershirt, lightly scratching him, voluminously kissing him. For a man who'd forbidden himself sex for so long, he naturally refrained from taking the initiative but dwelled on the last few pangs of remorse while she swept her arms up the length of his back, drew down his pants and boxer shorts, and ran her fine Anglo nose over the ridges and contours of his cock. After boyish maneuvers, off came her bra. He was content to feel her stiffening breasts gliding over his wintry chest, not even to handle them, certainly not to slide away her smoldering underwear. That was the sacred and final veil—and shouldn't they save that for after dinner? Wasn't the turkey getting cold? Wasn't she as hungry as he? But again she took the initiative, sliding off her panties and flinging them to the shadows, so his fingers that had glided over dampening fabric now combed through her fine and curly hair, slipping easily inside.

Thus everything began quite abruptly, finding Gurney then supine on the velvet love seat, his nose and mouth where his hand had been, lemony Jackie arched above, gasping the little honks of a Victrola. But when his attention wandered to the heavy falling snow and for a moment he lost track of what he was doing, the Victrola skipped, Jackie shifted. So he focused entirely on the task at hand, on all the funny things he knew that pleased her: lunch boxes, earthworms, privacy in Kraków; scholarship, honesty, connoisseurship; and this—and this! and this! and this! he thought, and this! and this! and this! What enjoyment to give her his full attention! What enjoyment to make her a wealthy young woman! This was bliss, licking her. This was bliss, tonguing her open, unzipping her like a purse. And although he'd refrained from touching himself, he took full part in her trembling pleasure as she raised her voice to the pointed ceiling and broke the spell of her shimmering temple.

Fuck me, Gurney! Fuck me, she said, as if she saved this word for special occasions. It hurt a little as she unrolled the condom, and the pain was good yet nothing so splendid as the deep prickly heat of easing inside her, of watching her ride up and down on his lap, illumined by candles from all directions. Looking him in the eye, studying his face, Jackie seemed satisfied and strangely schooled. This thrilled him, challenged him. He came too quickly and hastily withdrew, despite the sturdy German condom. She watched him shudder and heave to a finish, then collapsed her dead weight onto his chest.

Happy Thanksgiving, he said.

You're welcome, she said.

They listened to snowflakes pelting the glass. Everything was equal in the candlelight—the sloping dunes of her back and hips, the mounds and valleys of clothes and blankets. The earthworm book was just within reach. He picked it up and flipped it open.

What are these funny little holes? he asked, referring to the network of tiny tunnels drilled throughout its folios.

Wormholes, she groaned.

Bookworms?

Bookworms. The paper's pure silk. Bookworms love it, the little monsters. Look at the last page, it's almost unreadable.

Wait. Silkworms make it, and bookworms eat it?

I guess.

That's beautiful.

It's a nuisance.

Now he too found interest in the book. He refilled his wineglass and splashed some on her hip. Sorry. Wow. So this really *is* a living covenant?

Bother, she said, dragging her finger through the wine on her thigh, lightly running it along his lips. Please watch the book, she said groggily.

Just your skin, he said. The book's real truth is in its irony, don't you think? An irony beyond the book's control. As you say, the Covenant itself is very serious. And the writer of the book was serious, and so were the bookmakers, with their leather worm-straps and worm-silk paper and weird worm-ink. Not to mention the worm worshipers, who went so far as to eat the worms. No offense. But in the end they were just setting the stage for the bookworms to come along.

Not just the real bookworms, but bookworms like you, too, bookworms who'd just as soon eat it as read it! *Interpretation as wormholing*, you might say. Pretty cool. That's *my* theory.

It's very sweet, she said. But it doesn't make a lot of sense. Many *holes* in your theory.

I'm no scholar. I'm a dealer, and I've learned a thing or two about chance. Irony, as I see it, is simply the *interpretation* of chance. Pretty neat, huh?

She didn't respond. Before he knew it, she was asleep on his chest.

He was starving. She wasn't waking up. In the equanimity of this postcoital lull, he entertained himself by thinking about irony and luck. Could irony be taken seriously? Was there maybe a career in this? Could one devise, maybe, an erotics of irony? An ironics of eros? Jackie's low snores sounded something like a mourning dove. If he weren't so hungry they would have lulled him to sleep. Less delicately than he would have liked, he unworked her slender arms from his and managed to get himself to his feet. He picked up the bottle. Something about the fragile candles made him approach the kitchen slowly. He'd never really spent time in there—it was Jackie's magic laboratory—so when he groped the air and clicked the string he was shocked by how bright and cramped it was, agleam like an open refrigerator.

It was a mess. The chopping block was littered with dirty knives and vegetable skins. The counter was strewn with caked bowls, clotted beaters, lidless jars. Three cold pans stood waiting on the stove, their potatoes and gravy and creamed baby onions coagulated around respective spoons and ladles. He put on mitts and pulled the turkey from the oven. It looked fine, if not very warm. He felt bad for Jackie, for an elaborate meal that she'd drunkenly deserted right at the moment it would have been presentable. Whatever. Drunk himself and too impatient to carve it respectfully, he clutched the bird's slippery leg, winced at the ripping noises, and tore the thing away from the body. It was kind of tough. Still pink, but not really raw. He spooned lumpy gravy on it, making it tastier but messier to eat. He got a plate, poured some wine. He forked up potatoes, forked out stuffing, and sat down naked on a frail wooden chair. He ate.

A sheeny green bag hung from a nail that was painted the same mustard yellow as the walls. The bag was large, bulging. Christ, he said out loud, dropping the tattered leg to the plate. She'd carried it home, just like this? But what did he expect? He wiped his greasy hands on a dishrag, dried them on his hairy legs. He hefted the bag off the nail. Nothing stirred behind the curtain. His heart raced. His breath quickened. Unzipping it, he smelled the money exhaling from within. The floor looked clean. He couldn't resist. He upended the contents, which kept coming and coming, neat fat packets of hundred-dollar bills falling around his size-thirteen feet. He had no desire to count it out. He wanted to make it all disappear—but there it was, real as a turkey bone.

No doubt Jackie had plans for the money. No doubt she'd do something important with it, but he was the one to blame, and surely they would find him out. His prints were everywhere. He looked at the gristly turkey leg. He thought of Jackie knocked out on the couch, of Linda on the steps, his scene in the office, his fatuously holding up his fingers and mouthing the word *black*. He thought of the crap he'd blathered to Tomasz. No ironic distance here. The facts were blinding. Gurney was cornered, doomed. He restuffed the bag and returned it to the hook. He sat for a while, cogitating. Nothing really came to him except for that which was painfully obvious. He knew what he had to do. The next day he'd accept Wanda's offer and go with her, at her convenience, off to the dreaded cottage of her father. He had to. Unconcerned with the details, Wanda understood that her father held something that Gurney urgently needed.

Thirteen

IT WAS LATE NOVEMBER AND THREATENING TO SNOW. At last it was cold enough for Wanda's suede coat. She felt ten years older in it—the big, funky batwing lapels, one hand relaxed in its roomy pocket while the other held a cup of kiosk coffee. She was leading Gurney to her father's house, guiding him through the woods of the Ojców Valley. Patches of snow and empty beech trees, hills swelling up to the high horizon and meeting the edge of the ice-blue sky. Gurney was also looking older, with an old black coat and his own steaming coffee, tromping along with a sense of purpose, but she still couldn't help wondering if he was a virgin. He had that look. She'd taken care of her own virginity just one week before, when she'd bumped with Matek on the crummy bathroom floor, and now she saw the world just as it was. Now she understood the danger of her mission—the magnitude of getting out of town, the consequences of cornering her father—and she felt equipped to look after both of them. Little did her father know what she had in store for him. Little did Gurney know, trudging quietly beside her, that she kept his lost wallet in her inside pocket. But she had to be cautious. She'd given much thought to this risky plan, and she knew that when she gave back the wallet, under the shifty eyes of her father, she might set off unforeseeable violence.

Snow clouds were moving in.

She used to walk through those woods as a girl, imagining Hansel and Gretel trailing breadcrumbs as they went. She led him along the creek, tromping through frostbitten butterbur growth, and was pleased to think how romantic they looked, dark as ravens, hopping over logs and puffball mushrooms, white breath piling out of their mouths. But she had to correct herself: romantic it was not. She was leading Gurney into quite real peril, all the while taking advantage of his wish to claim some silly letters from home. Who was to say that Dick Chesnutt's evil fate, whatever it had been, couldn't as easily be Gurney's too? Who was to say her father's cottage wasn't a ginger-bread crematorium?

Suddenly she slipped and sank into the brook. Gurney dropped his coffee and caught her under the arms, swiftly swinging her onto the bank. Squishing her waterlogged boots on the moss, she noted how quick and strong he was, and she wished he hadn't unhanded her so quickly.

Good work, she said. Now get ready to throw him in the oven if you have to.

What?

My father, she explained.

At a point about two kilometers from the bus stop, the stream broke from the path and wound through the valley, spacing out three smoking cottages. The farthest one belonged to the Zamoyski family, its thatched roof barely visible through the orchard. She took off her mitten and touched the wallet. She was prepared to be disgusted by what had become of the cottage, expecting it to be frowsy and painfully rustic.

What's he do out here in the winter? Gurney asked.

Ask him.

Does he hunt?

Ask him.

She led him across the stream, past Grandma Słowokowska's cottage. They walked sideways through the prickly raspberry bushes and approached the blue cottage with its lemon-yellow door. Something was baking. The windows were steamed and frosted over. She knocked six knocks, then six more. She tried the pewter door handle and was surprised to find it locked. She edged her way to the frosted kitchen window and rapped a few times on the opaque glass. Tati!

Tati! She rapped and rapped until she thought it would crack. Rustling and slamming came from within, sounding like a nest of scared ground squirrels.

The front door finally opened, and her father appeared in exquisite style: purple paisley silk pajamas, a crisp canvas apron, a childish look of embarrassment on his face. Clearly confused, displeased at seeing Gurney, he trained his eyes on Wanda and abruptly asked if it was Sunday or Monday. She studied his shifty face. Either her father was consumed by guilt, she thought, or he had lapsed in his crude calendar keeping.

Monday, she said, squeezing past him into the warm cottage air.

It was marvelously transformed since she'd seen it last—impeccably kept, furnished in Scandinavian blond wood furniture. The little library, which her mother had made so humble and cozy, had been turned into a showcase of modern comfort, from the nubbly rug to the sleek black stereo to the Hundertwasser above the mantel, which, upon inspection, proved to be signed. In the corner crouched a broad-shouldered Sony Trinitron, toward which slouched two roomy leather armchairs and a stout leather love seat that must have cost a fortune. Her father walked in, followed by Gurney, and pointed a remote control at the stereo. The room filled up with the seasick Moody Blues. Wanda walked over and hit the power switch.

We came to visit, she said in English. Class was canceled.

Her father said nothing.

It's a new school holiday, she said with confidence, striding along the bookcases, pausing to glance behind an armchair. Even the baseboards had been wiped down. With the place so clean, why such delay in opening the door? She had caught him off guard, that was sure, and she would use this surprise to her full advantage. She addressed him from the center of the rug: It's a new holiday called Witkacy Jego. It's supposed to teach the teachers about the changes in Poland.

Her father looked pained. Gurney looked at books.

Pani Pieczara, for example, is spending the day on the street corners, visiting with moneychangers and the Russian *mafiya*. Pan Szczuka is visiting the new pornographic cinema. Pan Baran is on the express train to Warsaw, where she'll interview the publishers of a black-market-baby newsletter.

Her father smoothed his apron down, not nearly as scandalized as she thought he'd be. She continued: Tomorrow in school the teachers will report back to us, and the planks will fall from their Communist eyes.

Scales, Gurney said, correcting her.

Yes, scales. The scales will fall—will have fallen?—from their eyes. And thus she tried out Mateusz's plan for a new school holiday, Witkacy Day. But her father wasn't biting, so she baited him further: I think it should be called Dick Chesnutt Day!

Her father sighed. He said he had to check on a pie.

I said Dick Chesnutt, she called into the kitchen. I say that because he has recently disappeared.

He didn't respond. Things were far too quiet out here. She paused a moment, avoiding Gurney's eyes, then crept down the creaking hallway to the kitchen, where she found him making chubby gestures at the window—toward the garden? Was someone out there? Seeing Wanda, he tried to regain composure. He childishly put his hands to his face, but this only exaggerated the crazed blue eyes peeking out between his fingers. How obscene! she thought, advancing half a step into the kitchen. How obscene to catch him in such a state. This was very interesting. It wasn't his usual angry grandeur. It wasn't the spectacle that she had grown so used to. He peeked through his fingers and showed her the side he so painstakingly kept to himself, hidden away out here in the woods.

Stop it! she said. He dropped his hands, took a step back, darting his eyes between her and the oven. Had she brought him this close to crumbling already? Was he chirping in her hand like a defenseless toad? She looked away. When he turned to the oven, ominously quiet, she smeared steam from the window with her suede coat sleeve, but there was nothing to see. She remained standing.

He set a pie on the table. A perfect American pie. It was unlike him, first off, to bake anything, particularly something so completely non-Polish—but even more preposterously, the mess had already been cleared away.

The cottage is very clean, she said.

I try, he said. Life is much simpler here, you know.

Obscene, she thought, ignoring the chair he pulled out for her.

Drawn to the pie like a creature of the forest, Gurney appeared in the threshold of the kitchen, his big black coat slung over his arm. Tati took Gurney's coat in silence and hung it up in the hall. His hospitality ran almost as deep as his barbarism. He motioned for Gurney to join them at the table.

He held out his hand for Wanda's coat.

Not just yet.

May I assume, he said to Gurney, resuming his composure, that the Kasino also honors this Witkacy Jego? He poured their coffee, seemingly fortified by his own sarcasm.

Oh, no, Gurney said, smiling at a private joke.

But still here you are, and with my daughter.

I have time off.

Have you worked there for even two weeks yet?

How would you know?

It is no secret.

Father—

My roulette wheel's broken, if you need to know. He started to laugh but staved it off. But then, as if provoked by her father's silent stare, he broke up and filled the little kitchen with laughter. Wanda was amused, though uncertain at what, but her father didn't hide his disgust. He picked up the pie and held it well outside Gurney's range. When the laughter had finally subsided, leaving Gurney sputtering and shaking like a tractor, her father reluctantly replaced the pie, beside which he set down a needlessly large knife.

She watched her father slicing through the crust, tapping the blade against the glass pan and sliding it out smeared with red-black filling. She listening to Gurney still tittering with aftershocks, and she had to acknowledge the delicacy of the situation: these two men were volatile chemicals, purple and yellow, side by side in fragile test tubes. Was it really worth the risk to mix them? What did she hope to gain by it? She had to realize that, by producing the wallet as she had planned, her inspired and carefully administered plan would smoke and sputter into violent chaos, and what with that knife, and all those muscles, and all the blood surging through those muscles . . . she had to be very cautious now.

Actually, Gurney said, I had someone win big at my table last week. He dug into his pie and talked with his mouth full. Something like two hundred thousand dollars.

That's a lot of money! she said.

Her father shifted, not looking up from his untouched plate.

My manager thinks he can pin it on me, just because no one ever wins at the Kasino. Money goes in, nothing comes out. That should be the motto. Nice pie, by the way. But he's nuts. He thinks just because it's a friend of mine who won, it's gotta somehow be *my* fault—like you can rig a roulette wheel! Maybe somebody could, but I haven't the foggiest idea how.

Your friend? Tati said. Who's your friend?

She's an American. Named—Gurney swallowed—Jackie Witherspoon.

All the life drained out of her father's face. He got up without excusing himself, using the ladder-back chair for balance. He felt his way out of the kitchen.

They went on eating their pie without him. Cigarette smoke drifted in like an unwanted guest. Her father had stopped smoking on their 1986 trip to Dubrovnik, or so she'd thought. She slid the extra slice next to Gurney's smeary plate and turned to watch snow clouds tumble over the bluffs. She could feel Gurney waiting in her periphery. Probably realizing that was all the approval she was going to give him, he began to eat her father's slice of pie. She returned in her mind to the crux of the matter, that one hidden fact that would decide its outcome: did her father plant the wallet with intent to frame Gurney? If he had, she thought, he was a sinister bastard, and he would react with violence to the bungling of his plot. But maybe he had dropped it in the sloppiness of his anger, maybe while he was pissing in fear. If that was the case, he would melt like a snowball for all his horror and shame, and that was precisely what she wanted. Putty. Mud. And yet it sickened her to think that, at the bottom of it all, this was her father she meant to destroy. That was the part she couldn't get past. She got up and opened the strange new refrigerator. Sausage, butter, eggs, salad dressing, white wine, beet juice, pills, pickled cabbage—the everyday things that he'd always kept in there. The same old things that kept her father alive. Given the choice, she asked herself, would Mateusz do it, would he risk everything? Would Mateusz condemn his own father if he had to? She thought yes, and then no.

And after all, did she really *have* to? Did she *have* to know the truth?

Jesus Christ! Gurney said, rising on his hands and looking out the window. Jesus! But then he took a breath and sat back down.

What is it? What'd you see? She looked through the trees at the Słowokowski cottage. The overcast valley was empty and barren, but she searched it over hunterlike. What'd you see? she asked.

Nothing, he said, flexing his jaw. Really. I . . . my eyes must be playing tricks on me.

Tricks? said her father, standing in the door. His apron was off. His pajamas were unbuttoned and showing his undershirt. Violence, she felt, was very nearby, though her father wore an almost serene expression. Gurney looked long and hard at her father, then stubbornly went back to eating his pie. Wanda took another look out the window.

Her father sat down and watched Gurney eat. It's quite a thing, he said. It's quite a thing having an American man in your house. Leave the room to smoke a cigarette, and your daughter gives him your pie to eat. Her father stared at Gurney as if he wanted to hit him. History proceeds from moments like this, you know.

As if bracing himself against a blinding wind, Gurney turned to the window, then quickly to her father, then angrily down at his clenched hands, creaking them open and looking inside. Very weird, Wanda thought. Tati sliced himself another piece of pie. Gurney mashed a raspberry with his fork. Wanda kept an eye on the window.

It's quite a thing . . . her father began, then trailed off into his in-solent eating.

She listened to the exaggerated squeaks of their forks and won-dered how she'd gotten herself into this mess. Thinking she might cry or do something stupid, and not really caring what they did to each other, she buttoned up her coat and went outside.

The cold was just right. Standing behind the shed among weeds and brambles, she was overcome by the valley's windless quiet. She hadn't remembered it ever being so quiet. Back in the city, working up the courage to come visit her father, she'd anticipated some sort of noisy scuffle, shouting and struggling and maybe even blows—but then, for that matter, her whole life in the city was a noisy scuffle. Since she'd gotten to know Matek and his unstoppable friends, the volume had been turned up to a deafening pitch. And since that fate-ful episode on the bathroom floor, the whole city had turned into a boundless, blazing playground. Matek's breath hot on her breasts and belly, making her a little river mouth, a hot little river mouth that she'd guided him into, gripping and griping and complaining as he fucked her, careful though he tried to be. And then later on it was Dick Chesnutt's sofa, and Mother's big bed, under two blankets on the cold grass of the Błonia, rutting like rabbits among their friends in the flat, the air full of Matek's and Kuba's cigarette smoke, then living at the movies and cycling through traffic and drinking in cafés and shoplifting in shops. Matek was the mayor of this big noisy city and suddenly everything seemed possible now. She was a grown-up now, and she did as she pleased, so what on earth was she doing out here? This decidedly did *not* please her.

What the hell was she doing out here?

She opened the wallet. She wanted to toss it in the woods and be rid of it. She had no desire to show it to her father now. What did it matter if Tati were to blame? And who really knows what happened to Dick Chesnutt? It wasn't her risk to take. She started to cry, remem-bering the warmth of his blue flannel shirt, and she wanted to throw it as far as she could.

She was standing in the weeds, crying with the wallet, when something rustled on the other side of the shed. Putting the wallet in her pocket, she went to have a look. She stepped over hoes and shovels in the thicket. She tripped over fence wire and a tangle of traps, but all she found was the goat munching grass. Again she heard rustling in the place where she'd just been, followed by three taunting wheelbarrow clangs, but again, when she got there, nothing at all! She searched the bare trees. She searched the dead brush. She searched the white cliffs through the softly turning snow. A lugubrious whistle came from the other side of the cottage. Now she had it! But when she got there she found nothing but the munching goat. Good joke. Investigating more rustles, whistles, and snaps, she crisscrossed the garden and circled the orchard, losing all composure in the snow-whirling stillness. When the noises all of a sudden stopped (except for the goat, who didn't stop eating), she wondered if she'd been imagining it all.

Her father could be seen sitting in the kitchen. He looked even calmer now. He looked like a wolf digesting a sheep. She had to press Gurney on what he'd seen through the window. She went inside to begin the interrogation.

Where's Gurney? she demanded.

He's in the library. He's gone and hidden something in my records.

What did you do to him?

Her father sighed, not moving a muscle. She went into the library. Gurney was sitting cross-legged by the records, painstakingly removing them one at a time.

What did you see through the window? she demanded.

Co? Nothing.

You *saw* something. There's something out there.

We're out in the country. There's all kinds of stuff.

She didn't like his tone, but fuck him anyway. She went back to the kitchen and sat facing her father. After several minutes of dreadful silence, he fished a pack of cigarettes from the pocket of his pajamas. John Players. He uncharacteristically offered her one (she declined), then he lit one for himself. Ghosts, he said. I hardly make it through

the night out here without something terrible rapping at the glass.
And that's the truth. He looked solemnly out the window, as if he
hadn't just said the stupidest thing on earth. His shoulders slouched in
the rumpled silk. He dragged weakly from his cigarette.

There was a time when money meant nothing, he said.

What?

There was that winter when we bartered your mother's pictures—
for the basics, for grapefruit. You remember. Money was nothing
then. Money was just paper back then. You were a baby, you didn't
need much of anything. We were really living then. But it was more
than that. I'm thinking of you now, my daughter, Wanda Agnieszka
Zamoyska. You are a Zamoyski, and that's worth things even money
can't touch.

Bollocks, she said, using Matek's favorite word.

It's an old European value. It could never be fathomed by that
dolt in there, that American in there pawing through my records.

Give me one, she said.

He gave her a cigarette, even lit it for her.

You can see that I have trouble expressing myself, he said. Expressing my mind, expressing my heart. You know that's never been
easy for me. But right now, under such bad circumstances, I think you
should make arrangements to leave Poland.

What circumstances?

I am talking about where you should go to college. He took up her
left hand in both of his. He looked weak and old, but his firm, familiar grip took her by surprise. I am glad you came to visit this morning.
Nobody respects me here anymore. Not in Poland, but I have very
good friends around the world. Friends with influence. Friends at
Cambridge, at Oxford.

He paused to let the names of the universities sink in. He knew
what he was doing to her, seducing her with images of spires and dor-
mitories, images of lawns and early-morning crew teams. She imagined
making friends with the smartest kids in the world, sitting in lecture
halls and going to theaters, taking weekend field trips to London.

And I still have connections at Stanford, he went on, letting her imagine college life in California, amid all those rich and beautiful Americans, having bonfires on the beach, cycling by the bay, going to parties in the San Francisco hills. It was clear from the distant triumph in his eyes that he knew he had softened his recalcitrant daughter: with one easy offer, he was winning her back. But it was her *future*, the bastard! It was so hard to resist! She dropped the cigarette, pushed away the ashtray. She took a deep breath and tried to think of Mateusz. She didn't realize she had such strong desires.

They would adore a smart girl like you. And to be perfectly honest, they'd adore my money. We have entered a world where money is what matters. I've learned that one lesson, if nothing else. My child, he said, gripping tighter, regardless what happens to *me*—regardless of everything—remember I am making you this offer. As your father. Know that my offer always stands.

Regardless of what happens? she said. What kind of trouble are you in? She looked from her hunched-over father's hands to the heavily falling snow outside. She herself had been planning to get him in trouble, indeed in serious trouble. But even though he deserved the worst, and now more than ever she believed that he did, she saw the problem from a different angle. His guilt had a different look to it. It didn't look ferocious, not even scary. It was hopelessly flattened, beyond repair, a dead skunk sealed to the pavement by traffic. He was offering her a world of possibility, and he was offering it at the moment when his soul was most bankrupt—she could see it, his desperate soul—but she had every intention of turning it down. It was just another gift that she'd have to destroy.

She wrested from his grip. She went over to the counter with its egg-blue tiles. She couldn't reject him just yet, however, just as she couldn't show him the wallet. He lit another cigarette. Several years before, her mother had cut and lain those tiles, and she'd done such an impeccable job that the pencil lines of grout and gray mosaic trim showed no effort whatsoever. She swept her hand over the smooth cool surface. It had probably been wiped down a thousand times since then. In the next room Gurney cursed and shuffled. She looked at the appliances in a row along the wall: a four-slice toaster manufactured by Braun, a new food processor manufactured by Cuisinart, a stainless steel Italian espresso machine. But there was also one she couldn't identify, a white metal contraption with a couple of knobs on top. It looked like a miniature clothes dryer. She pulled it toward her—a bread-making machine! It was nothing much on the inside, just a metal canister. Its bold simplicity pissed her off. She picked it up, turned it over, shook it hard for no good reason. She swung it around, shook it some more, and raised it high above her head.

Do you know how badly Matka wants one of these?

I've never used it, her father said, not even flinching at the hovering appliance.

And you never will, after I smash it!

You may, he said, a look of ugly penance on his face, a look so ugly and genuinely Catholic that she was prompted to smash the fucking thing on the floor, or on the table, or even on her father's big soft head, when, all of a sudden, as if by a miracle, the oblong weight of it vanished from her hands. She turned to see Gurney setting it on the counter, leaving her feeling futile and embarrassed.

He assumed her place in the middle of the floor, his big body making the room feel cramped. His chest heaved. His eyes pitched about. Her father hadn't budged one bit.

Mr. Zamoyski, I wanted to trust you. When they weren't with the Shostakovich, I kept on looking. I opened all of them. I searched every last one, and the letters are gone! You know what they are. You know *where* they are. I demand them here and now.

Hic et nunc, hic et nunc, her father said, pushing himself from the table. You demand them in the here and now. I do find it interesting that a boy like yourself, who has waited several months to open these letters, should care one whit for what you call the here and now. Your here is not here, your now is not now.

But if you haven't seen them, how do you know I haven't opened them?

Simple enough. You wouldn't travel all this way otherwise. You haven't read them and they're controlling your life!

I'm not convinced, and you know why not? Because your raspberry pie tastes just like my grandmother's. Isn't that strange? And you know what I saw out there. You know damn well that my eyes weren't playing tricks.

What did you see? Wanda interjected, but he wasn't listening to her. He was crowding the table, crowding her father.

Who's in charge here? Aren't you in charge? If you aren't, would you please direct me to the person who is? I know who I saw, sir. I know she's hiding around here someplace—

At this, Tati sprang up and plunged himself into Gurney's open torso. He didn't tackle him but swung him around with the confidence of a man half his age, catching him in an ironclad cross-face headlock. Clamped between Tati's hip and the counter, Gurney could only push blindly against his thighs. These two men weren't Titans, Wanda thought, they were unruly gymnasium boys, and every bit as frightening—smashing, gnashing, and grunting as they were. Her father was clearly the one in control, such control that though he was flushed and winded, he spoke in a calm and even tone, tightening his grip with every phrase:

You are no teacher. You are no roulette dealer. Nothing about you suggests you are a father. Go shovel nuclear waste in Siberia, do something tough to build your muscles. You'll have to if ever you hope to go home. You'll have to if you think you can take on your daughter. Here is a Christmas warning: leave Poland. You Americans, your history lies in a shallow grave. Take the first train out of Kraków.

But then came the gruesome change: to Wanda's horror, her father began squeezing Gurney's neck with two or three fingers, and not until Gurney's mouth began making dry desperate choke sounds, not until Gurney's purple face bugged with fear, not until Wanda was trying to tear him away, did her father let go with one last shove. Gurney stooped and coughed and fumed.

Wanda edged sideways along the wall. Bracing herself for his next scary stunt, she pressed her back into the humming refrigerator. The kitchen sparkled with snowy hatred. Gray and blue surfaces trembled with danger. The sight of her father speechless and spent, his lips quivering, his face crisscrossed with streaks and wrinkles, assured her there was nothing more left for her here. Fuck the wallet. Fuck the truth. Fuck Stanford and Cambridge and everything else. She'd let Tati and all his ghosts run free, and she'd probably hope that he didn't get caught. But as for herself, she'd find her own way.

THE HEAVY WET SNOW was sticking to the ground, a wintry quilt that begged to be trampled on, but they walked a straight path away from the cottage. Birch smoke rose from the Słowokowskis' chimney. Naturally she felt a little dismayed, full of regret that nothing had gone as planned. But they crunched out boot tracks nevertheless, they mingled their breath clouds and didn't look back. Nothing had been resolved—neither the letters nor the wallet had been returned. And certainly nothing *good* had come of their visit, especially not her father's parting invitation that she join him out here for Christmas Eve. As they crossed the footbridge into new shallow snowdrifts she felt a confusing change taking place, one much deeper than losing her virginity. They didn't talk, leaving each other to think and unwind, and after a while their silence grew redolent, settling between them like wood smoke in the valley. Left to her thoughts, she considered this network of interlocking valleys and decided that it was just where her father belonged. Those chalky bluffs and hunching boulders, those deep and famous ice-water caves that for centuries had harbored deserters from the city. The valley belonged to an old Galician tradition. Centuries before, during the Tatar invasions, Krakovians had scuttled like rodents to the valley, deserting families and friends, leaving them to be enslaved in the city. King Władysław the Short had retreated there, too, cowering in a cave while the Bohemian king took over his throne. And more recently, of course, there had been heroes in the valley, as during the January Uprising of 1863 or the Nazi occupation of the 1940s, when brave young men regrouped in Ojców and plotted to reclaim their beloved Poland. Naturally, they had failed. She used to think her father was a hero. She used to think a lot of things. But now she could see he was just another man, another crazy Pole slipping off into silence.

After half a mile, Gurney spoke: I'm sure you're wondering, he said. She's just a little baby. Just over two months old. My daughter, I mean.

Wanda said, Oh, and he was gone from her side, nimbly hopping across the stream. He stayed at the other edge, silhouetted against the frosty mud bank, apparently waiting to catch her if she tripped.

Her name's Sarah! he called out.

That was all he said on the subject, and she didn't press it on the way to the road. Actually she hadn't been wondering about it at all, but now that she thought of it, it was kind of sad that he was in Poland, of all places. Was it that silly girl with the crewneck sweater? Had Gurney managed to get *her* pregnant? Remarkable. As they crossed the road, she suddenly understood why he always looked distracted. She felt sad for him, and as they stood rubbing mittens at the remote bus stop, she was prompted to hand over the wallet to him. He opened it and laughed to the treetops, leaping like a kangaroo toward the flurrying gray sky, which made her think of him carrying around an empty pouch, and then she felt sadder yet for this little girl Sarah, thinking that maybe someday soon she'd be old enough to enjoy having such a totally foolish papa.

Fourteen

GURNEY HAD ALWAYS liked complicated weather. But right then, as he waded through snow heaps that shifted like sand, and as he bumped the husks of holiday shoppers, the cold and filth were way too much. As a child he would run straight toward the towering thunderstorms that marched like elephants over the Iowa hillscapes. He would shrug through sleetstorms that made his paper route adventuresome and that, in adolescence, made driving hazardous. Even in the months since his coming to Poland, the sooty winds that played about town—mucking the gutters in October rains, tainting the light November snowfalls—had only piqued his imagination. But that afternoon he'd had enough. Two wrapped-up *babkas* fought with mittens, shouting at each other over a smashed decorated cake. Crap like that, at every turn, reminded Gurney that he was trapped in Kraków, slipping through Cocytus, sliding on the rink of frozen swill that was ruled at bottom by Zbigniew Zamoyski.

He was on his way to the warmth of Jackie's flat. That morning's events in Ojców were alive in his head. Zbigniew's lethal fingerprint lingered on his throat. Zbigniew's hushed threat while Wanda was outside, his threat to do the worst if Gurney ever saw Jackie again, hissed in his windswept ears. And the image of Jane, most haunting of all, appeared and reappeared in his mind's kitchen window, jeering at him through the naked fruit trees.

Greece—he could go there. Israel. India. He could sneak off alone, explode in the sun. But first he would have a word with Jackie and put some things in order.

It was two in the afternoon, maybe later. All he'd eaten was Jane's raspberry pie. He needed to eat something more substantial. He flipped open his newfound wallet—the bastard child lost at birth, raised by wolves in that grubby city—and he counted fifteen American dollars, more than 160,000 złotys, enough to eat like a king in Kraków. He had a sudden urge to spend and spend—on mutton stuffed with ham at the Wierzynek! Roast turkey and żurek in the Staropolska! Kielbasa and cabbage in a cozy beerhall! But he was so hungry that he settled for the nearest corner milk bar.

Outside, bright windows dripped with steam. Inside, the smell of burned butter and boiled onions rose up among proletarian patrons, all of whom, Gurney included, pushed and craned to get a good look at what was bubbling inside the day's big kettles. When he reached the fingerprinted glass, he said *dzień dobry* to the line of five *babkas,* all of them squat and in blue state-issue frocks. He pointed to what he wanted and they passed down his plates, ladling up kapusta, pierogi ruski, naleśniki z serem, biały barszcz, szpinak, kasza gryczana, mashed potatoes, such an excessive, if meatless feast that it already satisfied his savage gluttony—that is, until he reached the *kasa,* who appraised all of it at less than two thousand złotys. Less than twenty cents. He sighed, added bread and butter to the bill, paid with the crumpled excess in his pockets, and hauled his tray to a free place by the window.

He rotated his attention among the three big plates, between the pierogis, which he segmented into thirds; the blintzes, which he divided into fourths; the potatoes, which he leveled in strip-mine fashion; and the plateful of spinach and kasza and beets, which he evenly harvested in five narrow rows. Blurred figures sped past the window. Laughter and chatter all around. Partway into the soup his hunger subsided, but he kept eating out of an obligation to clean his plates while his head started working through problems again. It nagged at him that he didn't know today's date. It was Monday, this much he knew. Time had groaned to a halt, in effect, since his little interview with Herr Messersturm, who by now had probably found a replacement for him (if only loyal Tomasz weren't a Pole!) and had probably organized a deputation to hunt him down—lock him in irons, make him regurgitate every last dollar.

But sex had a way of swallowing time: they had been doing it several times a day for the past week, and it had been wonderful, like an ill-gotten honeymoon, but while Jackie retained her ambition and spent her days at the university, Gurney felt himself sliding into absurdity, circling the city on Jackie's bicycle, ripping more pages out of his little leather book. Was it an addiction? Was it paradise? The whole world was meaningless next to the taste of her body. It had taken all of his strength to climb on a bus and go with Wanda out to Ojców.

He soaked a piece of buttered bread in the *żurek*. He put it in his mouth. Good, sour *żurek*. He slowly counted forward from Thanksgiving—November twenty-second—but then as he rounded the weekend and arrived at that day's date, November twenty-sixth, he started and cringed, searching the dingy walls for a calendar and regretfully sinking back into his chair. Today was his mother's birthday.

Fuck him. Fuck him for wanting to run three blocks to the post office. Fuck him for even thinking about ordering a long-distance phone call, a task that could take more than a full day's effort. His mother's birthday—her forty-ninth? Her fiftieth? Fuck me. And my cousin having an affair with Zbigniew Zamoyski? And Zbigniew Zamoyski, Wanda's father, Grazyna's husband, Jane's lover, the same sorry creep who'd gotten Jackie pregnant? How hadn't Gurney figured that out before? Her at Stanford, him at Stanford. The facts had been there all along. He stacked his plates, economized his space. The person to his left, a falconine young man, spread out his dishes and got more comfortable. A woman in her early fifties, about his mother's age, draped with shopping bags and puffy winter clothes, unloaded her tray on the place facing his. A *babka* came and took his plates away. People with food looked for places to sit.

He navigated his way through the streets to Jackie's, getting colder and increasingly agitated, arriving exhausted at the top of her stairs. He pounded the heavy door. Jackie? It's me. Jackie? The knob turned freely, but the dead bolt was locked. Locked from the *inside*. This fact allowed him only two explanations: either she was incapable of reaching the door (maybe unconscious, maybe worse) or she was blatantly ignoring him (maybe angry, maybe not alone). But in any case, she was there, somewhere on the other side of the door, letting him freeze in the drafty stairwell. He pounded more. Jackie? Jackie? It's me. He pressed his face to the cold wood, but heard nothing at all. It would have been enough for her to send him away, but she didn't say anything, didn't make a sound. Growing angry, he tore off his gloves and rapped his naked knuckles on the door, rapped as if the wood were Zbigniew Zamoyski, or the mendacious Jackie Wither-spoon who'd pressed her body to the old Pole, or the mendacious Jane who did the same and then baked him pies. He pounded two fists and the occasional knee, creating a clatter that filled the stairwell. He pounded as if the door were himself and he was in need of a good hard drubbing for wrongs he couldn't even count anymore. It's me! It's me! It's me! he said, relishing the damage he was doing his hands.

He pressed his cheek and ear to the door. Nothing. His head be-gan to ache. His hands, cut and bruised, started throbbing around the knuckles. He was suddenly, hotly ashamed of what he'd done. Pum-meling the door of this dignified girl! Jackie Witherspoon! He hoped she wasn't home. He hoped she was all right. Gurney retreated qui-etly down the stairs, buttoning his coat, wrapping his scarf, gingerly regloving his messy swelling hands, recalling her sickening story of Zbigniew, how he'd destroyed her little turret upon learning that she was pregnant.

THE ZAMOYSKI FLAT HARDLY FELT LIKE HOME—but where else was he going to go? He let himself into the baroque foyer, which opened onto Grazyna's studio. Some sort of party was going on. His draft disturbed the laughter of several salt-and-peppery people, dressed in tweeds and black wool stockings. Behind Wanda's bedroom door, the Pixies drummed in fun defiance, relaxing him a little as he unlaced his slushy boots. He slipped into slippers but left his coat on, padding down the hall and through the kitchen, to the room he still technically shared with Jane.

On the way back to the Old Town he'd grown hopping mad at Jane, ready to rip off her wig and clown nose. But upon bursting into their room and finding her lamp-lit in the far corner (on the edge of her divan, rolling thick blue stockings up her slender legs), something about her made him stop and blink his eyes. She looked soft, at ease. She looked up at him and smiled—pleasantly, as if she liked what she saw. Why did this embarrass him? Why was he speechless? He was supposed to be angry.

Hey, Midas, she said.

Hey.

She pulled a black cardigan sweater over her burgundy blouse. Stranger, she said.

You too, he said, slipping his sore hands into his coat pockets.

How about this one, she said: Long time no see.

Not so long. His tone was snide, having seen her that same morning running through the garden, and having glanced back at the cottage upon leaving with Wanda to see footprints dotting the snow-covered roof. Jane's footprints. Still, that imp in the garden had no relation to the Jane who was sitting before him now. This one, his cousin, was plain old Jane, ignoring his bitterness as she laced her black shoes. Glad for the familiarity, he relaxed a little.

I got a letter from Gram today, she said.

Gram?

Gram. Our grandmother.

She sent a letter?

Yes, she sent a letter. And she sends you her love.

Me? Right.

Yes, you, silly cabbage. Do you want to see it?

No. I don't.

You can.

I bet she wants me to go home.

Home? Why would she want that?

He looked hard at her face, five paces off, its parted lips and earnestly open eyes, and he said, Never mind. What was up with her? Was she telling the truth? He could never tell. Right now, he was drawn in two directions, like the frail legs of a wishbone. One way, he wanted to flop down beside her and forget that that nasty day had ever happened, talk confidentially with his cousin about the great sex he was having, and his coup at the Kasino, and his new way of thinking, à la Jackie, that all was forgiven for a blind race of creatures who lived on their bellies and disappeared in the dirt (he felt she would have approved of this). The other way, however, he knew the real risk of taking Jane into his confidence, even the risk of a minor confession, like admitting having blown off his mother's birthday. After all, he could see how she'd spread her tentacles around this family, lovingly entwining Wanda and Grazyna while secretly fucking their patriarch.

That's quite a grimace, she said at length, walking to the bookshelf and removing a few books, behind which was hidden a fresh bottle of cognac. She handed it over for Gurney to open. Penny for your thoughts, she said.

He opened it and took a swig.

Take off your coat. Sit next to me.

He looked out the window onto the Rynek. Lights were coming on. A two-story-tall, three-dimensional scaffolding flashed the four-color greeting WESOŁYCH ŚWIĄT. Jane had told him that it meant Merry World. That was how they said Merry Christmas in Poland. Jane's big eyes watched in patient expectation as he took off his coat and draped it on a chair.

Oh honey! she said. What's happened to your hands?

Nothing, he said, and sat down beside her.

You've been hitting something. She lifted one of them, gently turning it over with her fingers. Ouch, she said. We'll need to put a bandage on *that* one. What made you so mad?

Never mind.

If you say so, sweetie. Remember that snowblower incident at Gram's? You were so mad you—

Please stop.

It's hard to stop such a good story.

Please do. I know the story.

You don't know my version, but I'll stop if you insist. She kissed the contusion and laid the hand in her lap. I bet you're *full* of stories, she said, from all of your wintry travels. In fact, it looks like one or two are pushing at your lips right now.

I went to Ojców this morning, he blurted out. Wanda took me. He wanted to check her reaction, but he kept looking at his hands.

And?

And my letters are gone.

What do you want them so badly for?

I want to answer them.

Write your own letter, silly. Say the other ones never arrived. They'll think the KGB ate them or something.

Do you have them?

Me? *Bzdura.* She lay back on the pillow. Her blouse separated from her skirt, exposing her white belly and the edge of her navel. You know I really *don't* take such an interest in your private life. And you know, for that matter, you're safe sleeping here if you want to. I miss you. I mean, this can still be home base, if things start getting dull out in the pleasure dome.

The pleasure dome?

The zoological gardens of Jackie Witherspoon.

What do you know about it?

Just what I've been told.

By whom? Zbigniew?

Bzdura, she said again, letting the name zip across her face like the shadow of an airplane. She raised her knees, pushed the skirt between her legs. I'm better friends with Linda than Jackie, as I'm sure you've guessed. And Linda's a talker.

So are you!

We talk.

You talk. What about?

Jackie. Zbigniew. You. Everything.

Right, and you take no interest in my private life! Home base, my ass, he said, standing up. He paced across the chilly floor. Some cousin. A fucking snoop!

It's just talk, you goof. You've heard me tell stories.

Yes, I have—and they're always true!

Stories, my dear, are never true.

All right, then, tell me a story about Gram's raspberry pie, how just this morning you baked one for Zbigniew. Then tell me how when we showed up you slipped out the back. Tell me that story.

Quite a story, but I'm afraid it's yours.

Are you denying it?

What's there to deny? Stories, as I've said, are never true.

It was hard to tell in the darkening room whether she was disturbed in the least. Her naked belly, the artfully mussed hair falling on her shoulders. Experimentally, he opened and closed his aching hands. He cautiously lifted the cognac bottle and found it to be surprisingly light. He took a drink and sat—not next to her on the divan but a couple feet away, in the big velvet armchair. He lit a John Player. Never mind *my* story, he said. Tell me one of your own. Tell me about Jackie.

Oh my. Where to begin? Jackie of the earthworms? Jackie of the money bag?

How do *you* know those things?

I bet you know a lot more than I do.

He had no good reason to feel like Jackie had betrayed him—those things weren't secrets. But now he felt jealous for the first time in weeks, very jealous. He wanted to know about Jane's secret informer. He thought of the turret door, locked from the inside, and asked her to tell him about Jackie and Linda.

Are you sure you want to know?

What's there to know? Stories are never true.

Precisely. She paused for a moment and then a smile rose to her face. Have I told you about the salt mines at Wieliczka?

They've got that underground church carved out of salt. Jackie told me.

She should know.

Just tell your story.

Jane swung her shoes to the floor, sat upright with that look in her eyes, but then, as if thinking better of it, she took a drink and went back to her languid sprawl. She spoke frankly: You know Linda. You can kind of tell from looking at her that she's more than half Galician—she's got that greenish blond hair, those big gray eyes. Well, sure enough, she has family scattered all over this area. But for some reason the only one she really cares about is her great-aunt Renata, who's like the widow of some World War II hero. Now, Linda's grandfather is this hero guy's brother, but shamefully enough he was a complete coward who fled the Warsaw uprising and moved to Chicago or something. I don't know what he did in the States—shoemaker, maybe. I guess he was so ashamed of himself that he lost touch with his family, and they disowned him, and he died miserable—it's too complicated to get into.

Tell me about Jackie.

Patience, boy, this is background. So the main reason Linda came to Kraków after graduating from Chicago, where, as you know, we had some mutual friends, wasn't because she wanted to teach or run away from something like everyone else we know. What she wanted was to patch things up with her extended family—an ill-fated effort, I might add. She wanted to patch things up with dear old Renata, who, as Linda would soon discover, was at death's door with some weird allergy that is unheard of outside the smog fields of Silesia and Galicia. Anyway, shortly after arriving here, having left scores of unanswered messages in Aunt Renata's mailbox and under her doormat down on Ulica Czapskich, Linda asked around and learned, much to her pristine American horror, that the old *babka* spent most of her year laid out on a gurney a quarter of a mile underground!

So Linda starts sending letters to the sanatorium, thinking, I don't know, that she can save the old wretch. After the first few letters go unanswered, she starts getting nervous, thinking her aunt's dead or turned into a mole or something, but just about the time she's given up on saving her family's name and integrity, she gets a letter from her aunt that tells her to do just that—give up! The letter was written in a shaky hand, on yellowy paper from the center of the earth, and in it the lady swore at Linda, calling her written Polish shitty, calling her grandfather and father American wussies, saying she had no need for a groveling great-niece coming around so late in the century.

You're making this one up.

You'd think so. Linda was delighted. She wrote back right away and insisted on an invitation to the sanatorium (she'd learned that security was pretty tight down there). And then the aunt promptly wrote back, offering an invitation on one condition: that she could spit in her brassy niece's face! Linda's more than a little masochistic, so she eagerly accepted the invitation, and somehow a date was arranged for three in the afternoon one day the coming week. Well, as the week passed, the prospects of having her face polluted by this vile old lady became more and more, um, literal, and daunting, and of course nasty, and so she went to Jackie and asked her to come along. Needless to say, Jackie and Linda had fallen out of touch lately, a fact that had Linda feeling resentful and Jackie feeling horribly guilty. It seemed a secret trip underground was just what their friendship needed. And that's just what happened.

What happened? When did this happen?

When did this happen. Let me see: since the vacant bus stop at Wieliczka was dusted with snow and coal flakes when they arrived there, it had to have been sometime over the past couple weeks.

Okay, then I know you're making this up. And yet, he reasoned, Jackie had left him alone on several occasions. He tried to think, but the days were blurry in his memory. He couldn't relax in the armchair. He wanted to light a candle, maybe another lamp.

As I've said, you'd think I was making this up. Anyway, they arrived well in advance of three o'clock, and Jackie, adventuresome and subterranean as ever, demanded they take a little tour of the mine's upper network. Linda consented. She'd never been, but of course your friend had been there several times before and made an excellent guide. Oh yes, and at the beginning of her tour she promised Linda a formidable surprise.

So our two girlfriends rode the rickety rattly elevator cage deep down into the center of the earth. When the lift operator left them there in the mine, he told them it was empty, that they had miles of rocky entrails to themselves, and that they should be careful. Remember the Maquoketa Caves? Remember how terrified you'd get when we'd follow those slick black cracks into the hills, holding hands, pinching our crotches we were so afraid? Well, these are so much deeper, so much creepier, and they're man-made, begun almost a thousand years ago. Linda clutched herself to Jackie's side. Jackie, proud to be in charge, started walking like she knew just where they were going.

What time was it?

Why does it matter?

Because, you know, they had to meet Aunt Renata at three.

Right. Three sharp, and you can bet Jackie was thrilled about that. At this point it was a little after two, but whatever, it was just another lift ride down to the sanatorium. They had some time to tool around. It's interesing to note that the Wieliczka salt mines are kind of like the Paris catacombs in that you have to walk forever, through farther and more crooked tunnels, getting hornier and ornerier with anticipation, until you arrive and are awestruck by the weird buried European treasure within. But whereas the Paris catacombs, as Jackie described them to Linda, who by now had worked her cold hands well inside her friend's coat—whereas the Paris catacombs eventually turn into elaborate walls of skulls and femurs that twist and turn under the city streets, illustrating how only the morbid French could turn their own dead into a corridor of Legos, the salt mines are a testament to Polish artistry, Polish ingenuity, and, God forbid, Polish piety. It's this Ripley's Believe It or Not museum full of salt statues, salt ballrooms, salt tennis courts, and, as you mentioned, a salt cathedral, standing in which Jackie the scholar dallied a bit too long, lecturing on the salt chandeliers and the intricately whittled salt altar. By now Linda was beside herself, dreading her aunt, wanting her surprise, but Jackie kept talking. Finally, she found a tactful way to interrupt, and she told Jackie either to show her the surprise or take her back to the elevator because it was a quarter to three and they were clearly lost.

As ever, Jackie had virtually no concept of time—or so she feigned! Her eyes were coy. Her lips were berries. Jane then started to speak in a confidential, husky voice that did bear close resemblance to Jackie's, making Gurney shiver: Thanks for giving me the choice, Linda. We could make it to the lift by three, we could. And we could go down into that disgusting hospital and let that woman spit at you, we could. But you know I hate the thought of it. I mean, really, Linda, you think you came here to fix your family, and you're so Catholic you think you can fix it by taking a hot goober of shame in your face, but c'mon. Get real. She's an earthworm. You're an earthworm. There's nothing to fix. No family. No responsibility. So c'mon.

Stop, he said.

Glad to, she said, swinging her feet to the floor.

No, stop. I mean stop mocking me.

Mocking you? I didn't know I was.

He sighed, stared straight ahead. His eyes fell on the stack of portfolios in the corner, then quickly glanced away. Whatever, he said. Just tell the story. Sorry to interrupt.

Thank you. She took a drink, passed the bottle, and lit a cigarette. So Linda's a little mad, a little embarrassed, but of course she wants to know what her options are, so she waits out Jackie's harangue, which of course has its intended effect because all the while Linda loses any desire to meet her aunt Renata, who's probably down there salivating at the approaching hour. And maybe Jackie detects this change of heart because her voice gets softer in the cavernous cathedral; she gets closer (Jane moves closer), her eyes get naughtier (as do Jane's), and she directs her friend's eyes down to her waist, to the little leather purse hanging there. The surprise is in here, she says mischievously. But I have to show it to you in private. We're all alone! Linda says, putting her finger to Jackie's lips, making her listen to the dull-flat silence of the earth. Not here, Jackie whispers, looking about the carven salt floor, the salt-pillar saints, the savage salty statue of Jesus, everything white and holy in the soft salt light. Right here! Linda insists, and then she lays out her coat and gets down on her knees. Not here, Jackie protests. Right here, Linda insists, ready to call Jackie a hypocrite if she doesn't agree, but presently, of course, she does agree and falls to her knees with her legs pulled ever so slightly apart (Jane demonstrates this, pulling her own legs slightly apart, pushing her skirt between them just as she flashes her black underpants). Linda can't help but to laugh—you see, all this while she'd thought they were finished together—

Why are you telling me this?

Pleasure.

Right. Whose pleasure?

Ours.

Ours? How so?

Isn't this fun?

I'm not sure.

Oh, yes it is. It's like we've always been. She put her hand on his knee, she reached up to kiss him—half on the cheek, half on the lips, soapy smoky brandy lipstick, warm breath exhaled from her nose. Now let me finish. (He wanted her to kiss him again. He wanted to touch her. He wanted to run from the room and never come back.) Both our girlfriends are kneeling there, right there on the cathedral floor. Jackie lays the purse on her lap—what's in it? Magic beans? Toys? Tricks? Treats? What? Linda watches Jackie's finger playing with the clasp. She reaches out to touch but Jackie brushes her away, saying, You can't have me for free, and I can't have you for free. It's going to cost us. We're going to be whores.

What?

Listen: it's going to cost you your family tree—cut it down, chop it up, build a fire, and every inch of my pleasure is yours. Then our shifty friend slides the purse between her thighs, snaps it open, and, plunging her hand inside, clutching something big, she says, As for me, it's going to cost me a lot of money. She removes a fat bundle of hundred-dollar bills.

No!

Yes! Listen, Gurney, my darling cabbage. Let me finish. At this point, Jane smoothly rose from the divan and shifted her bottom onto his lap, entwining a foot around his ankle, bending her arm behind his neck, letting a curtain of shampooed hair fall like rain across his face; though at first he tensed up all over, rigid as steel, at length his muscles seemed to accept that it was more comfortable, more pleasurable, to let themselves blend and blur with the warm relaxed contours of his cousin's enveloping body. Listen. His mind raced, demanding to know if the story was true, all the while knowing it was far-fetched and silly; his mind raced but his tired body made itself at home. His sore hands throbbed. Listen, she repeated quietly, and his thoughts slowed down. Listen to the rest. Jackie peels off three bills for starters, folds them over, and promises to pay the highest price in Poland. Get cold, she orders, indicating Linda's sweater. Linda removes it, then the bra—at which point she's so cold her shoulders go up and her tits stand out. Linda has a funny face but gorgeous tits. Jackie spends more, buys the black boots and brown corduroys, but leaves the socks and underwear. It's about sixty degrees in the chapel, chilly, and goose-pimply Linda, holding all this money now, looks jealously at the cozily clad Jackie, who buys a couple deep kisses, enough to get herself hot and bothered, then reminds Linda that she's a whore, too, and that since it's three o'clock her full price has been paid. So the roles reverse. At Linda's command, Jackie lays down her coat, doffs her cream cashmere turtleneck, unbuttons her jeans, lets them drop, unhooks her bra, lets it drop, and stands above Linda, her pubic mound bumpy and dark beneath her white cotton underpants. They pause for a moment, sobered by the noiselessness of the planet, and look at each other's naked bodies, illuminated by the dim electric lamps of the church. It's about right now that Linda notices the money strewn about the floor and wonders for just an instant if what they're doing is wrong. But who's there to accuse them? Who's there to judge? It's all up to them, and the very thought of being bad excites Linda, incites her to action, prompts her to pick up her stockings and gently blindfold Jackie. She spins her a few times, gets her disoriented, and leads her right on up to the altar. She stops there, admires Jackie's fine bones and her—well, you know her tits, small but shapely. Getting aroused watching her glow by the red devilish altar candles, Linda slides down Jackie's underpants and spreads her hand under her crotch, which in contrast to her prickly shivering thighs is as hot and wet as an underground sulfur bath. Blind Jackie starts making noise. Linda makes her swell and flow. Jackie's legs start to shake.

By this point Gurney had closed his eyes and had let the weight of Jane's body, warm as a furnace, soften him up like iron in a forge. He could not move, nor did he want to, nor had he any desire to interrupt the stream of his cousin's voice, gravelly and mellifluous, recounting a story that suspended his interest in all things factual, all things fictional, all things right or wrong. He was right there, underground, blindfolded, nowhere. He hadn't noticed the featherweight hand on his thigh until it had lifted and moved far upward, settling down open and easy, taking hold of how hard he'd become, and he likewise had no wish to interrupt its lapping, lapping like the edge of a calm deep lake, for this lapping seemed crucial to the story's progression. His pants were unzipped, naked fingers lapped him naked, and he listened:

Jackie's legs start to shake. Linda crouches down, kisses the base of Jackie's belly, the inside of Jackie's hip, passes her nose through the light brown mound of hair, and then, guiding her with a hand on the middle of her back, she bends her blind friend over her shoulder, you know, just like a fireman would. Jackie laughs—but not for long because just as quickly Linda lays her down, right there on the cold salt altar. Jackie yelps and squirms, almost like she was set on a griddle. Not here, she whispers. Right here, Linda says. Not here, she resists, but Linda ignores it, tells her to be a good whore, tells her to give her her money's worth. Jackie whimpers but then she settles down, which of course has nothing to do with a sudden relief from generations of guilt but, instead, owes everything to Linda's upturned nose searching Jackie's private parts, Linda's patient tongue growing more and more impatient until it can't wait a second longer and starts opening up your girlfriend like a sack of stolen treasures!

Again it felt like part of the same story, an illustration maybe, an accompaniment to his rush of pleasure at having Jackie sacrilegiously plopped down on the altar, when her lips brushed casually over his, which her faint tongue loosened ever so artlessly, making the effects of her lapping hand thump like a cello way back in his head. He lifted his sore hand to Jane's small breast, thereby making his own entrance into the story, gliding his hand under the cardigan and over the silk blouse, over the ticklish naked nipple within. Things progressed slowly from there and he enjoyed being cautious, deciphering her body's silent signals. By the time he had eased her onto the divan, beneath the dim lamp, her blouse was open, her eyes were closed, and her lipstick was so smeared around her mouth it looked kind of battered and bruised. He pulled back and looked at her, letting the amber vision of her face and torso, her raised knee and falling houndstooth skirt shimmer with his childhood fantasies of taking hold of his teasing cousin and kissing her, feeling her up, paddling her butt—but the fantasies generally stopped about there. Then and now, the thrill had the same rhubarb custard flavor—but now! Now it was almost real. His erection peered half out of his fly. Her chin lifted and her eyes opened to sly little slits glinting green in the lamplight, and he wondered if she would button herself up, laugh it all off, leave him to masturbate over the snowy city lights, but her hand went to her knee, pulled back her skirt, fell to her crotch, its fingers stroking the turgid black cotton. He took this as permission to touch himself, long distracted bowstrokes from bottom to top, and she did the same, sliding her fingers beneath the fabric, drifting the other hand over her breasts, releasing all sense of composure with one long rattly Janely groan.

What should we do now? she asked.

Huh?

Tell me what to do.

You tell me.

You're the man in this. Give orders.

Take all your clothes off.

It's cold in here!

So was the cathedral.

But that was a story, she said.

So is this.

She smiled approvingly, as if he were catching on. Here, he said, flinging off his shirt and shedding his trousers, I'll go first. Now you. He watched closely as she tossed aside her blouse and sweater, as she raised her knees and pulled her underpants over her rump, showing him her crotch, bushy for the winter season.

He unhooked her skirt, slipped it off.

The stockings stay on, she playfully grumbled, getting on her knees. Now tell me to give you head.

He paused. Give me head, he said obediently.

My pleasure.

Above him the dark ceiling was cracked. To the left clothes and slippers littered the carpet. To the right snowflakes caught on the glass, blurring the blue green red yellow lights of the main square. The world zigzagged. But then it stopped, and he felt the sensation of a non-believer who suddenly finds himself walking on water—resistance, distrust, confusion, dread, the enjoyable threat that his feet will fall through and he'll drown and disappear in a bottomless lake. She was very good at this. He had a sense that slick fingers were helping her mouth, giving the illusion of an impossibly deep throat, but he couldn't be sure. He couldn't hold a thought. Afraid to groan, he let out a chirp and passed half-feeling hands through the waves of her hair, brushing her ear, touching the downy sides of her face, touching the pulselike movement in the hollows of her cheeks. His fingers trembled there. But no, he couldn't resist touching the smooth base of his cock and heavens no! tracing it to that consummate rim where Jane's wet lips were closing over him. Jane's mouth! It was all around him, sliding from the head nearly all the way to the bottom, and she was letting him touch! Jane's mouth had a history, an inviolability, that over the years had grown more pristine with every simple kiss, with every public or private story, every long-distance telephone call; Jane's mouth, like Jane's quick wink, drew Gurney in close at the very same moment it pushed him away, but here it was now, dragging long on him, nearly swallowing him, consuming him, banishing him from the face of the earth.

But then she stopped, causing him to half-buckle with desire. She said nothing but held his eyes with hers and fell back on the divan, spreading her stockinged legs, running two fingers through her slaking pool. He watched. She watched. They stopped touching themselves and waited. It was up to him. So now he, in turn, fell to his knees and ran his nose along the fine wool stocking, lingering to kiss the white skin above the hem before placing his face directly between her legs. Jane smelled a bit muskier than Jackie, tasted more savory, less lemony, and unlike Gurney she freely voiced her pleasure, letting him know when he finally got it right. So at first he felt inadequate, amateurish, coughing up hairs that got caught in his throat, but the more Jane moaned and spoke in affirmation, and the more she flowed over his mouth and chin, then the more bold and masterful he felt, cleaving his tongue inside and out, working himself with his sore right hand, teasing the two of them just to the brink before he, too, stopped, fragile, and pulled himself back.

Well? she said.

Well?

Fuck me, silly. Fuck me silly.

Let me get a condom.

What? Fuck me. You're covered.

What about the . . . risks?

No condom's gonna touch our risks, silly. Fuck me.

And so he would fuck her, but not until his delicious horny fears had subsided some, not until he had of course regained some control. Jane waited, dilating there, while Gurney kneeled on the divan, hands to his sides, elephant cock upright, letting the chilly room give way to rising waters of oblivion, waters that blotted out all the people, places, and things that would make guiding himself into his cousin, which he gradually began doing, nonbelieving, which gliding was preternaturally warm, whose arms and hands were yes hot and guiding him in, guiding him in, whose rocking hips gave and took, and vice versa, vice versa, came and went, were successfully blotted out the deeper they rocked, back and forth, kissing cousins, fucking now, rocking like oil-well drillers on western highways, her saying my cousin, him seeing oil-well drillers, her saying her birthday, her saying fuck me my cousin, hush, fuck me I'm coming my brother, fuck me, fuck your sister, her father, her brother, fuck me, fuck us, fuck us all—

He pulled out, ejaculating on her belly, her breast, her hair, the cushion. He looked at the mess, avoided her eyes, and sat on the edge of the divan with his feet on the floor. He started to laugh, but felt fake and stopped. He dreaded hearing her voice, but she said nothing. She reached out for one of his socks on the floor and, sighing, used it to clean up his mess, quietly cursing the bit of it in her hair. She gathered her clothes and carried them to the bathroom, naked but for her falling stockings. The sky was orange, full of snow. Tiny lights glowed on the shadowy stereo and, not noticeable until now, tiny voices spoke in Polish. He supposed there was a lot he wanted to ask her, much he wanted to tell her, but now he well knew the valves had slammed shut, all chances for talking had been foreclosed. Jane was like that: when she wanted the last word, it was hers. For some reason he wanted to mention Dick Chesnutt, to see her reaction, see what she knew, but as he pulled on his shorts and undershirt he knew this fact was his alone, that the walleyed ghost was there in the room and was his alone, sitting, watching.

When she returned to the room both of them had dressed. She gathered books and winter clothes, and he stood by the window, pretending to ignore her when she announced that she was late for her night class and wouldn't return until after eleven. But in fact he took careful note of this, glancing at his watch as she closed the door behind her. He stayed by the window. He watched his cousin walk a straight trajectory from the door of their building, across the whitening flagstones, through the thinning crowd, toward the far corner of the Rynek, where the university rose in shiplike shapes behind the sulking Pałać Baranami. Halfway there her image shimmered and disappeared, but he kept on looking, giving her ample time to turn back, cooling the coils of wire-hot fury that hummed in the murk of his postcoital stupor. For he had to be smart now, had to make himself see clearly now. Banish chance, irony, pleasure, duty, anger, fate, fear. Draw back the dusty layers of curtains he'd hung over his towering outside windows, over his sunken inside closets. And no guilt. No superstition. No, he could not fancy the thought that it was not himself but instead the perturbed spirit in the room that tempted him to open those holy portfolios and read his cousin in all her candor. For it was in his control, and his reasons were well beyond curiosity now. He had need. Stifled inside the buried coffin of her stories, he had need to burrow free and read it just as she put it down for herself. Something in Jane's manner, her brazen nudity in the garden of snakes, made it seem as if she were always out in the open air, and he admired this, feared this, hated this, and he attributed it, enviously, to some sort of honesty and clarity of self. Better than knowing his own secrets, Jackie's secrets, everyone's secrets, Jane knew her own, knew herself, and fuck it all he would too.

Zbigniew's studio had at last been sanctified, an incestuous temple. This thought made him laugh. He'd been forbidden to see Jackie anymore—but would the old man approve of this evening's alternative? He cracked his neck, wiped off his palms, and went over to the crooked stack of portfolios. No longer treating it like a tabernacle, he thumbed through the folders with aching hands, found the black hardbound book, and took it back to the rumpled divan, where he plopped himself down beside the bottle of cognac.

Fifteen

❖THE LETTER A, DEAR EAVESDROPPER, may very well stand for the hordes of Animals and packs of Arseholes who've arrived in Vienna with Zbiszek and me—Angry Alpens with overlarge Appetites, Aardvark Artlovers glimpsing around and slipping slim tongues into every last Klimthole. Indeed, the letter A, which is everywhere, might as well stand for Österreich, but it doesn't. On this blackened afternoon, as we clink our cognac to the hair-raising oompahs of Bozo the Clown's Grand Prize Game, the letter A, lacking none of its fullness as the golden-arched Alpha of our western world, stands for A Sewer. For History, as I explain to my grumpy Polish pumpkin who stormily glooms over the fine black jacket that I insist he wear when attending my class reunion tonight, is nothing if not just that, A Sewer. Forgive me if I'm a little drunk. I am. But let me explain. Let me plumb the muddy depths of this matter. True, who can think of a sewer in a place so flash as this? In a baroque salon, so bright and modern with halogen bulbs, so airy to the ceiling with crystalline windows past which stroll pedestrians so delicate, so well heeled that one imagines them capable of going neither number one nor—perish the thought!—number two. In a place such as this, who thinks of a sewer? Me, I do, and much to Zbiszek's chagrin.

Just two blocks from here, nestled in the crotch of three proud commercial streets, some archaelogical expedition has opened a great hole in the unsuspecting pavement (this is true!) and has—exposed? unplugged? disemboweled?—extirpated a two-thousand-year-old secret from the deep urban dirt, the Pompeiio-Roman ruins of a different kind of city. A sewer city! An hour ago we stood there at the rail and looked past the lips of this asphalt wound into the sandstone entrails below—ancient rooms, ancient corridors, stairways leading nowhere at all—but almost right away Zbigniew turned around, wanting to retreat into the scrubbed nostalgia of something like this imperial café. I've humored him, of course, and so here we are at Café Sperl, but I will not keep quiet, for I think I know why this vision of a sewer shakes him at his very foundation. Watch him: He smokes. He smirks. He's adorable in that jacket—flawless lines, shimmer of worsted—it suits him. I kiss him, but despite all of this squirming and collar tugging I embark on a discussion of the profanities and slop he's tried to abandon upon entering Vienna—a city so unlike, say, Berlin—for Vienna, to look at it, is a ready-made museum. It looks just like History's supposed to look!

But I remind him: Historical Memory, especially in Vienna, which suffers from its keen obsession with *retention,* is hopelessly stuck in the anal stage. (I steal these terms from this very same psychoanalopolis.) But the poor mortal sphincter can only hold so much! Frightful quantities are flushed away—not into oblivion, and not into, say, the Mind of Europe, unless that's the name you wish to wipe off and assign to those kilometers of tubes and valves that grumble and squirt under the avenues of our beautiful bilious capital cities. No, the good part of History is all backed up, right beneath our feet, in the septic tanks of the here and now, and watch your step because it's ready to blow!

Why do I tell him this? Because, for one thing, I can see the poor drudge is being smothered under his reverence for power. He hates himself for loving Vienna—its immaculate streetcars, its neoclassical whiteness, its pencil-drawn men in Tyrolean hats walking their dachshunds through a Smithsonian sewer that's been swabbed of excrement and given a Windex shine. He hates himself for missing the boat that he trusts would have led him out of the sewer and into the channels of the blue Danube. And he hates his admiration for the Viennese ladies who walk their Chanel past the window, no prettier than Grazyna, no more aristocratic, but looking like they've never really given up their feces, bottling up generations of the stuff, holding it back out of respect for the sewer, allowing their pearly bottoms to leak but fine streams of Gewürztraminer and consommé into cold white porcelain bowls. He looks strangled, sitting there, ordering more cognacs with his two pudgy fingers, and so I tell him all of this because, for two, I think it might just throw him a line, save him from drowning in this unplumbable mess. I say something like: Blame not Kraków for going to the Twentieth-Century dogs, for going to seed after the Austrians moved out. Beneath every Vienna is a crappy old Kraków, so give it all up, and as I say this just now I scratch his furry jaw, smudge a kiss on his alcoholic mouth, and at least that gets a little rise out of him.

Anyway. Here's the facts. At forty-four years of age, Zbigniew Zamoyski, former professor and Communist loyalist, has come to Vienna on the eve of becoming a very rich man. Having secured a small fortune (approximately $260,000) through safe investments in Polish steel (his area of expertise), he has reluctantly taken the advice of his girlfriend (me) whose college comrade (and amorous attraction) may this very evening take him on as a junior investor in her brilliantly successful new business venture, the Kasino Kraków. The irony is, of course, that second only to speculation itself, the Kasino is for Zbigniew the most supremely evil temptress of the Western World, a strumpet he'd managed to icily snub until having the good fortune of making my acquaintance! Thus you can imagine his reluctance today, and you must admire my powers of persuasion. As I said, poor guy! Anyway, simple pleasure notwithstanding, this, my dear, is why we're here.❖

At this point Gurney looked up from his reading. A line of dim light was coming under the door. Grazyna and Wanda were talking in the kitchen. He sighed and took a drink and quickly found his place in Jane's thick black handwriting.

❖To conclude this brief session, let me mention why I'm letting you in on all this. It's didactic. It's a heuristic. If History's a sewer, and it is, I would advise Zbigniew, though he's a nervous little neophyte in the world of speculation and risk, to take your example and live gluttonously in the moment, to note how for you the moment's a French repast, the mad prelude to a Roman vomitorium, a feast to be devoured with relish and rapacity and no thought of the two tasteless ways to discard it (bucket or toilet—and I'll make this quick because I, too, have to use the loo!). Zbigniew wants to have his cake and have his cake. And if he didn't hate you so completely, I'd think to use you as a fine example since tonight we're off to just such a feast (you'd be a real success with these jokers!) but as it stands, it simply wouldn't persuade him. Now for *your* object lesson, and then I can go pee: Beware that septic explosion which as I warned you will surge from even the safest, whitest sidewalks. Walk swiftly, wear rubbers, and what fun you'll❖

October 16, 1990

❖Back at the hotel, one in the morning, Zbigniew sleeps, a spent bear, innocent of the remorse that awaits him when he wakes. I'm still up, sharp as a tack after coffee and dessert, almost sober enough to begin nursing my headache. I could fritter away your precious time, ticking off the luxuries of this Art-Nouveau-Riche boudoir—this dressing table's sleek bonetone Hoffman contours, that stickstraight pseudo-Moser high-backed sofa, the butterlike light sliding lilaclike down slick Loos-like walltiles—but that's not what you're reading for, and what a story I have to tell! Listen to this. By the time we reached the restaurant, half an hour late, Zbigniew and I were thoroughly wazzed. He was gnawing on a Montecristo, chugging out smoke like Spenser's dragon, and I was fumbling through my purse for a Certs. The maître d' fingered us right away and allowed us no time to compose ourselves before he whisked us away to the company of seven whose fourteen eyebrows were raised in alarm. Were we all right?

Had there been an accident? Yes, no, blah, blah, and we were seated opposite each other at the end of the table. The fois gras appeared and the conversation stopped, pausing to oilily recalibrate its engines from Viennese German to that clunky lingua franca with which I will continue to narrate this story. On Zbiszek's side sat two speculators with wives, on mine sat the toady Kasino manager and a gaunt gray ectomorphic lawyer. At the head of it all, looking lavish in her purple silk frock, sat the cosmopolitan Amazonian Eulalia, the chief stockholder, the handsome but ferocious mistress of ceremonies whom I hadn't seen in more than two years. I could tell straightaway that avarice becomes her—just as rage and envy become Zbigniew, just as lechery and self-hatred became our last eavesdropper, just as gluttony and sloth become you. Even though we exchanged just a polite hello, it was mutually charged, hot as a horsewhip, horny as a hummingbird vibrating there amid all the flowers left unsucked during the years of letters, faxes, and transatlantic phone calls.

Don't get me wrong. She isn't beautiful in any traditional way—her features are balanced but roughly hewn, her left eye's visibly larger than the right, but the excessive animus that glows like coals from her indulgent lips, her D-cup tits, her mighty arms, her steely legs, this singular heat had drawn me to her, slobberingly, witlessly, for the duration of my last long Hyde Park winter. In fact, back then, I dashed into that fire like a lovelorn moth, and not until I was scorched and tattered, not until I'd dumped a very nice girl, flunked three classes, sheered my sheepshead, even slept in my piss under the icy El tracks, not, that is, until I was nearly ruined, did I feel I had sacrificed enough to her excesses. I concluded that my only recourse, with a Slavic degree, was to move to Europe and on the double. At the time, Eulalia was a graduate student, getting her MBA up in Evanston, so she had to let me go, but her ravenously maternal spirit impelled her to help me out—finding me jobs, contacting friends, pointing out enemies, advising me that Linda was always good sport. And so even in my travels I've remained in her debt and always under her surveillance. (Never trust Linda, by the way, in case you haven't figured that out yet.)

You wonder now why I've never told you about Eulalia, why I've never confided in you. Simple: because Eulalia, like everything else you find scrawled in this book, is now, and ever shall be, none of your business.

Anyway, please feel free to judge me for this, but sometimes I do enjoy being her slave, and I'll admit tonight was one of those times. Tonight she was the portrait of benign mastery, and all of the table's attention, all but Zbiszek's, sloped in her direction with all the will of an avalanche. In spite of ourselves, we let her softly chatter ad nauseum about her new Land Rover (how brutally it handles the twisty roads of Crete!), about her designs on a villa in Upper Carinthia (how its trashy pink marble just has to go!), about everything but that one thing for which we buzzed around like bees—her budding orchid, the airtight Kasino.

I regret to say Zbigniew was a pill from the start. Unable to give up his damned habano, he sucked it like an infant through the truffles and soup, urging wrinkled noses and drumming fingers and the choicest looks from Frau Brunwald, a peacock lady to his immediate left. I assure you (and would have assured *her*) that he was raised exceedingly well, in true Zamoyski form, a little lord groomed for the *nomenklatura,* but that all his good breeding foams up like baking soda when mixed with liquor and red-faced vinegar. Not wishing to stir the cocktail any further, not wishing to pique my leopardlike Eulalia, I massaged his big ego with saucy smiles and managed to subdue his terrible pissiness. I went so far as to pose questions which concerned neither the opera nor the new fall fashion but which led us out of the city and on a sleepy safari through Z's favorite industrial wilderness—Austrian steel. But still he just sat there, benignly smoldering in the back of the tour bus, once chiming in with a weak opinion of something he called powder metallurgy. I was grateful to see him drifting off to sleep, but then just as quickly he was roused from his slumber by some grunting coming from Eulalia's toady (the Kasino manager—Herr Justus Messersturm).

The grunting was pointed across the table at the taller of the two speculators, a shrewd gentleman with a fluffy mustache who had stodgy concerns about the Kasino's security, but soon it ballooned into a stormy treatise coughed up for the benefit of the entire party. Abysmal English aside, the grunting went something like: "Perhaps you are afraid that one single gambler could, as you say, get lucky, *very* lucky, and walk away with your beautiful house, your wife's jewels, your children's future. This is a normal fear. But I tell you to have no fear. Only you, the investor, shall be lucky. I have known casinos the world over, and they are the very best of investments. It is the fundamental nature of the poor class and the middle class to freely spend ninety dollars, to freely spend one hundred and ninety dollars, with the hope of winning five. But I tell you, I promise you, I have never seen a people with more hope and less luck than those living and gambling in Poland. It is a winning combination, and that is a certainty. A Catholic casino, I promise you, *mein Liebling,* is one of this world's rarest treasures!"

Though he was obliged to scoff at the toady's chauvinism, the speculator presently loosened his posture and as if convinced that he'd already turned a profit, resumed with vigor his bright carrot soup. I couldn't look at Eulalia, who should have been ashamed but probably wasn't. I kept my eyes on Zbigniew, who, in the plump silence that followed, smashed out his cigar on his truffle plate. Wives recoiled. He got the attention of the entire table, a full minute of nervous recognition that allowed him time to toss off another glass, madly tug the chin of his beard, and, heaven forbid, rise from his seat! Now, before I recount his peregrinations around the table (which at length brought him to rest behind Herr Messersturm's chair), let me show you an adoring but less flattering portrait of the man I've known over the past couple of seasons.

Zbigniew Zamoyski, left to his devices, is nothing more than a sweaty little boy—see him there conked out in the damp fluffy bedclothes! This boyishness explains the whole of his character. To watch him now, clasped to the pillow as if to his potato-mashing mother, pinching his pee-pee as if in fear of his belt-whipping father, to watch him now, or whenever his guard's down, one would think he'd be just as well taking naps after lunch and playing with trucks in quick-snap knee pants. They're dead (his parents), but he's all the worse for that, because now that they're freed from their bedwetting bodies they've become two huge horrible monsters in his head, pathetic giants stomping around town like the ghosts of Poland's two sorest losers: Aristocracy and Communism. His mother rumbles in the hills, cathedral bells, castle walls; his father groans in the broken factories and corroded university towers—and all around their invisible feet, shuttling his useless little sack of beans, scampers the tiny boy Zbigniew. What beans? Why, the charmless beans of his inheritance—now hoarded, now planted, now put to market at closing time when really the best he could do with them would be to take them home, stew them up in a pot of chili, suffer the inevitable bellyache, then finally and forever let them go into that nether Sewer of his parentage. I've told him time and again that these days nobody but nobody buys, let alone climbs, those phantasmatic beanstalks! And I do believe it's dawning on him. But the man needs clarity. He needs power. Go ahead and judge me, you dog, judge me for helping him win back the clarity and win back the power that this century has wrested from his rightful clutches, curse me, cur, for leading this wide-eyed kid into a pit of speculators and bullies, but how else was he going to learn? I think he is learning. Tonight he tried to stick up for himself. Tonight he fell and skinned both knees, but I think he learned something along the way:

Standing there behind Herr Messersturm's chair, the loyal son took aim with his silly B.B. gun. Aim at whom? At all of us, even me. He fired: "Bastards! Orphans! Illegitimate world-class pickpockets! Let me be the first to admit I am no economist, I am no Nobel-laureate game theorist from the University of Chicago. *Jestem Polak*. I am a Polack. For what you know, I'm a superstitious Catholic blacksmith feeding my money to your reptilian Kasino. Fair enough. Let me be the first to admit that I have no clout at this gathering of thieves, I have no voice but that my money talks. But for this one reason, my money, all of you will listen. All of you will politely listen while I roundly insult you and, at the same time, press upon you my naive little theory of what must rightly be called orphan economics, orphan ethics. You will listen not because you yourselves are bastards, thieves, and orphans, and thus take personal stock in my theories. No, you will listen because you respect my money. You want my money. So I will be blunt. You are dressed beautifully. You look like prostitutes. You look like pimps. I, too, look like a pimp. And our hostess, right here next to her huffing rhinoceros, she looks like a posturing Louisiana debutante. Tonight in Vienna, we are gorgeous. We are wealthy. We are homeless. I can explain.

"You people have been raised by wolves, you've been reared by luck and schooled by greed in a social and political and economic wilderness. I will illuminate this point, and I will do so by posing two easy questions that will reveal you for the lonely orphans that you are: Where are your bloodlines? What is your ideology? Nowhere. Nothing. Look at you whores—you don't know! You have no beliefs, only drives. You are bound by neither blood nor nation. Your sluttish computers make faceless, voiceless, soulless connections, while you yourselves curry favors and make crackling promises on rented cordless telephones. You are like nameless little street urchins, passing off secret packages of drugs and contraband. You have no people, no family, no father, no patronym. You make suspicious friendships like we're making here tonight, and here, of all places, is where you get your sense of worth. Do we have an understanding? Do you get my meaning? Well, then, let us proceed."

Of course you can imagine the shock and mortification that followed. All during Z's ranting and raving, Frau Brunwald sat shaking, her eyes pinched up, a handkerchief pressed to her trembling lips. The speculators were stony, their faces frozen in twisted sneers— the lawyer was ready to pounce, the toady itching to swing himself around. The waiter whisked past with the entrée, but upon seeing Zbigniew snarling at the lot of us he irritably swept it back into the kitchen. In fact, of all people, Eulalia was the only one showing no visible indignation. Sympathy, maybe. And fascination. From where I sat, it looked as if she were trying to catch every word, as if she really *were* an orphan and what he was babbling were the gospel truth. Anyway, knowing Zbiszek as well as I do, I wasn't really surprised by his rakish behavior and stodgy ideas, but I was fully shocked by what happened next:

"Well, then, let us proceed," he said, reaching into his jacket pocket and producing his checkbook. He stood there for a minute, his eyes far away as if he were pissing, the anger all but drained from his face. He began to look boyish as only Zbigniew can. "I myself am an orphan. Much as I dread it, I understand you people. To be honest, I even lived in California for a time, in Palo Alto, on the edge of what they call the Silicon Valley, and that was where I truly learned the way things work. I learned by experience, by appetite, by my will to survive, just like any other orphan would. I will tell you what I learned. It is this. We do not live in an Ice Age, or a Stone Age, or an Iron Age, or a Golden Age. None of that. Nothing is solid. Nothing stays. There is nothing of value, nothing in the bank, and I regret that we must abandon such folly. We write checks and sign contracts, but this is no Age of Paper. We fuck with latex and swipe credit cards, but still this is no Age of Plastic. What I learned in California, and in airports around the world, is that we are a privileged race of frequent fliers, we drive on high-speed tires, we tuck ourselves in behind dual airbags, we walk on Nike Air, we talk on cellular phones, we fall asleep to satellite television. We spend numbers that are as empty as the souls of toy balloons. We live, therefore, in an Age of Air. Isn't that beautiful? It makes you feel buoyant. Ah! Here in Vienna, far from the Silesian smog that Jane and I call home, Air is a clean and simple idea, pure as the air we breathe, sure as the air we touch. Air touch! Air talk! An Air Age! Beautiful. Tonight I am prepared to enter the air, enter the Air Age, throw my fortune and caution to the wind. But oh, if only, if only—" His voice trailed off and he began to gaze—not into the empty plates and stemware but rather, as it appeared, directly into the fickle air floating over them. "If only—if only we could eat it! At home—what we call air at home is really so thick we slurp it like soup, and we do, bowls and bowls of hot black poison, when just a spoonful could kill a rat dead. But here, the air! Here, air! Austrian air! Here, sex isn't dirty.

Air slides its way with the speed of a snake, shining the aluminum contours of bodies, splitting the creases and loosening the gaps, slipping
like rainwater, sliding like fish, and just as clean, every bit as clean. Sex
isn't fucking here. It's clean. It's sterile. I'm not thirsty, mind you, but
I want it. Air so clean we know we can't drink it, air so thin we know
we can't eat it, but we want it. We want it, yes, yes, yes, we do . . . but
enough talking! You know my position. I shall proceed."

And then he reached into his pocket, uncapped a mashed-up felt-
tip pen, and after pausing to ask for the name of the wind tunnel that
would receive his shredded fortune-in-steel (his metaphor), pro-
ceeded to write out a sloppy, smeary check for the amount of two hundred thousand dollars. From where I sat, his signature looked like a
flattened blackbird. And then he left. I stayed on, polite and embarrassed, holding my peace as we hurried through dinner. Then, after
arranging to meet an unflustered Eulalia at four o'clock tomorrow afternoon, I gave my regards to each individual face and discreetly
bowed away from the table.

Zbigniew Zamoyski, thief and orphan, having invested a fortune
in a terrific quantity of absolutely nothing, went out into the cold Vienna air. One thing comforts me: he has finally released his secret self,
that insidious mole of a speculator soul which I'm sure has been
buried in there since childhood. His secret self, the shifty-eyed capitalist, emerged tonight from the Sewer of History. But what, my
dumb luscious, does he have to teach us? What do we have to learn?
Must we, too, cross our furthest limits? Must we, too, betray our
blood? You, yourself, have invested everything in nothing, nothing
which might yield something, and yet nothing which will probably
bring you nothing. But have you exhumed your secret self? Have you?
As for me, you know, it's not in my nature to learn lessons. It's more
like me to cherish my regrets.❖

October 17, 1990

❖I want you to see Eulalia through the eyes of Egon Schiele—
maybe because we're still here in his city, but also because I remember her naked body like that, with its prickly lines and jagged muscles,
its skin bursting with Crayola colors, its bruised painterly fruit. But
her clothes stayed on this afternoon. We didn't even touch. Her in an
armchair, me on the rug, flat four o'clock light, no colors. She refused
to rip up the check without Zbiszek's permission—a matter of honor,
she said, not greed. She said she liked and respected him, said that he
would be good for me, but he did remind her of that strange little man
both of us know who has a fallen chin and who dropped out of school
because the faculty refused his dissertation topic. Semen and economics. He's still at it, she said. He still theorizes the porn industry's
money shot, the family industry's sperm banks, the health industry's
condom companies, the reckless father's support check—he keeps
theorizing theories of surplus and waste, fertility and conservation,
ecstasy and debt, an unfocused project with no one's benediction, but
still he keeps at it. A good little wanker, she said. But money's not in
theory, she said, money's in action. Sure, she supposed, a casino is like
a penis. A casino, a penis, two hip-shot tools of risk and play. A casino
is a penis, and money is spunk, et cetera, et cetera. She went on and
on, but I must admit I started zoning out.

I watched her talking there, and well before she got disdainful
about penises and casinos, I could see how she was starting to harden
toward me—hard jaw, hard brow. I felt she was mocking me, but I
didn't know why or how, and then as if reading my mind she made
herself plain: "What is it about penises, Jane? What is it about men?
You're all about men these days. Does a good stiff penis make you feel
secure? Zbigniew, for example, is a plump little man, with a plump little cigar—now, does all that change when you've got him up? Does he
drain all the life out of you, out of everything, just so he can pump
himself up? I have to wonder." Her voice softened. "You're lifeless
these days, honey. You're flaccid. Is it the penises? Is that what it is?"

She wasn't looking for an answer, of course—it was clear she wanted nothing to do with me. But she must know that if men are really about security, then she herself is truly the man, she is the one who has the penis. She knows that all my men are hazardous, and she was mocking me for it. I wanted to lie with my head between her legs—she knew this. I wanted to sleep there, sleep it all off, but instead I got up on my knees and, bravely inhaling, changed the subject: "I have a cousin visiting me who needs a job." "Does this cousin have a penis?" "I presume so." "Then I presume you want him to work at the Kasino." "Can you make a place for him?" "Should I fire your man with the screwed-up eyes?" "Please don't." "Your man named Dick?" "Please don't." "Please don't." "Please don't mock me." "What's his size?" "Big and tall." "There's a change." "Please, he's my cousin." "Write down the details—arms, chest, waist, neck. I'll tell them to have it ready tomorrow." Then she walked off to make a phone call.

I want you to see her through the eyes of Egon Schiele. Not through my eyes, not as I saw her this afternoon through scratched-up lenses and October clothes, not through the static of erotic debts and dollar signs. See her in the winter of Egon Schiele, sketched on the nappy canvas of the past, and then you'll get it, then you'll see Eulalia qua Eulalia, cold and warm, cold and naked with pinched black nipples. What will you get? What will you see? Not her, but me. Over and over, you'll see the same senseless thing: a naked woman, sheets thrown off, radiator knocking, open window whistling, Chicago's bricks crunching with frost, all the Great Lakes stuck frozen together, and a woman lying there with the sheets thrown off. I know you don't speak German. Can you pronounce it? You have to pronounce it, to get the joke. Schiele. It's pronounced Sheila. Exactly like that. Now say it aloud. Repeat it: Egon Schiele. Egon Schiele. A gone Sheila.❖

October 25, 1990

❖We're alone, Eavesdropper, in the Ojców Valley. Zbigniew's pants are all in a bundle because the Kasino's already getting him rich (so I've sent him out to gather kindling), and you are finally getting a place in the world, having been working three good days now.

The sky is gray. The grass is green. The wind is full of red-black leaves. I've never felt so at home in Poland.❖

October 31, 1990

❖Wednesday morning. What is wrong with me? Why is it that, when Zbigniew and I are finally getting it down, I have to make trouble? One explanation might be that it's Halloween tonight. Or that I'm an inexorable bitch. Or that I'm hopelessly jealous. But never mind why—merely take for an example what happened this morning, before sunrise, as I was sponging him down in his steamy bathtub, lathering behind his pink little ears, slipping his sleepy prick through my fingers. I started off giving him instructions for the day (that he go shopping for a powerful German car, a powerful notebook, a powerful bank in Geneva or Bonn), instructions from which at first he shrank, loath to accept that he's suddenly rich, but instructions which he came to accept, much as he came to accept my fingers, lightly sliding, as they did, under his scrotum, fanning out to spread his thighs, one of them coming to rest its tip on the quivering mouth of his underwater anus—his anus which constricted, then heavingly loosened, then cleverly drew my finger inside to feel its small red angry pulse.

Zbigniew's arsehole has always made me jealous. For all the times I've massaged it with my—well, etc.—I've always known I was an intruder there. Not that he doesn't want me there—no, quite the opposite, he always guides me there, and I go there just to please him—but when I'm there I know he's not thinking of me. Early on between us, when all the stories were fun and free, he made the mistake of telling me about Jackie Witherspoon, how on the same day he first met her out on the Planty, after wooing the undergraduate all day with his nonsense, after flattering her with dinner at the Staropolska, they hired a dingy room, where, before they'd drawn the curtains, before they'd even kissed, Jackie opened his trousers, turned him around, bent him over the edge of the bed, and orally introduced herself to his nervous little arsehole. Such profanity, can you believe it? Why must Zbigniew keep whining and moaning that fucking her was such a sacred thing? What did she do to fool him? What can I possibly do differently? And how on earth could sex, that most base pleasure, be exalted to the sacred? Anyway, he made the mistake of telling me that Jackie's naughty surprise always put her in charge of their love affair, and so while I know I can master him with a digit up the bum, and times like this morning that's just what I do, it infuriates me, it humiliates me, to play the role of that sassy tart. I know why she liked it: one slip of the digit and the tyrant turns to clay, and you should know how it thrills me when my men are clay.

Now I've got Lazarus just where I want him, engorging, pulsing, shuddering, and I've convinced him how to begin squandering his fortune, but still I'm all heartless and mean with jealousy. Why, Jane? And why, if I'm so mean, do I lean over the rim and start giving him head, his ass getting tighter as his cock gets harder? Because then I can stop, ease my fingers free, and pause to remind him about Wanda's gift, a Discman we bought for her in Vienna. "Give it to her today," I say. "Stop putting it off." He grumbles, but I guide his warm wet hand into my robe, over my hip, between my legs. I throw off the robe and kneel down in the hot water, laying my head on his shoulder, my belly on his erection—I know he likes this, I know it comforts him. Softly as I can, I ask, "Do you think she's still a virgin?" I look at his face. There's misery in his eyes. It seems, for a moment, that this misery is enough for me. I lay my head back down. Riding him with my belly, listening to the roof groaning in the wind, I take charge once more with Jackie's naughty surprise. His whole body gives in. "You know you couldn't really blame her if she weren't one, unless you were to blame me, too. I was fifteen, you know, when I. . . . How old is she?" He starts going soft against me, but I slide another finger inside, I go deeper, where the walls are smooth and slippery like Jell-O, and like magic he gets hard again. He throws his head to both sides, like he wants me to go away, but his pelvis rises to meet me. "Is she seventeen already? When I was fifteen, as you can imagine, I was a bad little Lolita, and I threw my ballet teacher Sven into quite a state—I sat on his lap, I rode on his shoulders, I acted half my age, and very quickly it got out of control, out of my control. When it happened one day that he laid me after rehearsal, laid me, that is, with my childish consent, well then it was me, as you can imagine, it was me who was thrown into an awful state." He winces, he's listening. "I was ruined by it. I didn't catch anything or get knocked up or get abandoned by my friends, but I was ruined for anyone but men like you, old men, the only kind I've ever had. So here I am." This last bit, which I swear is true, gets no apparent reaction. I pull out, rise to my knees, and tenderly start to stroke him, holding him against my crotch, as if I were actually stroking myself.

I spoke throatily: "Boys my age made me feel dirty, only men made me feel sexy." It wasn't really relevant to mention the women I had been with—those affairs are about love, less about sex, and they have nothing to do with what I was getting at just now. And as I stroked him I was discovering that I had an agenda. Balanced midair above the sharp rocks of cruelty, the turbulent waters of intimacy, I just kept walking, my eye on the wire: "Dick Chesnutt, now he's almost as old as you. Almost. He made me feel sexy. He used to call me his crazy, amazing little fizgig, and somehow that made being young taste like a fistful of licorice whips, and it made me feel famous. He always came off seeming so dashing (especially for his walleye, strangely enough) that at first I couldn't feel young or famous enough to please him. Then it became clear that I wasn't young enough, couldn't be famous enough, because he started to compare me, a twenty-four-year-old college graduate, with this pubescent girl he gave guitar lessons to." Zbigniew grabbed my wrist, wanting me to stop stroking, but I resisted him and tried to finish my story. "Shhh," I said. "I know what you're thinking, and you're right. You're right. He wanted me to be Wanda. He wanted me to be your daughter. And I hated him for it." Zbigniew's reaction? Very strange. He wrested my fingers from his cock, roughly dragged me out of the tub, and plop! dropped me down, elbows and knees smack! on the tiles. (I have the bruises to show.) Then he soaked in silence, veins in his head thumping like drums, eyes in their sockets gray as ice chips. Rubbing my knees, I shrilly filled that silence: "I hated him for it. Filthy pedophile. Spoiled rotten old man. I wanted to choke his chicken-bone neck. But you know me, I didn't let him know. I teased him about it. I made him blush. I teased him about Wanda's dimpled little arms, her pouty little mouth, her blooming little boobs, and I tweaked his cheek until he squirmed, which I know turned him on because it made me into a naughty! naughty! naughty! little thing. Oh, I was naughty, honey, I was terrible, because I needed to know too badly. I needed to know if anything'd really happened. So I got him to trust me. I made it into a game. I'm sorry, sweetheart, I'm sorry, but I really wanted to know—and out of jealousy, I didn't even really care about your little girl. I didn't even know her then. But I did find out."

Poor, pale Zbigniew. Why do I do these things? He just floated there, unspent, beyond rescuing now. Short of breath, he croaked in Polish: "What did you find out?"

"I can't tell you," I said. But he just floated there, dead, knowing that I would tell him, since I always finish my stories. "Dick Chesnutt," I told him at length, "is a very needy man. He's not a kid anymore, and this kills him—first because nobody wants to cuddle a forty-year-old man, and second because he's made all the wrong decisions in life and now here he is, nowhere. But I did cuddle him, and I made him think his life was full of possibility, and so he trusted me. Then one day, when I had him at my mercy, I told him the story of Sven, the ballet cad, but I made this one crucial revision: I made Sven out to be my hero, a svelt thirtysomething magician who'd created me out of nothing with a wave of his wand, who'd given me poise, given me charm, and had turned this milky little pupa of a girl into a flapping purple-black moth of a woman. Ridiculous Dick Chesnutt enviously listened. He wanted to be my Sven. He wanted me to think that he was a magician. So he humbly looked down into his vodka, swirled it around in the glass, and quietly said: 'I think I've had just such an affect on Wanda.' 'Flimflam!' I said. 'But I do, I am, she's starting to shine.' 'What made me shine,' I reminded him, 'had nothing to do with bar exercises and pirouettes. It was the sex!' 'I know, I know, I know.' 'So are you having sex with the girl? Are you educating her?' 'Well . . .' he said"—but maliciously, so maliciously, I dragged this part out. I watched the foam go dry and pocky in the rivers of Zbigniew's beard. "'She's taken to me in a most interesting way.' 'Interesting how?' 'Affectionate.' 'Affectionate how?' 'Infatuated.' 'Ah! What do you plan to do about it? What have you done?' 'Not so fast,' he said. 'It's delicate. It's frightening. She adores my hands when I polish her chords. She closes her eyes when I'm singing along. Her arms and shoulders are sturdy and strong, but she's delicate when she's sitting with me, she's made of paper. Only once.' 'Once what?' 'Only once did I get at all close to her.' 'How close?' 'Too close.' 'How close?' 'We were sitting on her bed, no instruments between us, nothing, and even the air was close, jammed up with some punky song she was learning. We were *pretending*, at any rate, that she was learning the song, but really we were just trembling there together, our thighs almost touching. That's when I did it: I turned her chin with my fingers and lightly brushed her lips with mine, and she responded. We kissed like that for I don't know how long, and I felt like I was twelve, ten, five—all fresh lips and tongue!' 'That's all?' 'It was her first kiss, the best she will ever have.'"

I didn't bother to tell Zbigniew that, at that moment, I had forever turned against Dick Chesnutt and from there on out I had begun punishing him in all of my nasty ways. In fact, I said nothing more to Zbigniew, just watched him grow more and more piteous as he feebly groped the rim of the tub and tried to pull himself out. On his feet and dripping he stepped over me and felt his way out of the bathroom. He stumbled down the cold hallway, bumping against the walls. Finally, to my great pain, he fell down in the dark kitchen, and for a long time he shook there, wet and naked on the floor, sobbing, keening, like nothing I've ever heard. "It was just a kiss, it was just a kiss," I called to him from the bathroom tiles. But I stayed put, for there's no consoling a man in that state.

Why do I cause such trouble? I've had lots of time to sit down and think about this, ever since Zbigniew jumped in his car and left me stranded out here in the valley (not that I can blame him). I suppose I'll call a cab. I suppose I cause trouble for the sake of trouble. I can't leave bad enough alone. I snip red wires, push red buttons, flip switches, pull plugs, all for the thrill of not knowing what will happen next. I usually never find out. But this morning I have a sinking feeling, just sickening. This morning the desperate wind tugs at the roof, tries the windows, shakes the trees, but I'm perfectly safe, I'm curled up and wretchedly comfortable here on Zbigniew's Scandinavian sofa.❖

November 1, 1990

❖There's a real person, there are real places strewn in the shadows behind the shape of my cousin. I know them. There's his curly-headed father, the mild pharmacist, my mother's little brother, who at this moment is probably standing on his Victorian farmhouse balcony, drinking his second glass of Irish whiskey, or maybe wondering what's become of his son. And there's the mother, small and pretty, much prettier than me. A fourth-grade teacher. She has two of the liveliest blue eyes you'll ever see. She's loading the dishwasher. And then there's the town, Maquoketa, Iowa, whose surrounding hills are getting scruffy, whose trees are going naked, whose gables and steeples and trickling chimneys turn orange and brown then disappear, under the father's gaze. He's lived there so long he knows all the roofs, knows the names of the people living under them, knows who's taking what, and at what dosage. Antidepressants, mostly. Sometimes he knows their symptoms, too, but this is closer than he ever wants to get to this old and secretive little town. To look at the father's face, his big liquid eyes and generous lips, one can see that he has no interest in secrets, either in knowing them or in keeping them. He'd much rather live in a transparent world where everything's made plain.❖

November 2, 1990

❖No more games. Since you arrived here you have been harboring a secret, albeit an innocent one: you yourself are a father. And though there's nothing wrong with that, you fastidiously keep it to yourself, as if the secret, once known, might reveal how much you resemble your own father. And as if we didn't already know that.

Whereas some people travel in motorcades, having the right constitution for keeping secrets, you travel on foot, distracted by the sights, your every pocket an open target. There's something unforgivable about a tourist who forever worries about his money but still can't manage to keep it protected, and that's just the way you've been shuffling around town. I played along for a while—making you disguises, giving you aliases, rewriting your history—but in the end I just couldn't resist. I picked your pockets and blew the wad. One can only spend a secret once, especially such a silly secret, so one has to be extravagant, and I was. I threw a party in honor of your secret. I dressed you up as Midas, the reckless father who'd put it all at risk for money and magic, and I sent you out strutting across the stage. Everyone cheered, even the morose Dick Chesnutt. I told your story with all its glittery details, and you played the king, goofily beaming. But then when I did my fabulous trick, exposing the ass's ears under your crown, I was dispirited by the general ambiguity and confusion. Of course nobody understood, least of all you, who just tore at the things and wondered how they'd gotten there.

That's why I'm explaining it now to you, Eavesdropper. Now you're different, reading there. You've proven that you're invested in secrets: you care how they work, you know what they're worth, and you'll do anything to get your hands on them. I think you'll appreciate this now, in retrospect. The irony was gorgeous. Here you were, having been a pent-up jailbird in the claustrophobia of your secrecy, all at once basking in the free light of candor—not the candor of your treasured little fetish-secret, for no one there knew that you had indeed sealed up your daughter in a coffin of gold, but rather the candor of your deep secret self, that is, the secret that you are a young man who is incapable of keeping secrets, incapable of lying, and that you come off like a braying donkey when you try. So I did what I did, thinking you might get a clue.

But then you blew it. Yesterday morning I caught you under a big blue sky, fawning over Jackie Witherspoon, once again trying to be something you're not. Why lie to a sober little judge like Jackie Witherspoon? So I set her straight, just a bit, just enough to put you in line. Not meaning to delight her as much as I did, I simply told her that you work at the Kasino. Spring! went the ass-ears, and then the game was over. You told her something about me that is so confidential I dare not even to repeat it here. No sense of nuance, no sense of degrees, no sense of family. I was incensed. So then rudely I go, He's got a kid, and that was that, but no big deal. I bet even now, especially now, knowing Jackie and her taste for the truth, she's got you right where she wants you, facedown on the carpet of her tiny turret.❖

November 11, 1990

❖I hardly ever see you these days. Of course you're with Jackie, fiddling with her earthworms, and you can imagine how that hurts me. I see Zbigniew all the time. He's a mess, retreating into empty rooms, but he's a prodigal son buying out the town, and still the money keeps on rolling in. Quite a thing to watch, really.❖

listopad ?, 1990

❖Thursday evening and I'm proctoring an exam, a teacher's finest hour, when she enjoys all the authority but does nothing whatsoever to earn it. I relax here at my desk, doing nothing, basking in the anticipation of my students, my dear little people who will turn in their papers and then be free to speak Polish all weekend, go hiking with their friends, maybe attend to some drunk uncle. I'm going to the mountains in Zbigniew's new Mercedes and Gurney will be working hard at the Kasino. All is well. But concentrate, students. Make me proud.

I need not mention the air of entitlement with which nearly all the students in Poland cheat. This is no casual accusation. I've spoken with teachers from all over Poland who assure me that cheating is a student's given right, and most teachers allow for it, bend to it, gnawing their nails down to the knuckle or leaving the room to have a couple smokes. And so it will be in my classroom. I'm no missionary of American ethics. I'm hardly even a teacher at all. I'm just an impostor, a girl of twenty-four who shouldn't be teaching college students. Still, I hear some noise. I look around, and then look beyond their faces to the decorations on the back wall. During the day, this classroom belongs to a grammar school, so the desks, even, I think, the teacher's desk, are cute little miniatures. If you squint your eyes and look at the back wall you can see step-by-step instructions for making origami animals: *pingwin, gołąb, świnka, kaczka.* The room is full of hanging plants, religiously watered by some good teacher, probably unnoticed by all the kids, and here on my desk are three cacti, stubby guys who must have traveled a long ways to get here, such a long ways that they have lost their sombreros.❖

November 29, 1990

❖Here's a story, so listen up. Eulalia called today asking how responsible you are. Good question, I thought. Solid father, loyal cousin, good tenant. I told her you are very responsible. Then she asked me if I knew one Jackie Witherspoon. Thinking fast on my feet, I made the connection from Eulalia to Linda to Jackie to you to me, and knew that I couldn't lie. I said yes, and I also had to admit that you know her too. But I paused on the next question, whether Jackie is the responsible type, for I really don't know her very well. All I know is she's soaking you in bad wine, keeping you out to all hours of the morning, and flirting with you when she knows damn well you've got a kid and girlfriend waiting for you back home. Now she's caught you up in her nightcrawler cult, but don't even get me started on that. And since I'm endeared to Eulalia and estranged from Jackie Witherspoon, I felt compelled to tell these things.

According to Eulalia, on Thanksgiving night, exactly one week ago tonight, Jackie Witherspoon visited your roulette wheel—in a cocktail dress and stockings. A hussy or what? Our dealer hadn't given up a single złoty since opening up that afternoon, and I understand this is almost the routine there, but her showing up changed all that. Word is, she peppered your neck with kisses, slithered her fingers all over your tuxedo, and tantalized you with a purseful of poker chips. Blue chips. They say you're a dour dealer, that you go through the motions like a stiff old priest, but on Thanksgiving night, mesmerized by the vision of your Monterey Salome, you answered the powerful call of flesh. Pussy-whipped like a schoolboy, you told her the Kasino's most closely guarded secret. The croupier admitted to having missed the secret itself (it was obvious to me neither Messersturm nor Eulalia knew it either), but the fact is that you were seen making a certain gesture, a secret-society flash of the fingers that intimated some sort of hocus-pocus. We can assume that Jackie Witherspoon got your meaning, and much to her delight, for in less than ten minutes she was more than $250,000 richer!

That is the end of my story.

Now, how responsible are you? Let's see. Were I to write you a reference letter, which I wouldn't do given today's news, I would note that you had a paper route at age eleven (I used to walk with you on it, remember?), a Boy Scout badge for painting the front door of the Maquoketa Public Library (French's Mustard yellow), and in high school you had a group of freckled friends who scattered off to schools like Oberlin, Swarthmore, Reed, and Penn. The committee would be pleased by your sturdy roots. But then I'd have to fudge some stuff, ignore your chronic tardiness, overlook your years of promiscuity, and forgive the fact that, since going to college, you've lost all sense of worth and purpose. What's silliest of all, you hated yourself for missing out on Phi Beta Kappa by three-tenths of a percentage point. Now you wander the earth being nipped and bitten by that gadfly of inadequacy which reminds you that you're the sole heir of your mother's conscience, the megaphone conscience that shouts in your ear: You will always be mediocre, you will never do anything really well, and even for all your drinking and bankrobbing and Jackie Witherspoon–fucking you'll never really have any fun. Were I to recommend you, then, I would have to overlook your trademark tedium: dumb self-doubt.

He's tedious, sure, but is he responsible?

Responsible no, culpable yes. One thing I can say for him: he's the Roving Prince of Causality. But don't get me wrong. I'm not damning him with faint praise. Know that I admire the fact that in almost all cases you're the one to blame.

Could you expand on that, please?

I'll try. But I'm furious with him. I told you just now that I don't want to recommend him.

Fair enough. Well, since we've got you here, let's talk about you.

That's better.

You're furious. Because Jackie's rich and you're not.

Not at all! Because Jackie's rich and he's an ingrate.

You're furious because your cousin's ungrateful to you.

Flimflam!

So then, ungrateful to who?

Whom.

Of course. Now back up a bit. Look at it this way. You've lured this silly kid over to Poland, aware from the start that he doesn't know the language, doesn't even know himself, and that all he'll want to do is eat, drink, hide, and maybe get laid now and then. And honestly, do you do much more than that yourself? And aren't you, slut that you are, ungrateful to Grazyna and Wanda Zamoyska? Lay off the ingrate. Hypocrisy doesn't become you. Maybe you're mad because—ah, yes!—maybe it's because when you invited him here, you yourself were a haggard slut. You were looking for something wholesome in your cousin, the Bubble Yum breath of youth, a balmy afternoon back in 1978, a cheery little flame to get you through just one more long

Kraków winter, but then it turned out that he's just like you. Dead coals.

Twaddle.

Maybe, but you must admit that you're drawn to him. You depend on him. His Kewpie red hair got the little girl in you up and playing hopscotch again. It just about killed you to dye it black.

Okay, okay. There's truth in this.

More to the point, you're drawn to your fantasy of him. He arrived here, and for two weeks you horsed around like slumber-party kids. He in boxer shorts, you in panties, French fashion magazines all over the floor. But you're not little kids, you're dirty adults, and you know that if you fuck him

Stop.

you know that if you fuck him

Stop.

the fantasy vanishes, nothing left but a shriveled condom.

But that's not the point, so quit. You were wondering if he's responsible

Have it your way.

and I was saying that he's the Roving Prince of Causality. He makes things happen wherever he goes. He has the powers of a grown-up, the virility of a man, but it flies from his hands like a slapstick firehose.

And you resent him for this.

No. Have you heard a word I've said? I've told you that I myself am trouble. I'm the Scheming Slattern of Making Things Happen. But what makes me furious, though I'm not furious anymore, just weary and sad, what chafes me is, the boy has no sense of worth. I know, I know. I've dragged him off to a country where ten thousand crisp new złotys get you a wadded dollar bill, but even here, where numbers are just chaff, even here money's dangerous beauty, its quiet power, is the way it heaps and drifts like snow on all the living and the dead, elegantly freezing us to the bone. My cousin doesn't appreciate this power. But I do. I know the damage I've done to Zbigniew: the richer he gets, the more gold encrusts his heart like barnacles. I watch him sitting there restlessly flipping through the channels, and I can see the terrible work I've done. I simply don't care. But my cousin— Zbigniew calls him Johnny Appleseed—he walks the earth and makes things happen, sowing his seeds, swatting his gadfly, never bothering to stop and note that there's an absolute difference between a vital sign and a dollar sign. Whether it's the immaculate conception of Sheila's baby or the filthy conception of Jackie's fortune, he never quite knows what he's fathering, he doesn't even want to know, he just does his business and walks away. This is how he's irresponsible: he refuses to tally up the damage he's done, he refuses to appraise his trail of wreckage and junk. It's sad. If he keeps it up, and I fear he will, he's going to die never having met himself.

You're lying, Jane.

Tell me what I'm lying about.

You lie when you say you cherish your regrets. You lie when you say you don't care about Zbigniew. You lie when you say you've tallied up your damage. Two simple words can turn you to jelly: Dick Chesnutt. You writhe in your bedclothes and punch your pillow remembering the vitality that thrummed from his motorcycle through your numb and happy bodies, the easy vitality and gravel in his voice, the rigid vitality in his shoulders and back, the innocent vitality that waned and warped with every winter he didn't go home. You don't cherish the regret that he's dead now, and cold. For isn't he? You don't cherish having turned Zbigniew's heart into gold. You're a liar. Why? Are you embarrassed? Are you embarrassed to admit there's a sappy little girl in you who gets choked up just looking into a bird's nest? Are you ashamed to admit that, given the choice, you'd choose the booming avenues of life over the garbage-strewn corridors of death? No. It's nothing cheap like embarrassment. It's fear. You're scared, Jane, scared to even think of knowing life's value, its fragile strength, its absolute worth, for were you ever to let yourself touch life, console its blood and nerve and viscera, in that moment you would have to stand back and take stock of all the ruin that's yours alone.

Out of jealousy, you blame your lover. Out of fear, you blame your cousin. But these two men, silly as they are, have that one thing you fear more than anything else, which is that same one thing you need, yes need, so much more than you ever would own. And they waste it—waste it! But wouldn't you, too? Isn't that why you'll never let yourself have it?

Watch: Sheila sits in a warm apartment. ABC News plays on TV, the sound turned down. The refrigerator hums. The aquarium babbles. The answering machine patiently blinks. Her pajamas are open down to the navel, pulled well over to one side, and there an amazingly small baby with fine red curls patters little palms and fingers, tugs at her breast, tugs milk from her breast. Remarkable to think how alive they are—more than you are, Jane, more than you are, Gurney. Good to think how safe they are, for outside the air is razor cold. Outside, where we are, the sun's gone down and the trees are black. There are three of us out here shivering in the wind. A stupid kid. A haggard slut. A miserable killer. All of us sad and cold and poor in a dirty snowfall of paper money, falling meaninglessly, meaninglessly falling, on the corroded statues and the grinding streetcars, on the nothing that is not there and the nothing that is.❖

THAT WAS THE END of Jane's diary. He threw it down and sprang to his feet. He took three steps, looked back at it. What the hell did she expect of him? And how dare she? The room was too dark. He went from lamp to lamp, turning them on, tearing off shades, making the dirty, dusty room as bright as a blazing hospital. The smell of Jane's sex was still on his fingers, his battered knuckles, making him want to go take a shower. But not here. And he couldn't even think of going to Jackie's. So for a long time he squatted there, staring at the book, wondering if it was too late to get a flight back to the States.

He left the room just as it was, the lights shining, the book on the floor, and went out into the wet winter night. It was still early. Kids threw snowballs under colored lights. Mafiosi warmed their hands on street corners. Gurney walked through the middle of it all, thinking he could use a holiday drink, not vodka but whiskey, something to make Kraków feel like home. He rushed through the crowd and onto more remote streets, soon onto swervy Ulica Kanonicza, where he walked alone, crowded only by Jane's ringing writing voice, and the too vivid scenes still playing in his head. His eyes were attracted by a brightly lit poster, tacked to a placard in front of a theater. A brooding young nude squeezed a fat skull, as though he were testing a grapefruit for freshness. Beneath the nude was printed the word HAMLET. He knew that the poster had been drawn by Grazyna. He'd seen the sketches for it lying around her studio. Perfect, he thought. He bought a ticket and was let into the dark theater. He sat near the back. It took a moment for his eyes to adjust, a moment longer to realize he was listening to Polish and understanding nothing at all.

The scenery pleased him very much. It was done in the style of a Tatar court, an opulent style, beloved by Krakovians, which he recognized from the Czartoryski Museum. The action took place beneath a grand golden tent embroidered with royal blue arabesques. The actors lounged on flouncy silk pillows. The men wore ballooning hats and blue and purple robes. The women wore lingerie, which was coyly exposed through layers of sheer veils and gowns. A single nude actor reclined downstage, fanned by a boy made up to be Asian. Presumably this actor was Hamlet. Gurney too reclined in his seat and let himself be transported to the Dead Sea shore, where birds, he imagined, swooped over the tent and a hot breeze made the shimmering water delightful. He smelled the brackish air. He pressed his bare toes into the hard sand—but then it occurred to him where they were in the play: the Mousetrap, the dumb show, the play-within-the-play where the Prince is out to get the conscience of the King. The Players, who were ironically dressed in Jacobian style, had stopped talking. They were pantomiming the Murder of Gonzago. He sat up and watched. The stage lights dimmed. Afternoon orange became crepuscular blue, and a real sense of dread crept over him. Why dread? Because the man in the crown, embracing his wife, was marked for near and certain death. Gurney rubbed the nap of his pants and watched the rogue pour poison into the king's ear. The attendants appeared and took away the body. Gurney touched his lips. The actors started speaking again, as if ignoring the fact that death was nearby. But Gurney couldn't ignore it. Death was the muffled sound of the theater. Death was the bushy head blocking his view. Death was the perfume of the woman beside him. He wanted it to show its ugly face.

The King stood up, shouting for lights and disbanding the Players. Blackout. Shuffling on stage. Lights again. The King kneeled at prayer, and the naked pimply Prince hovered far behind him, a toy knife by his side, his muscles too feeble to do any real damage. He wussily tucked it back under his arm and went on talking to himself. Gurney wanted to get up at that point, go outside and do something real, but then the Prince turned to face the audience. Gurney sat back. The Prince cast his eyes about the dark theater, his mushy mouth prattling excuses, his droopy lids a total disgrace. Gurney didn't understand the Polish, but he knew bad acting when he saw it. But then what was it? The actor's weak eyes had a chilling effect, making Gurney feel dirty all over, making him want the house lights turned on. Under those watery, wimpy eyes he felt hundreds of miles away from himself, thousands of miles from where he should be—though he hadn't a clue where he should be—and he hadn't a clue how to get back there—

But that was a lie. That, too, was bad acting.

He knew exactly how to get back there.

There was no point in waiting around any longer. He knew what was destined to happen to this fool. He'd stab at something behind the curtain, he'd smut all over his mother's bed. Gurney stood up and put on his coat. Looking down over the audience, he recognized someone up by the front; she was lit by the stagelights and looking his way. Was it Jackie? It was Wanda, and it seemed she was sitting next to her mother. She smiled at him and gave him an excited wave. He waved back. He had to go. As he exited the theater, buttoning up, he wondered how much she knew.

December 3, 1990. 10:07 P.M.

❖How now? A rat? Dead for a ducat, dead! I've been feeling your steamy breath on my neck. I've seen your eyes through the slats in the wall. But now your prints are all over my prose, now my most pink and private secrets are sprawled out there in the middle of the floor, burnt and sweating in the incandescent light. Fine work, friend. Just fine. Never mind that I depended on you, never mind that I egged you on, never mind what a rash and bloody deed this is, for you should have known, Polonius, you should have known not to get too close. Your rent is past due, your time is up. Now consider yourself evicted, effective immediately. O, you are slain! Oh, yes, you are slain.❖

Book Three

Xmas Feast

Give me now libidinous joys only,
Give me the drench of my passions, give me life coarse and rank,
To-day I go consort with Nature's darlings, to-night too,
I am for those who believe in loose delights.

—WALT WHITMAN, "Native Moments"

Sixteen

HE WOULD HAVE HAD NO INTENTION of staying on in Kraków, even if Jane hadn't thrown him out of the house. The very next morning, while she was in class, he packed up his few things and made vague plans to head out even farther across the wintry continent—probably in a southernly direction, maybe to see what was happening down in Budapest or Istanbul. He felt youthful and intrepid, as now he had nothing more to lose, and it was with this cavalier attitude, hauling his heavy backpack down the Zamoyskas' stairwell, that he happily encountered Wanda and Matek. Their faces were pink, their heads encased by respective blue and yellow ski caps. They protested when he announced that he was leaving town, and when they had gotten it out of him that he had no destination they insisted that he stay with them in Kazimierz for the holidays. Dreary Kazimierz had never appealed to Gurney, but their good-natured invitation stopped him short. Wanda pleadingly tugged on his lapels, Mateusz performed a formal bow, and after a moment of playful resistance (their spirited generosity had already changed his mind) he walked with them into the blue December morning.

When they informed him, however, that they were taking him to Dick Chesnutt's apartment, his strongest impulse was to get off the crowded tram and find his way to the train station. Once more he felt his past doubling back on him, coiling around him, and what he had learned from Jane's diary had hardly helped the matter. But he kept these reservations to himself, and all the better, as it turned out, for once he had crossed into the old Jewish ghetto and had beaten back the mounting dread of encountering Jane and meeting Jackie and maybe having to finish all of his other business around town, he entered the refurbished world of Wujo Płujo and felt as if he could have been anywhere on earth. The windows were open, the coal stove roaring; steamy activity filled the garret flat. There were a dozen or more teenagers milling about—rolling cigarettes, playing backgammon, leafing through pornos and comic books. A couple of greasy boys tried to tune their guitars while Wanda's friend Piotr, big headphones on, hovered obliviously over two mismatched turntables and provided a soundtrack of furry, loopy funk. Gurney was given the hasty tour. He felt like a truant officer—finding pot smokers in the kitchen, sleepers in the bathroom, several kids in their underwear making out in the bedroom—but nobody seemed to notice him there, so why should he have cared? Mateusz made some space on the sofa, swatting away a boy and a girl who couldn't have been any older than twelve, and told him to make himself at home. Wanda went to make coffee in the kitchen. Mateusz flopped down next to Gurney and offered him a cigarette. Gurney considered it, then declined.

Dobre, said Mateusz.

Dobre.

Gurney didn't ask if anyone had come looking for Dick Chesnutt, assuming that it was a touchy subject, but then Mateusz launched right into it, saying: It is you who have took the job of Dick Chesnutt at the Kasino Kraków.

Yes, Gurney said. It is I.

People know where he is? At the Kasino?

Nope.

People come there looking for him?

Nope. Do people come *here* looking for him?

Nope. People hardly come here looking for him. Not at all.

Gurney thought about this and then told Mateusz that he spoke English very well.

As do you. But I have question for you. Now you do not work at the Kasino any longer? That is my question.

What's the question?

Why you do not.

Right. Because I was fired. Kind of. Actually, they never invited me back. They think that I may have helped a friend of mine win gobs of money at the roulette wheel, so they fired me.

Are they right? Did you do that?

Honestly, I don't know.

You don't know, Mateusz repeated, smiling, the cigarette stuck in the gap between his teeth. Gurney wondered if he did this cigarette trick as a joke or out of force of habit.

But this is why you leave Kraków?

Oh no, not at all. There's nothing left here for me. Anyway, my friend won the money fair and square. I don't have anything to hide.

Dobre.

When Wanda returned with a coffee service and a plate of poppy-seed cakes, Mateusz said something to her in Polish and both of them burst out laughing. She squeezed in on Gurney's other side, reassuringly patted his knee, and resumed the questioning in another direction, asking him why he was moving out of Jane's studio.

He had enjoyed the freedom with which he answered Mateusz's questions, but already he was a little concerned about the consequences. Did these kids need to know what happened at the Kasino? What happened in his life? Looking around the room at the general commotion (for some reason the guitar boys had begun grappling on the floor), he knew his visit there would be temporary and thus he could be as open as he pleased. This was just a detour, and the stakes of his honesty were pretty low. He tried out the same frankness on Wanda: We got together last night.

What does that mean?

We, um, got together, you know, we *slept* together, just last night. That's kind of against the rules when you're cousins.

You slept together. In the same bed?

What the hell. We had sex.

Wanda looked at him as if she thought he was gross. That's gross, she said.

You speak English very well.

You had sex with Jane?

Yes, he said, rather dramatically. I had sex with Jane.

She is your cousin.

She's my only cousin, my only first cousin.

Wanda spoke to Matek in Polish and they both started laughing.

You had sex with Jane and then she made you move out.

Something like that. I had sex with Jane, then I read her diary, and then she made me move out.

What is a diary?

It's, um, like a book that you keep to yourself, you write your secrets in it, private things. You know. It's also called a journal.

What did it say?

Nothing much. That wasn't the problem. The problem was that I had read it.

It is a good thing that I don't have a diary, Wanda said.

It's not like I go around reading peoples' diaries. These were special circumstances.

I think it is gross.

What part of it?

All of it.

She must have known that Gurney was embarrassed by his confession, for the next thing she did deftly put him at ease: she seized a soft and buttery poppy-seed cake and smashed it into his face and mouth. Gratefully eating, he wiped the excess frosting from his fingers onto the leg of her jeans.

He ended up putting his things in Dick Chesnutt's bedroom and staying on for a couple more weeks, during which time he began to see the city in a very different light. He would have been right to be paranoid—Herr Messersturm was out there pounding the bricks, Jane was somewhere hatching her schemes, and Zbigniew Zamoyski wanted American blood. And he had much reason to feel remorse— he had made no attempt to patch things with Sheila, he had really botched things up with Jane, and probably Jackie as well, and here he was squatting in Europe's saddest old ghetto. But he was having the time of his life, so it felt okay. Jane had schooled him in the pleasures of secrecy, the joys of doing whatever he pleased as long as he did it under the moral big top, but her way had left him feeling empty and ashamed. In the unabashed world of Wujo Płujo, this underaged Pleasure Island where the boys were sexy and the girls were macho, they kept their fun right out in the open. They sent out signals of sugar and noise, blood and guts, fun and games. Drinking in public was their political act, stealing from shops was their temporary employment, hockey on the Wisła was their recreation. Gurney couldn't resist joining in. Soon he too was wrestling in his underwear. Soon he too was stripping down without warning and enjoying a naked freedom that was as silly as it was youthful and European. Blissfully ejected from Jane's house of mystery, where lies and costumes were a way of life, he found himself basking in a paradise of skin.

One afternoon in mid-December, after he and Matek had returned from chopping down an evergreen tree, he holed himself up in Dick Chesnutt's garret and hung a sign on the door: WSTĘP WZBRONIONE. Entrance forbidden. He was ready to organize the man's mortal leftovers. The garret was an airy room with a low-slanting ceiling and chipped orange casements. Strewn all over the mushy bed, spilling like guts onto the shellacked floor planks, were mounds of letters and photos and tapes. It was all that was left of a forty-year life that Dick Chesnutt had once claimed to have lived by his whims. Gurney found a watch and some fountain pens, which he gave to Wanda. He found several sticky bars of wrapped hashish, which he gradually doled out to Wujo Płujo. The rest just seemed like paper and trash, but still he felt compelled to have a closer look.

Three people in the world knew that Dick Chesnutt was dead: Jane, his fink. Zbigniew, his murderer. And Gurney, now the executor of his estate. Besides them, only Wanda seemed even to care that he was missing. He felt some responsibility, having read Jane's diary, and he knew that a more civil man would have gone to the police. A vigilante would have tried to bring Zbigniew to justice. But it wasn't just laziness that kept Gurney from doing the same. He was simply following his own idea of justice. Granted, Dick Chesnutt was probably dead. But to judge from his letters, which Gurney pored over with almost prurient interest, he had been dead to his Stateside relatives for years. So what good would it do to put Zbigniew behind bars? It would horrify Wanda, mortify Grazyna, and it would maybe even implicate Jane. Would that be justice? Not to Gurney's way of thinking. From what he could tell, it had been a crime of passion—a jealous crime, a clumsy crime—and so if Zbigniew were capable of murdering again, and that would be a big if, he would only go after someone he envied and hated. Someone like Gurney. With the memory of Zbigniew's fingerprints still lingering on his throat, Gurney couldn't exactly laugh off the possibility, but it still wasn't reason to go bothering the police.

Dick Chesnutt was a man who had never protected himself. He'd left himself open on all sides, from all directions, asking to be watched and pleasured and fondled. Chase your desires, he'd said on Halloween, and when you die your life will have an interesting shape. Interesting indeed, Gurney thought, perusing clippings from old Polish newspapers, censored photographs of the Jagiellonian penis walk. In one popular shot he strutted down the stairs, his fist raised in protest, his face aglow, a small black box covering his junk.

Death, Gurney felt, had given shape to this life. Death had mercifully stopped the madness, though not before this weirdo's unflagging ambition had all but dwindled into lonely folly. If he had died before, say, 1985, at least he would have died with a shred of dignity. Some of his early pop songs were almost even touching—rough accoustic ballads in a paper-thin voice, songs about exile and drinking dodgy booze—though even that had gone pear-shaped sometime in the mid-1980s, when he started using a drum machine.

Among packages and portfolios of political photographs—mostly bad shots of Solidarity demonstrations—was an album that Gurney kept back for himself. It featured Dick and Jane naked around a pool. The quality was poor and the angles were awkward, but each shot was distinguished by their edgy attraction. In almost all of them, so unlike what he'd seen on Halloween, Dick dominated. One shot showed him jerking his impressively large cock. Another showed a submissive Jane being dragged like a rag doll from the pool. In an especially disturbing close-up, his hand pressed between her legs and bore down with its palm. The album was more of an artifact than a turn-on, but still it was riveting. When he eventually found the privacy to masturbate over it, he covered every trace of Chesnutt with tape.

One book in particular was clearly his prized possession. It was solemnly kept in a burnished steel box, and its front cover, written in medieval calligraphy, was immediately interesting to Gurney:

> Come one! Come all! Come serfs! slaves! swine! squires! scribes! sickos! sires! sirens! simpletons! sluts! Come, saints, and cast your judgments. Come, slobs, for the saddest ride of your life. Come for an unguided underground tour into the wonderful woes of the down and dirty, black and gritty—CITY OF JANE!

Jane!

Jane!

A brown envelope was glued to the cover, smudged with grimy fingerprints. On it was written:

START HERE, DEAR.

Inside the envelope was an unlabeled cassette. Gurney played it on a rattly Russian tape deck and was startled to hear Jane's distinctive voice, telling what seemed to be a confidential story. This is what he heard:

> I was sexually active at an early age. No big deal. *Excitable,* I should say. Of course I didn't have anyone to be active *with.* [Dick Chesnutt's voice responded, saying he thought that this was normal.] It's *perfectly* normal, she said. Boys love to touch their pee-pees. Girls love to touch their cunnies. Nothing's wrong with that.

But I bet *your* parents jumped all over you for it. I bet they got all Catholic on you and told you not to touch yourself. [He said he didn't recall being admonished for it.] Well my parents were *very* tolerant. Very modern. Especially Daddy. I remember one time in particular. I was eight or nine, no older than that. I remember the house had that Friday-night excitement. Baby-sitter was coming. My parents were running around getting dressed. I was soaking in the bathtub. I must have been soaking there for quite a while. I'd been masturbating for several minutes when I looked up and saw him standing in the door. I naturally felt embarrassed and rolled over on my side. I remember making a splash against the wall. For some reason the splash made me all the more embarrassed. But he walked right in like nothing had happened. He dropped his pants, sat on the pot, and started reading a magazine. I stayed there on my side, absolutely paralyzed, but after a little while he spoke up in his Dad voice and said it was okay to do what I was doing. I really shouldn't stop, he said, just because he was there on the pot. It felt weird. Okay, it felt *very* weird, but I started doing it again anyway. I didn't do it because I still wanted to, mind you. I did it because he said it was okay. It felt like the grown-up thing to do. But when I think back on it now it's not weird at all. Everyone thought that way in the seventies. And Daddy's always been a man of his times.

That was the end of it. He rewound it several times and sat back, listening. He thought of Uncle Sandy back in the seventies, his blond mop of hair and sweeping bangs, his bushy red sideburns and a terrific red mustache. That was how Gurney remembered him best. He was a banker, a broker, something like that, and he always let on that there was money to burn. According to Uncle Sandy lore, he came from a long line of rich Episcopalians, his grandmother having been presented to the queen of England. Jane herself could have been such a debutante hadn't Aunt Judy (Jane's mother, Gurney's father's sister) jealously forbidden it. In the light of Jane's taped confession, all of these aristocratic legends developed a sinister cast for Gurney. He recalled their countless visits to Wilmette, the two families having drinks on Uncle Sandy's terrace, Jane and Uncle Sandy always ganging up on Aunt Judy and teasing her for being such an Irish Catholic prude.

But who could disapprove of Jane and Uncle Sandy? They *were* very funny. And Aunt Judy *was* a prude—just like her brother! He used to adore them, viciously envy them, admire them for their exquisite sense of fun. They ruled the tennis court with club-memberly swagger, even though Gurney and his dad always beat them. They monopolized dinner tables with their dad-daughter travelogues, madcap escapades from Italy to India that always felt like they could end up X-rated. And after dinner they really broke loose, Jane abusing the baby grand piano, Sandy booming out old Gilbert and Sullivan, drowning out Aunt Judy's meek little falsetto. Once when Jane was about sixteen and drunk, she grabbed her dad, who grabbed her back, and the two of them danced such a biblical tango and cut such a mind-boggling image of incest that the whole family applauded in spite of themselves.

He hadn't really thought much of it back then. In fact, slouching in the backseat of the Galaxie 500, he would have guilty wishes that his parents would die, just so he could be taken in by Uncle Sandy and live happily ever after in the city with Jane. But his parents never did die. Very much alive on those Sunday afternoons, they'd drive him back through the western suburbs, back through tedious Illinois pastures, back across the mile-wide Mississippi, to soporific Iowa, where, amid the bosomy hills, they protected him from all the fun and games that the twentieth century had to offer.

As if! he now thought. As if Uncle Sandy would have adopted him! As if he would have let him live with Jane! Not a chance. He'd maintained a jealous romance with his daughter, a private romance right out in the open. He spoke to her in French. He showered her with money and gifts. He treated her like an equal, sometimes a better, and when he noticed that she was having too much fun with her cousin, he'd burst onto the scene like a big gallant baby. Once they were playing croquet and having a great time, acting like Kennedys and Vanderbilts, when prancing down the terrace came big Uncle Sandy, wearing a leotard, juggling tangerines, singing some damned Italian aria. Jane dropped her mallet and ran right up to him, leaving Gurney cursing under his breath.

Now Gurney imagined him sitting on the toilet. He had no doubt that the story was true.

He fanned through the glued-together Book of Jane. The right-hand pages were written in calligraphy. The left-hand pages were the maps and montages of an imaginary Kraków. He read the first page:

Late one afternoon the Village Idiot went walking through the Stare Miasto. He was following what Krakovians call the King's Road, that imaginary Path which makes a great arc through the City, from Florian's gate through the Rynek Głowny to the winding roads by the Castle and the Wisła. Preoccupied by the Story of Jane in the Bathtub, he didn't even do his usual Window-Peeping. He walked and he thought, and he tried to make sense out of Grown-Up Jane, and what he himself had done with Her. Inspired by the dripping old Buildings around him, he arranged the Fragments of this Damaged little Girl into a three-dimensional Map of the City. (Fig. A.)[1] By the Logic of the Idiot's walking and thinking, Jane's fractured Person became a vibrant Metropolis that smoked and whirred under the Tyranny of the Father. This is how he thought of it: at the Center of Jane was a great Market Square, where peasants and citizens and courtiers come together, peddling Meats and Fruits and Jewels, playing their Lutes and Pipes and Drums. That is, at the Center of it all, or so the Idiot liked to believe, was the chronically flirtatious and storytelling Jane, the loose and generous Girl of the People who sparked a Coal Fire in every Pub she entered, the foxy girl whose Siren-Song Letters beckoned Fools from around the Globe.

[1]Figure A, on the facing page, was an illuminated woodcut of medieval Kraków. Ambitiously but sloppily, Dick Chesnutt had pasted revelers and sodomites onto the area of the marketplace—graphic little etchings that he'd probably lifted from illustrated editions of Rabelais or Sade.

Gurney turned the page and read on:

> Surrounding the democratic Hubbub of the Rynek are those broad-shouldered Mansions Polacks called *pałacy*—Pałać Baranami, Pałać Krzystofory, Pałać Jablonowski, and so forth—houses first built for the likes of the Zamoyskis, ornate Houses with tall iron gates to shut out the ornery Hoi Polloi. (Fig. B.)[2] And in just this way was the Idiot shut out by Jane's high-pitched Braggadocio, which explodes like Cannons the drunker she gets—boasting of her Smarts, boasting of her Travels, boasting the purple Pedigree that sets her well apart. This was Palace Jane, Daddy's Jane, the one that makes the Idiot feel like Crap and believe he's Doomed to eternal Mediocrity.

Next page:

> But the Village Idiot knows it's not so simple. The Village Idiot could take you into the Sewers, the foul Corridors that undermine the Rynek and connect the Palacy and the cellars of the Village to the dyspeptic Bowels of Wawel Castle. (Fig. C.)[3] Down there!—that's where the Real Work gets done—the covert Economy of Goods and Information—the Guilds of Thieves who work for

---

[2]Figure B was an etching of the Pałacy on the Rynek. Glued to each palace was a different photo of Jane's disembodied face—laughing, winking, sneering, scowling. Prostrate before these jeering palaces, as if applying to get in, was a comical drawing of Dick Chestnutt–qua–idiot, a ballooning snapshot of his piteous face glued onto his kneeling, poorly clad body.

[3]Most of Figure C must have come from an antique anatomy book. For beneath a lithographic landscape of Kraków were pasted strands of large and small intestine. Some of them were apparently full of feces. All of them coursed with a variety of figures that had faces, in both black and white and color, pasted onto their cartoonish shoulders. All of them, men and women, had enormous penises hanging out. He'd seen some of these faces around the university, some of them even in Grazyna's studio. Dick Chestnutt was also featured there among them, and so, standing in shit, was Zbigniew Zamoyski.

themselves—the Gangs of Spies who work for the King—the Masonic Think Tank that understands everything. Power and Destruction and Money are determined. Pleasure and Sugar and Fluids are exchanged. Jane's high-pitched Braggadocio is nothing more than a Noisy Front, blaring to distract us from the Devastating Fact that, in spite of all her Social Flair, she is one Scared and Broken Soul. Down there is a World of mean and frightened Janes, passing each other in Dim Corridors, exchanging Lies and Flatteries, always suspicious of other Janes, always jealous of other Janes, always anxious in each other's Company because one Jane never knows for sure where—in whose Bed, in whose Grave—the other Jane will be lying next. Her best Disguise, quoth the Village Idiot, is to Flaunt her Secrecy in the cold Light of Day, under the very Noses of the People. Thus Underground Jane confides in her Eavesdroppers and announces Shocking Truths that resemble Pretty Lies.

Next page:

The Village Idiot knows what all this means: cheating and lies keep the city so prosperous, but there is one unavoidable Truth, one unswerving Fact of Exchange: the Tyranny, of course, of the King. The King will favor you for sharing your Secrets—but he'll Behead you if you keep them to Yourself. Thus we have the prominence of the Castle, perched on its hill like an ever-watchful eye. He puts a red crown on the Dirty Father's Head. He puts a big scepter in the Dirty Father's hand. (Fig. D.)[4] The little Girl's Pri-

---

[4]Figure D was simply shocking. It featured a large photograph of Uncle Sandy's face, a leering glint in his Jane-like eyes, a partial smile on his Jane-like lips, a ludicrous crown slopped on his head. He filled the sky behind a miniature Rynek Glowny, the center of which was a big clawfoot tub. Bathing in the tub, remarkably enough, was a photograph of Jane only eight or nine years old. Where had Dick Chesnutt ever gotten these things?

vacy, her inalienable Right to a Desire all her Own, is multiplied in the Idiot's Imagination and is evenly Disbursed throughout the City. The little Girl's privacy, in the Idiot's Imagination, becomes the Rights of a trusting People who sought the King's Protection against outside Threats. The Correlation is, of course, Exact. For doesn't the King do to the People exactly what the Father did to Jane? Nay! At some long-forgotten Moment in the nation's early History, the King lets himself into the Bathroom of the People and gives them Permission to go on Masturbating. The Dreaded Permission! The King is the Father, Man of Authority, Man of Generosity, who turns the people's Privacy into his own Commodity!

But it only works the First Time, of course, for the First King, for Daddy. Because once this King is knocked off his Throne, as he will inevitably be, the people are Ashamed of having trusted him, having trusted such a Clod with their unplucked Desire. Under the Tyranny of the Next and Next King, they discover clever ways to protect their Desire. They stow it away in more remote Cellars, where maybe even they will never find it again. They have no choice but to let Him into the Bathroom. They have no choice, and maybe they even Invite him in. And in time it becomes easier to pay Him His Taxes, pay Him Homage, lie back in the Bathtub and Masturbate for Him. But they know that whatever the New Tyrant will take loses all value upon being taken. It will be Fake and Empty and given in Spite, for the Valuables have been locked away Ages before, locked away and forgotten—never, perhaps, to be brought to Market.

That was the book. Gurney flipped through it, gave it some thought. Jackie's book of earthworms had the good stamp of history. Jane's book of herself, with all its little ruses, had foolproof ways of tantalizing its confessors while making sure nobody got too close. But this City of Jane thing went too far—making tedious penance for what he'd done with Wanda, giving shrill justification for his wild penis walk. Dick Chesnutt had clearly been so proud of his work that he'd had no desire to disguise his effort. Which is to say, it was hopelessly contrived—as was his activism, as were his pop songs and everything else he'd done. START HERE, DEAR! It had been put together with the vain expectation that Jane, in retaliation, would be sneaking around looking for it. As if she could have cared!

Gurney imagined a blurb for its dust jacket: The unblinking portrait of a man and his obsession—his devotion to the girl who wanted him dead, his devotion to the city that called him a pervert.

Poor Dick Chesnutt. He would have really grooved on Wujo Płujo—their guts and audacity, their jumping up at any excuse to throw off their clothes. But they were just kids, and he was an old pervert. But then again, he *had* known Wanda; his fatal error had been knowing her too well, getting too close, helping himself to her overflowing youth.

Of course this thought gave Gurney pause.

He packed Chesnutt's things into three cardboard boxes, preparing to ship them off to the States. The only address was some guy in Philadelphia, the only person to keep a correspondence with Chesnutt during his nearly ten years in exile. Wondering whether to include the Book of Jane, Gurney decided that he would not. He would shelve it away in the Biblioteka Jagiellonska and hope that Jane never happened across it. It was the least he could do. After all, he thought, who was he to make aesthetic judgments?

ONCE HE HAD THROWN ALL OF THIS TOGETHER, Gurney went searching the Cloth Hall and the rest of the Old Town for real Polish gifts to send back home. His father got a chess set, his mother got a tablecloth, and Gram and Aunt Judy and his ex-girlfriend Sheila all got hand-knit sweaters from Zakopane. He searched all over for the right baby gift, rejecting the frightening wooden dragons, putting back the stiff and itchy blankets, deliberating too long over a sleek red wagon that would have been senseless in every way. The right gift turned out to be made in Germany, costing more than all the others put together, a little grizzly bear with stars on its nightcap. He wrapped them all up in good Italian paper—not the usual butcher paper—and wrote the same cryptic message on each: WESOŁYCH ŚWIĄT. Merry World. On Sarah's card he drew a picture of himself with bushy red hair, making a cartoon kissy face.

By the time he got to the neighborhood *poczta*, they were turning away a grousing crowd that must have been queued up all afternoon. A little disappointed, he took his parcels around the corner to a state-run tavern, a place so big and cold and muddy that it hardly distinguished itself from the street. He set it all down on a middle table, calling out for a pint of Żywiec. The waitress was in her forties, wearing the usual flowered smock, her hair the usual lilac tint. Even at a glance he was attracted to her: her slender waist, her penciled eyes, her way of pursing her lips when she poured. When she looked up and saw him smiling at her, she dropped the bottle and let the foam rush up. He sipped it off and looked out at the twinkling intersection, the flashing yellow lights and aquarium-lit streetcars, the mothers and babies and limping drunks. He thought of the approaching holiday, and he thought that it could be taken a couple of different ways. Either he could yearn for it in the Maquoketa of his memory, a holiday strictly for the comfort of children, for fattening them up around a roaring family fire. Either he could yearn for that and enjoy his disappointment because he knew he wasn't going to get it, or he could accept the holidays as so many do, as most probably do, enduring long hours of sitting alone, and eating alone, because it's easier than trying to share the company of strangers.

Lines of bubbles rose in his beer. This year would be his daughter's first Christmas. And then there would be holidays every year to come. There would be wish lists, Christmas trees, the Peanuts special on television. For years to come, parents would fill elementary school auditoriums, watching their children acting their hearts out— watching his daughter acting her heart out, in construction-paper wings and a tinsel halo, sticking her chest out, singing her heart out.

Seventeen

ONE COLD MORNING Wanda decided to skip school, and it turned out to be in her very best interest. For right there in front of her on Warynskiego, while she was waiting for the tram to take her to Kazimierz, a woman racing along in a red Fiat Polski smashed into a man in a blue Fiat Polski. They jumped out of their beat-up cars shouting. Probably because the accident was obviously her fault, the woman swung first and connected with his face. He smacked her back with an open hand. She kicked him in the shin. He pushed her against her car. All of this happened in Thursday morning traffic, with all kinds of people gathering on the sidewalk. He cursed, she shrieked, the crowd cheered them on. Mateusz would have called the whole thing fun, using Gurney's favorite word, and he would have talked about it all day long. But she had a different reaction to it.

She enjoyed car crashes, and she enjoyed this particular car crash, but this was a sicker kind of pleasure. It moved things in her that felt like they should be sturdy, things deeper down than sex and skin, almost shaking bedrock Wanda. This foundation was rumbling more frequently lately, as it had that day in her father's cottage, as it did at the thought of spending Christmas alone and just about every time she came to Dick Chesnutt's. It was weird and scary because she couldn't keep it steady and she felt like she had to do something about it.

On that particular morning, when she'd gotten to the flat in Kazimierz, things were so shifting around down there that she felt as if she could burst into tears at any moment. But she hated crying. In a gust of inspiration, therefore, she decided to tear into Matek's new canvas and see about making a mess of her own. A mess in retaliation. She was no painter, that was for sure, but she clamped it up to the easel anyway, knowing she couldn't hang around just waiting to become one. Hoping to calm the subterranean rumble, she painted the first thing that came to her mind, which happened to be Crash of the Fiat Polskis.

The sky had been brown, so she squirted out orange and green and white, smashing out snakes and smearing them on the palette, then splurging stormy color all over the canvas. She made broad strokes with the knife, just as she'd always seen her mother do. Far too impatient for the sky to dry, she erected a coarse corner block of buildings, in sea green, burnt sienna, bloody brown stucco—not because the buildings had actually been those colors but just because those colors were handy. The tram lines had been black against the sky. She painted them, impatiently. The trees were kind of yellow, as though they'd been peed on. The snickering crowd was gray and black with Christmas flecks of gold and red, and they blended in with the dirty snow so as not to distract from the main event, which happened on the canvas all at once: Smash! Bang! Ouch! It all came back in one vivid crash. Piercing red traffic light, squealing black tires, the crunched-up marriage of red and blue metal. She got it right on the first try—the boxy little cars, the sharp angle of impact, the sheer smeary force slamming everything together. She wondered for a moment about including the drivers, kicking and slapping in the middle of traffic, but she decided that that would have been too much. So before she knew it, the painting was finished. At first glance it was brilliant. At second glance, a mess. Who cares? she thought, getting up to clean her brushes. She jumped at the sight of Piotr, leaning against the wall.

You jerk! How long have you been there?

Since you planted those yellow trees.

Jerk.

He smiled.

What do you think?

He made a serious face, squinting at the painting from several meters back. He came a bit closer and opened his eyes wider. He looked the whole thing over, and just when she started getting impatient he slowly nodded and started smiling again.

Well? she said.

Remember, I'm no painter.

I don't care. Do you like it?

Remember, I can't do much. I mean, I can put together little dance mixes. I can shoot little movies and do all right. My photographs are nothing like Matek's and Władek's. On a good day I can write an all right poem.

Right, sure, okay, shut up. Do you like it?

Did you like the omelette I made yesterday?

Smacznego!

I think I do that better than anything.

Please shut up now and tell me what you think. Do you like it? Does it stink?

Like I said, I'm no painter. So don't take anything I say too seriously. You should probably wait for Mateusz to get here. But here goes. I have a hunch that this is a really important painting and that, um, and that you've got some kind of rare talent. I think you're a genius.

Piotr! You're just silly. I painted this in less than twenty minutes.

Lucky you. You're a genius with a bunch of free time.

Lucky's the word. Beginner's luck, she said. She was hardly able to contain herself because she didn't believe in beginner's luck. But instead of contending with the preposterous idea that she did have rare talent or perhaps even genius, and instead of asking just *why* he thought the painting was so great, she gave him a shove, scooped up the soccer ball, and told him they were going out to play in the snow.

Dribbling the ball down Ulien Jósefa, passing it back and forth, bouncing it off cars and buildings and dumpsters, Piotr and Wanda took Kazimierz by storm. He dribbled down the cobblestones of Szeroka Square and she tended goal on the steps of the Mikveh, valiantly blocking his every shot. In no time at all her hands were blue, her lungs were fire, and her boots were soaked, but nothing, not even Piotr's pterodactyl wingspan, would stop her from running back across the square and scoring—one, two, three times—off the rattly gates of Bóznica Na Gorca. Pigeons fluttered overhead. Blasphemy echoed in the cold city air. When she'd had enough fun running him in circles, she lay down, breathlessly, on the tall stone wall. He sat down beside her, panting and spitting.

Remuh Cemetery? he proposed.

She lay there for a moment, still catching her breath. What about it?

Let's.

I have no desire.

Yes you do. I know you do.

No desire, she said, and she really did have no desire, but then she jumped to her feet and did something foolish. With Piotr in tow, she dribbled back in the direction of Ciemna and Lewkowa Streets. At the base of the wall of one of the oldest graveyards in Europe, kicking as hard as she could possibly kick, she sent the ball sailing into the land of the dead. It landed somewhere without a sound.

What were you thinking?

I wasn't.

We'll never find it in there!

We'll have to try. It's Kuba's prized possession. He'll kill us if we lose it.

Kill *you!* I haven't been in there since I was a kid.

Me neither, but we're still kids. We'll find it.

The entrance to the graveyard was hidden inside a sixteenth-century synagogue, around which had been built a shabby apartment building. She chose a door and dashed through mildewy hallways and stairwells, eluding Piotr, quietly trying more and more doors until she discovered the one that opened, with a massive hush, onto the colossal cemetery. She stopped short and looked out over its silent expanse. Piotr stopped behind her. What was it? The stones looked like a multitude of mourners and exiles, wet snow heaped like droopy hoods on their thousand dark and tired shapes. Apart from their breathing and a smattering of lit oil lamps, the place was preternaturally calm, a peace that had been piling up for centuries, a peace so large and old and solemn that it had probably absorbed Kuba's soccer ball as thoughtlessly as a whale swallows plankton. Wanda sighed. Piotr laughed.

Never in a million years, he said, walking on ahead of her.

She packed a snowball from the sopping, crusty snow. His silhouette was naked against the sky, an easy target, wide open, but she knew that if she threw first, he'd hurl one back at her, and then the calamity would spread all over the place, splashing off stones, tripping over vines, causing one blasphemous antic after another. She threw it anyway. It whizzed just past him and splattered on the wall. They both watched it fall. The wailing wall. It all came back to her in a rush, the story her father once told her of the wall, how it had been built from the remnants of Jewish headstones that had been shattered by Nazis during the war, how the wailing wall was a place for reverence and prayer. Nice going, she thought, shaking off her hands.

Quit it, was all Piotr said, taking a long hard look around. I remember this place being full of snails. Remember that?

It's winter. They're dead.

I bet they're hibernating.

They're dead. Nothing's living in here.

We are.

She started making tracks down a crooked little path.

You're never going to find it.

I'm not looking for it, she said, walking on. The tall black stones crowded in from all directions, their mossy surfaces dripping and cold, their inscriptions in Hebrew unreadable and sad. She was compelled to follow them deeper and deeper, knowing that any moment she could turn morose. She knew she was at an age when she should appreciate this place. She was at an age when she should pause and give it all some thought—the holy and forgotten remains of a culture, the beautiful remains of a persecuted religion that for hundreds of years had shaped their nation, bringing richness and wealth and wisdom and all of that. Nearly fifty years ago it had vanished, and yet it lingered in the stones and soil. It lingered in the stories and snow and shame. Jewish memory, her mother would say. Polish shame, her fa-

ther would say. And she was at an age when she could think for herself about those bones underfoot, ponder the fleeting gift of life, ponder the musky permanence of death. But in fact they were looking for
a soccer ball. And her feet were freezing. And she was walking with a
friend, whom she couldn't just ignore.

I wonder if Matek's ever been in here, Piotr said, walking up
behind.

Why?

I just wonder.

He couldn't have any fun in here, she said.

Gurney's been here. He says it's fun. He says he comes here with
his girlfriend sometimes.

His girlfriend? She turned around. Who the hell is that?

Her name's Jackie. I've never seen her, but I figured you could tell
me all about her.

I can't tell you anything.

This bothered her for some reason. She wasn't really jealous that
Gurney had someone, for to be fair she had a boyfriend and she was
crazy about him, but she was jealous because he hadn't told her himself. And after all she'd done for him, she thought that the bastard was
becoming her friend. Didn't he trust her? Did he trust Piotr more
than he trusted her? Piotr, too, looked like he was feeling uneasy. He
bent over to inspect a broad thin tablet that looked like half of the Ten
Commandments. What's wrong, Peter?

There's a snake on this headstone. The person must have been a
doctor.

What's wrong with *you*, not the stone.

Nothing.

Right. Never mind. But all at once she had a hunch, and looking
at her friend's pale pink face it occurred to her why he wanted to walk
through the graveyard. Why didn't she see it sooner? It was as plain as
could be. Piotr had a little crush on Gurney! Just as she did. Piotr was
jealous of Gurney's girlfriend, whoever this Jackie was, and it was eating him alive. A crush on Gurney! God, she was smart. She almost
started teasing him about it, because she wanted to know how anyone

else could possibly have a crush on Gurney, but she didn't know how well he would take it. She smushed a hot kiss on his soft cold face instead.

What's that for?

Nothing, she said, and bounded along the bumpy path, wondering how those two dumb lovers managed to have any fun in here. A thought occurred to her: she could hardly tease Piotr for liking Gurney, that would be unkind, but it would be okay to ask him one related question whose answer she was dying to know. He'd certainly have an opinion on it. Hey, Peter, she said.

Yes?

Do you think he really fucked his cousin?

Piotr wrinkled his face as if he'd bitten into a lemon. I doubt it, he said. But somehow he's gotten himself to believe that he did, and that's almost the same.

What do you mean?

He's a Catholic boy. You know how dramatic he is. I bet he wanted to do it something terrible, and I bet he got so scared by the chance that he just might do it that now he believes he really did. Such a pity. He got all the guilt and none of the fun.

This answer relieved her. She continued down the dismal path.

Happens to Catholic boys all the time, Piotr explained.

They even go looking for fun in graveyards.

And sometimes that's just the place to find it! He laughed and pointed way up high in the trees, where the soccer ball was lodged in between the branches.

Eighteen

BY THE TWENTIETH OF DECEMBER things were really happening. Gurney was up and bathed by seven in the morning, serving coffee to the kids who had spent the night. Over the past few days he had put himself at the center of the Xmas preparations. He had made eggnog for the masses, helped them string colored lights from the rafters. He had bought discount cans of unseasonable paints and helped them give the dingy old place a new coat. Make it a sex chapel, make it a circus wagon, make it anything you wish, he'd said, wanting to spruce up the funereal gloom. A real American giant, or so he must have seemed, he offered himself up as a skinny Santa Claus. Kids and hipsters jammed five to the couch and sat cross-legged all over the floor, passing the hash pipe, watching Mateusz hamming it up, admiring Piotr as he cooked up the turntables and patched together his holiday mix of Parliament, the mazurka, Ewa Demarczek. Wujo Płujo worked liked worker ants while stoned young Kraków poked around the tree, shaking gifts wrapped in pink butcher paper, coveting the pies cooling in the window, eyeing the stockings tacked up above the stove.

The closer they got to the holiday itself, however, the harder he had to work at having a good time.

He was firing up the percolator pot, making another round before returning to the *poczta*, when a messenger boy arrived with a note—in Jackie's handwriting!

He hadn't seen Jackie in over two weeks. He hadn't been over there since busting up his hands and then doing all that other stuff with Jane—but he had written her many notes, and he had called her number, sometimes several times a day. True, she had responded to none of this, and he realized by now that it was over between them, but he still called her his girlfriend when talking to Wujo Płujo.

And now there was a note! This could mean anything. It was written in blue ballpoint pen:

20. 12. 90

Crazy Gurney.

Sorry I've been so scarce. I want to see you, today, if that's possible. I have something for you, call it an Xmas gift. If you want it, meet me at Kleks, on the Rynek, at noon, or contact me with a better plan. Kleks means ink blotch.

Much love,
Jackie Witherspoon

Love! Love! Love! Love, Jackie Witherspoon! Did this mean she loved him? An Xmas gift. Did this mean they'd have Xmas sex? Xmas sex at Kleks? First he too had to get her an Xmas gift.

Hey Peter, he called out, rushing into the circus chapel. Where's Kleks?

Kleks? he said, looking up from the *Gazeta Wyborcza.* He crinkled his nose.

Kleks? chimed the other kids, giving similar looks of disgust.

Yes, Kleks. It means ink blotch, I believe.

Ink spot, Piotr corrected. Ink spot. The place is from my nightmares. It is a cigarette-smoke discotheque-restaurant. Don't you know it? It is in the building next to Wanda's, where you lived. It is on the second floor.

To jest syph, a hipster said.

Syph? Gurney asked.

Na przykład, syphilis.

The concrete post office was packed and edgy, people pushing him from behind, making him push the people in front, nobody really going anywhere. He daydreamed about what he was going to give Jackie. The problem was that she was loaded now, and he was coming to the end of his savings. He could never hope to match her generosity. Given more warning, he could have found her a rare book. A couple of weeks earlier, he could have bought her lingerie. Pushing back from an elbowing *babka,* he thought of Jackie's featherlight lingerie— cream silk cups falling from her breasts, low-slung briefs sliding off her hips—and he started getting aroused right there in line. He knew lingerie wouldn't do just yet. He would have to approach this with baby steps, get her hothouse flowers in the dead of winter; then if she rejected him it'd even be all the more romantic. But how could she reject that? First flowers, then chocolate, then the real Xmas pudding. They'd be back together in no time. Maybe they'd even leave Kraków together—go to Greece, the Middle East, just in time for the strike in the Gulf!

He entered the cold, relieved of his packages, ready to take on a new life with Jackie. The ice was sky blue, the clouds all marshmallowy, the blunt sun was cutting out yellow and green buildings like a child at work with safety scissors. Bad teeth, bent noses, bald heads, everyone smiling and full of Xmas spirit. Crossing the Planty he wanted music. All he heard was traffic and whispering trains, so he started whistling, nonsense at first, jumbled strains that turned into a Bach minuet that he used to play on the piano in grade school. A flower shop sprung up. He went in and bought flowers from the pretty shopgirl. Armed with flowers and whistling like a fool, he was ready for just about anything—Algeria, Alexandria, anywhere, anything.

The Zamoyski building was an ugly mausoleum. He walked on past, whistling with flowers. The sign for Kleks stuck out next door— a stylized black ink blotch, looking something like *Dating Game* flowers. He went through the glass doors, took two star-patterned stairs at a time, and emerged in a lushly carpeted black-and-white lounge. He looked for his date through the musty haze, drifting his eyes over the half-empty tables, past the wood-tiled dance floor, along the lacquer bar, along the bubble-mirrors studding the far wall, along the smoked windows that seemed to magnify the oddly medieval Cloth Hall and clock tower. No Jackie. Was he early? Had he stumbled into the pages of *Playboy* magazine? It was four minutes past twelve. Was she standing him up, as she had on Halloween? Leaving him standing there like an idiot with flowers? But just before his day turned dreary, a familiar touch lit on his shoulder.

Hey! she said, kissing his cheek.

Hello, he said, kissing her back. Merry Christmas!

Thank you! They look like California.

California Christmas in Kraków.

Have you gotten us a table? she said, a little too seriously. She cradled a formidable present in her arm.

Lots of tables. We'll pick one together.

By the windows.

Naturally, he said, sliding off her coat, a sealskin number that was new to him. He hung it up with his cap and coat and followed her to the table. Her body slid around in a gray silk dress. He was glad to see she was spending her money.

You look great. I like your dress.

She waved away his compliment and put the flowers on the table. They both ordered Cokes and looked at water-stained menus that, despite the swanky atmosphere, offered the same food as everywhere else. He chose roast chicken, in memory of the Thanksgiving they never really had, and looked through the grime at the sunny square. The view was exactly the same as Jane's, dominated by that dazzling WESOŁYCH ŚWIĄT sign. He wondered if Jane's studio shared a wall with this place. He wanted to tell Jackie that he was ready to leave Poland, ready to move on into the Merry World, but he didn't know how to make an attractive offer. He'd feel her out, wait until they were flirting full tilt.

You're living in Kazimierz? Her chocolatey eyes were easy, sandy hair freshly cut.

I'm having fun. I'm living with a bunch of Wanda's friends.

That's cool. Her voice was flat.

What?

That's cool, I said. What made you leave Jane's place?

The long answer is, we had a falling out. The short answer is, I wasn't having fun and now I am.

What kind of fun? I mean, why with a bunch of teenagers?

Teenager fun, that's all. You know Jane—she's always got an agenda. But with these kids, I don't know, they're a lot like you, what you see is what you get. And that's fun.

She reopened her menu and, lightening her tone, asked again: What *kind* of fun, you wicked boy?

You'd get a pretty good idea from the damage we do. Dirty shoes, skinned elbows, broken lamps. Good, clean fun. He could see that Jackie didn't share his enthusiasm, and so he let the smile fade slowly from his lips, trying to make it look natural. This was not the peanut-butter-and-jelly Jackie whom he had first flirted with on the Rynek. Something had changed. It would be delicate work getting them back in sync.

You and your damn irony, she said at length.

Am I being ironic?

Not that I blame you, really, but your whole worm-hole irony business almost killed it for me.

Killed what?

The book.

What book?

She looked surly.

Is that what's got you? Sweetie, I was just, like, rambling on that night.

Forget it. Drop it. It was good for me. It was liberating. I'd gotten to be such a kook about the thing that I'd started to forget that it's just a book—a moldy one at that. She waved to the waitress and called out, *Proszę!*

But you were a believer, queen of the cult. You'd eat the earthworms and everything.

Eesh. Don't remind me. Anyway, it was good for me. I stopped fetishizing the silly thing. I sent it home to one of my old professors, and he wrote back right away, saying we can probably do something with it. He's sure we can at least get a facsimile of it published.

That's great, he said, looking at his hands. *Proszę!* he, too, called out, and then to Jackie: You must think I'm such a kid.

You're twenty-two. You still *are* a kid.

But as she called out to the waitress, being a kid didn't feel right. It felt like wearing high-water corduroys. Wujo Płujo—they were kids, extraordinary kids, but he supposed he was supposed to be turning into something else. The reluctant waitress sidled over, pink hair and flocked smock. She looked out the window and smoked her cigarette, absently taking down their order. She walked away without collecting their menus.

I want out of Poland, he said.

Me, too, she said. In fact, I am getting out.

What do you mean?

I'm going home, going back to school, but let's not get into that just yet.

Right. So what on earth do you want to get into?

I don't want to get into anything, to tell the truth, but I have to.

What do you mean?

I've been a bad girl. She smiled when she said this. And there are some things I have to tell you. That's why I brought you here. And there's something I have to give you.

What do you have to tell me?

I've had an insane month.

Me too.

I mean really insane.

Me too.

Would you please just listen? Half of it's your fault.

Me? What did I do?

Listen, would you? And half of it is my fault, and that's what I'll start with. I'm sure you remember that one rainy day, that first rainy day. November first. You soaked in my tub.

Gee, what day?

I told you all about this professor I knew.

Zbigniew Zamoyski.

How did you know?

I doubt it's a big secret. But I just happened to read about it in Jane's diary.

You read Jane's diary? There was gossip in her voice, a hint of the old Jackie, but he wasn't biting.

I found out a lot of crap that way. A lot of crap I didn't want to know.

What did it say?

Let's not get into it. I'm just listening, remember? So continue. Zbigniew Zamoyski.

She looked very pretty as she collected herself, brown eyes darting around the room, her face changing from wily fox to furtive rabbit and back to Jackie Witherspoon. A bad girl. Would they get past this crisis? Was there still something there to work with? He felt ill. The *żurek* arrived, but as she talked he lost all appetite. Yet nothing prevented her from buttering her bread and spooning her soup in her familiar way.

I feel like a real heel, she said, spooning. I've been keeping things from you, and you know how I feel about secrets. I hate them. They eat you right up. Unfortunately, they do have their place, though. Sometimes secrecy's the safest bet.

Zbigniew Zamoyski.

I'm getting to that. That day in the bathroom was a big deal for me. I knew what Jane was wanting me to think. She wanted me to think that you were some sly dog who'd run off and deserted your little girl—and that's one interpretation for sure. But you, I don't know, *smelled* so nice, and you had so much fun—yes, fun—splashing through the puddles, remember? And you looked so funny in my cramped-up little bathtub. I guess I just liked you, and I had to find out for myself what you were all about.

I looked funny?

Well, you didn't exactly *turn me on* yet. Sorry. But I wanted to find out what made you tick. I probably never did. But I like you and I've found out that you're a lot like my dad.

Oh, Christ.

Hush, I never told you about my dad. My real dad. He got my mom pregnant when he was about your age.

You're getting off the subject.

All of this *is* the subject. Listen. Sometimes I think she did it on purpose, my mother, but that's beside the point because he didn't stick around. He moved to Boston for law school, then he quit that and moved to London, then Madrid, as if wanting to get farther and farther away. I think he was scared of ending up with Mom again, like, by default. But he always sent me cards, and Mom support checks, and he came back to visit me two or three times a year. When I got older I'd visit him and all that. It wasn't ideal, not at all, but it turned out okay. For a while there I was mad at him, hated him, but at some point I realized that's just how he is.

Where is he now?

Oddly enough, I'm in Europe and he's back in San Francisco.

Doing what?

Something with computers. I don't get it. She pushed her empty bowl aside and looked around for the second course. The point is, she continued, that afternoon I kept seeing this hunted look in your eyes. It bugged me until I realized I'd seen it in my dad's eyes. Here you were, Gurney and my dad, two boys who never would have *chosen* to have kids. You just wanted to go on being boys like everyone else, but surprise! You had these little daughters and you couldn't help but take them seriously—so seriously you had to rip your lives up by the roots.

You're making excuses.

For whom?

For your dad. For me.

Jackie scowled. I don't know what *you're* planning to do about it, but my dad kept coming back for me. It made a big difference. The more he came back, the bigger the difference it made.

Zbigniew Zamoyski, Gurney said.

Did you hear a word I said?

I'm not deaf!

Give it some thought?

Now tell me why you feel like a heel.

She paused while the waitress dropped off their plates. He looked at Jackie, aware that she was about to disappear. He looked at his chicken, potatoes, beet salad. Taking up her flatware in the European manner, Jackie went on talking and eating. He was feeling sick to his stomach, but he listened intently.

That day in the bathroom, as I've said, I had these strong feelings for you and my father. And I wanted to tell you about my abortion, so you'd know you weren't alone, and I guess so I'd know that *I* wasn't alone. I remember trying to make Zbigniew out to be an ogre, this Caliban who cornered me and made me kill my baby, but even as I was telling how he'd torn apart my flat, even as I was making him as ugly as I could, my feelings for him were coming back up. I couldn't help but feel bad for him, too. I couldn't help but see that he was just like you and Dad. Hush! Not *just* like, because you're not violent like that, not at all, but you do have this one thing in common: I figure for you and Dad it meant your boyhood and your freedom, and maybe for me it meant my girlhood and freedom. In any case it was a gift, a grave gift—to have a kid, I mean. But another child would have *cost* Zbigniew his wife and family. That's why he snapped when I told him I was pregnant.

What did you do?

I went to see him.

Gurney looked at his plate. The chicken wasn't food but a chunk of dead bird. When did you go see him?

That afternoon.

Right after I left?

Pretty much. I would have called him first, but he doesn't have a phone. So I took the bus and hoped that he would be there.

Wonderful.

Be nice.

Nice. What about Jane?

He told me about her sometime after I got there, but whatever, really. I was only going out there to clear the air, that was all. At first.

At first. Gorgeous. Keep it coming.

Well, I should have known that it couldn't be that easy. The minute I saw him there, working in the garden with his pants rolled up, mud all over his hands and knees, I realized I had all these unresolved feelings. Angry ones, tender ones.

So you jumped in the sack with him.

Not that day.

You gave him your little surprise.

What? What little surprise?

Nothing.

We just talked, that's all. I started with the abortion, where we'd left off, and I could see that he had been denying it ever since. I have this image of him crouching in the garden, all stressed out, stabbing his spade into the potato plants. We stayed there in the mud and talked for some time. He was completely changed. He had become all quiet and dreamy. He was like an old hermit out there in the country.

Do you really need to tell me all this?

Hear me out.

Get to the point where you two jump in the sack, then I can go.

Not so fast. He wasn't the cosmopolitan I'd known in California. He was just an old gardener, planting his garden—on the first of November!

The first of November, Gurney repeated.

Looking back on it, I should have seen how insane it was, but that day I was so happy to see him, Gurney, that all I could think was how sad it all was. He talked a blue streak about Wanda—his living daughter, he called her. I wasn't even offended. I got the picture he was consoled by her, proud what a great student she was and how talented and sociable and honest she was.

Is.

Sure, is. He kept comparing her to me, which was weird, and he said he wanted her to go to Stanford or some other American school like that. Wanda and his garden, that was his life, that was all he talked about. He was coughing like he was dying of pneumonia, so I put him to bed and made him some tea.

You put him to bed, then you left.

His place was all muddy. I cleaned it up and then I left.

But you kept on seeing him, even though you were seeing me.

It's not like we had a contract or anything. But yes, I did do that, and that's what I feel like a heel about.

Don't tell me any more.

There's more that I have to tell you.

I know too much already. It's plain as fucking day, all right?

Please calm down.

You and Jane are fucking this guy because it's the next best thing to having your fathers. And he's fucking you and Jane because it's the next best thing to having Wanda. I'm not stupid, okay?

Some women would slap you for saying that. I'm sure it's more fun playing Freud the Cowboy than it is to look at your own role in it all. But you must be pretty hurt, so I won't slap you.

My role? Slap me if you must, but I'm innocent.

Sure, you're innocent. Whatever. But listen, there's some stuff you need to know for your safety.

Right! There's stuff I could tell you for your safety, too!

I'm sure there is, but don't worry about me. I've stopped seeing him now, for good. The next time I saw him he was completely changed—again! He had on a cashmere suit and a fat gold watch. He pointed out his car down on the street—a big black Mercedes, scrunched in with all the Fiat Polskis.

He was at your place again?

Yes.

I bet Jane didn't know about this.

He said she didn't.

Did he know about me?

Not yet.

Why did you keep seeing me?

I was seeing him out of nostalgia, like I thought we had unfinished business together. I was seeing you because I liked you. The two were very different. He was history. You were now.

They can't happen at the same time.

Unfortunately they can.

Whatever. Tell me about my lousy safety.

Well, for one thing, a few days after Thanksgiving I started getting calls from Herr Messersturm.

What kind of calls?

Inquiring calls, nothing threatening. You haven't touched your chicken.

Pardon me, but I feel kind of sick.

You poor thing. He was very polite, but he asked some pointed questions about that night at the Kasino. How well I knew you, stuff like that.

And you told him?

The truth.

Wonderful, of all the people to be honest with.

You're right about that. He started getting very suspicious, until finally he came over and dragged along some detectives.

Detectives? And you're just telling me now?

It was *my* money. I thought I should take care of it. Anyway, they told me the whole story.

The whole story. This should be interesting. Fill me in.

Well, they sat on my couch and got all sarcastic, as if the details were just a formality. They acted as if I already knew them or something. I'll try not to take the same tone with you, but I can't help but think that you know them too. They told me how Jane had gotten you the job by seducing the Kasino's primary shareholder, some American lady.

Eulalia.

Is that her name?

You don't know her?

I don't, but see? *You* know her. You're all clued in.

Jane's diary. It's a fine resource.

Back to the story: they had spied on Zbigniew and me and knew that we had been hanging out, so they thought they would mention how Jane had also seduced Zbigniew, getting him to invest big money in the Kasino. Something to the tune of two hundred thousand dollars. I told them I hadn't heard of this and that it wasn't any of my business. They gave me these damn looks, I wanted to kick their bony shins, but I didn't. Then they told me something that was absolutely my business. Straight from the mouth of your croupier Tomasz.

Great. This has to be good.

Tomasz had said you'd been bad-mouthing the Kasino all night. Is this true?

I bad-mouthed the Kasino *every* night.

And he said you'd wished just one of your gamblers would win big. True?

Yep.

And he said that you told me how to bet, which I already knew, but he said that this was based on a trend that you knew well.

Did they tell you how I tampered with the roulette wheel?

Did you? They alluded to that.

Of course I didn't. Christ, Jackie! It's a roulette wheel. You can't rig a roulette wheel. At least *I* can't. So tell me, what did they make of all this coincidence and confusion? What was their *interpretation*, Ms. Earthworms?

They accused us all of being conspirators.

You and me?

And Jane and Zbigniew.

All four of us? He burst out laughing, not bothering to stop for quite some time. Jackie ate and waited it out. Conspirators! Moles! Spy versus Spy! Jackie didn't even crack a smile, but he couldn't stop the rolling waves of hilarity. The tremors subsided, and a chill came over him.

I can't see what's so funny, she said. The law is after us, thanks to your little trick.

What law? Polish law?

Probably. I wish you would take this seriously—take *something* seriously.

First of all, it was an accident, not a scheme. Second, you won your money fair and square. Third, not in my wildest dreams would I ever conspire with Zbigniew Zamoyski.

I believe that last part, but here's where your biggest troubles start. With Zbigniew. Apparently you and Wanda turned up at his cottage a couple weeks ago. Big mistake, but you couldn't have known that. He said you were riding him about those letters and Wanda was riding him about everything else. He felt cornered.

Of course he did. Plus Jane was out there hiding in the garden.

Jane? He didn't tell me that part.

Go on, please. Go on and tell me how I fucked up. Tell me how I brought up your name and told him you'd broke the bank at my roulette station. Tell me all that, then we can agree how stupid I was and then I can tell you some stuff you don't know—how he put me in a headlock and started fucking choking me, how he cut off my wind with his fat little fingers just like he probably did to Dick Chesnutt. I mean, really, Jackie, how can you sit there pestering me like this? So I lifted eight fingers and helped you win a fortune from a casino that's totally crooked to start with. So the fuck what! It was a gift! You're the one who's been lying since you met me and fucking around behind my back with that smelly hairy Polack murderer. I mean, really, how could you?

I'm not pestering you, and at least I'm telling the truth now. And what's this you're saying about Dick Chesnutt?

He killed him, Gurney said.

Zbigniew killed Dick Chesnutt?

Yes.

What kind of proof do you have?

The worst kind. Let's not mention it.

That's asking a lot. What kind of proof—

Just finish your story.

She finished off her Coke and gave him a soft look, a look she might give a donkey that was dying of starvation. Whether she believed him or not, it was clear she didn't want to know any more. She wanted to leave Poland with a clean conscience. So be it.

If Zbigniew is dangerous as all that, and I hope for your sake it's all in your head, you will want to take this seriously, if nothing else. After you left his cottage that day, he jumped in his car and zoomed into the city, straight to my flat.

What about Linda?

Linda? What about her?

Oh, never mind. What a town. What a crock.

He was still in his pajamas and he was asking about my money. I told him, yes, I had won some money, and it was held in a safety-deposit box at the bank—which was true. Then he asked about you, how well I knew you and so on, and I said not very well, which was a lie, not even consistent with what I'd told the detectives. My only interest right then was protecting you, Gurney, because he had that wild monkey look in his eyes, and I'd only seen that one other time before. Though this time it wasn't meant for me, it was meant for you. I made tea and talked him down. It seemed the detectives hadn't gotten to him yet, so he only had my version to go by. I said that from what I could tell you were honest, if, you know, a little rash.

You said I was rash?

I couldn't let on that I was protecting you, and anyway, what's the difference? Because it was just about then that you turned up yourself and showed the whole world how rash you were. I mean, Jesus, what a racket! Pounding and yelling, me inside, with this human time bomb, cupping my hand over his mouth. I said a little prayer that it would blow over, and for some reason it did. You went away. I took my hand away, and for a moment he didn't move at all. Then he said my name, and Jane's name, and Wanda's name. And then he said, and this is a quote, that if he didn't step in himself the pestilence would probably get to his wife and then the whole forest would be infected.

What pestilence?

I'm quite sure he meant you. But that's all he said. He didn't break anything. He didn't say good-bye. He just up and left and that's the last I saw of him.

He's the fucking pestilence. It's like he's got rabies, frothing around out there looking for me.

It's been a couple weeks. You can't be that hard to find.

It takes time to plot a murder.

Don't be silly. But I'm afraid he might actually be up to something.

Her plate was clear, her knife and fork resting in the four o'clock position. His untouched food had developed a sheen and looked as if it could last forever. Strips of beets forever tangled. Bones forever pushing through the straining wing meat. He hated it when people spread napkins over their plates, as if it were polite to bury the un-eaten. But he did wish he could make it go away. Nobody was coming to clear the table. In their silence he wondered if he should clear it himself.

Look, Gurney, like I said, I'm leaving Kraków. I'm going home for Christmas and not coming back. She moved the flowers to her lap and set the present on the table. This is for you. I have to admit I kept back a little bit for myself, like twenty thousand for student loans, but the rest is all yours. It only makes sense. To keep it would be stealing.

Never, he said. Never in a million years.

I have no right to it.

You won it. It's yours.

In that case, it's mine to give to you. Plus, there's something else in there, something that wasn't mine to begin with. I know I'm giving you a grave gift, and I suppose if you wanted to, you could leave it here on the table and walk away from it forever. But we both know how stupid that would be.

That's exactly what *you're* doing with it!

No, I'm giving it to you.

Same thing.

But that was that. The waitress brought the check, and they made their way out down the star-patterned steps and into the snowy sun-light. He was so hurt and angry that he turned his face when she went to kiss him good-bye—but then she was gone, and her gait was so light as she walked away that he thought she might easily lift off the ground. She had settled her accounts, cleared her books. Now all she had left was that featherweight bouquet, but even that would wilt in a couple of days. She rounded the corner, disappeared. Gurney didn't move. He stood there on the square, bound to the earth, an awkward bundle clutched to his chest.

THE SUN WAS BRIGHT, an enormous klieg lamp articulating Kraków's every crack and pebble. It followed him through town, bouncing off the snow into his eyes, showing the world the box under his arm. He pulled at his cap and dropped the box in the slush and had trouble picking it up with his mittens. Bodies bumped him, boots sloshed through shiny puddles. He thought of buying sunglasses but knew he didn't have enough złotys, only a couple hundred thousand dollars. He looked for the fun in his situation, he tried to focus on the fun, for here was this American in an Eastern European city, lugging a box loaded with money. It would have been fun in the movies. In the movies, his eyes wouldn't ache, he wouldn't have been hungry. He wouldn't have had to take a piss. There would still be the detectives, and there would probably be a fuckhead like Zbigniew Zamoyski. But it would be fun. Humphrey Bogart, Robert De Niro, *they'd* have known how to carry that thing as if stolen money really belonged to them. They'd pop some Tums, clutch the box, and keep fighting right down to the death. (He doubted there were Tums in Poland.) They'd have walked straight into the sun, puffed up with pride and lugging their money. He tripped on a curb and rammed into some people. But this money wasn't stolen. It simply didn't belong to him and he had to keep it moving through the crowd, where most men, he noticed, were the size of Zbigniew, many of them with short-trimmed beards. He didn't even know what the detectives looked like, but they probably didn't look like detectives. Messersturm didn't scare him, though. He could have fun with Messersturm again. And what was Zbigniew but Messersturm with a beard? Humphrey Bogart would have had fun with Zbigniew. Bogie would have run circles around him, but even so Zbigniew was quick; he could swing you around, go for the throat— Zbigniew had some weight behind him and he could probably strangle the life out of, say, Charlie Sheen.

He trudged along the avenues, bumping pedestrians, shifting the box from one side to the other. Soon he arrived at the Hotel Cracovia, an angular blue behemoth for Western tourists, ideal for a rich young American like himself. With its Stalinist mood and space-age shape it looked as if it had been built in the fifties or sixties, though it was probably only ten years old. At the desk, he requested a luxurious suite, which cost four hundred thousand złotys, about forty dollars. Up in his room, with the curtains open, he went to the bathroom and threw up what he could.

HE WOKE FROM A NAP and found the sun going down. He went to the window. The tomatoey light was gentle on his eyes, spilling from the clouds above Kosciuszko Mound, a pink pool of it forming in the snow-covered meadow that unrolled from the hotel like a broad, rosy carpet. A solitary tram rode out the meadow's length, inching away from him into the woods. He knew what he was looking at. Hidden out there in the forest above town, in the hills now blazing orange with sunset, was the zoo that Wanda talked about sometimes. He imagined the black trees sheathed in ice, throbbing in orange, shaking with the roars of a helpless lion. He went to the bathroom and rinsed out his mouth.

He called room service for soup and bread. He called again for a toothbrush and toothpaste. He ate at the table, watching the sky grow bluer and darker, and eventually got up to brush his teeth.

The present lay on the second bed. He sat down beside it. It was wrapped in midnight paper with twinkling silver stars, stubbed and ripped on the corner where he'd dropped it. Why had she wrapped it? She could have handed over the money and been done with it. But that wasn't like her. He thought of the way she'd left him on the Rynek, almost skipping. He had been counting on more from her, even though she'd blown him off for so long, for now that he was awake and sitting on the bed, her loss was devastating. Something had been scooped out of the middle of his chest, leaving him hollow and rattling like a gourd. Whatever he had expected from her, now he had her response, and it was hardly what he wanted. In the middle of it all, he'd thought they were invisible. He had thought that someday they would emerge into daylight, all clean and new like her damn night-crawlers. He thought his parents would adore her, his daughter would look up to her, but now he had to see the folly of it all. Those nights when he'd go home to drink and flirt with Jane, Jackie would tear off in Zbigniew's Mercedes for filthy pleasures all their own.

He understood why she gave it all back: she couldn't be compromised for any amount of money, except maybe student-loan money. But why wrap it? He sliced the room key through the paper, trying to be tidy but ripping off a flap that showed the top of a neat white box. Nordstrom. In Kraków? From her parents. Just like her lunch box and jars of peanut butter. He balled up the paper and shot at the waste-basket, missing by more than a foot. Nordstrom. He had to pee. He went to the bathroom and came back. He sucked in his breath and lifted the lid. Beneath a layer of wadded tissue, in four tight rows, lay packets of hundred-dollar bills. He ran his hand through his hair. The money was tidy and ordered and awesome.

He looked at the door, his reflection in the window. He shut the curtains and made a quick count—four rows of six.

$$24$$

Sliding his fingers between the money and the box, he counted its depth—five packets deep.

$$24 \times 5 = 120$$

One hundred and twenty? Right. One twenty times what? He counted out a single packet: two thousand dollars. Having collected this information, he slowly did the math in his head:

$$120 \times \$2,000 = \$240,000$$

Two hundred and forty thousand dollars. In cash. Fresh bills. Never spent. He fanned the inky-smelling packet with his thumb. The soup and bread fluttered in his belly. The telephone didn't ring. Nobody was at the door. He fanned the money. Two hundred and forty thousand dollars. That was three times his father's yearly income. And his father was forty-eight, more than twice his son's age.

$$22 \times 2 = 44$$

But the money wasn't Gurney's. Nor did it belong to anybody else. It was just plain money, a box of unspent, indignant money, and he happened to have it right there in his possession.

But what fun it could be!

He thought of the fun.

The world popped up in a full-color transit map, mechanical doors whispering open, trains and airplanes departing at once and zooming him away to the islands of Greece, the mountains of China, the musical streets of London and Paris, the tangled bliss of Tokyo and Hong Kong. Young Americans abroad with smarts and money sported slick passports unlike any other—passports glinting with the virtues of democracy—passports stamped with military might that ushered them into clubs and playgrounds, resorts and bordellos, any place fun was being had. For young Americans of Gurney's stripe, money meant action, jet propulsion—never mind the fine things money could buy, the sandbags he could fasten to his Jules Verne balloon, because money for fun meant lightweight luggage, a four-season wardrobe of versatile clothes, a wardrobe for enjoying all climes and terrains, spelunking into the minarets of Moscow, camel trekking the busy boulevards of Sydney, shaking martinis on the Kenyan savannas or stopping to fuck on the way up Mount Everest. Fuck fashion and property and all those heavy treasures, fuck Mercedeses like Zbigniew Zamoyski's. Money was the champagne fountain of youth, the blood of bicyclists, the sweat of sky divers, the kayaker's white water smashing into rocks! Money was fun, the lube of life, the jelly of joy, and just look how much of it he had there on the bed, in that box, in his hands, thrown into the air— into the air—like so many bricks of Black Cat firecrackers!

But what was this? He separated the money to see what he'd thrown up. Envelopes and letters, from Sheila and their parents. His heart sped up, his mouth went dry. He wondered how she had gotten them, how she had known, and he recalled having told her all about them once. He worked through the calculations: she'd swiped them from the records, snuck them home, and then given them back to Gurney along with the money—the whole thing thrown together in one messy Xmas gift. A grave gift. That was why she had wrapped it— so he would think about how grave and terrible it was. And that, of course, is just what he thought, the fun melting away like a snowman in springtime. Rats, he said. Rats alive. He picked up the two letters in Sheila's sweeping hand. He couldn't resist at least looking at Sheila's. He opened the first one, postmarked October 2, written more than a week after he'd jumped on the plane.

iowa city

gurney—

why do you have to be such a dumbass? only you could have pulled this off in such a graceless selfish bizarre dangerous victorian chuckleheaded way. i still can't believe you ever made it through college. the baby's fine, by the way—how the hell are you?

pissed at you,
Sheila

Chuckleheaded? he said aloud. The letter was so Sheila he had to smile, but the feeling it gave was anything but nice. He smelled the stationery. It smelled like nothing. She had always been able to read him like a book, and even though this letter only said the obvious, its impact was as hot as a blazing arrow shot from halfway around the world, piercing him—*thwak!*—right where he knelt on the carpet. Sheila was good, very good. He tore open the second one, ready for anything. It was sent October 8:

iowa city

nice going, dumbass—

    my dad wants to kill you and my mom thinks you're dirt. but knowing you you probably want it that way. your folks paid a visit to their new granddaughter yesterday, her name is Celeste, and both of them cried—tears of joy, i think. your name never came up. your mom started talking about Celeste's red hair but shut up about it before she said the obvious. i'm just writing this to let you know that if you want to be invisible we're all working hard to keep you that way. but you probably know for yourself what a damn shame it is that you'll never really disappear—it's already far too late for that. i'm too busy to write you letters so consider this it.

    still pissed but who cares,
    Sheila

Celeste? What kind of name was Celeste? A French name, he thought and let it go. It embarrassed him to think he'd sent a card to Little Sarah. A gone Sheila. A gone Sarah. He wouldn't be needing the other letters, he thought. All the facts he needed flickered in this one, flickered in the shadows. And letters from parents would be no fun at all. He read it again and put it away. He put the money in the box, four rows of six, stacked five deep. He stashed the letters under the money, covered it with tissue, and slid the box under the bed. He opened the curtains and stood for a moment, looking into the blackened window, looking out toward the zoo, when he realized he was looking at his own gaunt reflection.

    He thought of something Jane had once said about the illusion of looking at yourself in the mirror. However much you want to believe that you're looking at your own face, and however much it seems that you can look through your eyes straight into your soul, you're really just looking at a sheet of glass. You're really just looking at the reflection of a chump who thinks he's looking into his soul.

    Chump! he said aloud.

He looked from one sheet of glass to the other. He imagined how he would look if he were dead. He imagined how he looked to the other people who knew him and saw him in living color. To Sheila he was nothing but a chucklehead. To Jackie he was the image of her vanishing father. To Jane he was something like Zbigniew's shadow, a wild-eyed kid she could run in circles, tie in knots, put on trial. But it didn't matter how he looked to himself, for that was just a sheet of glass—trembling glass, shaking glass. Right then and there he really was invisible. Unless there was someone out there in the dark, someone who could see him from down in the meadow, someone deep in the frozen woods. Since he couldn't see himself, he really wished there was someone who could.

Nineteen

GRAZYNA LIKED KILLING TIME with the actors. With Julian and company it was all adult theater. Dirty jokes. Saucy looks. And if ever for a moment it started getting dull, they dumped their roles, slipped into new ones, and kept everything bubbling up like soda. They were so unlike Zbigniew's droopy old peers. And so unlike Wanda, her rebellious daughter, who had recently discovered that she knew how to paint and wasted her talent on screeching car crashes and close-up shots of blood-pumping needles. She was good, that was clear. But she applied the paint with mocking alacrity, and her cruel eye split the rosy surface of things, splintered the hidden bones of experience. It was exhausting to see. Grazyna had been quick to praise her, but it wasn't much fun to be around. And it wasn't nice having to accept that her daughter was growing up crooked, or that she, as her mother, was somehow to blame.

It was the twenty-third of December, and Grazyna was free. She had canceled Christmas. She had gift-wrapped acrylics and brushes for Wanda. She had spent the day before stretching out canvases and filling the freezer with cakes and *naleśniki,* and now her job was done. She had every right to enjoy herself. She had every right to run off with these people, this caravan of thespians on their way out of town, and kill the holiday in the snowy Tatry Mountains. She was the only passenger in Julian's red Wartburg. He was lampooning Saddam Hussein and losing to the steering wheel with winter-bitten hands. Their line of cars, six in all, pushed through ugly drapes of smog and crested a ridge of stubbled snow. Brittle farm plots checkered the landscape, jerking and vibrating along the white and gray horizon. She rolled down her window, breathed in rushing cold, and shouted out, *Świetny! Świetny! Świetny!* Saddam grabbed her chunky thigh and the car took a mushy swerve on the shoulder.

She always felt twelve on her way to Zakopane, since she had been twelve in 1960, when her mother had driven the four girls down to the Olympics. What a weird delight, all the world's most glamorous athletes just a two-hour drive from Kraków. Broad-backed skiers in skin-tight sweaters, soaring off their jumps and taking over their slopes. Wild-eyed teams of Scandinavians and Japanese piling onto those race-car sleds. And most breathtaking of all, that elite class of skaters, silent gods and ethereal goddesses who touched down on the rink to show all the mortals just how plump and awkward they all were. Indeed, for all its glamour, the Games had reminded pubescent Grazyna just how awkward she was, clomping around in her hard-rubber boots. They'd made her embarrassed for all of Poland, an object of pity in the eyes of all those rich, free countries.

But this was no time to be thinking such things! It was fine to be feeling antsy and twelve as she roared out of town with this gorgeous man, but it was no time for mooning over the Games. Had Julian even been born yet? She did the math and found that he hadn't, not by a long shot, so she decided not to bring it up.

Isn't it excellent to get out of town? she said.

It recalls my time with the libertines, he said, when we would ride out of Paris on piebald horses, gallop through meadows and woods to our villa.

Na prawda? I didn't know you lived in Paris.

Tak, tak, sure I did, we all did for a time. And on our way to the villa we'd kidnap virgins. They had such delicate skin, it bruised like peaches under the lash. Just splendid, getting out of town. We'd piss on them all weekend long. We'd sodomize them and, *może być,* kill the poor things if we weren't careful.

Then she caught the joke, laughed. Julian had good blood like Zbigniew, and she was inclined to believe much of what he said. He had promised, for instance, that they would be holding the Christmas follies in the family house of Stanisław Ignacy Witkiewicz—the fabled mansion in the middle of Zakopane designed by the notorious writer-artist-thinker. She had gone past the house many times in her life, marveling as a girl at its Byzantine ornaments, yearning as a student for its forbidden history and imagining herself belonging to the Zakopane circle, that halcyon moment of drugs and excess that somehow took place in this dark and tragic century. (Until, of course, in defiance of the Soviets, Witkacy up and killed himself.) But to think Julian maybe knew the Witkiewicz family! She liked to believe he was as noble as he looked, but she was just as happy to see morning light pressing through his eyelashes.

When they arrived in Zakopane, the mountains were cloaked by sepia clouds—very dramatic, German romantic. Couples and families filled the narrow streets, most of them well dressed and balancing on the snow, bowing in and out of chalet shops, stepping aside for irrepressible skiers and truck-sized sleighs hauling milk jugs and meat. Grazyna was dressed in a sweater and jeans, furry boots keeping her feet toasty. Julian Zagórski, young and slight, wore a long brown coat and smart beret and strode through town as if he had it under seige, a general from Budapest visiting northerly posts. Other actors played out their own fantasies: pornographic lovers, boisterous scoundrels, the vicar and his wife mad with grief when they realize they've thrown their baby on the meat sled, then laughing in relief when they discover that their baby is just a cow's heart. This one-upmanship was invigorating and indeed a treat, so long as they let Grazyna act like herself.

Magda Szczypczyk suggested they hop a sleigh to the Olympic park. Grazyna was quick to second the motion, and all fifteen pounced like hunting dogs onto the first one that came sliding past, tangling themselves in a goosing, tickling, hollering mass before dividing up and sitting around the edges. Magda Szczypczyk ended up beside Grazyna. She was always cast as an ingenue. She had buttery blond curls, dun doe eyes, and she warmed you up just by looking at her. She had played Ophelia opposite Julian's naked Hamlet, and Grazyna assumed she and Julian had at one point had a real-life history, judging in particular from the double entendres sparking throughout their get-thee-to-a-nunnery scene. But of course all these actors had histories together. As a group, she felt, they were all about incest. When Magda hooked her arm with Grazyna's, however, it was clear she was no ingenue at all. Grazyna liked the fear that they might let her join their incestuous family. So while Julian started up a brandy bottle on the other side of the sleigh, she went ahead and made friends with Magda. And while the horses tugged them out of the village and toward the base of the cloudy slopes, where the rings and torch were coming into view, she told her all about the 1960 Games.

Magda listened earnestly, naïveté rising like mercury in her eyes, her mitten rising to wipe her red nose, and Grazyna confided the story of a Spanish boy whom she'd met in the crowd beneath the ski jumps. Upon hearing the boy's name was Pepito, Magda clapped her mittens and exclaimed, Just like in *Madeline*! Grazyna said yes that this was just what she had thought at the time. Magda admitted not knowing that Madeline had been around so long.

The real life Pepito, Grazyna explained, was no ambassador's son. He was just a hyperactive brat. He got my attention by slipping past his mother and standing right under the lip of the jump. I remember him leaping up, pretending to touch the skis when they took off over his head. I wasn't impressed but I felt bad for him when the officials dragged him away. Later on we were sitting on a hay bale and we kissed. It was my first kiss. It didn't go anywhere from there because we didn't have a single word in common—except for French words that sounded like Spanish. He thought I was Swiss. I didn't correct him.

At this last part Magda laughed and clapped her mittens, but after that they rode in silence, Grazyna starting to feel old again. The sleigh stopped and Magda ran over to the group gathering around Julian's brandy bottle, in a patchy area between the speed-skating track and the gondola. Grazyna paid the driver and started drifting, walking sideways, toward the pot-belly slope curving out beneath the ski jumps. She got near enough to hear that old scraping down the runway, wind growling against superwide skis as a fluorescent hero shot off the jump and mounted way up high in the air, high above the fingers of Pepito. The knee-shattering slap slammed her back into the moment, but every few seconds a new one shot up, a rubber man bouncing out into pure air, oblivious to Pepito's fingers, thrusting upward toward a vanishing spot that hung a few meters beyond his descending arc. Craggy peaks broke through the clouds—black rocks, white glaciers, young and untamed against the gray sky. New wind blowing off the snow filled her neck and face and hair. Seeing the group inch toward the gondola, she ran back toward them, laughing and tripping on chunked ice.

They drank heavily on the gondola and even more so on top. Wind chipped at rocks and drew snot from their noses. Wiesław and Beata, both of them big and insulated, broke away from the shivering pack and, casting off their clothes, ran like polar bears along the barren ridge. The others, now flustered zookeepers with seven bottles opened, chased them down as if they wanted to eat them, and she was right there with them, so swept up in it that the thought of roast Wiesław even crossed her mind, and then when they caught the naked bears, had hoisted them on their shoulders and were portaging them back to their abandoned clothes, she joined in the somber chorus, chanting, Back to the zoo, back in the stew, we've had just about enough out of you! Poor polar bears, she thought, wondering if the city could be seen from there, were it not for hundreds of kilometers of clouds.

After the polar bear incident, everyone started stripping naked at random. On the gondola down, for instance, to the delight of their fellow passengers, they shed everything but their boots and swayed in the little car, fifteen bodies drinking and singing, and when the bottom came rising toward them, they rushed themselves into whomever's clothes were handy. Grazyna cinched up a pair of military pants, squeezed into a turtleneck drenched in girly perfume, and drowned herself in a sea-green parka covered all over with snaps and pockets. Magda Szczypczyk put on Julian's coat and beret, but Julian wore Grazyna's sweater and scarf, and on the sleigh ride back to town, he put her on his lap and said she looked like Russian *mafiya*.

Her affair with Julian had been a striptease in reverse. She first met him the day he was naked in her studio, posing as Hamlet, and he was naked for their next several encounters after that—again in her studio and then at rehearsal and then at the cast party after the play. From the beginning, his long white body was little more for her than a comical companion to his serious face. It only made her want to throw a blanket on him. She started contriving ways to meet him with clothes on. At first he made excuses not to meet her in cafés, and when he finally agreed to dinner at the Actors' Guild, she feared he'd show up naked just to spite her. But he didn't. He wore a nappy black suit with short lapels, a melon silk cravat bursting at his throat. He couldn't have been more handsome, but so shy he hardly spoke, and it would have been unbearable if the cravat didn't make her crave to see him naked. After that night, she ignored him when he was naked, just as she would a boy on the beach, and she fawned on him when his clothes were on. But she was never really sure what she wanted. They hadn't slept together yet, and apart from some heavy groping and kissing, they'd hardly even acknowledged that they were dating. But this trip to the mountains! These winter clothes! This sleigh ride on his hardening lap! All of it was heading in the right direction—apart from the fact that they were heading right past the notorious mansion of Stanisław Ignacy Witkiewicz.

That afternoon, were it to be remembered at all, could only come back in tattered scraps—a rudely eaten *obiad* in a roomy cedar hall, drunken snow angels, drooping snowmen, hockey players sword fighting with brooms on the ice. An exhausting exchange of wet clothes and underwear left most of them naked on the rugs of the lodge, napping under steamy windows, jagged mountains looming above while graylight and firelight danced on their skin. Three restless nudes stayed up playing cards. Drifting off to sleep in her briefs, she pulled his skinny leg over her hip and mouthed an automatic Hail Mary for her daughter.

Waking before the others, she removed his hand from her sweaty hair and maneuvered through the actors to the messy kitchen. Having tidied up some, she emptied the grocery bags and started slicing—tomatoes, black bread, dry salami. A few minutes later Magda Szczypczyk appeared and helped to spread the mustard and mayonnaise.

Smacznego! Magda said, feeding her an olive.

Dziękuje, she said, pouring them bull's blood. Both were still sleepy and didn't say much. Magda Szczypczyk's breasts, she noticed, were hard like little turnips, her nipples faint like pink snow peaks. She liked how hard they looked, the daisy tattoo on her teenagerly tummy. Before realizing all the wrong ways that question could be taken, Grazyna asked: What do you think he sees in me?

Who?

Julian.

Magda ate a handful of olives and cherries, wincing at the taste as she chewed them and swallowed. She spit out the stones one at a time, onto the Spanish tiles around their feet. Then she put her fingers, sticky with olive juice, into Grazyna's hair, over the nape of Grazyna's damp neck. I bet when he touches you here, she said, spitting out another stone, I bet he sees a woman named Zamoyska, a pretty woman with tiny wrinkles and beautiful streaks of gray in her hair. I bet he sees an aristocrat. But when he touches you here, she continued, sliding her hands over Grazyna's face and chest . . .

That's not what I was asking.

Yes it was, she said, moving closer, placing her hands downward on the base of Grazyna's belly. And when he touches you here—

Grazyna sighed but kept standing straight, refusing to resist.

—and he feels you like this, and he touches your hair and he feels you underneath, and he feels you wet like this—oh, Grazyna, you're wet, she laughed and Grazyna laughed, but she didn't stop, and she wasn't stopped.

Yes? And? Grazyna whispered. When he touches me like this?

I don't know. I can't remember, she said, still touching her. Aren't you going to touch me?

Grazyna touched her turnip breasts, which were softer than they looked, and her pink snow peaks, her teenage tummy, marveling how quickly she'd been taken in by this actor, this ingenue, but now the theater had fallen all around them and here she was touching Magda Szczypczyk, here she was being touched by Magda Szczypczyk. She stopped.

I'm sorry, she said. I can't. I guess I'm not an actor. She tried to laugh.

I don't understand. Magda looked hurt, mildly condemning.

This doesn't feel real to me. It feels like a play, and I'm not much of an actor.

Magda said nothing, but she looked so genuinely the ingenue, with her lips parted and eyes wide open, her golden ringlets so disappointed, that Grazyna wondered if she really *were* an ingenue, or maybe that she had played the part so long she had no other options, in which case her experience of the world might only be that of an ingenue, wonderously touching Grazyna's body, feeling and smelling it as if for the first time, at which thought something clicked deep within Grazyna: a rush, a thrill, a swelling throb that felt so private that she had no desire—or right—to share it with this girl.

No, she said, closing her arms over her chest.

Magda looked bashfully at her feet, and yet this time the gesture was so contrived, the acting so bad, that the spell was broken and Grazyna was set free.

No, she repeated, more firmly.

Magda pulled back, chilly. There was a stirring in the next room. Hungry actors started milling into the kitchen, helping themselves to plates of sandwiches, their hairy and lumpy and bony bodies filling the space between hers and Magda's. That morning she had felt a little bruised when Magda had run off with her story of Pepito. Now she felt fine, though she stiffened when Julian came in and grabbed a sandwich. Magda, she noticed, didn't change at all, just leaned on the counter taking big drinks of wine.

Grazyna knew next to nothing about that night's follies, except that on the drive down Julian had said that there would be no spectators, only participants, and that she would have to join in or take the first train home. It had seemed like a joke and she'd assumed that the follies would just be antics, like charades and truth games, but as the night wore on and Magda kept avoiding her, and as everyone's humor turned darker and dirtier, she got the feeling she'd been lured into danger—bodily danger or spiritual danger—a devilish anti-Christmas tradition that would call for the blood sacrifice of an uptight artist. She glibly shared this fear with Julian, whose complexion had grown unkissably rough. He responded by putting vodka to her lips and saying there would be no blood shed in vain.

Throughout the night, actors would disappear and reappear later, fully transformed into warty-faced friars, warty-faced harlots, warty-faced seamen—indeed, apart from Magda, who returned dressed as a smooth-faced belly dancer, presumably a costume from the Tatar court of their Hamlet production, there were many warts to be seen among them. They were cheered on as they entered and they responded in kind, harlots and seamen cursing and jeering, a hoary old hag weeping at being noticed, the belly dancer (or Salome, it seemed) slinking over to those who applauded her the most and acting positively slutty to Julian, who spent most of the night in a director's chair, silent and arch, as if appointed to judge them one by one. Drunk as Herod, yet he soberly ignored Magda's wiles. Eventually, only Julian and Grazyna weren't in costume. He called her over and calmly told her to visit the adjoining cottage, where she would pick out her costume with one thing in mind: she should choose one that reflected her role with him.

What do you mean, with you?

What is your role, well, with me?

My role in our love affair?

You could call it that. Take this. He gave her a bottle of bisongrass vodka.

The adjoining cottage, just an eerily lit shack, was connected to the lodge by a lane of trampled snow. She walked to it, the bottle bouncing against her hip. It was cold inside. Winter clothes, heaped on the floor, shifted in the candlelight. A dressing table and mirror stood in the corner. She went to it and had a look: her eyes were bloodshot, and her nose, she had to notice, was maybe a little piglike. She looked at the cake makeup and considered being Julian's pig, calamine pink and rudely oinking. Or, if Magda was his Salome, might she be his Herodias? Not likely, for how would she do Herodias anyway? She put on lipstick, ruddy brown, bringing out the copper in her hair, and she mashed her lips together. She tried to recall the taste of Magda's mouth, the damp touch, the wet sex, the surprise that Magda, or anyone at all, could feel that genuine and taste that good and yet also be so genuinely Ophelia, so genuinely Salome or whoever else she wanted to be. Certainly it was an art, or maybe an illness, but whatever it was Grazyna didn't have it. When she kissed, she was Grazyna, just as when she talked or cooked or painted, and her nose was always a little like a pig's.

She drank weedy vodka and searched the remnants on the floor, finding the same clothes she'd picked through all day—the sea-green parka, Magda's overalls, rank thermal underwear—but what was on the bar over there? She went to it, clothes underfoot, and found two costumes hanging on the rack, a red one and a black. The red one was big and plush, furry around the collar and cuffs, a black patent-leather belt. Father Christmas. Santa Claus. She laughed and opened up its front. Pinned inside were a fleecy beard and a meter-long cap with cottony ball. The black one was a uniform, ratty and small with tarnished buttons. Lifting it from the bar, she saw its red armband and threw it down on the concrete floor. She crouched down next to it and looked to see if it was real.

The wool was musty, eaten through by moths, but its epaulets and pins were still intact. She turned its sleeve and inspected the armband. It was larger than she would have thought and even more menacing, like four spinning razors or a poison black spider. Who were these kids? What were they doing with this terrible thing? It wasn't a costume, it wasn't a toy. Didn't they know that? She felt sick. It wasn't a toy, it was a thin black adder, one of a million thin black adders that slept and slithered in Poland, right there under everyone's feet, and these kids wanted to play with it. They didn't even know. And her own daughter! She spent her days playing in Kazimierz, where the hissing was deafening and unrelenting. Why there? What did she see in it? A sun-flooded painting, snowball fighters in Remuh Cemetery. Grazyna was somehow to blame for this. So was Grazyna's mother. Mother had stopped talking about it back in the fifties. She'd stopped describing the hush of the transports. She'd stopped accounting for Father's futility, how he'd cross the bridge to his office in Podgórze and see over the walls into the ghetto. She'd stopped talking about it early on, and Father had never talked about it at all. They'd taken their daughters to the movies, showed them the Olympics, introduced them to a new modern Europe, and let the stories sink deeper down.

She lifted the little uniform. Julian's skinny arms would stick out of its stubby sleeves. If it were real, she thought, it had been worn by a little man who had gone about his business in it. She'd always taught Wanda to look for the real, look hard without blinking, but had she really shown her how? Had she herself really known how? They'd taken her to Auschwitz I and II, they'd read her Jewish folktales and they'd taken her through the ghetto, but what were these things to a modern little girl? Museums and books.

Grazyna wondered what to do with the filthy thing—run it into the lodge and make them all look hard without blinking? Whatever these follies were, and they were looking like a celebration of Julian Zagórski's penis, sorrow had no place in there. She had to take care of it herself. She gulped her vodka and grabbed the hook and dragged the uniform into the night. She searched the pines and far cottage lights for a place to lose the little man. Bury him in the snow, said the wind in the drifts. Burn him in the fire, said the chimneys and folktales. Hang him from a tree. She pushed her way through needles and snow to a windless opening deep in the woods. No ceremony for the wicked, she thought, and hung him from a branch. She pushed her way back through the needles, imagining him running off like a gingerbread man.

SUDDEN SILENCE THEN WILD APPLAUSE as she entered the lodge, nude but for her boots and beard and meter-long cap with cottony ball. She gave the vodka back to Julian, who accepted it with true incredulity. What did he expect?

Go, she said. Get changed. It's almost midnight.

She played hard in his absence, tumbling right into the role of Herod, devouring handfuls of olives and cherries, shooting stones at the fire and the floor, tearing meat from a delectable wing and shouting *Kurdwa!* through a mouthful of food—at hoary sea hags, at slutty Salome, who was looking at her with renewed desire. She choked on the wing and a sailor haply clapped her back—out came the chunk and they drank to her health, drank to her beard, drank to the perky snow-peaked turnips bouncing on her belly-dancing daughter.

Julian came in, out of costume, and angrily looked around the room. The follies, it seemed, had taken off without him. He was asking around for something he'd lost but nobody could give him satisfaction: a pirate drew a sword to make him walk the plank, a drill sergeant wanted to press him into service, a harlequin in rabbit ears pestered him for alms, and Salome taunted him with castanets, tempted him with veils, babbled at him in tongues of fire. Julian stormed out with a blast of winter wind, and the follies flared up like a bellowed bonfire, a burst of laughter that probably meant there was really nothing to be mad about.

So the flesh had been torn from tradition's bone, whatever on earth that bone had been, but she surmised its marrow was usually the star of the season. And were he to strap on a jackrabbit loincloth, were he to stagger in there with locusts in his beard, she was sure he could be the head of the table and get all the attention he felt he deserved. But who'd made this excellent borscht? And who'd made the *uszka*? She sloshed and slurped it, Herod-wise, sopping her beard in hot beet juice. She grabbed passing Salome's wrist. You, my dear. You, my lovely peacock honey, you, my pink chunk of ruby-red rock wedged from the gravel with a knife or something, *moja pączek, moj pachołek, moja pantera, moja papryka, moj, moj, moj—toj pępek!* Your navel! So sour and sweet, like a lucky lemon drop, it will get you everything you desire in this world, my kingdom and then some, if only you'll do a dirty dance for me—dance a burlesque with your lemon-drop navel, buzz off the desert like a lemon-drop locust, rain down like lemon drops, manna, and boils. Come! Everyone! Panstwo—Jescemy! Tanczycemy! Mrowmieny! Let us eat and dance and swarm! Let's marinade his head in a bucket of bull's blood and get this Christmas off the ground!

A klezmer squealed and squawked the *oberek*, Salome danced with a horny vengeance, and the rabble formed a rowdy circle, welcoming strangers who'd come in from the night. Herod slumped in the director's chair, legs wide open, smile gaping, eyes blazing, beard snarled on her breasts like calamari. My Lord, she groaned, I've become my ex-husband. Strip away the veils, she called, strip away those terrible years and years! *Teraz!* she called. *Zaraz!* she demanded, and Salome stripped away lavender veils, uncovering her hair and shoulders and belly, uncovering her daisy, uncovering her ass, leaving panels of calico sheer floating on her face and peaks and sex, colors dancing a marvelous blur, giving but glimpses, embarrassing glimpses, encouraging Herod to give herself a touch—just one touch, there on top, one jolt of pleasure, which caught Salome's eyes and made her dance her way to the throne, dance like fire between Herod's legs, whip off her veils, drip down her veils, lower with applause down onto her knees, tear the veil from her face, lower that face between Herod's legs, and make the whole world explode into flame.

EARLY THE NEXT MORNING, on the train from Zakopane, she watched the mountains through darkened glasses, feeling them grate against the clouds. That night was Christmas Eve and there was so much left to do at home. Her head hurt so badly, so very badly, she was grateful for a first-class cabin to herself. Last night still chafed her like crumbs in bedclothes, images of it tickling her every time she got comfortable: Magda dropping stones on their feet, an S.S. uniform sulking in the pines, Julian appearing, bound in a loincloth, witnessing her and Magda with blanched dismay. A public sex act, she thought. She touched cool fingers to her aching forehead. And those follies would keep going on for days, going on and on in the mountains without her, rambling like the *kulig* toward some mythic land of joy. She'd never felt such pleasure in her life, and she'd never felt horror like she did right now. And tonight! Good Christ, she was throwing together dinner for her mother, aunt, daughter, and whoever else shows up. No matter how hard she worked, hers, she knew, would never touch the borscht that she'd spilled so gloriously over her beard last night.

The train stopped in Zab, a frosty concrete platform with a yellow stucco station house. Two boys in striped caps and hooded red ski jackets stood beside their tired father, white breath all around their heads. The conductor grabbed luggage, hurried their mother onto the train. Grazyna pulled her blanket in tighter, as if to protect her private cabin, but the door swung open anyway and let in the mother, who announced *Wesołych Świąt!* as she hurried to the window and eagerly waved. She slid open the glass and took hold of her husband's snowmobile mittens, filling the cabin with frozen air. Grazyna buried her nose deep in wool. Not until the train lunged forward did the woman let go and shut the window. She asked if Grazyna was going to Kraków. Grazyna nodded, pulled down the wool to show that she was smiling, and then put it back up. The woman said she, too, was going to Kraków, on emergency, because her sister was giving birth, and that her husband and children would have to stay in Zab, or in their house just a little ways outside of Zab, because they would only get in the way, what with the sister giving birth, but that was fine when all was said and done because she had already prepared the twelve courses and put them in the icebox and out in the snow, not to mention having wrapped all the presents and, *na prawda,* it wasn't too much to ask them to fend for themselves this one time—and what a special time, Christmas, to be having a baby.

The woman talked quite a lot, and she wore a funny scarf around her head, but her face was young and fresh and pretty, a face that had breathed only mountain air. She removed her heavy coat, under which she wore a purple acetate athletic suit. Julian would have associated her with the Russian *mafiya*. Grazyna noticed her shapely build and thought that, were it not for the headache, she might enjoy kissing her lips.

Do you have children? the woman asked.

A daughter.

You are going to see her for Christmas.

Tak, z przyrodzenie. We live in Kraków. The woman smiled and leaned forward, as if to encourage an explanation. Stubbly fields rose and fell and the cabin filled with stuffy heat. Grazyna opened her blanket and showed her sloppy sweater and jeans. She is seventeen years old, she said. She is a painter. I don't know where it comes from but she handles a paintbrush, *nie wiem,* like she was potting a plant, like it's the easiest thing to do but simply something that has to be done.

You must be very proud.

I think I'm jealous, Grazyna said, taking off her sunglasses. She squinted at the snow. I know that sounds terrible. But they worry me. Her ideas. She has one painting in particular—of Remuh, the grave-yard in Kazimierz. Her father and I taught her to revere that culture. We took her to the camps in Oświęćim. We took her to Remuh when she was just a little girl. We wanted to teach her it's an honor to grow up in a city that's dealt with so much pain, so much, *nie wiem,* histor-ical pollution.

The woman said nothing.

And now there's this painting of Remuh Cemetery. The painting's so . . . so raw, so frank, *otwarty,* in crumbly blues and blacks and browns, all of these colors close together. The stones are huddling. The stones even look like people, like they're huddling together. And that's just what they look like in real life, too, but I'd never noticed be-fore. The painting gets it all in: stones huddling around lamps like beggars, covered in snow and under trees. And the sky's a really first-rate orange. But she doesn't stop there. She doesn't practice good re-straint. She goes too far and puts in people, three of them, three kids, and they're throwing *snowballs* at each other! They're absolutely out of place in there—full of *zabawa,* full of wild pleasure like they're playing on a playground and not like they're disgracing Remuh Ceme-tery. One of them, maybe a boy, maybe a girl, actually *leaps* up off a headstone, *leaps* off a stone and throws a snowball with this terrible thrill all over his face. Her face. I can't be sure. But the stone. That headstone. I shrink when I look at it.

Grazyna squinted at the hurt gray snow. She rubbed her eyes and raised her hand to her mouth. Of course, she thought, letting the snow get brighter and brighter. Of course.

You must be very proud, the woman said at length.

I think I'm jealous.

Twenty

THEY DIDN'T HAVE TIME TO DROP THEM FROM AIRPLANES. Yet by one o'clock that afternoon they had successfully leafleted the whole city, sending invitations to its remotest corners, spreading the news, in Gurney's words, like a second epidemic of the Spanish flu. Reach street people and cardinals and money changers and hookers—get all of them in on our reindeer games! Tell them it's Xmas fun at Kleks! Xmas for X-rated expats and exiles! Wujo Płujo agreed that the more varied the crowd, the better their Xmas, and the randier their fun. So they split themselves up, hit everything they saw. The pamphlets they distributed were Day-Glo yellow, boasting the unruliest of XMAS FUN! They featured Matek's cartoon of Gurney dressed as Santa Claus: furry cap and collar, shaving-cream beard, a dollar-sign tattoo, and spinning green slot-machine eyes.

The day drove on and snow piled up and Wanda was amazed by the changes in Gurney. He was younger, yet older, like some kind of trickster, and still she trusted him. Working the streets, giving orders at Kleks, renting a suite at the Grand Hotel, he took charge with easy power that made everyone want a piece of him. They fell all over him to help him out, which would have been scary if he'd been some kind of fascist. But he wasn't. He was just a big kid. And then there was all this unaccountable wealth, cold hard cash that he passed out like candy. And still, at bottom, he was plain old Gurney—plain old Gurney with slot-machine eyes! She'd often suspected that he was sitting on money, that he was just *acting* poor like Prince Hal or something, acting so he could enjoy himself as everybody else did, and here was her proof. And how different he was! His voice flowed smooth as a babbling freshet. He moved around town like a governing father. His eyes were clear and confident and blue. In Kleks he poked fun at the smoky orange lounge, assuring them the right crowd would do the dump wonders. And he marveled at the Grand Hotel's eighteenth-century rooms, urging her to go overboard with an ambassadorial menu. You're the aristocrat, he said. You know what to do. He handed her a wad of hundred-dollar bills and told her there was plenty more where that came from. Spend what you have to, but make sure to go too far. Treat these scoundrels like lords and ladies and make sure it's good old *Roman* fun. He winked as he said this, and she got the picture.

She took it as a challenge. She was determined to match his pomp and verve and show him what money could *really* do. Sick as it was, she waved her family name around and got the attention of Chef Poniadzalek, the mustachioed prince of the hotel kitchen, who, upon seeing Wanda's ludicrous wad, wrested her away from his snobby staff. Posing before a wall of shiny pots and pans, he graciously called her Pani Zamoyska and started impressing her with his worldly extravagance. She interrupted and said she had just one wish: that their feast would make the guests preternaturally horny. His eyebrows shot up. His eyelids got heavy. He profoundly inhaled through his walrus-like lips.

Of course, he said. Of course we shall. That is the purpose of any true feast—but mademoiselle, this is such short notice! Three in the afternoon! I am not Jesus Christ! Some will be horny—nymphs! satyrs!—but I'm afraid the rest will just have to watch.

All, or none at all.

Of course. Come into my cooler. I've been meaning to avenge these pious little snails—excellent snails, you know, local periwinkles, but they've overstayed their welcome and they're notorious aphrodisiacs. We will start with them. For your special purposes, I must abandon that tired French peasant way, that sleepy butter-garlic way. I shall kill them with the lustiest sauce I know—a pepper-tomato puree, bright as a lighthouse, which gets its thrust from Spanish saffron. Buckets of saffron, a veritable storm. Why the look?

Saffron is very expensive.

Pani Zamoyska, are you with me or not? Saffron's the salt of sexual extremity.

Then saffron it is!

Bardzo dobrze. We need a soup.

I don't think anyone will be sitting down. It's going to be a mob.

Sitting, standing, ransacking the halls—mob or no mob, we need a soup.

Bardzo dobrze.

Piquant fennel soup with fat exploding shrimp. Are you with me?

Say more.

Fennel, first of all, goes straight to the loins, as does shrimp, and the soup I have in mind makes the most of these qualities, stroking the gullet with a dab of crème fraîche, sparking the nose with a jolt of Pernod.

Fine. Two kettles.

Ten tureens. *Teraz,* keep it light for the main course, keep them in top athletic form, am I right? Make it mussels and shellfish and something bright red. In keeping with tradition, there will have to be fish. Tomorrow night is Christmas Eve, after all.

Athletics over tradition.

As you like it. *Roglveugels.* A Dutch fish that will always be a mystery to me. Serve it with thyme and Dijon mustard and it turns the stuffiest midday meal into a scene from a bedroom farce. Once I served it for the bishops of Galicia, that and the fennel soup, and I will be damned if in an hour they weren't necking over their port. I haven't much of it in the freezer, so be sure it goes to your most frigid friends.

First come, first served, she said, and so went the rest of her culinary lesson: Chef Poniadzalek whisking her from kitchen to pantry to cooler to freezer, checking stocks, making lists, telling her how to coax the libido from a crowd of perfect strangers. There would be lobster, crab, and salmon sausages, squash ravioli and scallop tortellini, a magnificent quantity of ivory trout mousse suggestively surrounded by parfait spoons, inviting the guests to feed one another. But her education went beyond the strictly gastronomical. He told her:

A. Any orgy infamously fails without hordes of wine and liquor (a ridiculous supply, so much more than they could ever drink, such that it's an affront to their meagre mortal appetites).
B. Every element of the feast—the music, the furniture, especially the guests—must at least give the illusion, if not the promise, of edibility. The most successful feast, that is, falls just short of consensual cannibalism.
C. Most people are naturally frightened of their desires. They need a little wheedling. Hence, the host or hostess must be twice as demonstrably lascivious as even the most indulgent guest.

She was to pervade the rooms with the *quatre épices*—coriander, cinnamon, cloves, and aniseed—which not only invoked the holiday season (he realized this wasn't her objective, he said) but which were always dependable aphrodisiacs. As is jasmine. As is vanilla. He directed her therefore to a shop in the neighborhood (she already knew of it) that still flavored tapers with real vanilla beans. Most powerful is natural musk, a rare brown substance extracted from the abdomen of a certain young Southeast Asian deer, pounded into a powder, and which, to be safe, he would sprinkle imperceptibly over all the courses. If that didn't work, though he was confident it would, he would ambush the little prudes with his French Christmas roll, an unassuming cake that he would lace with *bood ambrette* (a lesser-known seed sometimes used in Turkish coffee) and ambergris (the intestinal secretions of a young sperm whale).

She was grateful for the education, but the more obsessive Chef Poniadzalek grew, invading her space with his sharp brown teeth, the less she knew just *what* he was. At first she'd thought she'd found an artist like herself, a maverick of the palate trained in Dijon, doomed to waste his talents on cheapskates and rubes. But the sleazier he became, looking down her shirt, playing with her hair, the more it

seemed he was a highly cultured pervert. Even this distinction, however, was put to the test, for in the privacy of the wine cellar, in the
cobwebby depths by the 1964 Bordeaux, he told her he could get his
hands on some of Poland's purest snow.

INVITING ZBIGNIEW HAD BEEN A STUPID IDEA. He'd just
done it for fun. He'd given a cabdriver twenty dollars, an Xmas Fun
flyer, and specific directions to the cottage in Ojców. Should he not
have invited his own murderer to the feast? What great fun if he decided to come! But when the cab drove off Gurney panicked, and he
waved his arms to call him back, but the cabbie was determined to
keep the twenty dollars. Now what choice did he have but to enjoy it?
Enjoy his paternal admonitions. Enjoy those fingers closing on his
throat. Running around and getting Kleks in order, he positively refused to worry about it. What a joke! he shouted to Piotr and Mateusz,
clowning around behind the bar. I laugh! he shouted across the club.
I laugh in the face of death!

We drink in the face of death! Matek said, raising the bottle of An-
gelica liqueur that Wanda had gotten from the hotel chef. She'd said
it was a rare aphrodisiac.

Now that he was in possession of so much money, Gurney hadn't
much to lose. More than intoxicated by its lusty power, he was en-
tranced, enraptured, saturated; he felt like that notorious fire artist,
that one who dresses up in asbestos and engulfs himself in roaring
blue flames. Everything he touched he torched, and the feeling was
neither good nor bad. Maybe Jackie had also had that feeling, and that
was why she had given all the money back. Maybe Zbigniew, drunk on
his Kasino, was likewise engulfed in thundering flames, and maybe
he'd show up and they'd kiss and make up and Kleks would go up like
the towering inferno!

Something was up, that was for sure.

He greeted the first guests coming up the stairs, a family of four:
the father was concealed beneath a tattered brown hat, the mother
was overeager in a sealskin coat, a sheepish son and daughter were

around his age. The mother presented an Xmas Fun flyer and he boomingly welcomed them into the lounge, wanting to kiss them in the European manner, urging them to eat and drink like lions. The mother and children knowingly nodded, but he was quite sure their primary language was Romanian. Could they see that his eyes were burning with money? Did they recognize him as the slot-machine Santa in the picture? Matek offered them their rarest hors d'oeuvres, snails in white cups with a sauce so red it reflected like embers off their hesitant faces. The girl was the first one to dump one in her mouth.

Piotr stood at the turntables for a trembling length of time. Back-lit like a priest, his hands at work under the amber lamp, he paused in the hush of crepuscular Kleks for a special Xmas transubstantiation, a miracle that floated through the warm pink lights, the big soft sound of La Vie en Rose—a fine place to begin, Julka seemed to say, squeezing Gurney's hand and leading him to the floor, leading him in a dance, pressed up against him, her brown hair smelling like clove cigarettes, her breath little bursts of garlic and liqueur, her fine brown sweater soft like cashmere, and before he knew it flames licked up and lapped out the pulpy smoldering orange—but then, like that, the song was over, bumping rudely up against the Beastie Boys, which caught the dancing Romanians off guard and brought more stairway people to the floor—still wearing snowcaps, too loud and boisterous, and shortly Julka was torn from his side, waving, disappearing into the holiday groove.

God bless Piotr, Gurney thought, grooving and drinking for an incalculable length of time, moving in and out of Julka's arms as a mishmash of music came and went, blending and blurring with unrefined dancing and carrying through the muscles of Poles and internationals. Wolfgang Press, Television, and Sly and the Family Stone, songs eternally at odds with one another were hewn together by industrial bomb-drop slop, fast and fatal techno gunfire, miracle fuzz and razor-cut horns, a mix so tough that even Janet Jackson crap, about which he could usually have not given a fuck, came off sounding practically respectable. Bless skinny Piotr for knowing just the right beat, encouraging such a generous outpouring of enjoyment, unbound by color, unbound by melody, rumbling through those bodies like electrical currents, coursing like the bloodwaters of DMs and dollars that rushed ever eastward through the poor parts of Europe, flooding toward the dry thirsty expanses of China. Currency, currency, currency, he thought. That night there was currency drumming him like a beat, sweeping through the crowd like the darkest intuition, bubbling up black from the deep cracks of history and carrying them along like the flashiest new fad, regulating a chaos of hips and elbows, putting a flash price tag on the cheapest shifts and bumps. But then— what incongruity! Curling through the gaps of this unrefined groove, Wanda could be seen guiding a grinning Matek, threading him through the crowd like film through a projector, selecting from all the bumping and scooping the delicate strains of a waltz. Gurney was mesmerized. He had never waltzed, and he had no clue what it would mean to lead. He stood stock-still when the contagion started spreading, when couples started forming from the midst of the fray and responded to an intricate Old World rhythm that Piotr had smuggled into the mix. A waltz! Who would have guessed? Watching the waltzers, he wished he could lead. One-two-three, one-two-three, he counted while watching. As if reading his mind, Julka swept him up and carried him down the current like a washed-away bridge, guiding the weight of his towering frame as easily as if he were a featherweight dwarf, threading him through the bodies with a touch of his waist, a teenage girl steering them through the waves of momentum.

Behind the bar, while watching the waltzing, Kuba was approached by a bespectacled young black man, one of the few people of *any* color he'd seen for some time. The man called himself Robert and asked in Polish—poncy, *good* Polish—who was in charge. Kuba wanted to ask him why he wasn't dancing, but the man had a fancy dictation device and appeared to have some kind of official agenda.

I'm in charge of the bar, Kuba said. But right then the music stopped. Hail to the Chief came on. The crowd parted for Gurney, who, dressed in a red robe and cheap twinkling crown, laughed and made peace signs with both hands waving. The man went straightaway to get an interview. Kuba went straightaway to bring Gurney a Jameson.

Robert had anticipated nothing like this. The crowd was under the command of a tall American man with fake raven hair. Were they mocking him? Was he mocking them? Why did they care? Several people called out Midas and begged him to touch them. He asked if they had been naughty or nice (invariably they said naughty) and he groped at them in a playful way. Robert pushed through and stuck out his mike, asking this Midas if he were in charge.

It's nobody's happening—and it freaks me out!

At your expense?

In a sense.

May I ask you some questions for National Public Radio?

NPR?

None other.

Shoot, said the King.

People gathered around as Robert raised his microphone.

I'm wondering what you, as an American abroad—you *are* American? (Robert had no doubts)—think of the impending war in the Gulf.

Say more.

You are aware that President Bush has given Saddam Hussein until January fifteenth to pull his troops out of Kuwait.

Tak.

Would you stand behind the President's decision, even though it poses a threat to you and other Americans abroad?

Mmm. Set me lee. We here in Kraków laugh in the face of death. We laugh if George Bush believes he can get anything done down there in that sewer. No plumber can fix that mess, never.

Sewer?

The letter A. It stands for A Sewer. The Sewer of History. The King's mouth simpered in a rather pleasant way.

Robert paused to let him explain.

A sewer, my man, a sewer. History is a great big backed-up sewer, and whatever's up between Iraq and Kuwait is just, like, well, so much sludge, and no matter how many American soldiers want to jump in and take a swim, it's still just sludge. Gurney reflected on his statement, blatantly plagiarized from Jane's diary, broadcast all across America on the Christmas morning *Morning Edition,* and he burst out laughing. He lost his crown under the bustling crowd. Robert wasn't so interested in this answer. He paused for the King to pick up his crown, though he never did.

But certainly you, as an affluent American, know that this war, if it does happen, would be more about money than, as you say, some sewer of history.

True. But money, I might add, also belongs there, all backed up in the sewer of history. Not at all worth fighting for. Money is the messiest waste of all. Flush it away, let it go.

The reporter gave an arch look, clearly associating him with the class of rich kids traipsing across the continent on Grand Tour 1990. True, Gurney had laid out one thousand dollars to the management of Kleks, two thousand to the Grand Hotel, and nearly three thousand to that slimy chef, all of which, at least in Poland, equaled plum gluttony by *any* party-throwing standards. So, true, if anyone understood flushing money down the toilet, it was the red-velvet brat with a smirk on his face. Drink, Gurney thought, tipping back Jameson to the ghost of Dick Chesnutt. He had no idea what he was doing or saying, but he couldn't help asking if the reporter had more questions.

Just one, Robert said.

Shoot.

There are reports that Iraqi forces are not only looting and burning in Kuwait, but also that they are raping and killing. Raping and killing women and children. Are these grounds for war? Insolence crept over of the King's young face, like a boy who had been wrongly accused of shoplifting.

Why are you asking me? Who am I to say?

You had answers to my other questions.

Those weren't answers—they were theories.

I see.

You think because I paid for this and you're holding the microphone, you think you can grill me on who to save, what to kill, shit like that. You're way out of your depth, my man, way out.

Maybe, he said, still holding the microphone. But you have to admit, money comes with responsibility.

Well, money's new to me.

Thank you, he said, clicking off the machine.

A British kid in a striped ski cap strode by, calling out X's! Es! X's! Es! Gurney rushed after him and tapped him on the shoulder. The kid swung around and said, Hullo, mate? Would'ja be buyin' an 'it tonight?

Are you selling?

Sure am.

Well everything's free here. No commerce. Sorry, mate.

Y'can 'ardly 'old a raver without a few Xers in the crowd.

A raver?

I'm just 'elpin' you out.

This isn't a rave.

Xmas fun, right as rain! The kid winked. But would'ja be wantin' an 'it tonight?

Gurney didn't know. He asked if it was Ecstasy.

It is.

Without a second thought, Gurney bought him out, twenty pills for two million złotys, keeping one of them back for himself. He told the kid to pass them around, starting with the deejay and the rest of Wujo Płujo. Much like sending a flyer out to Ojców, this was an experiment in God knows what. Still, it was fun. The reporter had gone. All around people were absorbed in themselves, his sudden celebrity having burnt off like dew. All the better. He looked at his pill. He took it. All around people danced like the dickens and Kleks's every atom was soaked in beat. Athletic bodies cranked up to the funk, but he was stuck there on the ground, still needled by the reporter's meddlesome questions. Impossible to order the clutter of his life: that tonight, at Kleks, he had a daughter: that here in Kraków on the eve of Christmas Eve a benign little drug was hatching in his belly and there was nothing to stop him from doing as he pleased. All these people, their shining hair, their gleaming skin, some stripped to bras and wet wife-beaters—they were doing great, just fine, strangers of the world rubbing up against each other, and wasn't that what he'd had in mind? Wasn't it good? Maybe even *the* good? It was certainly one way to blow his money. He shook out his hands and rotated his shoulders. He ran his dry tongue over his chalky lips. His hands, he rubbed them, took another look. No real ethic pulled all this together. He had a daughter, Celeste, out there somewhere, and here he was, licking his lips, balanced on the rim of pleasure and disaster.

An arm brushed meaningfully against his arm. A disco-pink aureole beamed about her face. Her eyes were so wide, her teeth so white. He was *so* glad to see her! What was her name? Linda! He said this and pulled her in with a hug: I'm so glad you came!

I got this flyer. I thought you were behind it somehow.

Nothing's behind it, really.

Is Jane here?

Jane? *God,* no. Actually—maybe she is. He looked around.

She ran long fingers through blond stalks of hair. Had he ever noticed how resplendent she was? Had he ever seen that blazing color, those glacial eyes, those roasting red tomato lips? He wanted to touch, but thought she might spank. Funny, he said, but didn't finish the thought, opting not to call her a seafoamy goddess. He did raise his hand, however, and slide his fingerbacks down the fuzz of her cheek. She flinched and looked suspicious, but why apologize? He was just being friendly. Do you see them? he said, looking around.

Who?

The faces?

What faces?

All of them. All of them are full of cheer. They're merry. It's funny, you know. I had this idea I'd escape the holidays and hide myself in this discotheque Xmas. I guess I thought that Christmas might kill me. But check them out. They're so full of cheer. Those humpity-bumpity loving bodies, isn't that just fucking *Christmas*? Kids in the classrooms with cookies and punch, workers at work with cubicles and booze. Booze boxes. You know? Feel it. *Sing it.* Humpity-bumpity, humpity-bumpity Christmas on its way! You're so easy to talk to, Linda. It's weird. You don't make it easy, you make it hard, but it *is* easy. It's funny. You're very pretty. Don't take that wrong. My mother is pretty. So's my daughter, or she will be someday. She's just a baby. Look how cheerful they are. I just want to touch them. Weighed down with all those clothes. Poor things. I've *gotta* lose this robe. Hullo, mate. Want this robe? Pure velvet. All yours. Forget it, really. Oh. *Air.* That feels good. So I thought Christmas might kill me and now here it is, killing me, all these gourmet faces and gourmet shoulders, and where on earth does Piotr find these tracks? Isn't he a genius? This one sounds like—a wedding march? funeral dirge? battle song? circus jig? He's such a goddamn sweetheart, Linda. I just *have* to introduce you to Wujo Płujo. I've told them all about you.

Me? What do you know about me?

Don't be sore. I don't know much. But it sure was charming that you took me to Auschwitz.

What do you know about me? Tell me.

Your family. You love your family. I bet you love Christmas.

I hate Christmas. What do you know about my family?

Your aunt or something. She's got this allergy and she lives in the salt mines.

Jackie told you that?

Jane did. You think Jackie told me?

Why?

So you mean to say it's true?

I don't mean to say anything.

Gurney gawked. It's true, he laughed. I thought Jane was up to her old tricks. But it was true. But was, like, *all* of it true? I hope so. Did you and Jackie, well, like that, on the altar? That salt altar? Did you two make commerce and currency and all that?

Shut up. You're on drugs.

He took a step back and took it all in. You're very cool, Linda. Too cool. I swear you're pure vanilla. One hundred percent. Damn. *Damn.* What a difference ten minutes makes.

Huh?

Just ten minutes and already we're vanilla.

She hated Christmastime and had never understood it, but she was having fun with this kooky Gurney. Maybe because he was flying on drugs, his pupils big as dog dishes. From the first time she'd met him, she'd taken his pleasure seeking for a front. She'd thought it was nonsense. Much as he tried to be a good sport, his big sad eyes always told the truth. And watching him gazing out the window on the ride home from Oświęcim had only confirmed what she had already known. But now she couldn't be so sure. He had the carnal abandon she would expect from a hedonist, as if he wanted to consume everything in the room. Running at the mouth, he innocently asked her to explain Jackie Witherspoon, why she could be honest in so many ways but then keep a string of secret lovers. He'd been clearly hurt by it, and Linda had been, too, but she never would have dreamed that they'd be talking about it.

Jackie's Californian, was her cool response. But she doesn't really like California. She'll be an expatriate wherever she goes. We all will be.

Are you from there?

Where?

California.

No.

Where you from?

She put back her shoulders and lifted her chin. Iowa, she said.

You? Iowa? Me too! Where?

Northeast Iowa.

No fucking way. Me too. Where?

Dubuque.

I'm from Maquoketa! Thirty miles off! Didn't you *know* that?

I guess not, she said, but he didn't believe her. He didn't want to push it, and he had no desire to play the name game. He knew why she'd been so cagey about it, and why even Jane had never brought it up: just like Wujo Płujo wanted to make moralist Poland vanish, the two of them wanted Iowa to vanish and let the world have its uncluttered fun. Girl from Dubuque! Cocktail Dress! He wanted to put his nose through her hair, tongue in her ear, hands on her legs and back and breasts. It was splendid having Linda there among the living. Yes! He could eat anything that money could buy, flaunt all the things, yes, that money couldn't change, strip back past and place and name until nothing was left but one throbbing nubbin—the here, the now, the *hic et nunc, teraz, zaraz,* so on and so forth. He led her by the elbow into the groove, where cold-weather people had torn off their clothes, piled them on tables and gotten to the skin, all at his expense, all to the delight of Zbigniew Zamoyski, who could show up any minute now baring his teeth.

Yes.

I want to kiss all of you, he whispered in English, running his hands over some sturdy guy's shoulders—a soft female waist—Kuba's wet T-shirt—Linda's wet hair—the ridges of Matek's soaking chest. Big gawdy smiles shone all around, for the X-man had faithfully done his job. All were turned on, democracy was afoot, circulating like blood and money through the crowd, spreading in five languages like the infamous rumor that Anything Goes at the Grand Hotel, Suites 310–312, Servers in Blindfolds Will Encourage Your Privacy, and the rest will be left to Wanda's discretion.

I want to touch you, taste you, fuck you—but then as if in rude response, the power cut out, black and silent. Many kept dancing amid whistles and screams. Nervous laughter, polyglottal chatter, voices by the windows saying it was black on the Rynek. Sweat and perfume packed the air. Everything murmured a casual Babel— casual, at least, until a chorus piped up and started calling out Terrorism—*Terrorismus—Terrorysować*—a freeze that blew through the crowd like freon, chilling warm sweat, tightening loose muscles, making them bump and gouge and curse and rifle in the dark for what clothes were theirs. What a damn shame, Gurney said aloud, imagining everyone scattering too soon, cowering away to their lonely little holidays. He acted fast. He soothingly groped his way to the bar. He got up on top and lit his lighter.

Państwo, mein Freundin, mes amis, my friends. Christ, I can't even see you from up here, you poor nervous cabbages, but oh, *mes amis,* there's nothing to fear, not when you smell as good as you do. Mmm! And you do. Smell yourselves. You smell like a big red bushel of apples, sweet and ripe, ready to eat.

Get to your point, mate!

My point! Indeed! Thank you for keeping this all on track. My point, *państwo,* is this, is this. So maybe it's a valid fear that terrorists cut the power, after all, after all, we have gathered here among us such a delectably diverse crowd of the world. If I were a terrorist, and I'm not, I'm an Iowan, but if I *were* a terrorist I couldn't imagine a more inviting place to plant my bombs or open fire and tear into all of our ripe fruit-flesh. I mean, what a statement that would make around the world. So I understand your fears, Freundin, and I even understand why you *like* those fears—just like you might like being in an earthquake or a hurricane or something else you might see on CNN, and I encourage you, if you wish, to run with those fears and go screaming across the Rynek like it was the War of the Worlds. Hell, if you do *that* I might even join you. But for those of you who are tired of being knotted up with fear, those of you looking for new, exciting *fun,* might I remind you—and where are my interpreters? Piotr? Linda? Mateusz? Wanda? Hey! I think some people are actually listening to this crap! All the better, because I want to remind you that here it is Xmas, and the lights are out, here where are all of us hot and bothered, so why waste it? Those of you who want to turn your fear into swampy fun, I suggest you reach back and lightly, tenderly—so tenderly—touch your fingers to an inch of frightened skin.

You're sick!

I know that voice. Is that Cindy out there? Oh, yes, I guess I'm pretty sick, a sick and perverted voice in the dark, but I am a pervert who speaks for the skin—my skin, your skin, all skin, all colors and textures and temperatures of skin, be it warm and wet or prickly and cold, be it tender on the belly or rough on the neck, it is skin, it is naked, and it is bracing for your fingers, wondering how to receive your touch. Take no more than your neighbor wants to give: what is bare, what is free, a shoulder, a cheek, that rare naked navel, you know, whatever, but remember you have no business under your neighbor's clothes—

Moralist!

—unless of course that's where your neighbor wants you. If so, dive in! Join your neighbor's reindeer games! I, for one, moralist though I am, want to find all of you here under my clothes, but I'm just a pervert and I speak for the skin, and so of course I want all of you right up in here—under my clothes, on my skin. C'mon. It's an invitation. Come up here. Don't be shy. Make my body your fingers' frontier.

And then, out of the mumbling heat of the crowd, while many could be heard leaving out the back, issuing words of harsh disapproval, a real-world miracle came to pass: there was a hubbub of voices, just like in church at the kiss of peace, and an octopus of hands crept up Gurney's legs, under Gurney's shirt, and with the gentle force of the tide rolling in, dragged him off the bar, into waves of hands—scaring him, sure, but challenging him, making him put his money where his mouth was. He stopped resisting and ended up on the floor, the object of affirmative hands and mouths that rubbed him here, kissed him there, made him writhe and giggle and squirm and make a good example for all.

BON VIVANTS OF EVERY STRIPE, STILL AMPED UP FROM THE BIG BLACKOUT, lowered their voices as they rushed through the doors, hushed and amused as they took it all in. The spacious front room, the center of the suite, was illuminated by candles and a roaring wood fire. The colors were alluring, like a troll's winter hovel. Surfaces were draped with thick purple cloth, and everywhere a feast of unusual foods. A Baroque-looking table in the middle of the room boasted an explicit roast of deer. Ducks and quails bathed in strange sauces. Cioppino-like soups steamed in tureens. Pungent red casseroles. Mysterious black pastries. Shellfish sausages formed the rungs of an enormous xylophone. THERE WILL BE NO NAPKINS, read neatly let-

tered place cards that had been translated into several tongues. WIPE
GREASY FINGERS ON NEIGHBORLY BODIES. Five busy servants
in black dinner dress, all of them handicapped by black blindfolds,
clumsily performed their wine-pouring duties, staining the guests
and carpets and making sure everyone got plenty to drink. The connecting room was locked, and on its door, also translated, was this
tempting notice: NO CLOTHES HEAVIER THAN UNDERGARMENTS,
PLEASE.

Linda couldn't guess what the party was for. She stood in the
doorway and considered going home. Kuba, by contrast, went straight
for the sausages, not even noticing the lack of napkins. Julka was riv-
eted by the Romanian family, who descended on the banquet as if it
might run away. But Roumiana, among them, was in a world all her
own, continuing her ongoing culinary experiments, comparing the
impacts of seed cakes and fish eggs, tasting things that jerked her
and tickled her, made her ache like food never should. Roumiana's
brother Andrei was stuffing himself, wolfing down truffles as if they
were dumplings, storing up enough calories for the whole family's hi-
bernation. Roumiana's mother, God bless her, was eating like a queen,
delicately starting with black grapes and cherries. Too bad Papa hadn't
come, she thought. Piotr thought he knew what mood Wanda was going for, and he eased everyone in with a suggestive samba. Mateusz
and Gurney (flying on drugs) graciously ushered in guest upon guest,
gleefully touching and kissing the strangers, who, in most cases, gave
thankful responses. And Wanda, the hostess, was everywhere at once,
locking and unlocking the connecting doors, buzzing around the party
as if she was plugged into the wall.

In her twenty-six years, Linda had been to countless parties,
probably a hundred or more, but she usually found herself standing
back and watching, a little annoyed at everyone's banter. Banter, she
thought, is impatience set to music. People got together, made noise,
went home. And she expected this night would be no exception. Even
when the power had gone out earlier, when Gurney had gotten up and
whipped them into a froth, those were just things that people did at

parties. It was nice in the end, when they exited Kleks and entered the sparkling winter air. Kids and drunks raised hell all around, but Gurney took her hand and led her through the streets, explaining how he'd taken the most pleasant drug on earth, asking her why she hated Christmas so much. (She didn't really have an answer to that.) It's rough being away from family, he offered, placidly smiling at the spangled snow. It would have been fine had they just kept walking, maybe in search of a quiet clump of trees, maybe even back to one of their places, but instead they had to come to the Grand Hotel, where everyone was acting like it was the end of the world. Everyone was there: people she knew, people she avoided, big bald Germans with tiny square glasses, polite Poles, shy Ukrainians, big blond Russian beauties, vodka drunks twice everyone's age. She took it all in, didn't like what she saw. She was just about to turn and leave when chunky, plucky Wanda Zamoyska slid off her coat and pulled her through the door.

Kuba had never seen anything like it. What a night! Not only was he in the Grand Hotel, of all places, but he and his friends had the joint *under siege*. The servers were blindfolded, just as they should be. The guests were completely out of control, and who could stop them? Piotr and Gurney were getting obscene, shoving chocolates and cherries in each other's faces. Julka and Wanda were undressing that blonde. Even that German licked sauce from his fingers, giving Kuba the knowing look, so he knew it had to be okay.

Andrei, however, was feeling a little sour. If only Mama would have gotten the hint, he thought, but he could hardly ask her to return to the station. It was clear she was having the time of her life, rooted there at the table, pushing those canapés into her mouth. So, as ever, he was duty-bound to look after her. Thank God Papa had gone off to his bar. One look at those blindfolds and they'd all have been sent home. Just once, he thought, I'd like to mix in with the Poles, the ones my age, and a chance like this would never come again. Never. Roumiana was doing just fine, of course, squeezed into that chair with three other girls. She wouldn't have dreamt of making Mama leave because she didn't care what Mama thought of her. Why can't I be more like that? He took a big drink from his sweet lemon cocktail. It collided with the dark chocolate cake he was eating. Just once he wanted to be those boys in the middle, the enormous black-haired fellow taunting that teenager, speaking in English, jamming his mouth full of cherries and olives and provoking the third one, Andrei's favorite, to dive at his waist and bring him to the carpet. They wrestled like school kids, their T-shirts stained with cherry juice and oil, their skin all sweaty and flushed and rug-burned. That black-haired fellow was a job for three men their size. Andrei wanted to jump in and help, and he knew that he would have, if it weren't for his tiny mother towering over him, always telling him he didn't belong.

Roumiana, by Julka's careful estimation, was somewhere between them and Linda in age. She spoke excellent Polish and had a yummy belly. She had terrible teeth, but huge brown eyes, and she knew right away what everyone needed. Linda's stockings were on the floor, and Wanda had started bossing everyone around when up came this funny Romanian girl, not drunk or stoned or anything at all, telling them they looked like three Greek beauties at a great Olympian beauty contest. Wanda said that if her assessment were true, then the mortal before them had to be Paris. Roumiana flashed her bad gray teeth and said she had no desire to judge them. Wedging herself between their bodies, she said that she was actually Helen of Troy, the mortal who was prettier than all of them put together. In the *Iliad* this would have been grounds for war, but in this case it simply called for tickling, and the three jealous goddesses went for the flesh, diving their fingers into dirty wool clothing, tearing through sweaters and blouses and slips and exposing the pale human being within. Her back had a fine layer of downy black fuzz. Her chubby little belly was jiggly to the touch. Linda got the idea, to Julka's surprise, to reach under the skirt to the top of her panty hose (smelly though those panty hose were), and strip them away as they'd done with her own. The girl protested, and Wanda looked worried, but Julka defused them with nice little kisses, sisterly kisses, as if putting them to bed on Christmas Eve. All of the girls were breezily relieved, and the girl's dimpled legs scissored and kicked, glad to be free in the cool candlelight.

THIRTY THOUSAND FEET OVER PITCH-DARK GREENLAND, nuzzling her face into a papery pillow, Jackie let go of a medieval city that hadn't turned into a dream just yet. She was excited to think, as she closed her eyes, that her mother and father and stepfather would all be waiting at the gate in San Francisco.

IN A SNOW-BLANKETED LODGE IN THE TATRY MOUNTAINS, as the actors once more fell asleep on the floor, Grazyna got up for a glass of water and stepped over the head of Magda Szczypczyk, who was locked in the legs of Julian Zagórski.

IN A SNOW-BLANKETED COTTAGE IN THE OJCÓW VALLEY, Zbigniew was awake in his Eames recliner. Jane was asleep in his bed. He was staring once again at the bright yellow flyer, needing to be sure beyond a shadow of a doubt that the cartoon depicted whom he thought it did.

AND HAVING DOZED OFF IN A CHAIR AT THE GRAND HOTEL, Maria was shaken awake by her son. A wild party was going on all around her. He told her he was taking her back to the station. Roumiana, however, would be staying on. She had met nice girls. She would be fine tonight.

PIOTR KNEW THAT SOMEONE had to make the first move. Wanda had laid out a brilliant game plan, but now she was so caught up in her fun that it looked like it was his job to get the thing moving. It was time to move these crazy foreigners out of the central feasting room and into the laboratorial middle room. Just beyond that room then, not recommended for the silly or shy, was the room on whose door was posted yet another sign: JUST SKIN, THANK YOU. The signs had also been Wanda's idea.

Just skin, Piotr thought, still thrilled from having groped Gurney's skin and sucked on his sinewy hairless chest. What a terrific freak he was, standing over there by the laboratory door, drinking milk with a Japanese boy, the two of them enraptured by a plate of chocolate truffles. A beautiful Japanese boy. He interrupted Gurney and tapped on the sign. We need you, he said, to speak for the skin. Gurney looked frightened, maybe not faking. His pupils were huge, like floating black planets.

Don't be scared, Piotr said, helping himself to Gurney's buttons.

Gurney gulped milk.

You laugh in the face of death.

I do?

You do, he said. He untucked the shirt.

I laugh in the face of death.

I scoff, said a German man, in the face of death.

I cough, said a Russian woman, in the face of death.

I sneeze in the face of death.

Shake keys in the face of death.

Make how please in face of the death.

Well put, Kuba! Gurney exclaimed, now down to his boxers and thin black socks. Oxford English! Good show, old boy. Off with the shirt and down with the drawers. That's right, off with them, strip and shimmy in the face of death—you too, and you—*jeszczemy*, ladies, let's go, *on y va!*

They were used to crowds. For decades the masses had gathered in their city. Thousands had filled the Rynek protesting martial law, pushing and shouting, Stop the lies! Stop the lies! Half a million Catholics had swarmed the Błonia, kneeling, praying, stretching two kilometers from the tiny little pope, clinging to every syllable of his interminable service. And in many ways this crowd belonged in that tradition—smaller, warmer, more fun and irreverent—but a crowd nonetheless, pulled from within by indeterminate force, drawn by a spirit no less noble or serene, deferring to the desires of the joyous collective that eagerly, nervously ushered through the door. Gurney policed them, making them undress, telling them to leave their cultures at the door. A reluctant handful slipped into the hall, but the rest fell in line and wiped hands on his body, some of them thanking him for standing up for the skin. Wanda and Julka brought up the rear, followed by Linda, who gave a sly look, and finally by the Romanian who had shown up with her family. He wondered where her family had gone. But it appeared she was having the time of her life, balancing a tray of cookies and condoms, her other hand dragging frosting across his ribs. The last one in, he shut the door.

It was dark in there, close and pungent. Someone butted Wanda's thigh against a table. She wanted her clothes back. She pushed against cold and heavy bodies, trying to get a little air. Her plan had been simple, her own little secret: pleasure in the Krematorium. But now it felt real and she wanted it to stop. That afternoon, when she'd gotten the idea, it had opened in her mind with origami perfection: sex in the Krematorium. According to the laws of natural desire, or just for a chance to see behind the door, people would gladly strip to their underwear, and once inside they'd be amply rewarded by sea sponges soaking in scented hot water. She could smell the cloves and jasmine and cinnamon. In mockery of the Nazi delousing chambers, then, these foreigners would lovingly bathe each other's bodies, of course not preparing each other for death, but preparing each other for absolute nudity, for sacrifice of privacy on the altar of delight! Now, however, crowded in the dark, her childish idea got all crumpled up. For this wasn't art, this was a terrifying orgy!

Tall bodies. Loud voices. Hot bloody smoke mixing with the air. The whole place started to chuckle in fear, not with concern that anyone would be raped, but with the racing sensation of boarding a roller coaster, the breathtaking thrill that they were bringing this on themselves. Germans laughing, Poles protesting, Matek's voice like a carnival barker's, telling them all to breathe in the heady smell, making an offer to scrub them all down—then *splash!* someone groaning under the sponge, and *splash!* someone else getting even with water, splashing Wanda, splashing Matek, splashing a chorus of laughing women, discharging a sponge on a muscular man, a rigid midriff shifting in firelight, Matek electing to sponge him down, buff his ribs, buff his pelvis, feel him get bigger in his dark tight briefs, push the sponge across his back, lay his face on this stranger's chest, see what it took to knead with his palm and make it rise up past the waistband, knob of the cock pressed flat against stomach, Matek's own cock pressed hard on the hip and then disappearing into the dark, leaving the man, Noah from Baden-Baden, feeling aroused and ashamed and amused, having been tantalized by a man in the dark.

Splashes of jasmine sent Roumiana back home, way back to her girlhood in Transylvania, back to early-morning baths in her grandmother's house. She ached for those baths and wanted them back, and now here she was, reclining in paradise, guiding Julka's heavy sponge to her back, spreading her thighs for Linda's warm cloth, bending her neck toward Wanda's soft mouth. It was paradise just to be clean again. She wanted these girls never to stop. She swallowed a sob and let herself be touched, let herself be bathed, the first real bath she'd had in months.

All this fire. All this pleasure. He wanted to touch them, sponge them all down, join each one of their reindeer games, but he strolled through the crowd like a dirty policeman. Someone had to take charge, right? He marveled at everyone's self-restraint, marveling at how, against all odds—even with strangers' hands in their hair, even with strangers' chins in their crotches, pleasuring their victims to the lip of destruction—everyone managed to keep such cool. Wanda had plotted this treacherous circus, but he'd put up the money, and as the man said, it comes with responsibility. But what did that mean? What needed doing? This lubricious hawk, here, biting this waitress, twisting his fingers into her pink bouffant, could have been a rapist for all anyone knew. True, she was squealing, and appeared to be loving it, and who, for that matter, wasn't loving it? None of these people needed an on-duty cop. Nay, they didn't need anything at all! So instead he made the rounds of a worried fireman, checking on hundreds of guttering candles, stoking the blasting sycamore fire and making it roar like lions in a cage. He himself was ready to go, combustible as twigs and paper and straw. Just one spark and he'd jump right in, let the whole business burn down around him. For who needed a pervert to speak for the skin? Desire, like fire, follows laws all its own.

Mr. Glass of Milk was poking the fire, his big Hephaestan body edged in light. A big man like that, Kyoshi thought, would probably have to be ridden like a donkey. Polish boy nudged him in that direction. A dare, Kyoshi thought, slowly approaching. He touched Hephaestan ribs and gave fair warning. Vulcan turned sideways with an inviting smile. Kyoshi mounted, arms around the neck, legs hiking up around the waist. The donkey was surprised but accepted his weight, dodging the featherweight kisses in his hair.

Matek stroked Gurney and thought about tasting him. Piotr took liberties with Kyoshi's briefs, baring his small ass, his dark little asshole, even putting his face inside. Matek got some spit and made Gurney even harder, leading him gently by the cock through the crowd. They parted like waters for the struggling beast: Matek, Gurney, Kyoshi, Piotr. Wanda unlocked the dark inner chamber. A few last people slipped out while they could, but the rest of them shed their last shreds of clothes, some throwing garments into the fire. A Holocaust of pleasure, she whispered to somebody.

Voices and candles followed them through the door, pillows and duvets got tangled underfoot. Gurney went slack in Matek's young hand. The heavy boy hard as a rock on his back panted at whatever was being done to him. This is your life, Gurney thought. They tumbled like acrobats onto the mattress. This is the outrageous end of your life. There is no telling why, but he felt an overpowering obligation— to the crowd, to his desire, to his sudden curiosity to feel how it would feel to get on his knees and be fucked by a man. In that one moment, rich as he was, surrounded as he was by holiday cheer, he confronted his need for something much more. He still felt the need for some impenetrable bliss, pleasure so great it was almost like death, and as the strange brick of a cock nosed up, knocking, knocking, and as his hands brought shaky blobs of spit back there, moistening the condom, stroking the boy, that lethal pleasure suddenly came, so white and sharp it burned like wire, making him say Stop, though the boy didn't hear, or didn't understand, or simply had no desire to stop, for again he said Stop, sure he would die if the boy didn't stop, but with slow determination he kept getting wider, the boy like a wedge splitting into wood, not funny at all, nothing fun about it, but another inch of agony and it started getting easier. He was full to the breastbone, releasing some breath, letting a little wash of pleasure in. He too was hard, up to his breastbone, 100 percent cock both inside and out, so big and hard he felt like someone else, but now with every sizzling exit, pounding entrance, burning exit, faster and faster in and out, to touch himself felt safe and secure, just like going home to Iowa, and the faster the faster the ripping pain—the boy collapsed on his downsloping back and Gurney came so full it was just like he was wetting himself, pissing hot splashes on his own chest and neck.

Shrunken boy slid out. Nobody was watching. He lay there awhile, wiping himself up, watching amazing sights in the shadows, enjoying the color of skin lit by fire. Nothing had changed. Nothing was different. He noticed that there was no music in the room, just murmuring and slapping, a raspy concerto of bodily pleasure. It was a privilege to smell so many having sex, a smell that would have been disgusting out of context—just as these people, lining up at the bank, would have been far too close for comfort. And it was a privilege to see so many having sex, their shoulders rolling like taffy machines, their hips slapping away like jackhammers. Some were beginning that universal search for something with which to wipe themselves off. One man jerked off alone by the fire; it was Chef Poniadzalek, too good for the others. And at the top of the bed, an arm's length away, Wanda straddled Matek's bony hips. Wanda Zamoyska! He felt dirty watching. She was fucking him slowly, one hand balancing, the other one touching her conical breasts. She was focused on his face, which was flat on its side, looking like that portrait of the dead toreador.

Gurney rolled over. The boy who'd been fucking him was down on the floor, with two Finnish women he recognized from Halloween. What a player! he thought. The boy was already kissing the breasts of the one, even as she received the tongue of the other. He looked around and noticed other Krakovian conspirators, some of them members of Jane's Romper Room Hollywood. He saw Ralph. He saw Andy. He saw Ted cleaning up. He saw Malachi groaning in Piotr's skinny arms and Michigan Melodye, sans plastic glasses, wetting the base of Steve's half-erect cock. Muscles shifted in Cindy's pretty back. Kabuki Christine was on the verge of coming. What fun, he thought. And what a privilege. They looked so much better without the velvet and suede. There was an elemental purity to all that bare skin, all that goodwill, something celestial and almost holy. He liked to think he had caused it all—or at least that he'd guided it, led it on like Julka had led him in the waltz. And he liked to think that Wanda had caused it, too. But he knew all these people had gotten there themselves, that they'd crawled on their bellies under the crossfire of morality, tumbling with squeals into this foxhole of delight. He would have taken responsibility, if he could. He would have owned the ones who nested in each other's loose arms. He would have owned the underage boys and girls, swapping their sloppy bodily fluids; owned the young women who kissed like movie stars; owned the middle-aged strangers by the fire, spooning as they drifted off to sleep. He would have owned all the warmth and ecstasy and trust that pulled this unusual family together—but he knew there was nothing more he could do about it.

Linda sat down next to him. Having fun? she said.

Fun, he said. I think we've got something much larger than that.

True, she said. How's your bum?

He hid his face, trying to laugh. It's okay. Now *that* was fun. Crazy fun.

If you say so.

She sat on her hand. Her legs made a perfect number four. He looked her body up and down, not feeling dirty in the slightest way. She was freckled and lean, with a little belly pouch. He was delighted to see that her breasts were cockeyed, just as they'd been in Jane's stories. He stroked one along the side with his thumb. She pushed her chest outward, making them rise, inviting him to touch them as much as he pleased. Was this really Linda? Was this really real? She had the softest breasts he'd ever touched. They held each other's hands and touched each other's bodies, deferring the moment when they'd finally kiss. They touched and stroked for a lovely length of time, as though they'd been on such terms for months, but still, but still—they didn't kiss. It soon got to where she was flowing on his fingers, and where he was hard to her flower-petal touch, and yes, and then, when they finally kissed, at first with a series of playful little darts, it seemed as if they could kiss all night, and it seemed as if soon they'd be down on the rugs—expatriates from Iowa, sliding in and out, bold as a couple in a salt cathedral. But something happened like a cold mist of rain. Their lips broke apart and they sat holding hands. They couldn't risk catching each other's eyes. They only listened to the murmur of the orgy, the variety of lovers, taking in the sleepy humanity all around, and they sat inches apart in careful silence, much as they'd done on that bus ride home. It was as if each had realized, with an unpleasant chill, that they were actually just two travelers out in the world, self-conscious strangers, Adam and Eve, two controlled by the absence of a third.

Twenty-one

ZBIGNIEW WAS DOING CHRISTMAS EVE, and he was doing it on his own. His grandmother always had her sisters to help, as had his mother, and Grazyna had Wanda and usually some friends, but he had gotten up early that morning and taken on the whole thing himself, all twelve courses. He'd begun with a trip to the *sukiarnia* for yeast cakes and poppy-seed cake and Wanda's favorite gingerbread, then home to make waffle dough, mash the potatoes for mushroom croquettes, grind the walnuts for nut croquettes. He did the maddening work of folding crumbly *uszka.* He did several rounds of dishes and started the almond soup and mushroom soup and then tested the borscht, which had been curing for five days now. All the while three carp swam circles in a washtub, and when tension got high—as when he scraped off the foam and found the borscht had gone putrid, or when he burned both thumbs on the cabbage pot, or when, as the neglected coal stove went cold in the corner, he found that he had let the boiled potatoes sit too long and get too dry to form croquettes—the carp went wild, splashing all over the wall and floor, flipping tails, smacking lips, such that one actually flipped from the tub and flopped and thrashed all over the tiles, its scales all sticky in his flour-caked hands.

Why take on twelve courses? Why make it so difficult? It is tradition, his father would say, solid as the walls of Wawel Castle, not to be questioned. But still he asked why, as the second batch of potatoes crumbled like the first and there was nothing solid holding him back, keeping him from wrecking everything in the kitchen. Why should he bother with all twelve? It was tradition—for Wanda's sake—and it wasn't to be questioned. So he didn't wreck the kitchen, for the sake of tradition.

The sun rode low behind the snow clouds, soft and budging along the ridge. The windows were frosted up to the top. Wanda could arrive at any time now, and with everything simmering, cooling, or ruined, he had nothing to do but sit around and wait.

He went to the sofa where Jane was sleeping. Her stocking feet were clasped in prayer. Her parted lips were draped with hair. He knelt there and rested his head on the velvet, putting his face to her faint sweet breath. He could have told Wanda that Jane would be joining them, but then there wouldn't be a chance she would show up. There'd be a scene, he could count on that. There'd be jealous tension (knowing Jane), and some violent outburst (knowing Wanda), but they had to resolve their differences somehow. He would be the one to keep his cool. For before he could ever ask Jane for her hand, Wanda had to know the truth about them, and this was as good a way as any.

He watched her from close-up, her eyes moving beneath her pinkish lids. Too much traveling, he thought, too much drinking. She'd gotten him rich and gotten him fat. He'd buried that menacing body out back. At fleeting moments like this, when he slowed down to reflect on where his life had led, he knew that he'd grown addicted to Jane—that she was slowing him down with trickles of poison, smothering his ambition under drifts of money, drowning him under waves of pleasure—but for some crazy reason, even knowing this, he wanted to marry her all the more. For when a man has completely ruined his life—and a murderer's life is forever ruined—addiction feels like the last frontier. And when two people are bound by that same addiction, it's some kind of romantic adventure. He brushed back her hair, kissed the side of her mouth. She half kissed him in return and nuzzled into the velvet. He stroked her firm leg, her narrow waist, each touch making him a little impatient. It was clear she wanted only to sleep.

Wanda? she murmured.

Co?

Is Wanda here yet?

No, not yet.

Are you ready for her?

How do you mean?

I don't know, she said, too tired to talk.

He went to the kitchen and poured out some vodka, trying to focus on practical things: twelve courses for three people. Fortune-telling for three. Christmas gifts for three, just Wanda and Tati and his wife-to-be huddled together on the oversized furniture. It would be very close. He was scared of having Wanda in his house, scared of her knowing that Jane was his lover. But if he managed to get through tonight, he thought, maybe it would start an early thaw. They could sit down and figure out her new computer. That would kill an hour or two. He'd gotten her a Toshiba laptop, just her size.

But where the hell was she? The cookies were smoking. He pulled them from the oven. Their bottoms were black, their centers raw, completely inedible. What a country! Rich as he was, in 1990, he couldn't get a phone for at least another year. The carps splashed merrily, egging him on, but they would get their due, he thought. He took a deep breath, drank some vodka. He knew he should have offered to drive her out, but he so was ashamed of her seeing his Mercedes that he took Jane's suggestion and hid it in the woods. He should have kept the old Wartburg for occasions like this. He put six new rows of dough in the oven, grabbed his cigarettes, poured out more vodka, and brought the burnt cookies out to the garden.

The mud in the garden was tipped with frost, like tiny Himalayas from far above. The wind faintly whistled in the empty woods. He dumped the dough on the compost mound and struck three matches before lighting his cigarette. She had probably gone caroling this afternoon, he thought. That was her favorite part of the holiday. Then she would have taken the last bus to Ojców. Jane had put her presents near the fire. And though she'd made some fun of the tradition, she had laid hay in portentous patterns on the table—yellow, green, brown, and black, the ends extending a bit over the edge. She'd covered it all over with indigo linen, just as Grazyna would have done. And she had given him space to work in the kitchen, honoring his crazy wish to make the twelve courses himself. They had worked well together in getting everything ready. From the darkening garden the cottage looked like home. He hoped it would look that way to Wanda.

Inside, he washed the smoke from his fingers and started setting the table. The last bus would arrive at six o'clock. If he walked fast he could make it to the bus stop by then. He turned down the oven, turned off the stove, and checked to see Jane was sleeping soundly. He bundled up with a flask and a fresh pack of cigarettes and went out to meet his daughter in the dark, where bare black trees covered the bluffs, poking here and there from a pasture of snow. Pine smoke rose from the neighbors' chimneys and loud icy water chattered in the creek. Wind chafed his cheeks and pulled tears from his eyes. The thought of his daughter alone in the dark, and the chance of finding her out in the woods made him walk faster past the hatchery and crucifix, swigging some vodka before crossing the river. But none of the shapes he saw was Wanda, nothing crunched in the night but him. He trotted as he came closer to the stop but paused in despair when his boots hit pavement. What next? He didn't drink, didn't smoke, not wanting to smell like that when she came. But after a long wait, maybe as long as half an hour, he had finished the bottle and smoked a couple of cigarettes and was cursing the blackness filling the trees. Just when he thought he'd missed the last bus, he heard the melody of grinding gears. Yellow headlights danced through the trees. The bus squeaked and stopped, its warm green glass dripping and glowing. The door crashed open, but nobody came out. The driver nodded, bored and impatient. He jumped on board but nobody was there. Nobody was sleeping between the seats, and the driver had seen nobody who fit her description.

Wesołych Świąt, they said to each other.

Jane was poking the fire when he returned, a sympathetic look on her worn-out face, a look that only made him sore and embarrassed.

He paced and drank and swore and paced. She asked what she could do, but they knew there was nothing.

Eight o'clock came and they were both rather drunk, a staticky tension filling the cottage. She said she was feeling peckish. He took this as a challenge. He announced it was time to celebrate Christmas. She cinched an apron around her waist, smashing the shapes of her pert little breasts in a way that made him unaccountably angry. He followed her into the too bright kitchen. He announced that it was still *his* Christmas Eve and pushed her aside a bit harder than he meant to.

She sulked by the counter, her apron still tied. He plunged both hands in the icy fish water, grabbed one hard. He bashed it against the chopping block—bashed it down, right where she could see. And when she said that was no way to kill the poor thing, he bashed it and bashed it and pressed it down dead, flapping and gasping with steely nerves. Good work, she said. You've killed the little guy. Cleaver whack, and there went the head. Upward strokes, and away went the scales, sequins sticking to his arms and pants. Slice up the middle and gush went the guts, zip went the bones, a mess of wet gore for their friend in the yard. The fish hit the butter and sizzled in the pan, and again she said, Good work, almost as if she meant it this time.

Pots roiled, steam came up, heat went straight to his empty stomach, but still he got the whole thing together, what was left of twelve hot courses. Blocking her out with his elbows and back, he got it on plates and put it on the table. She sat where he told her to and watched him uncorking, giving that soft, critical look of hers. He lit the candles and turned out the lights. He sat in his place. The dinner was done. He clutched his fingers and palms in prayer, but that was as far as he could go. Jane listened. The cabbage glistened. From where he sat, it looked nothing like food. Dry and burned, gobbed with fat, thrown like pieces of an abandoned board game, it was hardly a meal to be thankful for, but still he sat up and tried to pray.

What are you doing? she said. You don't pray.

It's Christmas. We pray. We pray for last year, we pray for next year, we pray for our families and fortunes and food. You don't have to help, but I'm going to pray.

I'll have some wine while you're doing that.

He looked about the table, trying to pray, thinking it looked nothing like Grazyna's Christmas dinners. It's hard to do, he said.

I'm sure it is. It might help if you stopped looking at the food.

Why? Why do you say that?

No reason. Think about Wanda. Pray for her.

That's just what I'm trying to do, so be quiet.

He looked up. She was slouching over her wine like a bored little kid, giving that look that made him feel old, but then she turned away, as if she didn't want to make him feel like that, and seeing her pretty profile relieved him a little. But then he saw that she was hiding a smile.

What is it?

Nothing.

Tell me what it is.

Go ahead and pray. I can wait.

It's obvious I can't pray, so be quiet about it.

Easy, Tonto, hold your horses.

I'm done.

She touched his hand with her icy fingers. She ladled the curdling *żurek*. She served curling filets and rocky croquettes, saying with a drawl, Praying don't flatter the likes of you, Tonto. Honest Injun, it don't. It just don't.

He took up his fork and tested the fish.

We got all night, she said. Jus' you an' me an' Christmas Eve.

Just you and me, he said. He thought once more of his wife-to-be. He looked at his plate as she cut her fish. He put down his fork. Her eyes looked drunk and uninvolved. The thought of a young wife worried him a bit. She could get sick of him. With Grazyna it had lasted twenty years, and if he hadn't blown it so completely with Jackie, maybe that marriage could have lasted twenty more, for Grazyna was Polish, of a good generation. But Jane was a risk, young and fickle. He took the poster from his pants pocket and unfolded it on the table.

This ought to make you happy, he said.

Both of them looked at it. She apparently knew exactly what it was. The artist had rendered a caricature of Gurney, a good one, a shaving-cream beard on his chirpy face, slot-machine limes spinning in his eyes, a dollar sign and question mark stamped on his head. All the markings of an American sham. Your cousin's here. Now you two can have some fun. Laugh at him, laugh at me—

I'm not laughing at anyone, honey. Let's have dinner.

You think they were trying to tell me something, don't you? Were they trying to tell me something about my daughter?

Let's just eat, sweetie.

What do you know about Wanda, Jane?

Nothing I haven't told you.

What's all this about Xmas fun? Does it have anything to do with Wanda?

Nie wiem. You're drunk. You should eat something.

He steadied himself, spreading his fingers on the indigo table-cloth. She ate in silence. He'd been uneasy from the moment he'd heard about Gurney. A younger cousin, her closest friend. It just didn't feel right. The feeling was darker and sleazier than jealousy. The cocky way she'd first said his name, winking that naughty wink of hers, gave him a glimpse into those dirty chambers that he knew she'd never unlock for him. Gurney was younger, Zbigniew was older, they both played different roles for her. And she stopped talking about him just after he arrived, right when she started sharing a room with him.

She tasted the *żurek*, tasted a croquette, said *Smacznego!* in her well-bred way. He relaxed a little. She was better bred than most Americans were. She, too, had aristocratic blood. She would make a fine wife, a fun companion, so why did he have such trouble trusting her? It wasn't her fault, he wanted to think, looking at the leering face on the poster.

She looked at it too, her eyes going sour.

He couldn't let it go. He asked her what the problem was.

I want to tell you something, she said, solemnly. I want you to know why I kicked him out.

I only want you to tell me the truth.

Never mind. You really don't want to know the truth.

I don't want you to lie to me. I want everything out in the open.

That'll never be possible. Her face lightened up.

Why?

We don't even tell *ourselves* the truth, you silly.

Entertain me. It's Christmas Eve. Tell me why you kicked out your cousin.

I told you it was because he read my diary. But that wasn't the reason. And it's not because he couldn't pay rent. We both know he's almost as rich as you. Stop it! Stop fretting, she snapped, and don't even *think* about getting jealous, especially after you had Jackie Witherspoon! Just be quiet. Be quiet. Have some more wine and hear me out. The day when they came out here like two little lovebirds, when I was out there dying of exposure, well he saw me through the window. You could have guessed that.

I don't want to hear this.

I know you don't. But I'm going to tell it. Leave if you want, and a big *Wesołych Świąt* to you if you do, but I'm getting everything out in the open. When he left here that day, I don't know, he went off somewhere and bloodied up his hands and then he came home and took it out on me. Nice, I thought. Very nice—

How do you know about Jackie and me?

How does anybody know anything around here?

Linda.

I don't want to talk about that.

What did she say about me and Jackie?

To continue: Why *not* take it out on me, I thought. Except that he's quite a big man. Pretty scary when he's hulking over you, looking like a bully with his hands all cut up.

Did he hit you?

Oh, you wish. He's never hit anyone. The thing is—and you just *listen*—it was the first time he ever looked like a man to me. I don't know, like a man who could protect me. Even like he could throw me around. It was *good* seeing him all grown up. I made him calm down and sit next to me. I'd known him since I was little, that's all. We used to play in tree forts, you know. We were friends and cousins. And now the first boy I really ever loved was this full-grown man sitting next to me. The boy who used to adore me for no reason at all, the boy who adored me as much as my dad did, was this beautiful man sitting next to me. Oh, Zbiszek, I'd brought him all the way to Europe, and I'd been *so good* all the time he lived here, but then I was afraid I was going to lose him. Don't you get it? You understand *that* much, don't you? I knew that you loved me then, and I'm glad you still do, but I just couldn't lose him, so I had to do something you'll hate me for. I know you'll hate me, I know it was bad, but I'm telling you anyway. Listen. You can hate me for what I've done to you, you can hate me for everything, but not for confessing. *You* know that confession is sacred.

What did you do?

Promise?

Tell me.

I climbed on his lap and I told him that story. I told him the one that you liked so much.

What story?

You know the one.

What story?

The cathedral story. The one with Jackie and Linda at Wieliczka. Honey, please—

He rose from his chair. He wanted her to stop. He crashed glasses and plates and food on the floor, he made a great racket and tried to get rid of it, but then he could only stand there and stare. He looked at the mess on the blue kitchen tiles, he looked for a message in the shards and slop. Jane stopped talking and let him look. Streaky canals joined oceans of red wine. Potatoes and pastries formed iceberg chunks. And as if the freak result of a tornado, two spikes of ceramic had been lodged in a croquette. Looking at the surface of this gastronomical catastrophe, he kept a steady balance between rage and despair, and feeling like he was floating above a ruined little world, a biblical world destroyed by nature, keeping his balance, he thought for a moment that he understood everything. But then it vanished.

Zbigniew felt no sympathy for her, though it was then that the spears started striking his chest—Jane's betrayal, his own betrayal, his daughter deserting him on Christmas Eve. And it was then that Jane picked up the poster and, brandishing the cartoon portrait of her cousin, told him what those kids really meant by fun. They had joined her cousin in his idea of fun. They had flouted their families and flouted themselves. They had leased a suite at the Grand Hotel, where, at that moment, they were gorging like Romans, where, she knew, they were fucking like rabbits.

He would see for himself.

Holding Wanda's gift under his arm, he dumped buckets of un-eaten food on the garden. He threw the gift in the car and went back inside.

Jane looked small in the messy blue kitchen.

Pushing past her with the sloshing washtub, he dumped that too on the infernal garden, leaving two carp thrashing away in the snow.

It was desolate and slippery on the way to the city, and the lousy weather dislodged his rage. Rising from the valley into big fields of fog, he sang *Przybliezli do Betlejem*—Quickly on to Bethlehem.

Oddawli swe ukłony w pokarze,
Tobie z serca uchotnego, o Boże!
Chwała na wysokości,
Chwała na wysokości,
A pokoj na ziemi.

The leather interior muffled his voice. The dashboard lights mocked his serious purpose. He wanted to boom it out in Mariacki Cathedral, his baritone shaking the baby from the creche: *A pokoj na ziemi! A pokoj na ziemi!* He had the smarts of ten men, the power of twenty, all of it strapped into his throttled machine, barreling like Tatars from the Ojców Valley, an army of men with swords on high taking Kraków by force, Christmas by storm. He knew this feeling. Men had known it for thousands of years—the taste of blood, the charge of duty, the presence of mind one needs to kill. *A pokoj na ziemi! A pokoj na ziemi!* Christmas feast! For thousands of years women tended fires, women made the feast, and men were held to that one great skill. Men killed. Men kill. I kill. And when I kill, I have ten thousand years' approval. When I kill with bare hands, I am exalted on high, above my cheap and wicked times. I may crash this car and I may burn my money but when I kill I know I am working, I know I'm alive. When I kill with my hands, *A pokoj na ziemi! A pokoj na ziemi! Peace on earth to men!*

He parked his car on the Mały Rynek, behind the cathedral's looming hulk. Two men were passing a bottle under the arcades. He walked the narrow streets of his neighborhood and entered the bright lobby of the Grand Hotel. He approached the concierge, a reasonable old Pole, and asked straightaway for the person in charge. The man derisively looked him over, probably seeing a common old drunk smelling of fish and covered in flour.

You are late, said the concierge. As of early this morning, we have excluded that man and all of your kind from our respectable hotel.

I understand, sir. And I shall go. But please be gracious and tell me the charge.

Libertinism.

Libertinism, sir? He felt for a cigarette. I do not know this word.

The charge, sir, is not with a fondness for eating and drinking. Poland prizes these virtues over the holidays, and the Grand Hotel naturally promotes them too. But drugs and orgies we do not condone. Our highest charge is against unnatural acts, the type for which Sodom and Gomorrah were burned.

I quite understand. Zbigniew found his cigarettes. He dropped his lighter. Do you have names of other . . . people in attendance. I'm from out of town and need a place to stay.

Strange excuse, sir. If you wished to lodge with them, wouldn't you already know their names?

Right. Very true. Smart man. I am looking for one person in particular.

Name?

Wanda. Wanda Agnieszka Zamoyska.

You have an influential friend, he said. You realize, of course, that she was in charge. She was the party who ordered the menu, costing over fifty million złotys. She's unquestionably the *agent provocateur,* well worthy of a police investigation. A fine young lady, however, exquisitely mannered, just what we expect from that dying clan. She made the employees in attendance wear blindfolds—a consummate aristocrat! They did so on a bribe, of course. But a plain beauty. I only wish I had been there to catch her myself.

The concierge winked. Nothing kept Zbigniew from poking out that eye. But he said only *Wesołych Świąt,* donning his hat and leaving the hotel.

Wesołych Świąt.

He returned to the car by way of the Rynek, pausing in front of his family's building. His studio windows were dark. Christ only knew what was happening in back. He went to the car and took out the gift. Unwrapping it under a flickering lamp, he split packing tape with his keys, tossed out bags containing manuals and cables. He tossed out batteries and Styrofoam frames and admired the hefty gray Toshiba computer. He jiggled it around, feeling its weight. He tossed it up and caught it. Carrying it a few meters, he smashed it on the stones of Mariacki Cathedral.

The meaty interior of his black Mercedes made him a silent but powerful predator, prowling like the Gestapo under yellow ghetto lights. That's what it took, that same dark feeling. The symmetry of this kill would please him very much. It would not be a simple repetition of the first, though the general circumstances were just about the same. It would be the second hit in a series. And it was not as if he'd gotten the wrong man first. On the contrary, he had simply hit a less valuable mark, and the merits were doubling as he approached the bull's-eye. He was moving toward the center, tearing up the roots. This creep was the taproot, this creep was the culprit who had gotten himself inside of Jane. He had rotted her out like a cancer, infecting the innocent with his American addiction. Maybe that could happen to Jane, but it would never happen to Wanda. He would rip the creep up by his cancerous roots.

He parked on the street. Lights were on behind the curtains. The top corner of a hulking block in Kazimierz. He entered the same alley and mounted the same stairs, taking two at a time, more full of the feeling than he'd felt before, the feeling that nothing physical could sway him from his rolling purpose. He cleared the top stair and in one fluid motion took two broad steps through the unlocked door and entered the bright activity of the scene. Everything was changed. Yellow walls, purple rafters. Shirtless boys drank and played cards. A mess of hundred-dollar bills on the table. *Wesołych Świąt,* the Słowokowski boy shouted, brandishing money in both his clutches.

Gdzie jest on?

Kto?

Amerykański!

Nie ma, said the boy, looking down. All the shirtless boys looked down. But he knew his way around. He knew where he would find him. He made his way to the kitchen, the bedroom door swung open.

Jestem tutaj, the American said. His hair was a mess. He was a contender in his tight costume of orange and brown. Santa Claus, I presume? he said with a smirk.

HE DID NOT SEE THE YOUNG AMERICAN MAN. It was not the rash punk whom he had met in his studio. It was not even the prick who had stormed into his cottage. What he saw in that moment, tall and clean, was no deplorable dishrag of a man. Dick Chesnutt had been harmless, a rotting tooth, sore and black and ready to yank. But this young buck, poised in a T-shirt, glowed like caps and money and sex, smirked like those dastardly fraternity students he had once secretly feared when teaching at Stanford. What he must have seen, then, in that prophetic instant, before going into the kitchen for a suitable knife, was a patch of healthy cancer he'd neglected too long, now fixing to rot this beautiful city. And judging from news of his little slut daughter, judging from those half-naked wayward boys, metastases had already begun to set in.

A deadly steak knife. Was that as big and deadly as they had? The first kill had been sloppy, done out of rage. The first one had been done for his own private pleasure. But he too had evolved, along with his prey, and now he was ready to kill with purpose. He was ready to teach. He tried different grips. He pointed it upward, for powerful cutting. Sideways for slicing, downward for stabbing. Downward, he decided. He would stab the motherfucker in the throat.

IT ALL HAPPENED VERY QUICKLY, they said. Tati came around on Christmas Eve. The three of them were gambling for clothes and money. Matek had devised a rule by which, if you lost a piece of clothing in a hand, the person to your left had to buy it from you. For some reason all of them were coming out ahead, which seemed to break some physical law. Anyway, they said Tati wasn't looking too good. His hair was matted, he smelled like fish, incredibly drunk for a man of his class. And he didn't even ask for her. He came right out and demanded the *amerykański.* They didn't like his tone, so they avoided the question, but then Amerykański must have been getting up from a nap because there he was, standing in the door. He casually announced, *Jestem tutaj*—Here I am—two of maybe ten Polish words he knew. Then came the weird part. Tati looked him hard in the face, like he was trying to read an eye exam, and then pivoting on his heels like Charlie Chaplin he carefully walked through the kitchen door. Amerykański gave an amusing look, as if asking what the hell was happening, and followed him in to see for himself. Wujo Płujo, alarmed by the noise, threw down their cards and went to have a look. They found Amerykański bleeding from his collarbone, kneeling there on poor Tati's shoulders. Piotr ran in and stepped on Tati's wrist and Kuba pried the knife away. It was a harmless dinner knife. The four of them lifted poor Tati and carried him out like a sacrificial lamb, offering to toss him off the catwalk. He didn't even plead or put up a fight. They set him down and laughed it off, saying his invitation had been revoked.

IN THE HOURS BEFORE SUNRISE ON CHRISTMAS MORNING, having left his things in a locker at the station, he must have walked several miles around town, nagged a bit by his bandaged shoulder. The snow was dry and fine as flour, snaking over cobblestones, giving the city a downy cover. There had been a great load off since the morning before, when they were herded like lepers through the Grand Hotel lobby, most of them stopping in the dark breaking daylight to kiss and laugh and go their separate ways. Linda hugged him before going home. Quite alert, given the night's excesses, he returned alone, feeling a solid and heavy sense of regret, though not really feeling all too bad. Naked in the brightness of Dick Chesnutt's bathroom, faint blue water filling up the bathtub, he watched the last quakes of it sparkle in the air and smelled Linda's mild smell rising from his skin. How incredible it all had been! How incredible that he had been responsible for that! After his bath he gave secret presents to Wujo Płujo, putting five thousand apiece in their stockings, keeping five thousand back for himself.

The rest he sent express to Celeste.

After that he slept for twelve hours, only to be awakened by his would-be killer, Zbigniew, who gashed his shoulder with a serrated blade. It was exhilarating good sport, and he even wished that the old man hadn't been so drunk, that they, too, could have settled their accounts, but what would have been the point? Really, they had both gotten off easy. Matek grinned and shook his head as he dressed the wound.

Gurney said his good-byes and began his walk through dark, quiet Kraków, able to see it now as if for the first time—not as the backdrop to the drama in his head, neither as Jane's nor Jackie's city, but as an old city, a juvenile city, a free and even comic city that did indeed laugh in the face of death. The castle looked mockingly down at the town. Insouciant Copernicus jeered at the university. The river wriggled by on its way down from Warsaw. Despite its layers of pain and pollution, this was a fine little city for children. At least in that moment he saw it that way.

But now as blue light blushed up in the east, and pushed up Christmas morning with it, that familiar panic started setting in. He had nowhere to go. He was leaving everyone behind. Even having sent off the money gave him no real comfort.

Ironically, it made him feel cheap.

He stopped at the station and took one last look. Rude old buildings hunched over the streets. An abandoned tramcar stood frozen in its tracks. There was no question that he wouldn't be going back there, but he was profoundly divided as to where to go next. That silvery choice was very much his own. He had put that leather book in his pocket, in case he had a thought for Christmas morning. He steadied himself, steadied his hand. He wrote with a crabbed script: *Life is an inedible feast. Life, Celeste, is an inedible feast.* His immediate impulse was to rip it out, as he had done with all the pages before, but he liked the way the sentence sounded. And somehow the words made him feel more grounded, a little bit less like he was floating away, though he had no idea where they were coming from. Someday she would read it and roll her eyes, just as any kid would do, but he didn't rip it out, and he hoped that he could continue on from there. He shut the book and kept on toward the station.

He pulled open the heavy door to the atrium. It was crowded with sleepers inside for the winter. When his eyes adjusted to the steamy light, he saw two kids who had come to the party, wrapped in one blanket and asleep by the wall. Roumiana was her name, spooning with her brother. Her hair was scattered across his neck. Their faces were beautiful and quiet with sleep and he wanted to join them under their blanket—curl up as if he too were their brother and sleep with them there on the cold tile floor. But naturally he couldn't. Would he ever grow out of wild thoughts like that one? He took out his wallet. He figured three thousand would get him by all right. He counted out the rest and wedged it between them, their bodies warm against both sides of his hand. As he walked away, buttoning his coat, he knew he could have given them nothing at all and he wouldn't have felt, once again, so cheap. He claimed his bag, hooking his sore arm through the strap. He shouldered it through the tunnel under the tracks, and as he mounted the stairs to the middle platform he enjoyed the last squares of a Ritter Sport bar.

Epilogue: Juvenalia

who knows what kind of trouble you've gotten into now, but i know for certain we can't accept your gift, or whatever you want to call it. keep trying, baby, you'll figure something out, but this just isn't it. celeste likes the teddy bear. take that as a hint.

s.

ps. not all of it's here. i've kept ten grand for student loans, etc. fyi: we're moving to montreal, I'm going back to school, will send the address to your parents when we have one.

The letter had arrived in early February, accompanied, amazingly, by a big box of money. Wanda had no clue what had become of Gurney, so she kept the thing locked in a safe in her wardrobe. She hadn't heard from him since Christmas Eve morning, when he had given her a fat envelope and said he would keep in touch. And then came this money, and that was the last she knew.

Now it was April, on the evening of Juvenalia, and all of her friends were in her room dressing up. She herself was nude under the pasties and veils, but she had made a big papier-mâché pig head to put on later. Matek was swimming in Gurney's huge tuxedo, to be topped by a papier-mâché donkey head. The prize for best costume, however, would go to the other four—Roumiana, Julka, Piotr, and Kuba—who had locked their ankles into real iron shackles that Kuba had gotten by some ill means. The girls had made them all black-and-white striped uniforms, just like the chain gangs wore in the movies. Her mother was bitching about chains scratching the floor, but what could she do about it? Tonight the kids were taking over the city!

She ducked into Tati's studio for a moment. It was almost a little sad now that nobody lived there, but it was nice and private. Her mother never went near it. Her thoughts turned to her father, as they usually did when she was in there. He wasn't that old, but he acted as if he was. She hoped that that would never happen to her. Sometimes she thought she was actually getting younger. And sometimes she thought about painting his portrait, though she knew she was too young to get it right. A portrait of her father! It was a tremendous subject. She entertained the idea quite often, in fact, knowing that, were she to risk it, and were she truly a genius painter, there was only one detail she would have to master—one winsome detail. It was a rare thing to see, rare like an eclipse, observable just once maybe every few years. She herself had seen it a few years before, sitting beside him at a concert in the Filharmonia. He must have been thinking he was alone in the world, for in that moment, just that once, as the cello played solo and warmed up the air, Tati let his pleasure rise to the surface and twinkle in his eyes like the lights of a town. In that moment, which Wanda had witnessed, all the heavy things that he pretended to be vanished. But that vanishing, she knew, was the most important part. And how could she ever capture such a thing with paints?

She opened the window and looked out at the main square and all the kids racing around down there. The sky was growing dark. The torches were lit. Undulant energy moved the spring air, coasting like fingers through her veils and hair. She was young. She knew this, and it made her very happy. She had always been young, of course, but she hadn't always known it, and she worried that it was the kind of thing you lost once you knew it. Of course not! Though the box in her closet was rather like that. It had a wonderful effect when she simply ignored it; it gave her the ferocious calm of a soldier. But it scared her to death when she remembered it was there. Being young, however, wasn't like that at all. Being young wasn't scary at all. Being young was sheer delight!

Acknowledgments

THE AUTHOR EXPRESSES GRATITUDE to the following people (and so many others, not forgotten) for their guidance and support in the writing of this book: Robert Balog, Sarah Bamberger, Stephen Beachy, Zoë Bond, Sarah Boushey, Melissa Clark, Jennifer Edwards, Molly Emerson, Kimberly Frail, Sandra Gilbert, Lev Grossman, Lisa Harper, Thomas Heise, Michael Hoffman, Tom Jenks, Glenn Keyser, Don Knefel, Thomas Lally, Fred Leebron, Jessica Magee, Clarence Major, Bill Martin, David Merson, Jude Rodriguez, Augustus Rose, Sandra Scofield, Melissa Stein, Andrew Strombeck, Elizabeth Tallent, Daniel Wenger, George Whitman, and the Ashby Avenue Groop. To Julie Barer and Tom Bissell for their friendship, brilliance, and unflagging commitment to this book. To Jennifer Barth, for her faith and last-minute gallantry. To Ann, Jerry, and Tom Beckman.

IN FOND MEMORY OF
MARC KISTING, MATTHEW ZAMOYSKI,
AND BARTEK ZUZIAK,
three who knew only youth.

About the Author

JOHN BECKMAN, a native Iowan, was born in 1967. He has taught literature at universities in Poland, France, and California and is currently an assistant professor of English at the U.S. Naval Academy in Annapolis, Maryland. This is his first novel.